The Toymaker

A novel by

James B. Brandt

The Toymaker

This book is dedicated to David Wegner and Duane Henry, who babysat the process of both writing the film and the subsequent novel, and to Travis Brandt and Girl, who kept me motivated...

I don't know why we are here, but I'm pretty sure
that it is not in order to enjoy ourselves.
Ludwig Wittgenstein (1889-1951)

If you are going through Hell, keep going.
Sir Winston Churchill (1875-1965)

We all agree that your theory is crazy, but is it crazy
enough?
Niels Bohr (1885-1962)

Courage is not the absence of fear, but whether the
judgment that something else is more important than
fear.
Ambrose Redmoon (aka James Neil Hollingworth
(1933–1996)

There are no passengers on spaceship earth. We are
all crew.
Marshall McLuhan (1911-1980)

James B. Brandt – *The Toymaker*

CHAPTER ONE
March 3-26, 1975
Flagstaff, Arizona

Samuels heard the car pull up but chose to ignore it. He could smell the Chief's cigar ten feet away and he knew His Royal Highness was puffing smoke like a dragon with indigestion.

"All right Samuels, what's so important that you called me away from a meeting with the Mayor?" H. R. Hoggensbach growled more than he spoke. "What is it, I said," he repeated before Samuels could speak. "I got no time for your big city way of beatin' around a subject. Just spit it out."

"Chandler isn't a big city, Chief. It's just a large suburb of Phoenix," Samuels said.

"Right. It ain't much of anything, but you still got a big city attitude."

"If you say so." Samuels begged off this fight; he had fought this skirmish before. "But this is right up your alley, Chief. Lots of press on this one."

"What's that suppose to mean," Hoggensbach demanded.

"Why, it's just that you need the press more than I do, boss, since you're a political appointee and I'm just an employee," Samuels said. "Besides, you tell me that the TV cameras always drop everything but my teeth and eyes; not a good image for the department, seeing nothing but a Jimmy Carter smile when the reporters want information about a crime."

Hoggensbach looked around and noticed the camera crews scattered around the small strip center, completely missing Samuels' sarcasm. The Georgia native clamped down on his cigar so hard he bit off the end and had to jump back when the rest fell from his mouth, ashes cascading down his jacket. There were the usual Flagstaff hacks, but the Phoenix stations were here in force and there was that girl from the University who kept up-linking things to CNN. Potential national coverage; just what he needed with an election right around the corner.

"Damn it, boy, what's goin' on? The Gov'nor get shot? And don't call me boss."

"No such luck. There was a burglary here last night." Samuels' reply was calm and even, despite the cultural reaction that Blacks felt when being called "Boy." Since the Chief was indiscriminate in his insults, Samuels pushed that aside along with the Chief's other abrasive mannerisms.

"Can't you handle a simple robbery? Looks like you called in the whole damned force for a simple snatch and grab. Damn it boy, we got a budget you know!"

"Not that simple Chief. Most of the strip's owned by Reynolds." Samuels nodded toward a well-dressed man talking to a small group of reporters across the lot. Hoggensbach blanched. Reynolds was one of the wealthiest men in Flagstaff and he was a "Native American" on top of that. For some reason he hated Hoggensbach and the candidate Reynolds had supported for mayor surely would have if he hadn't of been stopped on a DUI two days before the election. And there was no question that he would have knocked Hoggensbach out of the Chief's slot in a New York minute.

Hoggensbach's mind always raced whenever Reynolds was around.

"Put it on the line, Samuels. What happened?"

"It's been a bad night for the Reynolds Plaza. Someone hit the Reynolds Drugs, the S & R – that's 'R' for Reynolds – grocery store, the Radio Shack – owned by Mr. Reynolds – the card shop – owned by Mrs. Reynolds – and the used clothing place sponsored by Reynolds' church. They missed the Baskin Robbins, though."

"Reynolds own that?"

"Nope."

"It's just vandals," Hoggensbach said, trying to brush it off.

"I don't think so."

"What'd you mean!" Hoggensbach flared, angry over Samuels' audacity in disagreeing with him.

"Well, there were things taken from each of the stores."

"That's what a robbery's all about, Samuels. Or do they break in and *leave* things where you're from?"

"The list is more than passing strange, Chief."

"Smash and grab. They're in a hurry. They didn't go in with a shopping list. Reynolds has insurance. Damn, he owns a damned insurance company, doesn't he?"

"Oh, he's insured, but there was a lot of stuff taken, boss. And I'd be willing to bet they did come with a list."

Hoggensbach was beginning to get interested a little. Anything that inconvenienced Reynolds was always appealing to the bullet shaped man. He ran a handkerchief across his close cropped salt and pepper hair, then wiped his eyes. Maybe he would have something humorous to take back to the Mayor when this was over.

"The Radio Shack was hit the hardest," Samuels was saying.

"What'd they take?"

"Well, they left most of the electronic equipment in the stock room but took at least one each of everything that was on the shelves. Except for speakers. They took a lot of speakers. Actually, I think they took all the speakers but they left other stuff that's easy to resell, except for the computers. They took all the computers, but none of the software. Imagine that. MS-DOS literate burglars with discriminating taste."

"What else did they get?"

"They stripped out all the parts. I mean everything. All the resisters and diodes and transistors and capacitors and all that crap and all the kits with parts. Must have been a ton in bits and pieces alone. Just little things."

"But they left the component pieces?"

Samuels nodded. "Yeah, most of that inventory is still there. But they didn't just strip the shelves. They emptied the storeroom of everything on their 'list' too."

"Anything else?" Hoggensbach demanded impatiently.

"Nothing from the Shack, but they got a whole truck load of food. Bits and pieces there, too. Kibbles and bits, rather. They took all the pet food left most everything else, including the booze."

"Dog food and not beer?" Hoggensbach turned to look at Samuels to see if the black officer was playing games with him, but it was obvious Samuels was laying it straight.

"Yeah. Cat food, too. Every bit of it. Along with bandages and some things from the pharmacy. But the stuff a junkie'd take – you know, the mind and feely drugs – they didn't touch. Weird. Then a few odds and ends from the clothing store, reference books and novels – mostly classics – from the bookstore, typing paper, computer paper, envelopes, and other stuff like that from the card shop – but no greeting cards. Let's see... yeah, about three hundred pounds of unground glass from the optometrist. Reynolds owns that and part interest in the bookstore. They're still taking inventory, but that's the idea."

"What'd they do, bring in a semi?"

"Reynolds estimates it would take at least three semis to haul out all the stuff they unloaded from the center. It'll be a few days before he's sure what all was taken."

"And no witnesses."

"None."

"No alarms."

"All bypassed by a professional. From the looks of what they took, there must have been two dozen or more pulling the job. And they had to be fast. It was all done in less than two hours and no one saw a thing. Not even the two in the cruiser who have this beat. They're down getting polygraphs."

"This ain't real."

"That ain't all, boss."

"Don't call me boss."

"Right, boss," Samuels said, needling the chief, who hated anything Samuels called him except "Sir." "But that's not even what's weird."

"What could be stranger than this?"

"They left all the cash. Yeah," Samuels continued when the Chief just stared at him. "None of the cash drawers were jimmied, none of the safes were blown, and not even the take-one-leave-one pennies were touched, as far as we can tell."

"Like the robbery at the auto salvage yard last week."

"Right. All they took there was the electronic parts, one engine, belts, gears, weird shit like that, and all the tools, including the grinders and drill press and other metal fabrication equipment. But they didn't touch the safe."

"Yeah, weird shit. McPhearson here?"

"He's off."

"Get with him since he's working the salvage case. Compare notes. See if there's any connection besides the strange shit." Hoggensbach took out another cigar and lit it slowly, deliberately, then looked up and saw Reynolds starting across the blacktop. "And tell everyone I want a complete report in my office by four. Have something for me then."

"Yes, sir, boss, sir," Samuels said to Hoggensbach's retreating back.

"Damn, that Reynolds's gonna give me trouble," Samuels heard the big man say as he retreated to his car and motioned the driver to start up.

"In a pig's eye we'll have something by four o'clock you horse-faced bastard," Samuels muttered through clinched teeth. "This is too weird, man, and you ain't gonna leave this detective out to dry."

Samuels turned and intercepted Reynolds, who was fuming over Hoggensbach's hasty departure. But Samuels was a pro and this was one emergency he knew he could handle. Finding answers to the previous night's events, however, was something else entirely.

CHAPTER TWO

June 6 and 7, 2002

Phoenix, Arizona

Paul winced even before he stopped; anticipating the bone-chilling, metal-on-metal squeal from the front brakes that inevitably set his teeth on edge. It was past time for repair, but brakes were well down on the list of priorities; somewhere below repairing the car's air conditioning but above lunch, though nothing on the list was anything he could afford.

When the car finally rolled to a stop, Paul sat looking at the three bedroom home baking in the late afternoon sun. The oppressive heat of early June crawled through the open car windows, seeming to reach Paul's inner being, compressing his emotions into a tight knot, squeezed even tighter by the pain of returning once more to the house that was no longer a home.

Resolutely, Paul rubbed his face with the towel he kept next to him in the car, carefully wiping around his eyes before replacing his glasses. He reached for the small, brightly wrapped package that had fallen from the passenger seat to the floor after a sharp turn; he straightened out the bow and brushed off a few grains of sand. Paul put on his best smiley face and stepped into the shadeless street, bracing himself for the coming confrontation while at the same time wondering why he bothered. Of course, he knew why he bothered. It was the same reason he had the package.

Taking a deep breath, he started up the walkway to the welcoming shade of the front porch. He stepped over the broken trike, abandoned in the center of the path, then stopped to set it on the dried brown grass that spotted the dirt and weed-covered lawn.

The sprinkler system must be broken. Again. He thought as he stepped back toward the house. Or Janet's just saving money on the water bill.

He stood for a minute examining the house. The paint was peeling, the citrus trees wilting, the flowers drooping. The house resembled nothing more than a Dali portrait of middle class neglect. Paul almost turned back to his '87 Cherokee, but reminded himself that he was on a mission and strode up to the porch.

The front door was open and Paul felt the moist breeze forced out of the secured screen door by the evaporative cooler. A decade before, the cooler had worked well. But no longer, with the humidity that years of urbanization had inflicted on the once dry valley. The new comers from back east had to have their grass lawns, even in a desert.

All this ran through a small part of Paul's mind as he stood looking in through the screen door, watching the three-year-old happily piling miniature wooden logs together in strange architectural shapes. Paul's father had made the blocks in his home workshop and they remained Jeremy's favorite toys. Paul's dad didn't send many toys for Jeremy any more. Janet wouldn't let Jeremy see his grandparents except during the summer when Paul had custody and had told them to stop sending things for the kid.

Even the summer visits were shrinking. Janet had already found ways to postpone it twice this summer and the fall monsoons were almost here. Just a couple more weeks before pre-school started, Paul recalled having heard something about back-to-school specials at Wal-Mart or K-Mart or some-mart, even though the official back-to-school date was not until September first. Somehow he thought it should be a crime to have back-to-school sales before the forth-of-July sale. Like starting Christmas before Halloween or something.

But Janet had already announced her plans to commit their son into the hands of the educational system, a prisoner until aged nineteen before voluntary incarceration in college. Paul had started saving for that already. Forget that Janet had a good job, she would expect him to fork out for college. She already was demanding the four-grand for the first year of pre-school. Starting September one. Then his little boy would start the process of becoming a little man. To Paul it seemed like a major turning point, like the end of a millennium, and why Janet couldn't wait until the kid turned five like normal kids was beyond him, unless she just wanted him out of the house for some reason.

At least, that was the theory. This would be the first summer since the custody battle and Paul had no confidence that Janet would allow even that meager visitation. He no longer had the will to fight Janet's desire to punish him for not being everything she wanted, for not being rich enough to support her in luxury, for not being a person who could ride white chargers and tilt with dragons, for not being more than average. If it came to more court battles, well, she would win, no question: everyone said that men only received custody about twenty-percent of the time and seldom won as liberal visitation agreement as did women who lost custody. Hell, Paul had asked for a month in the summer and been given two weeks at his ex-wife's convenience.

Janet had a job with the government, steady if not great, and she was a fine-tuned sycophant. He figured she was a passable mother – the bitterness and fighting still had not sunk in enough to change that opinion even in light of her mood swings – and, anyway, he didn't have the money, or the will, to carry the fight to court again, which Janet promised she would do if he "misbehaved." Maybe that was her reason for starting this pre-school business: to keep that hole in Paul's pocket leaking cash.

He swallowed thoughts that seemed to pile one on top of the other in rapid succession. Forcing a new smile, he rattled the door a little to get Jeremy's attention without disturbing the whole house – which would happen if he woke-up the dog who was probably sleeping on the foot of the bed in Jeremy's room, a place he took up residence the day the crib came down and the bed went up. He was, after all, here to see Jeremy, not to worry about Janet.

Jeremy looked at the door and saw Paul silhouetted against the cloudless Arizona sky. It took him a minute but when he recognized Paul his entire face lit up with a huge grin.

"Daddy! What you doin' here?" Jeremy asked, getting up and toddling to the door. "Is it Satday? Ice cream! Movies!"

"Hi, babe. It's not Saturday, but I thought I'd drop by and surprise you. I brought you a toy so you could play with it in the pool tomorrow," Paul said, holding up the package.

"Got a toy? Gimme," Jeremy said, trying to undo the lock that was just a little too high and too complicated for his baby fingers to manipulate. But he did rattle the door hard, and that noise was heard by the dog, which came bounding into the room, barking excitedly when he saw Paul. That brought Janet into the family room, hair pins in her mouth, rollers in her hair, but still everything in a woman that Paul had ever wanted.

"Jeremy? Jeremy, what's the matter?" Janet asked as she stepped into the room. She saw Paul and immediately froze, strands of her long brown hair falling over her eyes from where she held her hair up waiting for a roller. Paul looked back. She had on a short pair of jean cutoffs and her long legs were well displayed. Small breasts, freed of the constraints of a bra, pushed at a white T-shirt semi-transparent where water from the sink had splashed on her chest.

Paul felt his stomach knot and a lump grow in his throat.

"What do you want," Janet demanded in a voice so cold the knot in Paul's stomach turned to acid and the lump dissolved in bitter waves.

Jeremy froze, too, incorrectly assuming the anger in his mother's voice was meant for him. He looked back at her, all the joy draining from his face like sunshine running down a funnel.

"I, uh, brought a toy for Jeremy," Paul stammered, now uncertain, caught someplace between love lost and hope discarded.

"You've brought something over here every other day for the past two months!" Janet screamed, jutting her chin forward and planting her hands on her hips in a slim parody of the Blue Ridge Mountain-born behemoth that was her mother. "Save it for visiting privileges, you hear! Now go away!"

"But..."

"Maybe you wouldn't be so generous if you had to store things! Go. A. Way."

"I only wanted to see Jer. Besides, it's still early and..."

"And I have a date tonight," Janet interrupted, secretly rejoicing over the stricken look that flashed over Paul's face, marking in her precise way the slight touch of gray that crept into his complexion. She moved to the door and picked up Jeremy, glaring at Paul though the small mesh of the screen. "So please leave and don't come back until you're supposed to!"

"Do you have a sitter?" Paul asked, his eyes wide and hopeful at the prospect of, maybe, being able to spend a few hours with his son.

"Yes and good-bye!" Janet slammed the ornate wood door – the one Paul had so painstakingly finished for her a few years ago – with such force that the living room's large picture windows shook. While he stood there open-mouthed, Janet closed the J. C. Penny mini-blinds. Faintly he heard Jeremy crying, yelling for his toy with Janet screaming at him to be quiet and for the dog, Morgan, to shut up. The noise muted as she moved Jeremy to his room deep inside the house and slammed that door against his growing wails. She closed off Morgan's rising excitement as well since she shut the dog up with the child. Paul stood staring at the door until he realized that he probably looked foolish. So he closed his mouth and turned to leave, bracing his shoulders because he felt Janet watching through cracks in the blinds.

Paul stepped out into the sun and remembered that he still had the package for Jeremy. For a moment he hesitated, almost turning to put it outside the door. He half turned and took a step to the door, but indecision had him firmly in its grasp. He turned back to the street, then looked over his shoulder at the door again. He no longer saw Janet looking out from the blinds. But just as he took his first step he saw her silhouette against the breakfast alcove curtains, obviously still watching for a false move. That firmed his resolve. He strode to his car, the package swinging in his hand. If he left the toy, bought at an expensive shop in Scottsdale, it was problematic that Jer would ever see it anyway.

Paul slid into the driver's seat and slammed on the engine and pulled slowly away from the curb, never once looking back. He hoped his bearing showed determination and not anger, but inside he was seething with a mixture of volatile emotions that boiled down into a soggy mass that left him weak and shaking. By the time he reached Black Canyon Highway, just a few blocks from the house, he felt like a piece of wilted lettuce.

Paul was not a drinker but John was and at five-thirty on a Friday afternoon, Paul knew exactly where he could find his best friend. *No*, Paul thought to himself: *his* only *friend*.

Paul made a beeline for Henry's Bar.

Henry's atmosphere enjoyed the same ambiance – with the French pronunciation "on-ray's' – that brought the original Boston Cheers to the attention of Hollywood and could easily have spawned a hit show every bit as funny as Boston's inspiration. Phoenix, however, was too close to Hollywood for Hollywood producers to frequent. It was too much like being in their own backyard; only good enough to capture exteriors, like Mel's Diner, for tacky – not classy – sitcoms like *Alice*. The bulk of that show was even filmed in LA, the producers just sending a second unit crew to Phoenix to shoot exteriors. So there were no large crowds of sightseers or people grasping for the nearness of fame flocking to Henry's, cluttering the coolness of the bar or the cozy, private booths that surrounded patrons like the protective walls of a fortress. Just a friendly place, where everyone knew your name.

Fortunately, Henry's was not a brightly-lit movie set and the subdued lighting fit Paul's mood. The tone was enhanced by classical rock, piped in at a level just high enough to be heard and to keep conversations from being over-heard without being so high it impaired discussion. In his present state of mind, Jethro Tull's "Locomotive Breath" rang like a self-portrait. "And the all-time winner's got him by the balls," Paul mouthed silently, thinking of Janet and her pig of a lawyer.

Paul stood in the door and let his eyes adjust to the shadowy interior. Then he walked around the bar, glancing in the booths, looking for John. His heart sank lower as he made the circuit and, finally admitting defeat, moved to the bar and hitched himself up on a stool. He nodded to the bartender –

who knew Paul's name but whose name always escaped Paul – and ordered Ginger Ale on the rocks with cherry juice (Paul firmly refused to call it a Shirley Temple). He absently played with a water ring on the counter top until the drink arrived.

Paul stirred the soda with the straw, watching the cherry swish around the rim of the glass, but did not drink. He was looking for the meaning of his life in the effervescent bubbles. He had seen that in a movie once; he had not understood it then and he was not finding it now. But he still spent his most depressing moments trying to capture whatever magic lived in the dancing fountain found in sparkling carbonated drinks.

He had slowly sipped the soda down a third when John walked in and swung up on the stool next to Paul.

"Hey, buddy," he said, full of enough good cheer to make Paul's stomach flip. "What's new?" John asked. Then, not waiting for Paul to answer, he called out for a mug of imported on-tap beer, needlessly, since the bartender had drawn a glass as soon as John entered.

"Oh. John," Paul said, coming out of his lassitude. Then, whether foolishly, "What brings you here?"

"Boy, you sure are down in the dumps. What always brings me here? Beer!" John downed a large mouthful and wiped the suds off his lip. "What's eating you?"

"I went over to see Janet today."

"Oh, man, whatever for? That stuff'll kill you."

"Actually," John said a little defensively, "I went over to see Jeremy. Janet just happened to be there."

"So? She usually is. It's her house now, you know."

"Yeah."

"Well, what's wrong? The kid sick or something?"

"No. Janet wouldn't let me see him. Told me I had to wait until I have my 'rights.' Hell, all I wanted to do was give the kid a new toy."

"What you need is a break in the routine," John advised sagely around another gulp of beer. "All you ever do is think about that kid and Janet. It ain't healthy."

"I love Jeremy," Paul protested with more energy than he had thought was left after the way his earlier encounter with Janet had drained him.

"Sure you do, but thinking about it all the time won't do you any good. You're going to have to live with things the way they are, not the way you want them." John polished off the mug. Before he could set it down, another full glass appeared on the table in front of him. "How much have you written since the divorce?" John asked, seemingly changing the subject abruptly.

Paul looked away and pretended to drink his cherry Ginger Ale.

"Well?"

"I've started a few things," Paul mumbled evasively.

"But what have you finished," John pressed relentlessly.

"Well..." Paul hesitated and John leaned toward him, pushing his face into Paul's personal space, daring him to invent something. "Nothing, I guess," Paul finally sighed.

"There you have it! What do you expect to live off of? Your good looks?" John chuckled at his own joke, then continued less smugly. "You're a passable writer, but what else do you do? I've tasted your cooking, so that's out. You're a terror with cars, so skip the mechanic bit. Electronics? Photography? Well, maybe, but you can't stand other people's kids. Store clerk? Not your style."

Paul waved away John's list of jobs at which Paul had already failed. "I'm not hurting right now," he said. "Alice just sent a check for an option on *Vault of Power*." Alice, Paul's long suffering agent, had been ruthless when she called to tell him about the option on the script. He was not at all happy that he had failed to produce anything new in what she called a "geological age."

"An option? She's sold a bunch of options for you, but nothing ever gets produced."

"At least I can sell options to my scripts," Paul shot back sullenly.

"Yeah, but the big money's on the screen and the independents who buy your script options never seem to find the money to actually make the movie. How much was the option?"

"Three thousand," Paul mumbled knowing full well that John knew exactly how much was in the check since he did Alice's counting.

"Yeah. Not even industry standard. Less the agency commission, that's this month's rent, back child support, back car payments, and what? Fifty, sixty bucks left over? You can't rest on that. Hell, *Vault of Power* was even written before the divorce, wasn't it? Well. Yeah, don't say anything. I know Guild rates. Better start turning out some copy or you're right back where you were: broke, abused, abandoned, and lonely. How about an unwed mother story? Seems to me you were selling those pretty regularly."

"Can't think of a plot I haven't used. Besides, the editor found out I wasn't a girl."

"Like I said, you need a break," John sighed, and waived off the waiter before he could pull down another mug – the poor soul was conditioned to John's normal four or five drafts. "Don't fill another one, Clint. I'm running some errands for Alice" he called, then turned back to Paul. "We're having a cook-out tomorrow with a group of friends. There should be some nice girls there."

"Not another one of Beth's matchmaking schemes?" Paul protested. Beth, John's wife, was always trying to set him up with a girl. It had started as soon as he was separated and accelerated once the divorce had finalized. Beth firmly believed no man could survive without a woman looking after him.

"Not this time. She wanted me to ask you, but not for that. This time we really do have more unattached ladies than men. Just worked out that way. I love it!" John polished off his drink and set the mug down with a thud. "So, what kind of toy'd you get the kid."

"It's one of those tub and pool toys."

"Excellent!" John said, standing up from the stool. "It's a pool party tomorrow, so bring your trunks and we'll give the toy a try."

"Hey, I didn't say I was going."

"Sure you did," Paul said as he stepped to the door. "See you about one. Be there if you want to collect for the beers!"

John vanished into the blinding light that streamed through the doors. Paul blinked once or twice and then it connected: John had left him with the tab. For some reason, that brought a smile to Paul and he left – after paying the bill – feeling much better than he had when he arrived.

CHAPTER THREE

June 8, 2002

Maryvale, a suburb of Phoenix, Arizona

John's house was in a part of Maryvale that had not reached the rundown levels that would one day blend the little community into a mass indistinguishable from Glendale or South Phoenix. Maryvale's principal builder, John F. Long, only believed in single car driveways and no fenced yards. While this helped keep costs down for young families, as couples grew older, the number of cars multiplied to accommodate the desires of teen children. Soon, there were cars parked on the streets and sometimes in the front yards. Laundry flapped in backyards through a hodgepodge of fences or bare walkways, decreasing property values by several points over those developments that came equipped with double car garages and standardized fenced lawns.

Fortunately for people like John, some of the smaller developers in Maryvale opted for more than just bare boned sub-divisions. John's ranch-style four bedroom blonde brick house sat under tall shade and palm trees in a row of neatly trimmed houses of similar design. John's, however, had the dubious distinction, on this day, of having several cars parked along the sidewalks. Neighbors had grown used to Beth and John's Saturday parties and no longer looked worried at the possibility of their neighborhood turning into an imitation used car lot.

Paul was late and had to park down the street, under the dark glare of two suspicious children watering the lawn with a Slip-and-Slide. He set the emergency brake and reached over to grab the paper bag containing his change of clothes, a towel, and two huge buy-one-get-one-free bags of chips from Bashes. He wiggled out of the car and, still clutching the bag, leaned across the seat and slid out a six pack of Dr. Pepper and another of Shasta Black Cherry Soda. He managed to slam and lock the door without dropping anything through the expedient method of holding his keys in his mouth and clamping the bags of chips to his chest with his chin.

So burdened, he started back down the street to John's when he suddenly remembered the toy. He struggled with indecision for a moment before settling on taking it. By propping a six pack between his leg and the car and gently lowering the bag to the ground by gripping it tightly between his thumb and the side of his forefinger, Paul managed to unlock the door, lean precariously into the vehicle, retrieve the package from the floorboard, and re-lock the Cherokee without spilling anything.

Paul figured he could grab the bag, flip it in the air, and catch it with his arm before it hit the ground. He stowed his keys in his pocket and reached down, gripped the bag between thumb and toy package, and yanked up, only to come away with a perfect semi-circle of brown paper. Paul tried again, this time stuffing the toy in the bag first and lifting the bag slowly to waist level before launching it the final few inches he required for his attempted snag. Up went the bag. It paused for a brief micro-second in free-fall before starting back down, just long enough for Paul to wrap his arm around the chips.

But the towel and clothing had their own inertia and, as they dropped, they pulled the bag with them. Quickly, like a juggler catching a falling plate, Paul stopped the bag from hitting the ground by shoving a knee under the bottom. With a little breathing space, Paul again wrapped his arm around the bag, but this time tucked a supporting hand under the bottom.

Inordinately proud of himself, Paul's face broke into a huge grin. When one's whole life appears as stable as a crumbling sand castle built at the water's edge at low tide, even minor successes like juggling groceries are welcomed. Paul looked around to see if anyone had observed his amazing feat of agility. The first thing he saw was the two children. They stood stock still, large solemn eyes like the dark pools on the kids from the movie *The Children of the Damned*, mouths slightly open like – to Paul – wolves salivating before springing, motionless in their play like rejects from an *Addams Family* casting call.

Paul felt the first brushes of high tide against his castle. If leaving the scene did not seem marginally worse than moving into the comfort of John's air conditioned house, he would have bolted from that awful gaze back to the safety of his car. Instead, he forced his lips into a quirk of a smile and walked on down the street.

Paul stood for several long moments at John's front door trying to figure out how to ring the bell. The children were still watching, having moved to the edge of their lawn so they could keep him in sight without crossing that invisible line that marked their territory from the rest of the universe. So.

Pushing the little button with his nose was out of the question, he thought.

Paul was saved the pain of that decision when the door suddenly swung open and a blast of cold air swirled around his legs. Paul blinked, trying to see into the dimness of the foyer, and managed to push his glasses back up on his face from where they had slipped on the sweat lubricating his nose with his right shoulder, but it was still too dark to see with eyes set for Arizona daylight.

"Uhhhh..." he managed to articulate.

"Hi," came the greeting from inside, full of vibrancy and good cheer. The words were followed shortly by a body stepping out of the house and into the doorway where the full sun splashed on a bikini-clad figure that was fully tanned wherever Paul could see, which was most of it. "Come on in! I'm Joan. You must be invited. I can tell."

She cocked her head like a spaniel; sunlight cascading in ripples down sun bleached blonde hair that spilled over her breast. "Well, don't just stand there," she said into the lingering silence. "Come on in!"

"Oh. Uhhhh, is John around?" Paul said, trying not to stare or be too obvious with his suddenly tongue-tied behavior. Joan was stunning, a Kelly Bundy, only taller and with a slight hint at something occupying the space behind green-eyes-flecked-with-gold-and-brown that sparkled like intriguingly flawed jade from Mexico caught in an early morning dew.

"Sure," Joan said, standing straight so Paul could squeeze past her and into the house where loud music seeped through from the pool area in back. Her attempt at good posture, however, only managed to throw her breasts out farther into the doorway. "He's out back with everyone else. Need a... hand?" Janet added with just enough brashness to make the offer to help with the bags and sodas sound like an offer for something else entirely.

"I... uhhhh... I can manage. I... uhhhh... thanks," Paul said as he turned sideways and attempted to slide through the door without touching anything in front or scraping off too much skin in back. It was a tight squeeze that got tighter the more Paul tried to wedge through without brushing against her boobs. Joan was enjoying every minute of his discomfort though Paul knew if her nipples stood up he was brush and blush.

"Out back?" Paul asked lamely as he stalled at mid-point.

"Uh-huh." Her eyes twinkled, Paul noticed, even in the dim light of the foyer. And she smelled good. Not womanly good, but like hamburgers and chlorine.

Well, Paul thought defensively, sometimes chlorine smells good.

"Out back," he repeated lamely.

"Yep," she said with a large smile, leaning into Paul a little so that her breasts made the potato chip bags crinkle.

"Yeah. Well, see you later," Paul said, hastily popping out of the doorway and the rest of the way into the house.

"Bye," Joan called, silhouetted by the light streaming from the door, her hourglass figure brightly etched against the glare.

"Bye," Paul mumbled, turning around to look back at her and stumbling into the wall. "Uh, glasses fogged from the AC," he added with a gulp, backing into the living room, where he promptly stumbled over his own feet. Quickly, before Joan could come to his rescue, Paul was up with the groceries gathered in his arms. He flashed Joan another smile and retreated rapidly around the corner and into the kitchen.

"Bye," Joan called again to Paul's slowly fading after image.

The kitchen was deserted, so Paul walked to the family room and stepped out onto the covered patio. It looked like a "happening" party and right then he felt like a virgin at his first high school dance. Hell! He was a father! Why was he so nervous around women? It wasn't like he had never been around pretty women before.

The pool was crowded, probably exceeding the Fire Marshal's maximum load limit, Paul thought, then amended that by noting that pools probably were not fire hazards. People made him nervous. Crowds always did, ever since he was a child, a point which his mother took fond pleasure in reminding him.

As Paul absorbed the madhouse atmosphere, he felt a strong urge to just set down the chip bags and the drinks he had brought and just leave. There were about forty people in and around the pool, most in their mid-to-late thirties. There were a few "beautiful people" centered around the portable bar and a few regulars from the bar. Beth also worked at Alice's small talent agency – she handled models, clowns, and other talented people and Alice dealt with actors and literary properties while John took care of the books and reviewed contracts and SAG/AFTRA regulations. He was often busy trying to collect from slow paying clients – and his parties were regularly sprinkled with models who came in hopes of meeting photographers or producers.

A few feet away, a smoking barbeque grill attracted an older crowd, paunches hanging over swim trunks on the men and varicose veins sneaking past one-piece monstrosities that served as swim attire for the more timeworn female guests. A few of the younger, presumably single, crowd were playing piggyback wars in the pool. No, not all single. That was John lumbering under a stunning redhead who, Paul thought, was married to... somebody, but that somebody did not appear to be here.

The noise level was enough to assail the senses, but Paul did note the presence of the nearest neighbor's teenaged kids and he thought that he had noticed that the house next door had papers piling up in the lawn. Probably the neighbors in the back were gone or here, so the volume was unlikely to attract police. Paul corrected himself again. That tall, black haired Clark Gable look-alike from the agency was a cop… and he was talking to a heavy-set retired detective who also fancied himself an actor, stuntman, writer, producer, and whatever other skill that was currently in demand whether or not he had possessed the necessary requirements.

John sure covers all the bases for these things, Paul thought sourly. And just why am I here, he wondered.

He was about to do an about-face, dump the chips, and make a hasty retreat when Beth walked out of the house carrying a tray piled high with raw 'burgers.

"Oh! Hi, Paul," she began in her typical rapid-fire, aggressive New York accent. "Glad you could make it. Good, you've brought a change. As soon as I set these down I'll introduce you around. Oh, what's in this box your hiding in your bag? Well, never mind that now. Did you bring more chips? Good. How'd you know we'd run low? You always think of the right things. Here, let me take those... there... just slip them in my fingers... now don't argue... the drinks go in the cooler... and go change for heaven's sake! The men are changing in the guest room. You know where it is? Of course you do. Just don't be a naughty boy and go in the master bedroom. That's where the girls are. Now hurry back." Beth leaned close to Paul and finished in a pseudo-whisper. "There are some really cute girls here and I want you to meet a few of them. I mean, meet them here, not in the changing room."

And before Paul could get a word out, she was gone. He wandered over to the grill, dumped the drinks into the tub of ice, and exchanged a few pleasantries with some of the agency people. Then headed back to the house to either change or make his break. He still wasn't sure which.

As he walked toward the Arcadia door, the piggyback wars reached a new high. Paul looked over his shoulder to see who was the dunking victim and stepped right into Joan, who had just turned around from closing the screen behind her. As he felt her fully loaded bikini top flatten against him, his eyes grew large and his mouth dropped. He was too stunned to move back, though he felt his ears turn red. But Joan didn't move, either.

"Hi again," she said brightly, looking up into Paul's eyes, putting her hands lightly on his chest.

"Uh, hi," Paul responded, inching around her in a futile attempt to reach the door, desperate to break the direct eye contact.

"I think you'll do just fine," she said.

Paul floundered for an intelligent reply but Joan saved him the trouble by wiggling – well, it was more like jiggling – past Paul and moving out to the party. She stopped at the edge of the patio and smiled back at him coyly then ran to the pool, her shapely butt swaying in the wisp of a swimsuit bottom precisely as she knew it would.

Paul swallowed, controlling his chemistry by telling himself that she was too young no matter how old she was. In desperation, he bolted into the house and down the long hall to the guest bedroom. He had no idea what she meant when she said he "would do" and he wasn't sure he wanted to find out. Or maybe he was sure he wanted to find out *too much.* Whatever the case, the easiest answer was to dodge the whole issue.

Paul took his time changing. He sincerely hoped that Joan was not the person Beth had wanted him to meet. Granted, he had been single and celibate for almost two years and Joan looked willing, but Paul thought he should ease back into things. A

Bonneville was more in his line than a Ferrari, something built for comfort, as he recalled from the song, more than speed.

After he changed, Paul stood at the window and watched the party around the pool for a few minutes. There was a lot of activity, but Paul thought he knew most of the men there, at least in passing. Some of the women were new, but there were always new women at these parties; females came and went from the agency with an astounding frequency. Their lack of loyalty and "staying power," as Beth called it, had always bothered Paul. The models he met were excited enough when they signed with the agency, but when the job proved to include actual work, their determination rapidly paled. Pounding the pavement to meet potential – though often uninterested – clients was not fun. Waiting in endless lines with a thousand other hopefuls at a casting call was tiring. Making the rounds for free was painful. They stayed a while and, if their career was not stellar or they hit a few rejections, they moved on to another agent in the belief that all they needed to do was sit at home and wait for the phone to ring.

Since Alice handled all Paul's film, television, and novel writing and Paul and John had become good friends, both in and out of the agency, Paul had seen many would-be stars come and go. Paul had hooked up with John on Columbia's *Used Cars*, where Paul had a bit part, augmenting his writing income when Beth was backed in a corner trying to find a bearded lawyer-type. She had called, Alice had called, then John threatened to take violent action if he didn't agree to help. But the beard had gone during the custody battle. Still, Paul did what he could to help out at the small firm in areas besides just his writing and knew quite a bit about the much maligned business of "agenting."

The ten or fifteen percent that Alice earned was often less than the effort cost to collect the fees. With Screen Actors Guild rules limiting commissions on residuals, collecting on a past-due union account was often not worth the long distance phone calls, so Paul's volunteer work was appreciated. Paul remembered one time when Alice had spent over twice what her commission brought in just on phone bills, travel, postage, and secretarial time, trying to collect a day rate from a major studio production in Tucson for an actress/model who walked of the agency as soon as she pocketed the check. Alice never even had the opportunity to breakeven with commissions from the other work she had lined up for the girl – those the girl's new agent pocketed. Paul remembered with some satisfaction how her new agency had dumped her for a younger, taller model later that year.

So, anyway, Paul's interest in having an involvement with anyone from the agency was not high. While there were exceptions, he admitted, but the ladies who frequented the modeling and acting professions were more often shallow, self-centered, dishonorable, back stabbing... oooops, that sounded just like Janet and Paul knew he was getting carried away. *Mustn't stereo-type*, Paul reminded himself, especially since he knew he was also far from perfect. Besides, Janet was a pencil pusher, not the least bit artistic.

Paul shook his head and scanned the party again through the window. There was one blonde talking to John... maybe he should get out there. He grabbed the toy from the bed and unwrapped it on his way to the pool. In the package it looked like a thin ovoid fish made from bright blue and green and red and yellow plastic. But when Paul pulled away the annoying form-fitting hard plastic packaging, the center section swiveled freely.

Intrigued, Paul stopped and looked at the fish closely, his curiosity aroused by the unique design. He went back to the trash and pulled out the package. Yes, it actually said that the fish swam in the water, but there were no switches or obvious places to put batteries. There was a small hole in the bottom of the fish, presumably to allow water to leak into the lower body which would then act like a stabilizing keel. The oval center, which remained vertical while Paul was holding it, probably swiveled out horizontally in the water to keep the fish floating upright. Paul decided the oval would look like a fin. But how did it move? Where were the motors and power supply? Was the package labeled wrong?

Paul walked out to the backyard, wrapped up in the toy, his apprehension was over-shadowed by this curiosity. He sat on the steps in the shallow end of the pool and set the fish in the water. It immediately began to travel across the pool, making a slow, lazy turn to the right. Paul retrieved it before it ran into the water volleyball game just getting underway. He took it out of the pool, looked it over closely, then put it back in again. Off it went. Paul spent the next five minutes in happy oblivion, trying to figure out how the toy moved without any moving parts.

A rush of waves and a suggestive shadow falling across the toy finally distracted Paul. He looked up at

Joan who, to Paul's eyes, looked much like a braid-less Bo Derek from 10. She had that other blonde, the one he noticed earlier, by the arm.

"Hi again," Joan said with a little wiggle which nature only graces to well-built teenage girls.

"Hi," Paul replied, squinting in an effort to see better in the sun's bright glare without his solar-ray glasses.

"This is my sister, Elizabeth. She likes fish, too," Joan added with a mischievous grin.

"That's nice," Paul mumbled, trying to hide his growing embarrassment. "Nice to meet you," he said, finally regaining his manners and some composure. Paul set the fish down to shake hands and it immediately started to swim away.

"Actually, I prefer real fish." Elizabeth's voice was almost dry enough to empty the pool. It was an obvious message to her sister: *Why have you brought me to this clown who plays with toys*, the tone demanded.

"Oh... ah... well, you see, I, ah, bought..."

"You two can talk all night long," Joan said, turning away. "I'll see you later. You be nice to my sister, you hear?" Joan threw the last comment cover her shoulder with a light laugh as she moved back over to the volleyball game.

"Joan!" Elizabeth was not at all happy with her younger sister. The truth was she was not at all happy at being forced to come out to the party. She had come for a family visit, not to meet a bunch of empty-headed strangers polluting the atmosphere with the odor of burnt meat and beer. But Elizabeth's frustration with Joan struck just the right cord with Paul; it made him bold.

"Another Beth. I hope I won't get confused."

"Not Beth, Elizabeth. I don't like the informal version."

"Oh, sorry. Well, that will help keep things clearer, anyway. I usually have to worry about Beth playing intercessor at these things," Paul said, laughing at Elizabeth's distress which so matched his own. "It's refreshing to find that someone else has the same fear of her evil matchmaking ways. Care to join me on the designated victim's stoop?"

Paul pointed back toward the pool's stairs that were empty now that the volleyball game had moved into full swing.

"Sure," Elizabeth said, resigned to her fate. Joan would pay for this later, she vowed silently, but now was no time to be rude. At least this wasn't a date. Elizabeth could always escape back into the party later.

As she stepped away, Paul assessed this older sister. She was probably in her early-to-mid thirties and shorter than Joan, but she did not give up anything on looks. She had the same hourglass figure, tight muscles, sun-bleached blonde hair, and gracefulness in the way she walked. Her figure was, perhaps, a little more settled, but that was probably the figure she would carry for the better part of her adult life. That was much better than plucking a ripening version, like Joan, and worrying if she was going to go to seed in a few years. Of course, if genetics meant much, after seeing Elizabeth, Joan had nothing to worry about over the next decade as her mind grew to match her figure. *If her mind grew to match her boobs,* Paul thought drolly.

Paul sat down next to Elizabeth, feeling the warm water wash into his lap. Suddenly, he had nothing to say and the silence grew.

"You're losing your catch," Elizabeth finally said, pointing to the fish which was swimming with grim determination against the waves from the volleyball game.

"Oh." Paul watched the toy for a few seconds without moving. "Look at it go!"

"You'd better catch it before it gets sunk," Elizabeth said.

"Right."

Paul made a shallow dive, skimming rapidly across the pool to grab the fish.

"So, what kind of fish do you like," he asked as he sat down again next to Elizabeth, holding the plastic fish up so the water could drain out the hole in the bottom.

"All kinds. I'm a marine biologist."

"In Arizona?" Paul asked incredulously.

"No. I live in La Jolla. I'm only here for a visit. Joan wants me to move back here so she throws every man she can find at me." Elizabeth was silent for a minute. She realized how bitter – how cruel – she had sounded and felt bad. "What about you," she continued in a lighter tone. "Why the interest in plastic fish?"

"This? I bought it for my son. It's whether an interesting piece of workmanship, actually."

"What do you mean?" Elizabeth relaxed a little. If Paul had a son, he was probably married and probably safe. *Ha! Joan blew this one!* she thought.

"Well, for one thing, it moves by itself," Paul said.

"What?"

"It moves on its own," Paul repeated, trying to find words that were more descriptive. "There's no power supply, no batteries, nothing to wind up. You just put it in the water and something makes it go. That's what I was trying to figure out when Joan came along, towing you behind. How does this thing operate? I don't know."

"What else?"

"Well, it costs less a lot more some of the other toys even if it doesn't look like much but, well, I don't know. It has a different feel to it, something new, innovative. I just think the kid would like it better than some of the other things he has."

"So, why don't you test it out on him instead of playing with it here?"

"Oh, I will," Paul said with a nod, "in a few weeks."

That was not the answer Elizabeth expected, she admitted to herself. "Why wait?" she asked.

"That's when I get the kid next. Oh! You don't know," Paul said when he saw the puzzled look on Elizabeth's face. "I forgot that Beth didn't introduce us. That's part of her standard introduction: 'Meet mister Paul Johnson, recently divorced and a nice – but lonely – man who misses his son who his ex-wife – the bitch – won't let him see.'"

"So now I know the whole story."

"Pretty much. What about you? Come on," he coaxed after a few seconds of silence.

"Not much to say. College, then work on my PhD. A few romances, but never the right one. Now I spend my vacations visiting my land-lubber sister in Arizona."

"Say, are you free tonight?"

"Free for what?"

"Well, if I know Beth, there'll be enough food here today so we won't be hungry for a week. But there's a *Star Wars* revival at the Palace this weekend. One ticket buys the entire first trilogy and a late night breakfast at the IHOP. They ran the second trilogy yesterday and it's scheduled again for tomorrow so you can see the show in chronological order or release order. I want to see the first ones again – they were the best, anyway - but I really don't want to go alone."

Elizabeth thought for a few seconds – just long enough for Paul to believe she was sorting through excuses – before answering. "Sure, why not? I must be the only person in the world who's never seen any of those films."

"Wow. Then we'd better do dinner and dancing tomorrow night."

"What?"

"Well, if you've missed *Star Wars*, then you must be socially deprived and I feel it's my civic duty to rescue you."

"My, you do work fast," Elizabeth laughed.

"Fast? Well, you said you were leaving soon for California and I didn't think there was much time for a cure."

"I never said I was leaving soon. Only that I was here for a visit."

"Oh." Paul's sudden spurt of confidence and inhibition suddenly left him. Depression and self-doubt settled in like an old friend. "Well, can you think of a good reason to wait?"

"I suppose not," Elizabeth said, surprising them both. "What time's the movie start?"

"How about eight? It's an all-night festival that starts at ten but we can get dinner first if you don't fill up here and play some pinball if we're early.

"OK. But I have to be in before dawn or my little sister will ground me."

They both laughed and Paul felt a weight lift from his shoulders. He was looking forward to someone with whom he could talk, perhaps enjoy a little romantic by-play. Naturally, sex hovered around the edges of his conscience, but it was not part of the main equation. Unlike the stereotype that most men tried to emulate, Paul avoided one night stands or short-term relations just to have a mere bed mate. This was a habit that preceded his marriage, not a result of the divorce. He wanted a companion and, if he could keep his raging hormones – too long suppressed – under reign, Elizabeth looked like someone who could make some interesting conversation.

"Hey, you two," John yelled from across the pool. "We need some help over here!"

Paul looked up. While he and Elizabeth had talked the volleyball net had vanished and piggyback wars were again the main game. Joan had landed John as her mount and they were badly outnumbered. Paul looked over at Elizabeth. She looked about as eager to join the melee as Paul. Still, John was insistent and Joan was mercilessly teasing so, bowing to the pressure, they joined the others.

Before Elizabeth climbed up on Paul's shoulders, Paul dropped the fish back in the water. It scooted off about six feet then began making lazy figure eights through the waves and the revelers.

CHAPTER FOUR

June 14, 2002

West of Flagstaff, near Clay Springs, Arizona

Angie Tucker bolted out of the house on West Graphite Road and was running down the street before the screen door slammed against the stop. She turned around when she was sixty feet down the road, and skipped backwards down the slight hill.

"Hurry up! We'll be late to the movie!" she yelled to her twin sister who was only just leaving the house.

Barbie waived at Angie impatiently. Her older sister was always in a hurry, always bossing, as if three minutes really made that much of a difference. "I'm coming!" she yelled back. "Just wait a minute, will ya?"

With all the dignity that her thirteen years could give her, she tailed after her sister. She walked with slow decorum away from their family's neatly trimmed split-level home tucked away in the woods right at the eastern edge of Clay Springs, Arizona.

Behind her, with absolutely no dignity at all, Buffy, their ungainly Saint Bernard, burst out of the house and bounded down the street after the girls.

"Barbie! Look out behind you!" Angie screamed. "You let Buffy out!"

Barbie turned just in time to catch Buffy's front paws on her chest. The rambunctious beast knocked the hapless girl on her tail in a fit of squeals and laughs. She tried to wrap her arms around the dog's huge neck, but Buffy had spotted Angie and bounced off Barbie toward her indignant sister.

"Will you hurry up! We're late already! I told Randy that I'd meet him at the show!"

"I'm trying! Help me with Buffy. He's coming right to you!"

"You let him out; you get him back!" Angie retorted hotly, but made a grab for Buffy's collar as she dodged past her, head high and tail circulating like a propeller pushing her faster. She snagged her and tried to yank her back toward the house, but the Cujo clone just stood her ground and slobbered over Angie's new sneakers.

Barbie ran up to Angie, bubbling over with laughter and nonsense. After a brief – and heartless – argument, the twins agreed that the only way to coax Buffy back to the house was for both of them to go home together. They pulled and yanked until they had her huge head aimed in the right direction and began urging her home, but she jerked away when a pair of low flying aircraft shook the house with a window-rattling sonic boom.

The girls jumped at the sound and Buffy almost pulled free from them but they managed, somehow, to hold on to her despite her wiggling and squirming, even though it meant they had to roll around on the neighbor's grass just to keep her from slipping away.

"Did you see that?" Angie asked, awe making her voice husky.

"Yeah. What was it?"

"Them. It was a them."

"Well, then 'them' was probably just some hot-shot military guys from that base in Nevada where they invent stealth bombers and stuff."

"Yeah, I guess. Look! They're coming back!"

The two ships shot into view over a stand of trees behind the last house on the block and came to an abrupt stop. They hovered a brief second, then settled into the trees.

"Planes can't do that!" whispered Barbie with more than a little fear.

"Yes they can."

"No they can't, smarty. Remember science class. Things can't stop that fast. It's one of Newton's stupid laws. They can't break a Newton law. Be still, Buffy!"

"Yes they can."

"No they can't."

"Can."

"Can't."

"Can too, and I can prove it!"

"Oh, yeah? How?"

"They can do it because they just did it."

Barbie glared at Angie. That was irrefutable female, unassailable pre-teen logic and Barbie certainly could not refute it if she was to uphold the honor of kids worldwide. What was right was right and it didn't matter if it didn't make any sense or some old guy had made a rule about it. Rules, made by adults, were made to be broken. *That* was a rule all teenage girls new instinctively.

"Smarty."

"That's because I'm older," Angie said smugly, topping it off with a look that would have made a cat envious. "Besides, I don't care. Come on. I'm late and Randy'll be mad," she added hotly.

Angie stood up and released her grip on Buffy. That was all she had waited for. Like a shot she broke from Barbie's grasp and ran to the woods.

"Damn! Come back here you stupid bitch!" Barbie spat out, though in a voice that was meant not to carry.

"You'd better not let momma hear you talk like that or we'll both get tanned!" Angie was quick to correct her "younger" sister and Barbie was just as quick to point out that Angie was the one who taught Barbie how to swear.

"And besides," Barbie insisted, "a female dog is called a bitch and momma always says we need to use the proper terms for things and not slang."

"But 'damn' is still gonna get you switched," Angie retorted.

"OK, OK," Barbie submitted, this time ignoring her normal rebuttal. "But Buffy's gone now and if we don't get her back, momma'll tan us for that, too! So you'd better help me get her or you'll never get to the school."

Angie glared for a second, caught up herself in the absolute logic of the situation and hating Barbie for turning her own tricks against her wasn't going to help. After all, Barbie was the younger sister and she was supposed to be stupid! Barbie and Angie stood for a second and looked at each other. Finally, they both realized that there was no help for it and, agreeing non-verbally as they so often did, they turned and ran after Buffy. Besides, the big lumbering Saint Bernard was headed toward the woods where those planes had landed. There were probably a couple of cute pilots hanging around that might prove more interesting than the going to the town's only elementary school where they showed old films during the summer in the gym. Randy wasn't that cute, anyway.

The twins entered the woods on a trail that wandered over to a man-made pond. Buffy liked the pond in summer, the thick Saint Bernard coat more suited for the winter snows. Scrambling down the well-worn path, the girls pelted after the dog. If she made it to the pond and got wet, they were done. She would need a bath to get rid of the pond stink and they were going to be the groomers for sure. They followed the sound of Buffy's excited barking but stopped when her normal deep, slow woofing turned into a series of quick and savage sounding barks.

"I hope she hasn't found a skunk again," Barbie whined, wrinkling her lightly freckled nose at the thought.

"If she has, you have to wash her!"

"I did it last time," Barbie protested, turning on her sister and planting her hands firmly on her still-girlish hips.

"Let's not stand here and argue. Let's go and get her." Angie was aware that time was passing and Randy was not one to wait and maybe the cute pilots would all be *old*. Angie knew she was cute and could have her pick of the guys in town – not that there were many when school was out – but Randy was the hot number this summer and she wasn't going to lose his attentions by standing him up on a date!

Suddenly, Buffy's growls turned into a scream of pain, followed by a yelp and a whimper and then silence.

"Come on! It was over here!" Barbie grabbed her sister's hand and pulled her into the brush, headed for a clearing a little east of the pond. Buffy was her special friend and confidant and sometimes defender when Angie got a little too rough.

The girls pushed through the tangled undergrowth and into a small clearing under tall Ponderosa pines. Barbie, who was still in the lead, froze in horror. Buffy was a quivering mass of gore and torn skin lying in a widening pool of blood. The bright red liquid sparkled in a shaft of light that squeezed through the twilight created by the pines' branches. Suddenly, the sun went behind a passing cloud and the clearing was plunged into an eerie half-light, making Buffy hard to see in the shadows.

"What is it?" Angie asked petulantly as she stepped into the clearing next to her sister.

"God, no!" Angie gasped, as her eyes adjusted and she could see the dog more clearly.

Angie stumbled past her sister toward Buffy, drawn and repulsed by the sight of fresh death. She covered her face with her hands and staggered against a tree, trying not to throw up all over her good cloths. Suddenly, a scaled hand reached from around the tree and grabbed her by the throat. Angie gurgled a brief protest, her eyes wide with fear. Then she stepped back from the tree.

Slowly, Angie turned toward Barbie, who was still standing where she had stopped, as frozen in place as if she was rooted there. As Angie moved,

Barbie saw the blood running down the white undershirt Angie wore beneath the brightly flowered blouse she had bought with her last allowance. The blood streaked in runnels down the ribbed fabric, running freely from a throat that was ripped completely out. Angie began a slow, shuffling walk toward her sister, her body not yet aware that it was dead.

"Angie? What...?" Barbie took two staggering steps toward her sister, unable to pull her eyes from the mask of terror that twisted the face of her dying sister. Then, suddenly breaking free from the spell, Barbie turned to flee back down that path. But as she turned, a scaled hand with wicked claws slashed through the speckled sunlight, ripping into Barbie's chest just below her neck. The hand jerked down, shredding Barbie's thin blouse, a claw catching in her bra. With a vicious jerk, the hand pulled away her blouse, her training bra, and her left breast, leaving behind four parallel groves in her body almost two inches deep.

The hand swiped a second time, this time laterally, ripping open Barbie's abdomen. She stood for a moment, watching her intestines fall onto the ground, marveling at their length and the steam rising from the cool, moist mountain air. She tried to speak but no noise made it past her lips, only a few weak, small sounds caught in her throat. Slowly she sank to her knees, her arms held out in front of her, elbows tucked into her sides. Behind her, Angie finally stumbled, falling into her kneeling sister. The pair toppled backwards next to Buffy, forming a mass of ruined bodies.

From the bushes, three individual pairs of silver-clad legs moved into the clearing, which was suddenly cold and dark and silent, except for the soft buzzing of gathering flies. A fourth pair stood in the path to the clearing, the direction Barbie had tried to take to escape back to the road. Off in the distance, a dog began to howl.

CHAPTER FIVE

June 15, 2002

Henry's Bar, Phoenix, Arizona,
and Clay Springs, Arizona

"Still playing with toys, I see," John said as he slipped into the booth opposite Paul and picked up the toy fish.

"Huh? Oh, hi, John. Yeah, I'm still playing with it."

"Well, if it brought me the kind of luck it brought you, then I can understand the fascination."

"Huh?"

"Articulate today, aren't you? I meant Liz. Lizbet. E-liz-ah-beth. From the party. Have fun?" John asked, turning the conversation to the latest girl he had thrown in Paul's direction.

"Oh, yeah," Paul said, finally pulling himself out of the world where his thoughts had taken him. "She's a nice girl."

"Stacked, too."

"We didn't get that far."

John just smiled. "Beer on tap. And run a tab. Ah, put it on his tab," he said as the bartender nodded in John's direction. "Come on, what happened? You were out all night, I hear."

"Remember her?"

"That girl with the PhD? That *is* the stacked one we were talking about. Right? Elizabeth? You didn't change topics on me in the middle of the conversation?"

"No, no, the one I met at the party. Yeah. Elizabeth." Paul seemed to shake himself out of a fog. "Sorry. The mind is elsewhere."

"Yeah, I remember her. You ended up with the wrong girl. She was much too intelligent for you, buddy. Should have taken the younger sister, Joan. Or what about Helen? She was stacked too. Just my type. And smart, so your type, too."

Paul snorted. "Maybe she had brains, but she didn't act like it. Helen I mean. She ran into that tall, bald guy when she headed back North. Remember? Forget his name. She married him. I mean, she was married when she was at the party." Paul paused to take a drink of his tea, then set down the glass. "That date with Elizabeth, we went to the *Star Wars* revival. That's it, just the movies."

John sighed and shook his head, turning a baleful eye on his friend. "I'm worried about you, buddy. All night with that girl and you didn't even get her shirt off?"

"I wasn't in the mood for more than company."

"You're not turning, you know..." John asked, wigging his hand.

"No, I still prefer girls. I went to see Janet after the party, before I picked up Elizabeth."

"Stupid." John shook his head, an expression in his eyes that said more to Paul than volumes.

"Yeah. Well, I told her I was researching a story and I needed to look at some of Jeremy's toys."

"I'll bet she loved that."

"Yeah," Paul said, punctuating it with a hard chuckle that was more groan than laugh. "She nearly blew the roof off. She had another hot date. I mentioned that writing was how I paid child support and she couldn't collect what I didn't make. It took a little arguing but she finally let me in the house to go through his stuff and only after I promised to be out long before her date arrived. Jeremy was a bit of a problem. He didn't want to let anything go. I guess his mother has been punishing him by taking away his toys."

"Ouch."

"Yeah. Anyway, I promised to bring everything back. And I had to swear it was just so I could see what he had before his next birthday. I told him that I didn't want to duplicate anything."

"That worked? Thanks," John said to the bartender as he set the beer down. "To casting agents! They keep the beer industry flowing." He took a long drink, closed his eyes, and sighed.

"No, of course that did not work."

"What's all this stuff then," John asked, waving his hand over the collection of toys Paul had laid out on the table.

"Well for Jeremy I had to promise to buy the 'whole collection.' You know how he is. He doesn't want one Ninja Turtle, he wants them all with all the accessories."

"A true kid."

"Right. A little too like his mother sometimes: it's all about him."

"Kids grow out of that. Most guys do when they realize the girls want it all and if you want what the girls have you have to share a little. But speaking of women, did Janet give you any shit about taking the stuff."

"Nothing but. I think she was worried I was going to hock it or that I had a new girlfriend who had kids and was being cheap."

"So, how'd you get that wonderful ex-wife of yours to act like a human?"

"Well, I told her that I was working on this article on kid's toys and I wanted to see what companies made the most of Jer's toys, the special ones I had bought, to see if there were any trends. I told her that if I didn't finish the research then there wouldn't be any money for child support this month. Money goes were reason fails. Anyway, she 'allowed' me to ask Jeremy and of course I had to negotiate with him, too. But he said I could rummage through his toy box after I promised to buy him something special the next time we went out and that I really, really was not going to punish him and keep anything. "

"Did *that* worked?"

"He's a good kid, but I think he has a materialistic streak as wide as Janet's. Anyway, I was in a bit of a hurry since the negotiations took longer than I expected. Then, of course, Janet needed to make sure I understood what a low-life I am before she'd let me in the house."

"And?"

"What you see here."

"All this from your kid's toy box?" John asked, looking over the dozen or so toys scattered across the table.

"Plus a few things I picked up from a store in Scottsdale later. The same place where I bought the fish and most of the other things I scrounged from Jeremy's toy box."

"So is this the 'entire collection' of these super toys you wanted to look over?"

"No. Jeremy only had a few but it was easy enough to recognize them. You know, I've bought that kid some real neat and unique stuff in the past few years. Almost no one else has these toys. They all came from the Black Forest, that exclusive little toy shop in Scottsdale, not the mass marketers. I bought the rest of these there. They're all from the same designer and they're only sold in small, privately owned stores, not the big chains. They're expensive, but not too much."

"So? What's the news value of these things? Designer-label toys for the rich?"

"'So,' he says. Watch this."

Paul took the toy from John and held it up in the dim light of Henry's, ignoring his half-finished drink that was slowly becoming too waterlogged from melted ice to drink. He twirled the center disk and watched the multiple colors sparkle in the dim light, then put the fish on the table.

"You say this started it all?" John asked, watching the fish stand upright, the twirling center disk acting as a gyroscope.

"Yeah. A week ago. It's the first time I really looked at the toys from the Black Forest outside the boxes, but I first found these marvelous toys about a year ago. Never really looked at them before, you know; not until the pool party," Paul answered, adding more sweetener to his waterlogged glass of ice tea.

John reached across and picked up one of the other toys Paul had scattered across the table. John examined it closely, but could see nothing special in it. It was a small plane, about the size of his hand with a four inch wing span. He handed it over to Paul.

"Show me."

Paul nodded eagerly and held the plane up at eye level.

"Fly," Paul said to the plane. The tiny propeller began to spin. When it reached its full throttle, Paul set it down on the table and released the plane. It dove off the end, then recovered and increased its altitude. It flew in slow figure eights above the table.

"Straight," Paul whispered, and the plane began a gentle curve and then flew out toward the center of the near-empty tavern. When was over the long bar Paul whispered "land" and the plane made a perfect touchdown. It taxied over to a stack of glasses, turned and sat, its prop slowing to idle, looking for the world like a Piper by a glass control tower and, somehow, smug with its own cuteness.

"Cute, Paul," the bartender on duty called out, "but this is a bar, not a playground."

"Yeah, sorry," Paul muttered. Then: "return." And the little engine revved up and the plane launched itself into the air and made a beeline back to Paul's table, where it landed with the same precision that it showed on the longer runway of the bar.

"Voice activated?" John asked.

Paul nodded then sat still for a long minute just staring at the toy before reaching for a small crystal ball that was nestled in a black holder. The entire unit looked like a hand holding the ball in a wadded up velvet handkerchief.

But John had picked up a wooden dragon and a knight in armor from the pile and set them facing each other. He was playing around when he tapped the dragon once on its head. The knight immediately attacked the dragon with sword and shield.

"Hey! What the hell!" John yelled as the dragon fought back with a blast of fire.

"Nothing to worry about. Watch."

Paul waited until the dragon had backed a few steps and reared up, preparing to strike again. Just as the beast belched forth a blast of fire, Paul stuck his hand in the blaze, deflecting it from the knight as the flame bounced back at the dragon. A few tendrils seeped through when Paul opened his fingers a little and the knight took cover behind the salt shaker.

"Paul..."

"Nothing happened." Paul displayed his unmarked hand for John's inspection.

"You weren't burned. But I saw... How?"

"Some kind of miniature holographic projector built into the dragon's head, I think. And there must be a visual feedback loop because you saw how the flame reacted to my hand – like hitting a brick wall with a flame thrower – then seeped through the cracks in my fingers. It makes Disney look downright primitive. They'll fight as long as you want. The directions say neither will ever win nor get hurt. It's non-violent violence, I guess." Paul tapped the dragon again and both figures reverted to their original positions and then froze. "The knight's slaved to the dragon."

"Where's the battery go?" John asked, picking up the knight and examining it.

"No batteries."

"Where's the power come from?"

"Don't know."

"Well, let's take it apart and find out."

"It won't work. According to the instruction book, the toys are made from a new synthetic. If they're damaged, say by a knife trying to get inside, they dissolve."

"Hummmp. You believe that?"

"Yeah. I lost a really neat flying pterodactyl that way."

"But the dragon's painted wood!" John protested, trading the knight for the winged menace of legend.

"No, it only looks that way."

"What about these other things?"

"Well, the dragon obeys voice commands, but the pair will fight back and forth just like the give and taken in a real battle. Oh, and the dragon can fly too, if you ask it."

"Get outta here," John said in a passable New York accent.

"I'd show you but I already pissed off the bartender by using the counter for a runway. But look at this, it will blow you away."

Paul moved the crystal ball and its elegantly carved base in front of John.

"OK, give. What is it?" John asked after a few seconds when nothing happened.

"It's a toy."

"Yeah, but what happens?"

"This is a real toy. An educational toy. It does what all toys are supposed to do: it teaches while the children play with it."

"It's just a clear ball," John said in disgust.

"You have to turn it on."

"How?"

"Ball. On."

Instantly the ball filled with a swirling mist shot through with bright flashes similar to sheet lightening. A rich full voice resonated from the ball's black base. "Topic?"

"Maze," Paul said.

"Level?" asked the crystal.

"One," Paul said, then to John: "I'm not good enough to play the advanced games yet."

"Choice?"

Still looking at John, Paul asked, "What's your favorite cartoon?"

"Ah... Dog Ranger and the Space Patrol?"

"Good choice. Ball: Dog Ranger and the Space Patrol."

"Your mission," the crystal said, "is to rescue the Princess of Galactica from the evil clutches of the Aeolian Lizard People. You must escape from the Aeolian prison, where you were captured, locate the Princess in their Headquarters, and find a way off the planet before time runs out or you are captured. Do you wish further instructions?"

"No." Paul looked at John. "'Start' activates the program."

"I'm not sure I dare."

"Start," Paul said, not giving his friend an option.

The ball cleared and a projected box about a foot and a half square sprang up around it in a shimmering blue field. A clear representation of the floppy-eared Dog Ranger appeared in a Dark Ages dungeon complete with flickering torches, scurrying spiders, and lurking rats.

"The object of the game is to find a way through the booby traps, the guards, assorted weird creatures, and a castle that's right out of Poe's worst nightmare," Paul said, eyes bright.

"It's just a video game?"

"No. More than that. See, you start out with five million points. You lose points for every creature you kill. There's a non-violent way through the maze, but you can use your stun gun – that only costs a single point – but if you just think about it and figure out the maze, you won't even need that. This is a real brain teaser. It's a game of logic and strategy as you try to work past the guards and monsters and such without killing anything. More than that, you can build points by rescuing other creatures the bad guys have stashed in cells and cages. The more of them that reach the end with you, the higher your score. It promotes logical think, problem solving, non-violence, and humane treatment of all living creatures."

"In a video game?"

"Yeah."

"That's… un-American. Killing things is required." "

"One of the first things I learned is that there are times when you should stop and help some creature in trouble even if it takes up time. It will recharge your stunner or give you a time bonus. Of course, if you can figure out how to free the creature, you get the points at the end."

"No extra life?"

"You can't die. You just get captured and thrown back in jail."

"That's weird."

"The only downside is that the bad guys are really bad. They tend to cook the creatures they kill. Some kind of reptiles with big teeth. They are sketchy, not enough to create nightmares, but they are distinctive enough. I sure wouldn't want to meet them on a dark night. When you finish the maze, the Space Patrol arrives, rescues all the creatures, and tosses the bad guys in dungeon." Paul took another quick drink. "I tell you, I get the weirdest feeling that the people who made this game have been there, seen these things, and probably have t-shirts to prove it.

"Watch." Paul gave the start command then watched the crystal closely. The images moved in 3-D; John had a good view from his side of the table. As Ranger Dougie Dog moved through the dungeon level, Paul would call out directional commands and occasionally give the crystal specific instructions like 'go through the trap door,' or 'lock the door behind you,' or 'take the guard's sword and throw it down the well.' The game responded to his voice, moving the character through the dungeon maze until Paul took a wrong turn and ended up in the guards' chamber. He tried to leave quietly, but took a wrong turn again and was captured. The guards marched him back and threw him in a different cell; one Paul said had a more difficult escape path. John watched enthralled.

"I usually get a little farther at this level. I've only beaten the easy scripts so far. The action changes, guards move, things are never the same except for the layout. The game works on memory skills, since the castle stays the same, but there are so many random elements that each time you start, it's a new game. You have to remember the dead ends and the secret shortcuts to win in time. There are twenty different games in the ball. Some are two-player, like 3-D chess. The instructions say some will take up to six players, and a team game that has some wonderful graphics of space ships in a major battle for control of some solar system that's not ours, if you have multiple balls. I think it will take unlimited players at once or in separate 'quests.' I haven't tried that since these little suckers are *very* expensive. I'll save if for when Jeremy is a little older. Maybe because they're all voice command and it's hard to pull multiple player commands from a group of kids all yelling at once, but the instructions say multi-ball games need to have the balls separated by at least six feet."

"Why haven't I seen this advertised?"

"It's a prototype, I think. The owner of the store where I bought the other toys was testing it for the distributor. I had to leave a fifteen hundred dollar deposit to take it and he wouldn't have given it to me even then if he hadn't have known me from before. And if I *still* had to promise his store a prominent place in my article. This line of toys is *very* exclusive and the owner was concerned about losing the franchise. The toys are *expensive* – did I mention that? – come in limited quantities, and sell out in a few weeks. Christmas? If you're not there the minute the toys are delivered, forget it. But this is a little different, which is why a few were sent out for beta testing. They weren't sure if the kids would like a portable six-inch crystal ball as much as their television set video games."

"Some people you have to hit with a stupid stick to get them to wake up. Kids... hell, adults, will eat this up. And I think this could be modified for training simulators for military and police forces," John said, catching more than just a little of Paul's enthusiasm.

"I think so, too. I promised a second article on just the cube and the testing program when I'm finished with it. He hopes the company will release the mass produced version in a few months. Well, mass production as defined by this toy maker. Let one of the major electronics companies get a hold of the specs on this and the video ball'll corner the video game market, especially since you can change the game pack by changing the base. There's supposed to be twenty different bases with twenty different games each when it is released. It's not supposed to cost a whole lot, either, and one of the game packs is an educational version with an encyclopedia updated through an internet data link, atlas, math, science, foreign language, and reading tutors, everything your kid'll need to pass high school."

"Where were these things when I was flunking German?"

"You flunked German?"

"Yeah. I wasn't supposed to know how to ask the teacher to sleep with me in German. I guess I got the question right but the phrase was a little vulgar."

"That new blonde that started in your senior year?"

"Yeah."

"Don't worry. Half the kids in school tried to fail her class before she married Dorfmann."

"The algebra teacher?"

"Yeah. There's no justice in life. It made graduation bearable, though." John had been a senior in high school when Paul was a sophomore and Janet a freshman. John had not liked Janet even back then. Paul reached for another toy, shaking his head, pushing thoughts of his ex back into the closet where they belonged. "This one is a holographic martial arts battle. You stand on a pad and fight ninjas and other bad guys. You need to learn the proper moves. The pad generates an electrical field that picks up your moves and translates it to the challenger fighter. It's a fun way to exercise. It works in perfect sync. The only thing that would make it better would be if you could feel the blows you strike on your opponent."

John picked up a pair of keyboards linked to a small black box, examining with a worried look wrinkling his forehead.

"That one's interesting," Paul said, responding to John's unspoken question. "It's like a land version of Battleship. When it's on, a black screen appears between the players. You set up your army up with the keyboard on one side to protect the fortress and your opponent sets his pieces on the other side to attack. Once the battle starts, it's like a real war, nothing works as planned. It teaches strategy, quick thinking, and the futility of violence. There are twelve scenarios from ancient China to England to a battle on the moon with the problems of low gravity, and several that take place on strange planets with weird creatures. It's all done with holography. Once the battle starts, it goes fast and furious."

"Voice controlled?"

"Not this one," Paul said. "You are right across from your opponent who could hear everything you said. So you need to learn computer skills to keep your tactics and strategy secret."

John looked at the array of toys before him, picking one up and setting it down, then moving onto the next.

"These are fantastic," John finally said.

"More than that, they're...well, they're magical!"

"OK. You found some super magic toys. What's that got to do with anything?" John asked, playing his favorite role as devil's advocate.

Paul took a deep breath and let it out slowly. It came out in a hushed tone, how the hints – nothing real – had come from his preliminary research, some of which he spread out on the table between them in the form of a chart, showing links between retailers, distributors, and, finally, through shipping records, back to Flagstaff. The electronics for the holography came from three different firms; no one had the complete diagrams for the whole unit. The parts were assembled at a small plant in Ohio that received the molded parts from a company in Germany, electronics from Taiwan, and the plastics from Mexico. Once assembled, they would not work until they were sent to a small chemical firm in Flagstaff and dip-coated with some obscure combination of common chemicals and a catalyst that the final assembly company received directly from the designer and that they couldn't analyze.

The individual manufacturers were sometimes eager to talk, sometimes reluctant, but they all eventually told Paul the same story: they had never met the designer; everything was handled by mail, including the royalty payments from the distributor in Chicago. Nobody knew who designed the toys and provided some of the special parts, but they all hoped Paul could find the answer: they saw major profits in spin-offs from the products and wanted an edge over their competitors. All the company sold was toys of their own design. And no patents. Patents can be research. And so far, no one had been successful in reverse engineering any of the toys well enough to duplicate the processes.

"Whoever is making these things is making a fortune, but they are doing it at a nickel a time and it is just a *small* fortune. If they branched out into other goods, or increased the production runs, the sky's the limit," Paul said. "These are the best selling toys in the stores that carry them – I called a few. They're not widely distributed. It seems they began to hit the market about fifteen years or so ago. Just one or two are first, handmade, and very limited runs. Then about twelve years ago, the manufacturers were brought in and production increased dramatically. So did the number of designs. The designer must have been making a bundle, you know, even with small production runs, but once things increased he spread out across the country. But it's all still small run production compared to a Mattel or such and only sold in independent or small chains. If he ever authorized major mass production – I mean, mass as in Toys 'R' Us or KayBee, you know, the big chains – this guy could own the toy market. Or the defense industry, if you stop and think about it."

"So you're going to write a story about an eccentric inventor who had money to begin with and now has more. For what magazine? *Fortune*? *Money*? *People*? Who?"

"In Motion."

"The television and movie magazine?"

"Yeah. They want to know if the holography has commercial applications in a larger format and how it'll impact production of features and video. I like that editor. She has vision. Nobody else is interested. I made a lot of phone calls this week."

"Allison?"

"Yeah. Super lady. So after I talked to her I began thinking about a film angle. Keep in mind, the toy started me thinking but I did not get really into this until after I saw took Elizabeth to see the *Star Wars* trilogy."

"Huh?" John asked, taken back by the sudden change in subject.

"Elizabeth hadn't seen them. Here, look at this."

Paul passed John a full color picture of Mimas, Saturn's seventh moon.

"Isn't this Mineos, Mymoss… Kinda looks like the Death Star."

"Pronounced 'MY-mas.' Discovered in 1789 by the British astronomer Sir William Hershel. But the photos were not taken until November of 1980."

"Yeah. That was… Oh. Wait. The first *Star Wars* was released in 1977. The photos weren't taken until three years later."

"That's my point. Whoever designed the Death Star had already seen Mimas, I'd bet dollars to donuts on that one. And it was one of the Titans that Hercules killed, while he was saving the *Earth* from destruction."

"You're trying to say that the designer saw this and for some strange Hollywood reason with mythical and metaphysical insight put the thing in a *movie*, for God's sake?"

"No. It's not that bad. It's just more than passing strange. What do we know about Mimas? It orbits 185,520 kilometers from Saturn, has a diameter of 392 kilometers and masses 3.80e19 kilograms. It has a low density, about 1.17, so the brains figure it is composed mostly of ice water with only a small amount of rock. But what if it is ice on the outside for a water supply and inside is made of metal and hollow spaces? That would keep the mass down.

That crater, incidentally, is almost one third of the diameter of the entire moon. Its walls are about 5 kilometers high, and parts of its floor measure 10 kilometers deep. The central peak rises 6 km above the crater floor. OK?"

"So?"

"So, scale those down to a model that you can buy in the comic book shops and they *identically* match the proportions on the Death Star. Identical, with less than a one percent deviation. How about that?"

"Coincidence?"

"OK, add this: The surface is saturated with impact craters. Look at the pattern of craters canyons. Now match it with the pattern of gun emplacements on the Death Star and the pretty much match," Paul said, perhaps a touch smugly, as he passed over a publicity photo of the Death Star. "Even the 'canyon' that they fly through to blow the thing up matches a long crack on the back side of Mimas that the experts are calling a stress fracture."

"Are you suggesting that there is a *Star Wars* Death Star in orbit around Saturn that everyone thinks is an ice moon?"

"Well, not exactly," Paul temporized, "but what if someone was trying to tell us that there was danger from that direction that could eventually destroy the Earth."

"Ha! Got the hole in your conspiracy theory!"

"What?"

"The moon orbits Saturn, right?"

"Yeah."

"Saturn orbits the sun, right?"

"Yeah. Sure.

"That means that the direction is constantly changing. If we draw a line from the Earth to Mimas and say danger comes from that direction, then it will be constantly changing. We only know that there is danger from 'out there' somewhere."

"Well? Isn't that enough to get started?"

"Paul, Paul, Paul. If this was real, why hasn't it hit the press yet? Why are you the first person to put it together?"

"Someone got to Lucas," Paul said flatly.

"Yeah. And who would that someone be?"

"The same people who put the lid on everything dealing with space. They guys with the black helicopters."

"Who?"

"The men in black suits."

John looked at Paul like he was some sort of talking amoeba himself. Paul new he sounded completely off his track, but it all fit together so well.

"The infamous Men in Black," John said with a shake of the head. "OK. I'll bite. Why haven't these men in black found your inventor yet?"

"They're the *government* John," Paul said as if that explained all sorts of inefficiencies.

"The government?"

Paul nodded.

"Give me a break," John said, taking a deep swallow of his beer. He was beginning to worry that his long-time friend had slipped a gasket or three. "Another Area 51 conspiracy?"

"No," Paul insisted. "This isn't a Roswell or a secret alien autopsy. Besides, everyone knows the aliens are really kept in Dayton, Ohio, anyway," Paul went on, waving away John's objections. He point at the toys, forcing John to take another look at each one, then waved the publicity photos and the NASA images of Mimas in front of John's disbelieving eyes.

"Dayton? That's nuts too. Dayton is duller than Cleveland."

"Exactly my point," Paul agreed, nodding his head. "I don't know what's there, but it's something the government – the government, John, never forget those people – it's something the government wants buried deep. I'm ex-Air Force. I know these things. These things are real. The toys are real, aren't they?"

"Toys are real, your conspiracy theory is not."

"Look, it's not a conspiracy theory. It's not even well thought out. More of a 'what if.' Maybe there's something I'm missing, like a time element that's lost somehow. Maybe a date. Something. But there're just too many coincidences for me to let this slide as *only* a coincidence."

"I guess you're saying this came from your infamous 'toy maker' person." John did not quite scoff at the idea, but his tone made it plain that he thought the idea was ridiculous. "Give. What does this have to do with anything?" John asked perplexed. "The movie was made, what, three years before the radar image was taken?"

"Well, Elizabeth said something that got me thinking, and I guess my mind has been more centered on the toys than the movies anyway," Paul replied slowly. "After the show, she mentioned that the Death Star was an almost exact copy of Mimas. She thinks the *Star Wars* fortress was copied from Mimas in exact detail."

"That's impossible," John scoffed. "We already figured out that the timing is wrong. They couldn't have seen it before the movie was made. It's like the faces they found on Mars. Nothing but a coincidence. You told her that I hope."

Paul waved off John's protests impatiently. "I said her comments made me think. So I called around. The design for the fortress was bought from an outsider before the film went into production."

"Did LucasFilm confirm this?"

"No. They won't tell the press anything about anything if it doesn't fit with their own marketing goals. They've got that kind of power. But I have a friend who works in special effects. He heard from the sister of a designer on the film that the drafts for the fortress arrived in the mail during pre-production with a note suggesting that a touch of reality would lend credibility to the story line. They came with photos of Mimas... three years before there were photos of Mimas. But nobody checked on that. LucusFilm ate it up. The design work was cheap and whoever sent the Mimas stuff didn't ask for screen credit, either."

"Let me guess. The designs arrived from Flagstaff?"

"Yeah. From Flagstaff. And nobody knows how the designer found out about the story in the first place. Those scripts are guarded like Fort Knox."

"So what are you trying to tell me?"

"One more point, then I'll get to it."

"What?"

"The measurements, the ones I mentioned about the dimensions?"

"Yeah," John said, his voice saying plainly that he expected a trap.

"Radio images were not available on Mimas until the late seventies and not released in time for the design work to have been made before they reached the producers. And…"

"And?"

"The photos of Mimas were not taken until 1980, remember, when the measurements were confirmed and refined. And…"

"Oh, God! Another 'and'!"

"Yeah. *And*, the stress fracture on the far side was not known until November of 1980 *and* it is in *exactly* the same place as the canyon is in relationship to the central peak of the crater. This *can't* be coincidence."

"Yeah. I'm afraid to ask, Paul, but exactly what is the punch line?"

"We have an alien living in Flagstaff."

John began laughing and then couldn't stop. Try as he might, all he was able to say were a few "oh's" and "I's" and "No's" and an occasional "Oh, God." But Paul sat quietly, letting the laughing fit run its course. It wasn't as if it was unexpected.

Finally, John managed to swallow a few times and take a couple of deep breaths.

"I'm sorry," he said around chuckles. "It's just that I know some people in the Communications Department at Northern Arizona University. I could have told you there were aliens in Flagstaff a long time ago, and not just lawn guys from Mexico."

"I'm serious, John."

"Yeah, right, but don't tell anyone else or you'll end up in the nut house at 24th Street and Van Buren."

"Can you explain this any other way?"

"Well, there are a lot of fairies up there in San Francisco, too. Maybe they got some elves to help them cobble up the toys. Or maybe Santa Clause moved south for a while. I don't know. But this is nuts. God! And I fell for it."

"I'm serious, John. These toys are too advanced, too unbelievable for any other explanation."

"Look, if this is going to get you back on track, if it will help you write, then go look for aliens. It doesn't matter. You know the basis for research: set your hypothesis and then change it as the facts are revealed. You're not going to find any aliens, except illegal aliens from south of the border, in Flagstaff, but if it will get you going again, then go look. Just don't be disappointed if all you turn up is some eccentric old geezer or a ten year old genius. Look, maybe there's a movie script in this somewhere, something about men in black chasing down aliens with a way to hypnotize people into forgetting whatever it is they think they saw or something."

"They did that. It was called *Men in Black*, remember?"

"Or maybe it's a real fantasy, like pretending there's nightlife in Dayton," John said, waiving off Paul's Hollywood conspiracy. "Don't get hung up trying to prove your theory, though. That'll just get in the way. Let the evidence speak for itself."

"I know that. But everything points to Flagstaff. I've checked the trade magazine ads and articles, made the phone calls, and branched out into other areas. It's all in toys: this new stuff isn't appearing in military hardware, transportation, anything. Just toys."

"Look," John said, growing seriously." You have enough here to tell you that something strange or unusual or wonderful or weird is going on. Whatever. It's enough to make a start. What are you going to do about it?"

"Do about it?" Paul echoed, perplexed. "I hadn't planned on doing anything about it."

"What! I thought after Sunday night your blues would be over! Of course you're going to do something about it! Write about it! Go to Flagstaff and meet this guy!"

"Alien."

"Alien, guy, whatever. Go! This could be the biggest story of the decade. Imagine the title: Eccentric Inventor! Backbone of American Toy Industry A Martin! God! That's good enough for inquiring minds even if *Playboy* turns it down. Maybe even a Pulitzer!"

"I know I can sell the article," Paul said, beginning to catch John's excitement. "Allison will take something. But do you remember Saul Goldstein?"

"Yeah. From International Machine Products?"

"Right. He has kids and knows about the toys. He was one of my contacts to see if the technology had been spotted in other products. He said he would pay ten thousand dollars for an inside lead on the designer and he knows a venture capitalist who would pay big bucks for an introduction to this toy maker. Saul thinks that, if he can save enough money, the inventor will turn his attention to business products as well as toys."

"Makes sense. If the technology behind the toys will work on a larger scale, the possibilities are endless."

Paul sat silent for a long moment. The toys were years, maybe decades ahead of their time and Paul found that somewhat frightening. He knew the companies that were handling the bits and pieces were eager to get their hands on more. There were people like Saul, who built some of the machines that the manufacturers used to assemble the products, who wanted a bigger piece of the action. Some of them would wave more than money around. Paul was legitimately worried about stepping into an industrial war where the rules changed with the players. People could die in that environment. Or they could be first in line and be set for life. Paul had an advantage, and he knew it: he was native to Arizona and had contacts in Flagstaff. Most of the industrialists didn't even know where the tourist town existed.

More than that, the toy maker scared Paul. The idea of a mind that could see so far ahead and then develop the technology to reach those goals was chilling. The choice of toys, of reaching out to children, also carried an ominous ring. Like the Pied Piper, Paul thought. Only where was this piper leading the next generation? The toys looked innocent enough, but was there something deeper, more sinister?

"You have to go," John was saying, pulling Paul back to the conversation.

"Look. I'm just a poor writer. There are companies out there that received these designs that make modern technology look like paintings on cave walls. Don't you think they've tried to locate the designer? Don't you think they have people out trying to find this guy? Professionals. If they can't find him, what makes you think I can?"

"You're not a professional," John said with bluntness that stung.

"What?"

"You're not the government. You don't know what can't be done. You don't know what is normal and what isn't. You'll look places they wouldn't even think of or would think were the wrong places. You're a writer. You're a creative person. Most of your life you deal in 'what if' and that's not the same reality that private detectives and industrial spies lived in, not at all. You might succeed where they fail simply because you don't know how to do their job. You'll do yours. You track down leads as a writer all the time. You know how to research and what to look for that in finding a story. That's what you're after: a story. They want a man. If he hasn't been found by now, then maybe these professionals are taking the wrong path. Try it your way. What can you lose?"

My life, Paul answered silently, but gave John's words serious thought. Motivation was Paul's problem now and he knew it. This was a story he wanted; but he needed a push and John was certainly pushing.

"Flagstaff's only a couple of hours away. It's not like going back East of something," John went on relentlessly. "I'll look after things while you're gone. Water the plants and all, collect the mail. It won't take you more than a few days to run down any leads up there, then you'll be back to write it up."

Paul sat for a long time, letting the silence drag out. He was uncomfortable under John's gaze, but he could feel his hesitation crumbling. Finally he agreed to leave the next morning, promising to drop the keys off at John's office. Once the words were out, he felt a great weight lift from his shoulders. It was a beginning, something new and exciting, something he had put out of his life ever since Janet walked out: it was a will to live and a belief in the future. It felt good. If it would only last.

"In the meantime," John said with a wicked grin and twinkling eyes, "you can buy me another beer."

Sheriff Ed Rogers stood with his arms crossed and legs spread, a solid block of a man whose presence and authority made him appear much taller than his five-foot-seven. His cold gray eyes followed the coroner's assistants as they loaded the two shrouded figures into the ambulance. Where his eyes touched the gawking curious behind the bright yellow police scene ribbons, those innocents shivered as if they had walked through a ghost.

"Boy, I don't want no word of this to get to the news until we've had a chance to find out what done it," he said quietly to the tall deputy standing at his side.

"Sure, Pa," the young man answered back. Mark carried the same gray eyes as his father but they did not have the same hard edge, the killer's look, that his father's eyes carried. Moisture stood on his upper lip and he wiped it off with the back of his hand. If his father was sweating in the afternoon sun, he had no idea. The set jaw beneath the brown beard streaked with silver gave no sense of discomfort. "But ain't it an animal?" he asked, hoping his father would agree and shatter the knot of fear that settled in his stomach. "Looks like they were mauled."

"Can't say fer sure. Ain't no animal signs 'ceptin' for a few scavengers and a coyote or two. Ain't no coyote killed that dog though. Not even a pack." The Sheriff was silent for a while as he rocked back and forth, changing is weight from one leg to another.

"What do you think it is," Mark asked, fear creeping into his voice. Clay Springs was a quiet town, a friendly town. Nothing exciting ever happened. The drug dealers from Phoenix hit Flagstaff but stayed out of the little villages where everyone noticed a stranger and the local people had been quiet ever since they hauled young Curtis Watkins off to the juvie home a couple of years ago. Murder and mutilation were not Clay Springs' style. He took the deputy position a year ago after graduating from Clay Springs High because it was what his daddy wanted him to do and it looked like a cushy job that paid well. He never expected to land in the middle of trouble. And the long delay in his Pa's answering was setting his nerves on fire while he felt himself break out in a cold sweat despite the heat.

"I think that it's that same group of weirdoes who's been killin' off the livestock 'round here," Ed finally answered in the same flat tone that Mark remembered from childhood. Heaven help whoever crossed his Pa when he used that voice. "Some kind of ritual killin', maybe."

"You mean Devil worshipers?" Mark almost whispered, the shadows in the woods seeming to grow darker in his eyes, the high, thin clouds passing over the sun suddenly feeling as dark and massive as the storms the proceeding the evil hoards in so many fantasy novels.

Ed stood quietly nodding and chewing on the inside of his cheeks, frowning at the retreating lights of the emergency vehicles pulling out of the pristine yard that typified this wealthy section of Clay Springs. "Probably some of those Hippie nature lovers."

"Pa, ain't no Hippies now."

"They got some other name now, but they're still here. You see 'em passin' through all summer. Sedona attracts more weirdoes than Santa Fe. But you keep quiet. I'll handle this my way."

Rogers looked over at Brian Chompers, the police chief for the towns of Heber and Overgaard, which shared the costs of some essential services, being good neighbors and all. Chompers was young and he looked a little green, but at least he knew enough to follow-up on strange events when strange events were happening in his jurisdiction, too. He had heard the call about the twin's death and had driven down to see what was going on. There had been reports of missing pets, mutilated livestock, and a group of missing campers in his area, and now this.

This area was supposed to be quiet, but lately someone had been hunting outside the limits in Rogers' backyard and that had him a little ticked. These hunters weren't the proper type, going after sheep and cows and dogs and cats, and leaving the remains to attract scavengers and flies. He had been nosing around for weeks looking for a clue, visiting the site of one livestock mutilation after another, and coming away with nothing. Chompers had talked to him already. Rogers knew the hills or northeastern Arizona better than his own backyard. He had been batting around them for over fifty years and he had been Sheriff for a good chunk of that. Coming up empty-handed had ruffled his feathers right proper.

These girls like they had met the same fate as the livestock. It looked like the killers were taking a step up the food chain. Not that killing two little girls was much of a challenge. There was a connection, but what? He looked over at the Chief and decided that it was time to share that thought with this pup. Then he'd probably call the State Police, who would foul things up. His best hope would be from the Injin reservation. They had trackers to beat anything. He wondered if there were problems on the reservations. Them Injins were a closed-mouth bunch, especially the Apaches, but he got on well with their lawmen.

"You keep quiet about this," he directed Mark, including Chompers in the comment. "I'll handle this my way. And don't you go spoutin' nothing' to no damned reporters until we get the varmints that done this. Don't want no city slicker posse up her trampin' through the woods. Not 'till we know what's what."

"Sure, Pa," Mark answered lamely to his father's retreating back. Ed Rogers was going back to look at where the bodies had been found by a group of six-and-seven-year-old boys playing cowboys in the morning's cool shadows. But Mark had no desire to go back into the once friendly woods and he was just as happy when his father motioned to another deputy to accompany him into the gloom that marked the trail from the woods to the creek. There was more going on in those woods than a few lost Hippies and Mark had no desire to meet up with whoever slashed up those little girls and that large dog. No, sir, no desire at all.

CHAPTER SIX

June 17, 2002
Flagstaff, Arizona

"I see you've got your fist out, say your piece and get out, I guess I get the gist of it but it's all right," Paul joined the Grateful Dead just a little off key and at the top of his lungs. The Phoenix classic rock station behind him faded in and out of the static as the engine labored up the foothills surrounding Flagstaff Mountain but no problem: Paul knew the lyrics. "Sorry that you feel that way, the only thing there is to say, every silver lining has a touch of gray. I will get by. I will get by."

Paul graciously ended his concert by stuffing a Dunkin' Donuts mini in his mouth and washing it down with a Seven-Eleven Super Double Big Gulp Dr. Pepper, mumbling the final chorus line "I will survive" through the mush the soda and donuts made in his mouth. Paul felt good – better than he had in a long, long time. The classic rock had lifted his spirits as only Zeppelin and Cream and Tull could; his blood was flowing and body felt alive. He reached over and patted the list of names and numbers he had pulled from his research the night before. He was on a roll and he knew it.

Finally, the Phoenix station faded into oblivion. Paul listened to the Sedona country station, vainly hoping for some McMurtry or John Stewart or Waylon or Axton, but all he heard was whinny women or men with nasal problems. Flagstaff had a rock station, but they played an over-abundance of pabulum so Paul dialed until he picked up the university's alternative rock station which, despite the kids on the air, hit a mix of Pearl Jam Nirvana and Classic Rock that was better than the commercial stations in the area.

His first stop was at the local YMCA. Naturally, he almost missed the exit and dumped the remaining donuts on the floor as he braked hard to squeeze in behind a motor home with New York plates doing all of fifty when everyone else was adding ten to the seventy-five limit.

After booking a room at the Y and tossing the remaining donuts to a hungry looking alley dog, Paul found his way to Flagstaff's remaining newspaper. There are still newspapers in the country that have legitimate Morgues and this was one of the holdovers. With interactive cable and instant news services, printed papers have all but vanished and the Morgues now are little more than computer satellites with printers. Paul liked the old style – the news felt more real with the smell of old papers and the feel of the pages between Paul's fingers than the scan lines in a computer. Paul had never shaken the feeling that some computer hacker could change the news in a data bank; it is infinitely more difficult to change the faded yellow press of old fashioned newspapers, to fake a single story in the middle of an aged edition of the press.

The Morgue clerk looked over Paul's list of issues without saying a word.

The newspaper was old and the Morgue probably dated back before the turn of the century – the last century, the one with the 18 in front. It was a study in sepia tones; brown waist-high paneling, indeterminate paint that was something between tan and dirty yellow, news clippings faded into parchment, the brown wooden shelves and counter top, the reading carrels relieving the sameness only where the brown veneer had been scrapped away to reveal cryptic saying in dingy off-white clapboard. The room even smelled brown, full as it was with the musty odor of rotting paper, stale cigarette smoke – though the building was long since a smoke-free environment – and the dust that is everywhere in Arizona, even in the majestic forests around Flagstaff.

Even the clerk, when he returned, had a dusty cast to him as if unsure whether his ancestry was white, Hispanic, Indian (oh, Native American, Paul corrected himself.)

Paul took the stack of papers, absently thanking the clerk, a little bemused at the direction of his thoughts, and walked over to the nearest carrel. He dropped the papers on the desk, then looked around guiltily when the wooded rods down their spines – the binding common to many old newspapers – make a loud *clunk* on the table.

Paul worked over his stack, sorting through the stories, taking notes, doubling back to check facts from an earlier date or to note inconsistencies that cropped up and never seemed to be corrected in later issues. When he finished his first batch, he went back for more, slogging through the old papers at his limit-fifteen-at-a-time pace until the sun was slanting through the dirt-grimed window and the clerk began fussing around the counter in a not-so subtle it's-time-to-go-home dance. He poured over one last story, a sordid follow-up on some scandal dealing with the owner of a strip mall that had been the victim of several mysterious robberies.

He finally stood and stretched, feeling his back creak in the process, then picked up his last limit-fifteen-at-a-time pile and returned it to the service desk. Surprisingly, there was no one around. He waited a few seconds, then left the stack of papers on the counter and left with his notes tucked safely in his jacket pocket.

Outside, the chill evening air that marks the high mountains around Flagstaff even in the height of summer had settled over the area. It was surprising crisp after the closed and stuffy environment of the Morgue. Paul looked around the parking lot, having briefly forgotten where he had parked his car. Life looks different after the sun goes down.

The lot was practically empty and he had no trouble spotting the Cherokee. He started across the lot, but the bright neon of a greasy spoon across the street caught his eye. It had been a long time since he had tossed those left-over donuts to that skinny dog outside the YMCA. Now, he half-wished he had saved a few of the stale ones for himself. Instead of wasting time on regret, he decided, he would take a stab at the place in sight and hope the heartburn would be no greater than the Denny's downtown had generated the last time he was in Flag. Stopping by his car to grab a Flagstaff map was his only delay in appeasing his stomach, which was suddenly letting out loud protests over any delay. Its pathetic demand to receive a donation rivaled the look that earned the dog his doughnuts.

There were only a few patrons scattered in the tattered booths and at the stool-fronted soda bar. It was relatively clean, but it had seen better days. Well, clean was more than he could say for a lot of fast food restaurants he had been in recently, and that Kyoto Hot Pot in Tempe had been something else entirely. He decided this would do and, taking the advice of the sign suggesting customers should seat themselves, he did just that.

He glanced quickly at the menu that was propped between the museum-quality jukebox terminal at the table and a half-empty bottle of Heinz Ketchup, then put it aside in favor of his notes and the Flagstaff map. In seconds, he was bent over the map and had his nose stuck in his notes. So much so that he did not notice the waitress walk up until she grew tired of standing and asked if there was anything Paul wanted.

"Huh?" Paul asked in his best imitation of a Nobel prize-winner. "Uh, Stacy," he stammered, reading her name badge, "do you know where the old Caruthers place is?"

"Three miles from where I live," Stacy replied, a little impatiently. She was alone out front and there were other customers that must want something, she figured, and she didn't have time to play word games with a mousy-haired tourist. "But what I meant was: are you ready to order?"

"Cheeseburger and fries. And a glass of iced tea, no lemon," Paul answered absently, concentrating on his notes and the map. "Where did you say you lived?"

"Cheeseburger, fries, iced tea ..." Stacy looked up from her pad and gave Paul a lopsided smile. "... and I have that question asked three times a night at least."

"Oh." Paul glanced up from his notes, actually *seeing* her for the first time. She looked like she was a few years younger than he was, though with women one could never tell. She had light blonde hair, maybe strawberry blonde if the sun was right, small breasts, long legs, and just enough extra fat to make her look soft but no way did she look chubby. Good cheek bones, Paul thought, with a strong face. Not the type of granite face that a lot of hard-used blondes effect by their late – meaning no hint of bitch. She was not a "power woman," as Paul's Hong Kong friend like to call business women who thought the world revolved around money and influence. A rather nice package Paul thought, somewhat set back from his boorish behavior a few minutes before.

"O.K. Where's three miles from your place," Paul said, not one to back down, even when he knew he was behaving less than politely. "I need to find the Caruthers House and I can't find it on the map. It's on …"

"Oh, I know where it is," Stacy cut in. "And you won't find it on any map. That's a private road and the house is set back at least a quarter mile in some trees. What do you want with the Caruthers place, anyway? It's pretty run down and more than a little creepy. It's supposed to be haunted."

"Haunted," Paul asked, his attention suddenly picking up. "Nobody lives there?"

"There's supposed to be an eccentric millionaire living there, but nobody's ever seen him" Stacy said, losing interest in old gossip. ". You want everything on that burger?"

"I need to get out there and talk to the owners and if it's not on the map I could use some help finding it," Paul said, letting the hint drop as broadly as possible. "Yeah, everything and some mayo for the fries."

"Uh-huh, a mayo-and-fry kind, are you?" was Stacy's only reply, not rising to the bait.

"Look. If you'll tell me where the Caruthers House is I'll leave a big tip. Bigger if you draw a map. If you take me there I'll ..." Paul suddenly stopped. He had no idea what he'd do if she actually went with him. "I'll ... I'll, uh, take you out to dinner," he finished in a rush, feeling a little more than juvenile.

"Well, that's at least original," Stacy laughed. "I work tomorrow."

"Day after? I'll be at the running things down or at Morgue again all day tomorrow."

"So, let's see. You are running things down and then visiting the Morgue? That sounds a little premeditated to me."

"No, no, I don't mean run down like run over. That's run down like, uh, you know, find answers. I'm ... well... uh... you see, I'm a writer and I'm researching some material for an article I am working on, for a magazine. It's like a feature article, not like the checkout stand papers. OK? I need to talk to the police, the Morgue I mentioned is the newspaper archives, then check out a shopping center ..."

"I know which one that is, I'll bet."

"... and run out to Clay Springs and see to a few other items. How about it?"

"Sounds like you've a busy day ahead of you."

"No, I mean how about helping me find this Caruthers place?"

"This is the strangest conversation I've had all month," Stacy said, but she was smiling and there was a sparkle in her eyes. As nice as Flagstaff was, it was still – and probably always would be – a small town. There wasn't a lot to do on a hot June day except watch the million or so tourists who flocked to the city every summer or fight the crowds around Sedona's famous Slide Rock Recreation Park. A break in the monotony would be worth a little risk.

"I really need to get this done," Paul pushed, seeing the tiny break in her armor. "I could use the help."

Stacy pretended to think about it, but she had made her mind up even before he had suggested dinner. "OK. But I warn you," she said, right on the verge of laughing, "I watch the reruns of 'Kung-Fu' so no funny business. Here," she continued, pointing to the map. "There's a mom and pop grocery store at this corner … here … see? I live on this street behind the store, third house on the right from the corner. Day after tomorrow, nine AM sharp or I'll write you off as just another flake."

Paul quickly scribbled a note in his day planner and circled the location on the map. "Is ten o'clock OK?" he asked, thinking that that might be a little early for someone who worked the nights, but Stacy's smile and agreement assured him that was no problem.

"Now," he said, flashing her is best Robert Redford. "Can I have that cheeseburger?"

CHAPTER SEVEN

June 18, 2002

Flagstaff and Clay Springs, Arizona

The Flagstaff Police Department headquarters was housed in a building that looks like it was built in the 1881 – the year Flagstaff was founded - and not redecorated since. It was a brownstone semi-Gothic styled building, impressive in its way, though not overly large. It had a solid feel; like the mountains that surround the city, something that has been there a long time and will never change.

Of course, everything changes, even mountains. A large chunk of San Francisco Peak near Flagstaff is missing, the victim of volcanic activities about four hundred thousand years ago. And the area is still active; Sunset Crater erupted sometime between 1040 and 1100 and the crater is less than fifteen miles from downtown Flagstaff. Not to be outdone by mere nature, the inside of the building was stripped and rebuilt in glass, chrome, and steel. It has as modern and up-to-date as any city police headquarters in the country. Flagstaff was not a city that experiences much crime. It is a sleepy little town most of the year, nestled around the upper slopes of the twelve thousand six hundred foot Humphreys Peak. Some theorists think Flagstaff Mountain was once the tallest in the Western hemisphere until it blew its top, most likely frightening the dinosaurs in the area at that time. Now, it shelters a pleasant little community and even the students at Northern Arizona University are not known for blowing off their tops very often.

The biggest need in Flagstaff for a well-equipped police department is the summer tourist trade. The young people who flock to the cool reaches of the high elevations are prone to rowdiness and an occasional – dare we say, nightly? – over indulgence at one of the city's bars or taverns. Surprisingly the winter crowds, who come for some of the best skiing in the United States, are less of a problem. Popular belief is that NAU students are known to study more than Arizona State (which has more than once made *Playboy's* list of top party schools) or University of Arizona students. Maybe thirty inches of annual snow has something to do with that, but, for whatever reason, the Police are just as happy not to have frequent calls during the winter months when the evening temperatures are hanging out around sixteen degrees.

As these things happen, the almost-criminal heat on this steamy June day was kept at bay by the department's more-than-adequate air conditioning and Paul was glad he was inside. So was Richard Samuels, police lieutenant now on loan to the detective division – with a paperwork promotion to "detective/homicide" to boot. He was decked out in his formal black suit. Outside in Arizona in the summer, even in the mountains, it is not comfortable anywhere in the state in a suit. So he was more than happy to talk to this Phoenix writer, inside and away from the heat. Perhaps he could stretch this out until time to go to lunch – some place that would also be cool.

"Yeah, that was twenty-five, thirty years ago now," Samuels said to Paul's question about the

Reynolds Plaza robberies. "Strangest case I ever worked on. Still haven't a clue after all these years."

"You say that almost every store was hit and that what was taken didn't make any sense," Paul prompted, looking over his notes. So far, it all fit with the newspaper accounts.

"That's right. They took all kinds of crazy things; everything from dog and cat food to electronic components." Reynolds stood up and walked over to a battered gray filing cabinet where he kept his personal files, mostly information on known crooks, his personal snitches, and the few – thankfully, very few – unsolved cases still attached to his name. It was a thick folder, none-the-less. "Got a list here, someplace. Want to see it?"

"Yes, I would." Paul set down the Dixie cup he had just drained of tepid cooler water, stood up from the latter-back chair and walked over to Samuels, taking the bundle of stapled pages Reynolds had handed out. It was an impressive list, neatly typed in two columns over 12 pages. "And you never could find out who did the robberies?"

"Funny thing about that. We not only never found the crooks, but none of the merchandise ever surfaced. At least, not that we've seen. Not from that one or the seven subsequent robberies that happened all within a period of a few months." Samuels moved back to his desk, letting a little chuckle slip out. "That's what got the old Chief fired. Eventually, things worked out to opened up this slot in Detectives that I got, even with the case still open." Samuels paused for a moment, reflectively. Then he flashed a huge smile at Paul. "All in all, it wasn't such a bad case."

"How'd they get into the places? Weren't they all alarmed?"

"Every single unit was bypassed. And there were some fancy alarms, too. The center was new then, and there were none of the outdated alarms we find in other places. And after each incident, the alarms became more elaborate. In fact, the last one happened with two security people patrolling the area and neither reported seeing a thing. Both passed lie detector tests, too. But they stopped after that one. Strange."

Paul looked back at his notes, scribbled a comment in the margin, then looked back at Samuels, now sitting with his feet propped on the desk top and his tie loosened.

"That first one was on, what? August the 27th, 1975?"

"I think that was the day they discovered the losses. It happened that morning or the previous night. It's all there in the file," Samuels said, tossing the rest of the file over to Paul. "Do you think that will help your article?"

"I hope so," Paul answered distracted, flipping though the seemingly endless series of reports and notations that made up the Reynolds file. "Actually, I don't really know what I am looking for yet. There are a lot of strange things that happened in this area, starting at about that time. I'm just curious. Maybe it's just a coincidence." Paul looked up and gave Samuels a wan smile. "If there's something interesting, I'll write a story that connects everything together just for the fun of it. If it's really juicy, maybe I'll base a book on what I find."

"I guess writers can get away with anything," Samuels said, not acting very interested any longer. An early lunch was beginning to sound good.

"It's called 'artistic license'," Paul said.

"Well, if you are going to dig, follow the money."

"What does that mean?"

"Reynolds collected on everything that was taken from the insurance company."

"So you think he set it up?" Paul asked.

"One might think so, but Reynolds also owned the insurance agency. They took a big hit and lost some of their carriers. Then something strange happened." Samuels snorted. "Like you said, some very strange things are connected with this case."

"What happened?"

"About ten years ago, the insurance companies started receiving payments for the cash toward the cash they laid out. Reynolds even received a cash gift in the amount of his deductibles."

"You're kidding!"

Samuels shook his head. "No. The cash for Reynolds was left in a box on the door of his insurance company. He called out the bomb squad. What a surprise it was to find bundles of tens and twenties and a note thanking him for providing 'much needed supplies' over the past few years."

"Covered all the deductibles for all the robberies?"

"Plus a decent interest. It was a big box."

"And no clues?"

"None," Samuels acknowledged. "Even had the FBI lab guys looking at the bills."

"And no idea who sent the cash?"

"Well, sure. Someone connected with the robberies. But no clue who. Find who sent the money and the rest will fall in place."

"And you say the money came in ten years ago?"

"About that."

"Interesting."

"You got something?"

"No, nothing really. Maybe just another coincidence," Paul said. "The story I am trying to track down seems to begin around ten or twelve years ago. The robbery was just for background color. But it might be interesting to see if there is a connection. Follow the money, like you said."

Samuels suddenly sat up, his attention squarely on Paul, his nonchalance completely gone. "Look, man, if you come up with anything connected with these burglaries, let me know, I wouldn't mind another promotion."

"Was it that big a deal?" Paul asked.

"There isn't much crime in Flag," Samuels said, still dead serious. "Clearing up a case that's gone on this long would make some eyes open. Important eyes."

"That might make a story in itself," Paul laughed. He picked up is cup and looked at the drops still in the bottom, but decided against another trip to the water cooler. He stood up and tossed the cup in a waste basket by the door. "Thanks for the water. I'll keep in touch."

"You do that," Samuels said with a smile – a smile that never rose above his lips.

"Oh, do you need this list back?"

"Keep it. The one I handed you was a copy."

"Thanks," Paul said, reaching for the door. But he stopped again as Samuels spoke in a low voice.

"Be careful checking this out. Whoever did those jobs was slick. They didn't leave any tracks that we could find. They might not like civilians snooping around." Samuels paused for a moment, letting what he had said sink in. There were indications there that Paul would need to consider – like the possibility of police or other high-ranking involvement, something it might be difficult for someone inside the department to ferret out. "Besides," Samuels continued, once he saw that Paul had begun thinking about the ramifications of a huge case that no one had cracked after years. "What makes you think you'll find anything when we couldn't?"

"I have a friend who thinks that sometimes people fumbling in the dark can do better than people who know what they are doing."

That brought the smile and easy manner back to Samuels. He leaned back in his chair and gave Paul a measured look. "I've got the same theory about young girls getting knocked up at drive-ins."

Paul laughed at Samuels' witticism. "Well, we'll talk later."

"Sure," Samuels said. "Just let me know what happens."

Paul nodded and walked out the door, letting it close behind him with a soft thud. That door closing sounded like the crack of doom to Samuels, for some reason. A sudden wave of foreboding washed over the detective. In a long life of playing hunches, this had all the earmarks of a major event. He buzzed the outer office and called in one of the uniforms, quickly scribbling some instructions on a Post-it note while he waited for the officer to saunter in on his own good time.

"Here," Samuels said as soon as the officer came in. "Have this guy checked out."

"Now?" The officer whined. "I'm just going off-duty."

"Just get it done," Samuels said, his patience a little thinner than normal with the urgency of his intuition hounding him. "I want to know who this guy is, over, under, around and through, upside down and inside out." Samuels paused just long enough for the officer to wake up to the mood of his nominal superior. "Understand?"

"Yes, sir!"

"Then get with it!" The officer – Fisher – stammered something unintelligible and reached for the door. "And I want it in my hands as soon as you have it."

"Yes sir!"

Fisher turned to the door and somehow forgot it opened in. He slammed into the closed door before he could recover.

"Fisher!"

"Sir?" Fisher responded, turning back to Samuels.

"He's asking about the Caruthers House."

"So what? It's not like the owners are a pillar of society or anything. I don't think anyone's seen the owner since the new people moved in back when I was a kid. Hell, they still call it the 'Caruthers House.' I'm not sure anyone even knows the name of the new owner and they've been there pretty near twenty-five years."

"Whoever owns the house has money, no matter how they keep the yard. They have a lot of money. Let me repeat that – they have a *lot* of money. A lot of money flows from that house to businesses here in town, especially through Reynolds's TV and Appliances. They purchase electronics and scientific equipment by the truckload. And the feed store is always taking a delivery of pet food there, so I wouldn't be surprised if their security system has for legs and a lot of teeth. They don't want to be disturbed. If that guy becomes a nuisance, we need to stop it fast. Got it?"

"What?"

"Let me paint you a picture," Samuels sighed. "There is a bucket of money associated with that house. Word gets around. Bad people hear about it. That guy seems legit, but if he *is* planning on making a move on the Caruthers house, I want to know it. I want to stop it before there's a problem. Now do you got it?"

"Yes sir."

"Oh, and Fisher."

"Sir?"

"He says he's staying at the 'Y.' Have someone verify that and then see about putting a tail on this guy if I think I need one. Got it?"

"Yes, sir. Right away, sir. Immediately, sir!"

Fisher stumbled out the door and let it close a little harder than it should have. His mumbled comments were lost to Samuels, but he did not need to hear them to know what was being said. He had been in the force long enough to know how the uniforms responded to any orders from the Detective branch. Fisher, Samuels thought, might just be looking for some extra duty if he didn't watch himself.

Paul followed the winding back-country roads through Flagstaff's particular brand of outback. If he stayed on I-40 long enough, he would end up in Show Low. But he needed to find the turnoff to Clay Springs long before then. He just hoped he had the research right: Clay Springs was in the middle of nowhere and a good ninety-six miles from Flagstaff if not a full hundred with the serpentine route the road took through the Northern Arizona mountains. There had been strange sightings – UFOs? – and reports coming from Clay Springs for a few years in the mid-seventies before they tapered off, now they were back. But why Clay Springs? There was nothing out here except a couple of buffalo ranches. Rather, bison, not buffalo. As if there was a difference.

Paul finally saw the exit and pulled off, heading north for Clay Springs. The ride was pleasant, through the high country with its towering pines and rugged mountains slowly giving away to the bare beauty of the red rocks that dominate much of Arizona. One thing Paul noticed though… there was nowhere to eat. From what he could tell, there was a Mormon Church, a library, and a post office, but no Taco Bell, Arby's, Burger King, or McDonalds to be found. For food, movies, and fun, one apparently left town.

Clay Springs, back before the publicity, was a typical one-horse town, complete with a hitching post in front of the sheriff's office and a boardwalk. It had not changed with the tourist trade. The town showed a touch of the Old West, and Old West attitudes still clung to the buildings like dust clings to a horse's hide. It certainly was clinging to the bearded lawman sitting in front of the Sheriff's office with his feet propped up on the hitching post rail.

Paul stopped the car between an old, dusty, white Plymouth with Clay Springs Police fading out on the side and an equally newer if just as dusty as the Navajo County Sheriff's Office four-by-four truck. . He stepped out and stretched his back until it popped, only half-surprised that Clay Springs actually had paved streets. Years ago, he had a girlfriend from Cincinnati with a typical Easterner's attitude about the West. The first time she had come out to Arizona she could not stop gaping at the trees and the multicolored mountains. She had said, more than once, that the state looked like something out of a movie. That was fair enough; most of John Ford's panoramic epics were filmed in Monument Valley, which boarded on Arizona and Utah. The classic mountains were what made *She Wore A Yellow*

Ribbon and *The Searchers* classics more than the acting or directing. She never could recover from the idea that Arizona was real and the movies were staged and was happy enough to return to Ohio where she quickly became lost in a world of drugs, sex, and failed relationships. After the first few weeks – well, months actually – of the break up, Paul had never looked back. He wondered if he had learned his lesson with Janet or if his luck with women would always be the same. His swapping a horse-faced Ohio tramp for a saccharin-sweet small-town Georgia belle who hid a vindictive and cruel streak as wide as Sherman's march was long put a lot of questions to his ability to pick a good woman. At least Janet had given him Jeremy, but even that was a sore spot, with Janet doing everything she could to keep him away from the boy.

While Paul was relieving the kinks in his back from the drive, a Deputy Sheriff stepped out of the office and moved to stand next to the Sheriff, a younger, though somewhat taller, version of the man sizing Paul up from his chair. *If the Sherriff isn't that kid's natural father,* Paul thought, noting the scraggly beard trying to catch up with the older man's full bush, *then Northern Arizona is a lot more like Southern Georgia than I'd thought.*

Paul stepped forward a little hesitatingly, then stopped all together as the Sheriff sent a black stream of tobacco juice at a lizard scuttling along the edge of the sidewalk. He missed and punctuated his efforts with a few choice words. He also ignored Paul's offered hand when the younger man stepped up to the rail.

"Uh, my name is Paul Johnson. I was looking for the Police Chief."

"Ain't here," the bearded one said.

"We're just waitin' for him. He's the Sheriff and I'm the Deputy," added the Deputy, only to earn a scathing look from the Sheriff.

"Well, if you're the Sheriff for the county, maybe you can answer some questions for me. I'm from Phoenix and ..." Paul began.

"Another damned reporter from the big city," the Sheriff shot over his shoulder.

"Why can't ya'll jist leave us well enough alone," the Deputy asked, his voice whinny and droll. "We kin handle our own problems without some nosy reporter from outta town pokin' his nose in ev'rything."

"Actually, I'm not a reporter," Paul began, trying to pick up his momentum after the rather abrupt way these two had dismissed him out of hand. "I'm ..."

"Then what do you want," Sheriff Ed Rogers cut in, not giving Paul any time to get his stride back.

"I just wanted to ask about some sightings you had here a few ..."

"No damned reporter, huh?" Rogers cut in again. Then why do you want to know about them flyin' saucers? We've had fellas up here ever' day since we reported that a week ago. I can't see why we should tell you anything more than we did the others ..."

"And we didn't tell 'em nothin'," Mark broke in on his father, but quickly cut off when Rogers glared at him.

"So you can jist git back down to the Valley and quit wasting' honest people's time."

"Yeah, and we'll find out who kilt them girls, too, with nobody's help," Mark punctuated Rogers' comments with a smirk.

"What girls?" Paul asked, bewildered.

"He didn't mean nothin'," Rogers growled, giving Mark a look that had a world of promises in it.

"You had some girls killed?" Paul asked, further off track than ever.

"Run across a rogue bear is all. Happens sometimes up here. Especially since them damned Liberals began movin' grizzly's back into Yellerstone."

"Yellowstone is a long way from here and on the other side of the Rocky Mountains!" Paul exclaimed.

"Bears cain't read no maps," said Mark, as if that was the end all and do all of the matter. "Almost drained out all their blood, too." He couldn't help but add.

"What!" Paul was well startled. He had never heard of bears killing for blood alone.

"We found them ..."

But this time, Rogers' interruption came quick and final. "Shut up, boy," he growled before turning back to Paul. "We'll track it down in the next day or so. Ain't no need t' git worked up or carried away.

Jist put in your story that were workin' hard on trackin' that there bear."

Paul tried to cover his confusion, and his sudden interest, by taking a slow look up and down the sleepy town street. "Well," he said after a moment while silence seemed to settle over the town like a blanket of oppression. "I came here for some other information, anyway, and it's only tangentially related to the sightings and I hadn't heard anything about the death of any girls. Just a couple of questions, please."

"Like what?" Rogers asked, suspicion leaking from him like the heat radiating off the hood of Paul's car.

"You saw some flying saucers here last week?" Paul asked.

"Said so, didn't I," Rogers retorted.

"Yeah." Paul hitched himself up onto the rail and pulled out his note pad, using one thigh to steady the book. "Could you tell me about them? Actually, I came up here to talk about the meteor that landed a few years back and the sightings that followed that. There's nothing documented much past the initial reports and I hadn't heard anything about these more recent reports, either."

"That a fact?" Rogers asked, flatly, suspicion still apparent in his every move. "What kinda reporter are ya if you don't even read the papers?"

"I'm not a reporter," Paul said reasonably and somewhat truthfully. "I'm a novelist and magazine features writer. Not the same thing at all. I've been researching some material in Flagstaff lately and I've spent most of my time going through some old newspapers. I haven't paid much attention to the current news in a week or so."

"Well, that weren't nothin' back then. There was jist this big light that flashed through the sky and hit the side of the hill back yonder," Rogers said, gesturing vaguely over his shoulder.

"Same place nearly the other hit," the Deputy added.

"Oh?"

"Weren't the same damned place. Just the same damned mountain," Rogers stated flatly, sending another glare at the Deputy.

"Did you see it?" Paul asked.

"I did," the Deputy answered, excited at the potential at seeing his name in print in something other than a tabloid. "I was out with my girl ..."

"Up to no good," Rogers snorted. "Another ten minutes and you would'a had to marry her, too. Meteor probably saved your hide, boy."

"Pa!" Mark said, outraged that his father would bring something this personal up in front of strangers. "Anyways, we was parked out on the ridge when this thing flew past and lit up the night sky. We thought it was a plane on far and high-tailed it back to town."

"Why'd you think it was a plane?"

"Well, it didn't act like no falling rock. It kinda ..."

"Boy's not the brightest," Rogers offered, obviously wishing Mark would decide he was needed elsewhere. "Scientists didn't find no wreckage, so 'tweren't nothing but a rock."

"Didn't find no rock, either," Mark offered, sullenly.

"Is there any way to see where it landed?" Paul asked, a little embarrassed at this inter-family bickering.

"Can ya ride?" Rogers asked with a smirk, which quickly found a match on the Deputy's face. This was clearly something that had worked to discourage others in the past.

"Ride?" Paul asked in all innocence.

"Yep. Only way up there's on horseback. Cain't even git a four-wheeler up in them mountains. Believe me, there ain't nothin' there to see," Rogers finished as if that ended the topic. "An' you don' wanna go no how. That's up in Apache land and that there mountain is sacred to a lot of tribes.

"Do you know anyone who's been up there who might give me some information?"

"Nope. An' like I says, that Injin territory. They ken shoot you for traspassin' and ain't nobody gonna say a thang. And they ain't gonna go there themselves because it is where the Gods live. Elders and grandmothers would skin any young buck who offered to play guide."

"Maybe I can talk to the tribal leaders," Paul said, pushing the topic. "I think they have an office in Leupp don't they?" Paul said, more to himself than to Rogers.

"You kin ask, but it'll be horses only, iffin' they even let you go. Said it was sacred, didn't I?" Rogers was getting testy. This Valley reporter was denser than most, it seemed. Just couldn't take "no" for an answer. Like that Kolchak fella on the television.

"Maybe if there's no way a car can get there I can make it in a Jeep," Paul said.

"Nope," responded Rogers.

"Then a Hummer or a quad?" Paul asked.

"Not hardly. Not even with one of them three-wheel jobs. Dirt bike, maybe, but the Apaches don't allow no mechanical things up on their mountain. You go by hoof... yours or a horses, don't make no nevermind."

"Well, maybe I can find someone who will take me on horseback. I can ride a horse I guess," Paul insisted.

"Lots of someones could. But ain't no one goin' ta. We don't upset the reservation people unless it's real important like, then mostly all we do is call the tribal police an' hope they take care of the problem. They're friendly 'nuf, most of the time, but ain't nobody gonna cotton to some stranger messing 'round their sacred places, ya know."

Paul nodded. The Middle East had been a hotbed for centuries for just that reason. That and pure, stupid, human stubbornness.

"OK," Paul said, reverting to Plan B. "Do you know anyone who's been up there that might talk with me? There are some things happening in Flagstaff and I think it might be related to whatever happened up in the mountains. I am not sure, but if I can't track down the information I'll never know."

"There we some guys up here from NAU. An as-tro-phics or something and some geometry ..." Mark offered helpfully.

"Geology?"

"Yeah, some geology people. They took a lot of pictures and hauled off a lotta rocks."

"Was that for this time or the last one?"

"Both I recon," Mark replied, more than a little confused. He was around in 1975.

"Thanks, I'll try to find someone at the University later," Paul said, pretending to add something to his notes that was already there from his earlier research. It didn't hurt to make people like Rodgers think they had done something special. "You say after this last meteor there have been more sightings?"

"Yeah. There's been a bunch of them flyin' saucers around here lately."

"Easy, boy," Rogers warned, still not sure of Paul.

"Around here," Paul prompted.

"Mostly over where the meteor landed, but they been crisscrossing the mountainside a lot. Almost like they was lookin' fur somethin'. Jis like they say happened in '75."

"Junior." This time the warning carried dire overtones, but Mark was no longer listening. Paul was too good an audience.

"Pa, that's what they've been doin'. Jis like the Air Force did when that National Guard plane went down a while back. Those lights was makin' the same kinda patterns. And ya know the old medicine man says its dem same evil spirits that was here in '75. An' there was a big crash on the mountain then 'cepten the Apache's wouldn't let no white people on the mountain because it was winter and the storm god was there then the Zuni Pueblo wouldn't let 'em come in the summer 'cause all their gods are in New Mexico somewheres for summer. Like summer vacation or sumptin'. And the Zuni's didn't want nobody walkin' 'round up there with no gods to keep watch."

"Boy, you are thick," Rogers said, easily picking up on Mark's confused, and incorrect, description of the Indian Reservation locations. Everybody knew it was the Navajos you had to watch out for.

"But they let the University people go this time?" Paul asked.

"Oh, no. Don't nobody asked the Injins this time. Jis came with those big Army helicopters and took over for a few weeks, is what they did. Them Injins is pissed. Wouldn't think no white boy would go up there iffin' he was smart. Them Injins have ways of making accidents happen, ya know."

"Boy."

"They was!"

"Then maybe it was the *Air Force* you seen flyin' around looking for a crashed *Army* helicopter. Let it ride, boy!"

"And what about all them dogs we been gittin's calls on, jis vanishin' off the ranches? Huh? We've had more reports this past month than we've had in a 'coon's age! And the cattle and sheep and stuff?" Mark was truly worked up now. Visions of late night sci-fi movies flashed through his head. There was something here. Hadn't they made that movie with Captain Kirk nearby, *Valley of the Spiders*? If there were killer spiders nearby then anything was possible!

"Those pets were probably kilt by wild animals! Coyotes kill dogs all the time, and with that bear loose ..."

"The same bear that killed the girls?" Paul asked.

"We ain't never had not blood drinkin' animals 'round here before!" Mark was warming up to his topic nicely, and the hotter he grew, the colder his father's eyes became.

"You've said enough," Rogers fairly shouted. "This man jis wants to know about the meteor 'cause there ain't no flying saucers or vampire bears." Rogers turned his attention back to Paul who would just as soon have continued to go on unnoticed by those gray eyes, *Killer eyes,* Paul thought. "I think you've found out all you need to know. Why don't you run back to the city before someone takes a notion to arrestin' your ass for disturbin' the peace."

"I'd just like to look around. I'm not bothering anyone," Paul protested.

"You're disturbin' *my* peace, boy. Git my drift?" Rogers asked, voice as cold as an Atlantic iceberg and promising as sure a disaster as the Titanic if Paul did not rapidly change course.

"Yeah, I guess so," Paul said, struggling to keep the sarcasm from his voice, "thanks for the hospitality."

Paul went back into his car and made a u-turn, neat as you please, since there was no traffic on the street. He watched the Sheriff tilt back in his chair, prop his feet back on the rail, and tilt his hat back over his eyes like it had been when Paul arrived, for all the world the picture of an 1850's Western Officer-of-the-Law.

"You got no sense a'tall, boy," Rogers said through his hat as soon as he heard the car pull away. "The last thing we need is a bunch of city folk pokin' their noses around here. We'll find those weirdoes who've been killin' off the dogs and cats. And we'll find whoever kilt them Tucker girls, too, and take care of them in our own way. We got things out in the woods that ain't nobody's business but our own. We don't need no big city reporters or in-ves-tee-gators nosin' 'round. Understand?"

"Yeah, I understand, Pa. But he said he weren't no reporter."

"Boy, sometimes I worry 'bout you. I really do. If he was a reporter, did you 'spect him to tell you?"

Mark gave this a lot of thought. It was an interesting concept. He wasn't sure he had the answer, but he knew the better part of valor. "Sorry, pa."

"Sorry, my ass. Git back to work. I got to think about tonight. Chief's out there snoopin' in the woods now. We'll wait here until dark and see if he comes back."

"Can I use the truck, pa?"

"What fer?"

"Wendy lives near here."

"Boy, you keep fergettin' what I always tell you."

"What's that Pa?"

Rogers threw his hands up in the air. Idgit forgot again. "It they's under eighteen, they's off limits or your ass will go to jail."

"Pa! We ain't gonna do nothin'! Not if you're goin' huntin' tonight."

"Yeah. Just make sure the screwin' you're gettin' is worth the screwin' you're getting'."

"Pa, you think the Chief is OK?" Mark asked, changing the subject because he was sure hoping Wendy would put out. "He ain't answering his radio."

"If he's out in the hills he kain't hear nothin'. We'll give Chief Langsford 'til 'bout eight to show up. Then we'll go catch ourselves one of them aliens from those flyin' saucers of yours and see if they ain't no wetback or Yankees from the AT and F or pot-smokin' Hippy. And if the Chief ain't back before it gets dark, well, we'll just go with our ownselves."

"OK, Pa. You do the figurin' and I'll do the head bashin'. Jis like always."

Rogers just grunted.

Paul slipped out of town like a ghost in a stale Gothic novel. Nobody seemed to notice. In fact, nobody seemed to be around at all. Clay Springs was a very sleepy little town, so sleepy that Paul doubted that anyone had the energy to commit murder. He wondered briefly if even the local animals would have had enough motivation to attack anything, much less to active girls. Well, that was not on track. He was *not* a reporter and two dead girls were not connected to his story. Were they? No. The story was in Flagstaff, he was sure, and the reported UFO sightings were nothing more than an interesting side trip. Not likely that anything would bother to visit the town, in any case, Paul decided. There was nothing there of note or in the surrounding area, of that Paul was sure, not even a convenience store.

Murder and mayhem were not on Paul's agenda. Neither were strange sightings of lights in the sky, though the first ones seemed to herald the arrival of the toy maker and the second ones came shortly after he had released a series of new toys. It was probably a coincidence, but the *Star Wars* designs tossed into the mix made 1975 a very weird time for northern Arizona. Still, it is not like anything out of the ordinary would bother with Clay Springs. No, the story was in Flagstaff, the rest just a distraction. There was nothing in the town. Nothing to attract aliens. No apparent connection to the toy maker, just a lead he thought might help, just in case his toy maker had arrived in a crashed space ship. Ridiculous concept. John had said so. He turned off Old 160 onto SR 260 and aimed back toward Flagstaff. He was just wasting his time out in the sticks. Maybe.

As that thought crossed his mind, a flight of three Apache helicopters slipped out of the trees a few hundred feet in front of his car and sped a quarter mile along the highway before peeling off North and back into the woods again. Paul was so startled that he almost drove off the road. Those Apache's could be quiet buggars! And they had been at tree top level, if even that high.

Paul eased off on the gas and cruised past the location where the deadly attack 'chopper had passed from sight. No road or trail break was visible and he was pretty sure that the top branches of the nearest pines had been clipped. Either those National Guard boys were hot dogging with total abandon or there was something going on in the area that put a lie to the sleepy look of Clay Springs.

Whatever, it was grist for another mill. Paul was determined to focus on his search for the toy maker and not be distracted. He had let too many other projects drop since the divorce to not realize a pattern. He was determined to grind away at this one until it produced flour and not husks.

Starting with the meteor strike in '75, the inconsistencies began to build. First, from his research, there was no evidence of a meteor strike ever discovered by researchers or reported by the natives, though the falling star had been seen by dozens of witnesses. Well, those were sacred grounds so maybe the Indians wouldn't say anything even if there had been something there. Connected with all that were reports of strange lights crisscrossing the skies in the Clay Springs area in '75, which could have been the National Guard searching for debris; but right after that, the reports of strange burglaries in the Flagstaff area had begun to appear in the newspapers. What was really weird were the reports of cargo hijacked from moving trucks; no witnesses or evidence that the sealed trailers had ever been opened before their destination. These were thefts of electronics, which was understood, but also truckloads of cat and dog food. Nothing was ever reported as surfacing on the black market, either.

Then the designs had been sent to LucasFilm that rumor said had resulted in the design of the Death Star; the designs that apparently mirrored photographs NASA had not yet taken. By 1978, the first mysterious toys began to appear in select stores around the country. Paul had learned that from one of the store owners who was eager to talk about the highly profitable novelties. As the toys became more available, the thefts of electronics tapered off and the business section had mentioned some closely-held enterprise at the Caruthers' House that had purchased a large quantity of electronics. Was there a connection? That was one item on Paul's list of the weird, which he had compiled while researching the toys.

Then, there was another meteor – or something – strike on the same mountain as the one in '75. Lightening striking twice? Whatever, this one was also accompanied by strange lights in the sky. This was a little different though. Now, the lights appeared first, then there was some kind of explosion in the mountains that the papers attributed to a meteor strike. Then more lights and an apparent lid slammed down on any information about the site. Paul had spent a lot of time on CompuServe and in libraries looking up old articles on the area. His gut said there was a connection with the toy maker because of the lights and the timing. But there was no proof. He wanted proof to back his article or he may as well sell it to Asimov's *Amazing Stories* but he wanted to sell it to Fox News.

Paul stepped back on the gas and centered his thoughts on Flagstaff. He knew his story was in the city – what he had found pointed to the Caruthers'

House – but something nagged him about the Apaches. He couldn't shake the feeling that there was something out of the ordinary in or near Clay Springs. While it felt more like an Arkansas family reunion than the *Stepford Wives*, there was still something very odd about Clay Springs. A mystery for a later date, Paul decided, but not too much later. Had he glanced in his rear view mirror and seen the two F16D's flash across the road coming from almost the same spot where the Apaches had vanished – the Falcons, like the helicopters, well below the 1000-foot minimum peace time limit mandated by FAA safety rules – he would have to move that priority up a few dozen notches. He realized that what appeared as sleepy may have just been buttoned up tight.

Night fell on Clay Springs like a blanket. The oven-heat that baked the town during the day was replaced by something more alive, pulsing, as the stored energy radiated back from the rocks and sand and buildings and tarmac that had stored it throughout the day. The cloudless sky would allow all that heat to escape back into space, and bring on a chill that is surprising only to those who have never lived in the desert. By midnight, all the reminders of a sweltering summer day will have vanished. Jackets and sweaters would be in order. But at nine o'clock, with the sun barely vanishing somewhere over California, the night was still warm and Mark Rogers was prepared to take full advantage of the situation, that time when cotton blouses were all the protection from the night air that a girl needed, a few hours before sweaters and jackets would be on display.

Mark had pulled a bench from inside the sheriff's office earlier in the day. He drove his old, batter ford pick up to the gas station and picked up a six pack of Coors and a bottle of Annie Green Springs, then he had pick up Wendy Lakeworth about three blocks from her house. It would not do for the fifteen-year-old's parents to see Mark picking her up. No indeed. Now they were sitting on the bench, Mark with two Coors down and Wendy sipping on the almost-wine. Mark was dutifully trying to run his hand up that thin cotton blouse. Wendy was not wearing a bra and there was just enough chill in the air to pull a reaction from her nuptial nipples. But not from Wendy, as she pushed Marks hand away … again.

"Com'on, Wendy. You'll like it," he whispered into the flow of her honey blonde hair while his hand moved to play with the buttons on her blouse. "You know you will."

"You leave those buttons alone or else I'll scream and your daddy'll get mad …"

"Now why would you wanna go and do a thing like that?" Mark asked, pulling back just a little, but not stopping trying to work the most interesting button loose with one hand.

"Because Norma told me all about you," Wendy said with a pout. "All you want to do is get a girl's clothes off and then try to get her in trouble."

Mark moved his hand away and squirmed. Norma was fourteen but looked seventeen. And she hadn't been a virgin since twelve. But he never thought she would be telling all her friends. "Now, Wendy," Mark protested weakly. "You know I ain't like that."

Wendy reached over and lightly slapped his hand. "Then leave them buttons alone," she admonished him. Then she leaned over and continued in a whisper: "At least until we get some place alone." She gently guided his hand up to her breast. "But outside's OK," she finished.

But that put her in control and Mark didn't like that. He jerked his hand away and sat in a sulk while Wendy smiled at him and had another sip of wine.

"But it ain't as much fun," he pouted.

"It's just until we can get the car …"

"The last time I took the police car I forgot to set the brake and it rolled into the lake," Mark admitted, remembering too well his father's response. But the temptation was great. He knew how much Wendy was turned on by riding in the car with the lights flashing. "Pa's not 'bout to let me have it again for months. He like to never got the sirens working again."

Mark had more to say, more on the edge of his mind that he knew would melt her resistance, but he was distracted by a pair of bright lights flashing across the clear desert night.

"Oh! Shooting stars!" Wendy exclaimed.

"Those ain't no shooting stars," Mark said. "See?"

The lights had stopped suddenly and hovered for a second. Then they began to sink slowly behind some nearby hills.

"They're landing! Look! They're landing!"

Mark jumped off the bench and rushed into the office, all thoughts of Wendy's fine young breasts forgotten. Wendy, who had almost been knocked to the ground when Mark sped off, followed meekly behind.

"What'd you want now, boy," Rogers asked, not looking up from the board where he and Amos Burke had a hot game of checkers raging.

"They've landed!"

Rogers looked at Amos and shook his head. "I swear that boy's distracted." He looked back down at the board, not giving Amos an inch of grace, but spoke distractedly to Mark. "Who's landed, boy?"

"The lights! The lights are back," Mark shouted, hardly able to contain himself. That jerked Rogers' attention away from the board just enough to allow his white-haired opponent to switch a couple of pieces. "Those same ones we been seein', Pa, they came back! They done landed!"

Rogers was out of his chair in a flash and over to the gun cabinet, the checkers match completely forgotten.

"Don't just stand there, boy, tell me where!"

Rogers pulled a pair of shotguns from the cabinet and a holstered 45 revolver with a carved mahogany handle. He tossed one of the shotguns to Mark and strapped on the sidearm after checking the load.

"Looks like over by Potter's Hill."

"That's near the Tucker place. Where the girls were kilt," Rogers mused, stuffing his pockets with shells. "You get on home, Wendy," Rogers said, coming to a decision. "Amos, you put them pieces back the way they was before I get back. I seen you switch 'em."

Rogers grabbed his hat and headed out the door, grabbing the second shotgun from the desk as he went. "Com'on, boy, let's go."

Rogers burst out the door and Mark followed. Wendy stood in the middle of the room, wondering how she was going to get home this late without a ride and how she would explain why she was not at Suzie's house doing homework, like she'd said. No way was she walking home with strange lights in the sky. Amos glanced at her once, then pocketed the few dollars that were sitting by the checker board. He looked back at Wendy, who was still standing in the middle of the room, confused and more than a little frightened. She sure looked good in that thin little cotton top. Maybe he could give her a ride home himself. He knew where Mark kept the spare keys to the truck and if he acted quickly enough, she wouldn't have time to get mad at Mark for dumping her like that. In fact, she might even be grateful to an old man …

There is something special about mountain woods at night; something eerie, even on a good night. The mountains of Northern Arizona are especially eerie, laden as they are with the mysteries laid on them by the Navajo and Pueblo and Cocopah, the Pima and Hopi and Tohono O'odham. Stories about the Sinagua and Anasazi and other vanished races; or stories like the Lost Dutchman's Mine are common. There is a reason the Hopi hold Flagstaff Mountain sacred.

It is the tall pines that twist in the breezes like they are reaching for something just out of grasp and the fireflies that look like thousands of malevolent eyes watching from the tree limbs can make even the most innocent night a Halloween experience. When the object is to track down a mysterious murder, then the high woods can be an experience like no other and not a pleasant one. That fact sunk into Rodgers and his son about a hundred yards away from where they parked their Jeep. They slowed their rush to near a crawl and began acting like two school boys playing Cowboys and Indians.

They crept thorough the underbrush, believing themselves quiet as church mice, secure in their woodcraft as only a white man can be, not at all aware that any Boy Scout would laugh at their efforts, much less a Native American. But it was not Boy Scouts or Injins they sought, but murdering butcher Hippies who were probably too stoned to hear anyone coming anyway; or so they thought.

"You sure you seen them lights?" Rogers demanded in a harsh tone. He would not admit that the woods at night gave him the willies. He was country bred and raised. He had spent many nights sleeping under the stars and tracked everything from polecats to bears in his time, even a few human fugitives. But the mountains at night still made his skin crawl and this night he had the distinct impression that every hair on his body was straining to race back down the mountain to the safety of the town lights.

"Sure I'm sure," Mark insisted, miffed that even his own father doubted him. It was bad enough that the kids at school had thought him brain dead, but his father never gave him credit for anything. "They've gotta be 'round here somewheres."

Rodgers wasn't as sure that they were close but he sure as sure didn't want to spend any more time in the woods than he had to. Damn! Forget the lions and tigers and bears. There was ticks and chiggers and no-see-ems. Them was the worst!

"They'd better be, boy," Rogers said in a voice low and thick with the promise of the woodshed. "I'll bet we're gonna find us a whole parcel of Hippie witches or somethin'."

"That's a coven, Pa."

"Huh?"

"A coven. Witches come in a coven."

"Don't you know nothin', boy," Rogers snorted in disgust. "A coven is a family of quail!"

They pushed on in silence for a while, Rogers mulling over his fate in fathering such a stupid son and Mark still mulling over the difference between a coven of witches and a covey of quail. It was in that state that they pushed through a thicket of shrubs into a clearing and stopped dead in their tracks. Here was something more interesting than quail or witches dancing naked in the moonlight. Something more interesting, something more unusual, and something much, much more deadly.

Rogers had taken Mark to the air shows at Luke Air Force base in Goodyear, Arizona, when Mark was younger. They both remembered the Air Force T-38 Talon, a sleek trainer that looked like nothing more than a very, very deadly mosquito. Sitting before them on stork-thin legs was a pair of beefed up T-38s with very sinister ancestors.

The craft before them had the T-38's swept-back wings, streamlined fuselage, dual independent ailerons, flaps, rudders, and other flight control surfaces that marked normal aircraft. But they were bigger, much bigger than the T-38, which allowed an instructor and student to sit in tandem in the pressurized, air-conditioned cockpit, and there was something about them that suggested that the T-38s 55,000 foot ceiling was a baby step to these babies. These two craft had the same stinger design, but were much longer than the T-38's 46 feet, with the space to hold a dozen or more passengers in comfort behind the cockpit, which, coincidentally, was still built to seat two, did not at all make the craft look bulkier or less deadly.

The T-38 needs as little as twenty-three hundred feet of runway to take off and can climb from sea level to nearly thirty thousand feet in one minute. What squatted before the two dumbfounded humans obviously were vertical lift craft since the clearing was no more than three hundred feet in diameter and the pair just about filled the clearing from stem to stern.. And for all that, thirty thousand feet in a minute looked slow for these stub-winged craft with the over-sized engines that were still radiating heat into the chill mountain air. And a T-38 never had external weapons.

Oh, sure, the AT-38-C had been modified to carry external weapons, but nothing that looked like what hung below the craft sitting in the clearing, challenging the crickets with an occasional ping of cooling metal. No, nothing that humans made looked quite like these. Not at all; these looked like something Buck Rogers would have given his eye-teeth for in a heartbeat. Either the Air Force had grown up very, very quickly, or these T-38 clones were anything but trainers. And anything but American, Rogers figured, suspecting a Russian invasion or, from the writing on the sides, something A-rab.

The moon cast a pale glow over the clearing, starkly outlining the craft and casting deep shadows around their base.

"Shit," Mark breathed, exhaling after a long minute of not breathing at all.

"Oh, gawd. Look at them!" Rogers swore softly. There was no way these could have landed in this clearing, no way at all. Yet there they sat, obviously not wrecks and obviously not natural. "Well, let's check 'em out," Rogers said, finally, hoping seriously that there was nobody at home.

Rogers and Mark approached the two craft, not yet realizing that the craft were extra-terrestrial in origin.

The closer the pair drew to the craft, the larger the planes appeared, eventually dwarfing the pair of human intruders. Rogers reached out a hand and touched the skin of the nearest craft. He expected it to be hot, but it was very cold. So cold he jerked his hand away quickly – not so much in pain as in surprise. Up close, it was obvious that the pinging was coming from the exhaust in the back, not from the body of the vehicles. Much like a car engine pings when turned off after a hard, fast run, he thought. But the skin of the plane should not be cold. Friction heated metal, right? And moving through the air pretty fast made some good friction, right? So why cold?

He reached out again to confirm his thought and was rewarded by more chilled fingers. But the surface was not metal. It was soft and very slick, almost slimy. Whatever it was, it was not metal or plastic or ceramic.

The pair skirted the craft and rounded the back. There had been nothing on this side of the craft that resembled a door or hatch. Maybe on the other side. They ducked under the engines and walked under the fuselage hunched over and craning their necks to see ahead. Rogers refused to walk behind the craft, being fully aware that they would quickly become crispy critters if caught in the blast of those mammoth engines coming to life. As such, they saw more of what was on the ground below them – nothing interesting – than what was in front of them – much more interesting. When they stepped out from under the alien fighter, they were almost as surprised as were those they stepped out in front of. That gave the humans just a second to realize that the creatures they faced were not Hippies. In fact, they were not human at all. And, conversely, those they faced took a second to realize that the humans were not... not... now whatever, either. The scene was a frozen tabloid like an establishing shot from a Quentin Tarantino movie.

Rogers automatically raised his rifle, despite the shock, and Mark automatically turned to run, once he had recovered from the shock.

"Run, boy," Rogers screamed, not noticing that Mark was already abandoning his father for safer surroundings. Rogers then added with more wish than reality: "I'll hold them off!"

Mark had taken two steps when a scaled hand snaked out and clamped talon-tipped fingers around his throat. Mark gurgled a few syllables and grabbed the arm as he was lifted bodily two feet off the ground and shaken like a rag doll. A second later Mark had the remarkable sensation of flying seconds before he cracked into the second craft, snapping his spine and ending all sensation a scant second after the young fool realized he should have been watching for someone coming around behind them. His father would be pissed at him forgetting the basics again.

Rogers was still finishing the swing of the rifle and squeezing his finger on the trigger when he was stabbed by a lance of searing light. His mouth opened in a gasp of surprise and his eyes looked down at the smoking hole in his chest. His finger never completed its pull on the trigger. The creature before him stepped forward and swiped its arm in a viscous half-circle, slamming a clawed fist into the side of the dying Sheriff's head, knocking it clean from his shoulders. His body stood still for a second, then toppled over, draining blood onto the forest floor. Through it all, the creatures had made no sound, shown no emotion, and never looked at the two men as anything more than dinner invading their campsite.

Amos was back on the porch, nursing a sore jaw. Hell, all he'd done was slip his hand down the front of her blouse. There wasn't any need to have slugged him so hard. He'd thought she wouldn't mind. She let Mark cop a feel whenever he wanted and Amos had given her a ride to keep her from getting her pretty little ass whipped for coming home late. But no, she wasn't grateful at all, and snippety, too. Maybe, Amos thought, he should have spanked that little ass himself. She might have been a little more willing then. Drop her knickers and slap those cheeks a few times and she might be beggin' for a little more than just a quick feel, yes indeed!

As he fantasized along the lines of Aqualung, "eying little girls with bad intent… Watching as the frilly panties run," two bright stars fell *up* from the woods and hovered for a few seconds. Then, with amazing speed, they fell east. Strangest falling stars he'd ever seen. Amos wondered how Rogers and that good-for-nothing son were doing and what they'd made of those star things. Shrugging off the peculiarities of astronomical anomalies, Amos scratched his crotch and moved back into the police office.

The Caruthers House was set back from the road about a hundred yards. It was surrounded by a growth of first generation pines that towered over its three-story frame structure. Built in the late eighteen-hundreds, its style was a mixture of Gothic and Victorian, sporting a wrap-around porch and several tower rooms topped with conical roofs set off from the steep-pitched roof of the main house. It was on a large tract of land, accompanied by a small barn or garage and two outbuildings off about twenty or thirty feet from the house. It was well separated from the middle class neighborhood that had sprung up down the road a mile or so and the farms that touched two other sides of the property. A large stand of pines, part of the national forest, separated the house from the rest of humanity on the north side, stretching several miles before Flagstaff poked out toward the towering Flagstaff Peak.

There were farms touching two sides of the property, and another across the road. Drive a few hundred feet north and the road to the Lowell Observatory marked the edge of the property. There were no other houses in the Thorpe Park area. A large stand of pines, part of the national forest, separated the house from the rest of humanity; stretching almost a half-a-mile before Humphrey's Peak thrust up through the clouds. North and west of the old mansion, then, was generally deserted grazing land. The location was as isolated as one could be inside the city limits.

The house was bathed in a pool of moon and starlight, but the rest of the grounds were sheathed in the black that only country living can give, far from streetlights and neon. It was silent, dark, empty, and deserted; dead and abandoned, at least, to the casual eye though not to the sensitive instruments that were scanning the outskirts of Flagstaff from just inside the clouds that scuttled over the moon.

Two streaks of light flashed over the house. Mark's falling stars had arrived from Clay Springs. They quickly stopped, then darted back to hover over the house. One pulled back a little, much like a cop backing his partner at a questionable stop. From the nearer, a soft red light quested out of the craft, touching the outbuildings, sliding over toward the barn, bathing it in a soft glow for a few seconds, then inching toward the main house. As it neared the house, a light blue glow sprung up around the structure. The red light splashed on the glow, engulfed it, but did not penetrate. Satisfied, the two falling stars fell away again. The glow left the Caruthers House and all was once again silent and dark. But everything had changed; and nothing would ever again be the way it was.

CHAPTER EIGHT
June 19, 2002
Flagstaff, Arizona

Paul sat on the edge of the bed in the hotel and toyed with his phone card. This was a call he both looked forward to and dreaded. He always liked talking with Jeremy, even when his son recounted every second of the most recent episode of *Transformers* or the one-hundredth replay of *Scoobie Doo*. It was not exactly stimulating conversation and Jer's vocabulary was not great, but it was Jeremy and even if it made him sad and lonely, it still gave him a warm glow to hear his son's joy and eagerness whenever he called. Bitter-sweet, but filling, Paul labeled it.

On the other hand, there was Janet. He did not understand why she wanted to punish him for falling in love with her, for asking her to marry him. She could have said no, after all, but somehow this was entirely his fault and she was not about to let him forget it. *Every* time he called, it was something else, some little thing that he had said or done that warranted rehashing and capital punishment. Like tossing out a three-day-old, half-empty can of Dr. Pepper left sitting by the TV or on the dresser or in the shower. How often had she ragged on him for *that* crime? It's not like she was actually ever going to finish it!

The less time he spent on the phone with her the better. If not for Jer, he could do with never talking with her again. This nonsense about being good buddies was just that: nonsense. Somewhere, sometime, she would have to forgive herself for all the things she had done to destroy the family before she could begin to be a decent human being again, at least where Paul was concerned. But that wasn't likely to happen, not with her friends – people Paul had never met – reinforcing her feeling of being victimized – how horrible that she had missed out on all the good things in life, like being single and dating the sleazebags her friends met in bars – and, of course, this was all about her, wasn't it? Nothing at all about Jeremy or the family.

That had been the hardest thing for Paul to understand. Yeah, he had made some mistakes. He had paid for most of them with interest and moved on in his life. But she held every slight to heart, like it had been a deliberate plot to make her miserable. And life was all about her; always had been, but Paul had been too blind to see that, too caught up in working to help the entire family to see her focus on things Janet and Janet only. Of course, she never said or did anything that hurt anyone else. No, not Janet.

He had talked to some other men he knew, men who had been through a divorce. He had never met or even heard about a man who had not been caught totally by surprise by a wife with a dozen knives aimed right at his back. Men, it seemed, just felt crushed and wanted to move on with their lives. Women, the ones who divorced, seemed to enjoy the crushing and wanted to make that a lifelong career objective. That left a man only two choices: stay in contact and tolerate the abuse, or vanish into the sunset. Vanishing seemed a good idea, but how do you do that to your child? He could never understand men who abandoned their families. Well, maybe he could. Sometimes dealing with the ex-wife was just too much. Sometimes the desire to strike out... Yes, if there was no way to limit the contact, maybe leaving and trying to repair the situation with the children later was less destructive than the tension and angry words every time custody was traded for a holiday or weekend or vacation. If it was about the kids, then dealing with the ex should at least be polite. Paul had not seen "polite" from Janet in years.

Janet probably had some legitimate complaints, but had just never voiced them; only the petty little things that Paul believed one learned to live with if love existed in the relationship. He would not have divorced her over the soda cans or the cap off the toothpaste or any other minor irritant. There was always a fresh can of soda in the refrigerator, Paul, who drank mostly iced tea, made sure of that. He had always put the lid back on the toothpaste and never made it an issue. You just deal with that stuff from the people you love and move on. It was not like someone cutting you off in traffic. But perhaps that was the rub; maybe there had never been any love in the relationship at all. Maybe it was, as he suspected, just Janet being in love with having someone being in love with her. Outside her romantic ideal of a never-ending courtship, the reality of marriage was as strange to her as replacing the empty toilet paper roll.

Paul sighed and put his thoughts to rest. He would deal with Janet as little as possible, figure out some way to see Jeremy with only brushing contact with his ex wife. Maybe tonight would be an exception and she would not complain more than ten or fifteen minutes. The child support was on auto pay, so that, thank God, was not an issue any longer.

Paul picked up the phone and hit nine, then dialed the long distance access code from his Sprint card. He squinted at the number on the back and punched in the PIN, then Janet's home phone. Tomorrow would be better. Just get through the next few minutes and then have a good chat with Jeremy. He could forget Janet. Until the next time he wanted to talk with his son, that is.

The phone rang three, four, five times. Paul was about to hang up and try again, on the theory that he had dialed the wrong number, when a small voice picked up with a "Hallo?"

"Jeremy? Hi, this is dad," Paul said, instantly buoyed by his son's voice and his good luck at not having to speak with Janet. "How are you, buddy?"

"OK."

"Hay, what's the matter? You don't sound too happy," Paul said, noting the lack of enthusiasm that usually accompanied on of his calls home.

"Where are you, daddy? Mommy says you go away."

"Oh, I'm just in Flagstaff on a business trip. I'll be back in a couple of days."

"Bring me sumpin'?" Now the excitement was there.

"Of course; don't I always?" That had been one of Paul's biggest mistakes, and perhaps biggest joys, the rendering of gifts after each trip he took. Sometimes he worried that the automatic reaction from Jeremy was akin to giving a dog a treat every time you walk in the house. Naturally, the dog is happy. He was just fed and all he had to do is act excited. Not that the stupid human would ever guess that the mutt was happy about the treat and not seeing the human; no, never that.

He worried that he was creating the same response in Jeremy. Janet said he was buying his son's love. That took a lot of the joy out of Jeremy's excitement when he saw his father. She never understood that he was not buying love, but buying joy: his son's happiness, which in turn made him happy. Paul fully believed you could not buy love but you could purchase a little happiness. Janet did not understand the idea of delight in the pleasure of others.

"Good. Mommy put all my toys in a box and gave them to some men. I don't gots anything to play with."

"Gots." Oh, Lord where did he pick up that piece of gutter slang! And a dangling participle! His son's English was going right to Hell and he wasn't around to do anything about it. Good grammar took daily work. But what was this about boxes?

"Why did Mommy do that? Were you a bad boy?"

"I didn't do nothin'!" And Paul believed that. The indignation was too real, not hedged a bit.

"Well, what..."

"Give me that," he heard Janet say in the background and he could almost feel the temperature at the other end of the phone drop. Janet had the phone; life just took a very unpleasant turn. He had hoped... But unsurprisingly, life was never that kind.

"Paul, is that you?" Cold. Arctic cold. God, why was she angry now?

"Yeah. I was just talking to Jeremy. What's this about his toys?"

"They're packed."

"Packed? Why?" Paul knew a hundred answers to that, but none of them made any sense. Suddenly, the room was swirling, spinning. The universe had taken a sudden turn and gone out of kilter.

"We're moving. I hadn't wanted you to know yet, but I guess *your son* gave it away." Paul could just see Jeremy cringing from her tone.

"Moving? But…"

"Look, I wrote you a letter and sent it to your attorney today. It'll tell you what you need to know now. Later, I'll let you know when we get settled."

"What do you mean? You can't…"

"Well, I am. I'm getting married again and I don't want you interfering with Jeremy getting to know his new father."

"Wait a minute, the court…"

"Gave us joint custody?" Janet interrupted, finishing his sentence for him. "I'm not going to stop you from seeing Jeremy. Just put it on hold for a few months. I'll give you an extra week in the summer. We're going to take a trip then and I don't need the kid around to get in the way."

"You can't…"

"That's the way it is."

"You have to notify the courts where you are. You have to notify me!"

"I did both in letters that went out today. Don't bother trying to find us. The address is temporary. We'll really be there to keep it legal, then move again. I can stretch this out as long as I like."

"Where are you going? How will I see Jeremy?"

"You probably won't for awhile. I'll tell you this much: we're moving back East, so even when I get an address, don't expect to see him. And when I get married, I don't want you around at all."

"You can't…"

"Stop telling me what I can't do. It's already done. The packers are just finishing now. I paid extra to get it done while you were out of town, just to make sure you didn't interfere. We'll be gone before you can make the drive from Flagstaff. Thirty minutes tops, so don't bother trying." Paul heard some noise in the background, a door slamming and a large truck starting up. "The movers are gone now. We'll be gone before you can make another phone call. Just live with it, Paul, and don't piss me off or I'll make it impossible for you to see Jeremy ever again."

Click. The phone was dead.

Quickly, Paul went through the process of calling again, misdialing the calling card numbers three times before the phone connection went through. He let it ring until the phone company sent the call to an intercept that politely told him that his part was not answering and would he please try again later. Paul hung up the phone. He could see it in his mind's eye, the phone sitting in the middle of an empty living room, cord snaking to the wall where it lay unplugged beneath the jack. Or maybe just the cord, the phone having gone with Janet.

What could he do? Not a hell of a lot, and that was what his friend John told him when Paul called a few minutes later. John would call some friends on the police force, but if Janet had planned the move this tight, it would be pure, blind luck if they caught up with her or if anyone in the neighborhood had even noticed the name of the moving company. It was probably someone with a plain panel truck that took her things to storage more than a regular moving company, John said, based on what Paul told him. If she had planned things out this well and this far in advance, she wasn't about to leave any traces.

John said he would start the ball rolling and call an investigator, but that would take time. How much? As long as it would take for Paul to finish his business in Flagstaff and then some. But John said he would bet it would be months before they could track Janet down and that would take a lot of money; money Paul did not have.

It was a long time before sleep arrived, blotting out the flashing neon light painting images on the motel ceiling. When Paul did fall asleep, he dreamed of monsters, some of them very human.

With falling stars, a few miles of woods count for nothing. A few thousand feet count for even less. Across the road and down past a stand of mixed pine, fir, and elm, Sabertooth, a mix all his own of timber wolf, malamute, and Doberman, set up a howl that quickly changed into a non-stop marathon of furious barks and growls. Chuck Biscotti was not in the mood to listen to his dog set off the neighbors one more time. Biscotti, a manager at the Wendy's on Highway 89, Flagstaff's main strip, had just managed to slide into bed at 3:07 am. He was tired, irritated, and in no mood for the inevitable phone calls that Sabertooth generated on a much too regular basis.

He pulled himself out of bed, cursing the dog, but mainly cursing a job that required a minimum two openings and two closing in a 50 hour week. It's not like anyone could develop a decent sleep pattern with such a schedule, much less a normal one. He was always tired, always short tempered, and always aware that he was trapped in a job that could vanish in one bad week of drive through times and he could not easily quit and go somewhere else. His paycheck was already only 89% of his expenses and he was constantly fitting odd jobs into his few hours of off time just to make ends meet. Drop the main income – forget that it was at least $5,000 a year below the average range for restaurant managers in the area – and he and his family would be out on the streets in less than sixty days. *That's life in fast food,* he philosophized. But if he hadn't knocked up his closing cashier, Beth, and been force into marriage … First a bitch now the damned dog. The more things change, the more they stayed the same …

Chuck shuffled to the back of the house and into the kitchen. He peered out the back window, but he could see little beyond the pile of trash he had piled up next to the door. He really should have carried it to the community trash bin three days ago. But he could see Sabertooth straining at the end of his leash, yapping his head off at the woods. *Probably another damned skunk,* Chuck reasoned, and that brought resolve. The last skunk had sprayed the dog down good. It had taken six days and three gallons of tomato juice before the smell had finally gone away, even though he still thought he caught a whiff now and then. No, if there was a skunk out there interested in Beth's small garden or Chuck's large pile of trash, then better to end the discussion right now before things were carried any farther!

Chuck threw open the back door and aimed a few choice epithets at the dog, but Sabertooth just ignored him. Something certainly had the dog's attention out there in the woods.

Chuck flipped on the kitchen light, but he really should have known that the inside light would do nothing more than destroy his night vision. He hit the back porch light, thinking that might frighten the... whatever... away and give him a chance to calm Sabertooth, but all that did was cast a pale yellow bug-light glow across the backyard up to the tree line. If anything, it set the dog off even more. But wait, something moved out there, something man-shaped. A bear? Maybe, but a very skinny bear. Probably someone skulking around in the woods looking for something easy to steal and pawn. Well, not his stuff and not tonight. If it was a thief, Chuck thought reasonably, then it would give him some ammunition against the neighbors who were always complaining about the dog's nightly howls.

Chuck stepped boldly out onto the back porch, his plaid bathrobe flowing out behind him like Darth Vader's cape. He picked up a handy hoe and advanced a step or too, once more admonishing Sabertooth to shut the hell up. He just about jumped out of his skin as two objects flashed over the house and settled into the woods just beyond the tree line.

Well, maybe that explained things. The Army National Guard out playing Boy Scouts in the woods. Those helicopters sure were quiet though. Not like the ones they normally flew around here on Guard weekends. Those could wake the dead and shake the pictures off the walls.

Well, if there were 'copters in the woods, then whatever was bothering Sabertooth was a non-problem. He would just drag the dog in and shut him in a closet if that's what it took. Still gripping the hoe with one hand, he reached down and gave the chain a tug.

"Shut up, dog, and get your stupid ass inside!" he requested in his best restaurant manager voice. And, in his best *no hablo Inglés* manner, Sabertooth kept right on barking. So Chuck jerked again and just about fell over when there was absolutely no give at all. The dog was putting his whole 125 pounds into stretching the chain just a few more inches.

Chuck peered into the woods. Nothing. Gripping the chain loosely, he walked out to the dog, just a little nervous that the angry animal might turn on him in frustration at not being able to break free. Speaking a little softer now, coaxing, he tried to calm the dog and work him back into the house. But Sabertooth was having none of that.

There, at the end of the chain with the dog, away from the direct glare of the bug light, Chuck tried again to see what had the dog so worked up. And there was something there. A man-shadow, deep in the woods, not moving, just standing and watching Chuck and his frantic dog. Well, that was enough.

Unless this was something out of that old stupid sci-fi movie *Mimic* – and Chuck knew damned well it wasn't – he was ending this once and for all. Now, Chuck was really pissed. And the other dogs in the neighborhood were beginning to pick up Sabertooth's agitation and voice their own complaint into the night. It sounded like the dog chorus was in full voice, from what little he could hear over his own dog's vocals.

"Is there someone out there?" He called, noticing angrily that his voice cracked just a little. Taking a deep breath, he shouted out again, making sure he was heard over the frantic dog. "Who's there!?"

That brought a reaction! The shadow was moving forward, into the light. Chuck gripped the hoe more firmly. If it was a tramp, he'd have him off right quick. Anyone wanting a little mischief, well, working in fast food built up a lot of anger and frustration. Chuck would welcome a release and woe be to anyone he started on since he knew he wouldn't stop until that person was a bloody pulp on the ground. That was not ego. He just *knew* he was invincible when that flood of restaurant anger was released.

But what stepped into the light was not a bum or illegal immigrant or drugged up teen. It was not even a man. It was something straight from a nightmare or the special effects of Universal's make-up artist Bud Westmore.

The … thing … walked right up to Sabertooth, just right out of reach of the dog's snapping, salivating jaws. But he was watching Chuck every second. Then, lightening quick, it brought its arm around and back then slammed his clawed hand up against the dog's head.

Chuck thought that maybe, just maybe, Sabertooth had made a shot at snapping that flashing hand. But if so, he had failed. The dog flew sideways, marking a half-circle at the end of his chain, to fall in a crumpled heap a half dozen feet away from the creature. No chance. No chance at all. And by the ruined look of his head and shoulders, Sabertooth would not be making any more noise at night. Not ever.

Chuck took a staggering step backwards, his rake held crossways before him like a deformed halberd, his pajamas and robe splattered with Sabertooth's blood and gore.

"Saber … saber …" Chuck choked out, not wanting to believe what his eyes were telling him. Frozen by fear, he did not even notice the warm trickle down his thighs as his bladder let go. He backed up to the porch and stopped when his heel hit the edge of the concrete. Whimpering a series of soft "no's" he just stood there, his hoe held at port, while the creature advanced. He made no move when the creature reached out and grabbed his throat, lifted him single-highhandedly, and tossed him back against the screen door, incidentally keeping hold of a good portion of Chuck's throat in the process.

The slam of the door into the house finally roused Beth from the warmth of her bed. Either that or the cries of her baby, now awake after sleeping through Sabertooth's night-song. Leveling her 240 pounds out of bed, she slipped on her slippers without ever opening her eyes. She tossed a "be quiet" at the child and stumbled into the kitchen, ready to give Chucky the what-for over all the noise.

The light was on in the backyard and she could see someone moving around out there through her half-closed eyes. Pulling her pink robe tight, she wandered over to the screen and looked out. What was that man doing out there? Where did he get those outlandish silver clothes? And what was up with the stupid dog? He looked funny, just lying there when someone was in the yard. She could not see Chuck where he was slumped against the side of the house, but she finally opened her eyes enough to realize that the figure now walking up to the house was not Chuck. Not anyone she knew. Nobody, and she had given blow jobs to darn near everyone in town before Chuck finally took the fall and had to marry her.

Frantically, she began trying to latch the screen door. The wooden door would give her some safety, but she had to latch it so the screen door would not open. First the screen, then the solid wooden door. First the screen. She couldn't close the other door until the screen was latched, could she, because that was not the proper way to do things. First the screen, but it wasn't latching. Not at all! There, that was it! The screen door was latched.

Now, semi-safe behind the screen, she looked up at the creature standing in the yellow glow from the bug light. Some kind of walking fish. She screamed. But only a second. The clawed hand ripped away the screen and reached through for her. She stepped back, but tripped over the dog's water dish. But she could not fall with the claws dug into her throat. Unlike Chuck, she was not lifted, but pulled through the screen door, ripping it off the hinges in the process. The creature turned away, leaving Beth dangling over the corpse of her dead husband, held in place by the bottom half of the door that was still firmly latched to the jam.

The creature turned back to the woods and walk away, following a pair of like beings who, having snapped Sabertooth's chain, were carrying the dog with them back into the trees.

A few minutes later, three falling stars fell back into the night and vanished across the low hills below Flagstaff Mountain. With their going, the few lights that had snapped on at the noise went out and the neighborhood dogs went back to restless watches, none sleeping until dawn crept fearfully into a clear morning sky.

Paul put on his best game face. John had called early. He had rousted Paul's attorney the night before and gone over the details of the situation with him. There were options, but none of them good. The best professional advice was to file a contempt charge against Janet for taking Jeremy out of state, but Paul's divorce papers did not specifically prohibit that. If she was bouncing around a little, she was probably covered as long as she sent certified letters with each new address, never mind that they were outdated by the time they arrived. A private investigator would cost upwards of three grand to track her.

Best to wait until Janet surfaced and stayed put for a few weeks and file a summons then. That would only cost a few hundred and if she skipped before she was served they would at least have the beginning if a trail. Right now, there was nothing of value that they could do; John repeated several it times until Paul stopped protesting. Just get on with his life. If she was really planning a trip with her new husband (and, God, didn't that hurt whether he wanted to acknowledge it or not!) without Jeremy in the summer, she'd have to contact Paul then. Perhaps they could summon her for a time when she would have to leave the trip to go to court. Petty, but if she missed the court date it would help if Paul decided to file for custody, which he had about a one-in-ten-thousand chance of winning. That was especially true if she went back East and not to California, where men were beginning to see some success in winning custody battles.

In the clear light of early morning, his options were bleak and he knew it. Whatever happened, Paul could look forward to years when he only saw his son occasionally and probably, judging by Janet's behavior in the past, only by jumping through whatever hoops she put in his way. That is, if he could manage to see Jeremy at all. Paul's only reasonable option was to move, go with the flow for now; but they didn't know anything about this newest partner in Janet's revolving-door bedroom. If he was military – and Janet tended to lean toward me in uniform – then they could expect them to move every three years or so, and Paul would have to move to stay near Jeremy, even if it was an overseas assignment. And it would probably take three or four years at best to clear things up with court ordered psychological and sociological exams, appeals, requests for delays, moves, and lord knew what else Janet would devise to keep Paul away from her and, incidentally, Jeremy. The attorney estimated a minimum of fifty thousand in legal fees. There went the kid's college.

Or he could wait and try for something – John wasn't sure what – when they had a solid line on her. No, kidnapping Jeremy was *not* an option. Or, and this was the big *or*, he could get on with his life and do what most men were forced into under these circumstances: do his best to see Jeremy when he could but not fight the tiger. In other words, he had no go choices at all, though for some reason the thought of a gun kept picking at the back of his brain. He could use a gun. And he remembered an old man he met saying it was easier to bury 'em than divorce 'em. But what good would that do Jeremy if he was stuck in prison?

One thing that was abundantly clear and had been ever since Janet told Paul she had wanted a divorce: none of her actions were ever in any way connected to what was best for Jeremy. It was all about what Janet wanted and all she wanted to do was punish Paul for stealing the best years of her youth. She had told that to her lawyer after the custody hearing, not noticing that John had stepped out of the men's room behind her. But by then it was too late for everyone, and John had never told Paul about that conversation, until just now; it was hearsay evidence, right? Why help spread the pain, he had said, until Paul could deal with it more rationally? But Paul knew divorce was always emotional and never, not ever, rational.

Get on with your life. Live with the reality that it would be a long and hard road to before he ever saw his son again. And forget buying a gun. It wouldn't help in the long run. After all, John reminded him, Paul was not a shooter and just as likely to shoot himself as he was to hit Janet.

So Paul worked at putting on that game face. He dressed with care and shaved with great deliberation. He firmly shoved everything behind him and was determined to make the most of the rest of the day. John and his lawyer would do all they could to help. Good friends were hard to find and more precious than gold. It would work out or not, but now he had work of his own and he needed to make the most of it. Should this eventually lead to a long court battle, then this research might go a long way toward funding the legal fees. Articles, maybe a book. A few thousand, anyway. Probably no movie deal, but maybe someone would take a look at his other work with the publicity.

But he couldn't shake the feeling that he should go to the nearest pawnshop and put down a couple of hundred for a gun and do it *today*. Or maybe a .50 caliber machine gun. Or a bazooka. Or something. Anything. And do it *now*. There was an overpowering feeling that he would need to shoot something, someone; just kill a can or two.

Instead, he stopped at the Y's front counter and bought a couple of Snickers that he threw in the glove compartment before heading out.

Paul eased his car to a stop next to the curb, careful not to stop too close to the fire hydrant. There were too many police around to be anything less than prudent. He wondered if he had the right location and, being the studious journalist he was, he double checked the address. Right. No mistake. This was a nice, upper-middle class neighborhood. It was not the type of setting where Paul would have expected a half-dozen police cars, two emergency rescue vehicles, the coroner's car, a few assorted fire trucks, and a couple of what looked like Air Force blue military sedans parked off to one side. Even problems in Phoenix's rougher neighborhoods didn't pull this much muscle, and you can throw in a bust on a Coyote's human smuggling stash.

Paul had a strange feeling that everywhere he turned these days, he was stepping into something that smelled... well, not like fresh-cut grass but more like something left by a cat. The Sheriff in Clay Springs had been less than eager to help, that cop Samuels – and yes, Paul could see Samuels in this mix of authorities and the morbid curious – had given him the third degree behind polite smiles and free coffee. Northern Arizona was beginning to feel an awful lot like the badlands, up around Las Vegas, New Mexico, where they'd cut your throat just for being the wrong shade of tan. Of course, there was a large insane asylum in Las Vegas, that tended to turn the inmates lose in the daytime, so at least they had an excuse. But what was happening here?

Paul spotted Stacy standing a little off from the crowd. This was certainly the right corner, it must be the right time, but something was certainly off center in this version of the Grinch's Whoville.

Even though his reporter instincts were aroused, he did not want to become involved with whatever was happening. He did not want to be sidetracked from his main story. There had been a growing sense of urgency ever since he had left Clay Springs and that had compounded with Janet's bombshell last night. He felt that he had to land this story and land it fast or lose it. Besides that, his eyes were certainly not hurting when he look at Stacy. She had on a white blouse and a tight jeans skirt that set her long legs off nicely. Not that the blouse detracted any, either.

Paul told himself that it was impolite to stare – well, he just didn't want her to catch him staring like a teenager at a topless beach – so he shook himself and set out across the street just in time to catch Stacy's eye as she turned to scan the road.

It didn't take much for Paul to see that Stacy was very upset. Worry lines creased her face and her eyes were red. She walked over with her arms crossed under her chest, constantly throwing glances over her shoulder toward the activity around a rather ordinary looking house. Paul stopped by the front of his car and waited for her to cross the street. Something told him that he would be better served away from the action so he let her approach him just to put more space between them and the milling police.

"What's going on," he asked when she was still a few feet away. He wasn't sure he really wanted to know, but that was the natural question and it jumped out before he could think of a more original, and perhaps more appropriate, opening line.

"It was horrible," Stacy said, turning back to look at the crime scene, repulsed and attracted at the same time.

"What was?" Paul asked. For some reason, his mind was not working as well as he had hoped. He was a little old to be tongue-tied around a pretty girl, but for the life of him he felt like a teenager out on his first date.

"What happened," Stacy answered absently, not really paying attention. "It was awful." Her elaboration was just about useless. She obviously thought that Paul should know the whole story. After all, he was a reporter and this was news. Never mind that he had just arrived and did not know Flagstaff at all. He should just *know*. That, Paul would say, would be female logic and nothing he could never argue with successfully.

"What was," Paul asked, allowing his curiosity to overcome his desire to not know and not be caught up in some local tragedy.

Stacy absently waved back across the street, where there was some more activity with the paramedics. They were pulling a couple of stretchers out of the ambulances and wheeling them around to the back of one of the houses, trampling the flowers that lined the driveway in the process.

"What happened, it was awful." Her mind was still not focusing on the fact that Paul had no clue what was happening in the yard behind the white house with the blue trim, the one badly in need of a lawn mowing and a little attention to some minor repairs. On a closer look, Paul thought the house was a little less respectable than its companions in the area. It was a house obviously owned by someone with less pride in the neighborhood.

"All right," Paul said, letting just a little exasperation creep into his voice. "It was awful. But just exactly what happened?"

"They're not sure," Stacy answered, still not paying much attention to Paul. She was totally caught up in the activity, just as surely as she would be hooked on a daytime soap opera… that is, if she allowed herself the vice of watching any daytime television. "But they think they were killed by a wild animal. A mountain lion or a bear or something."

"Wild animals? Here?" Paul asked incredulously. "I hadn't heard of Flagstaff having problems with animals." Paul looked at the scene with more interest. People dead and talk of wild animals. Maybe there was something here for him after all. That would be a strange background for his toy maker story. Maybe it wasn't animals but some robot-like toys that were running wild, Paul thought, then discarded the idea as being too much like science fiction. He was, after all, not a novelist but a journalist, a writer of features, and documentaries, and news, not a fiction hack. Still … "Who were they?"

"The Biscottis. Both of them. But it left the baby alone, though. Just killed the two adults and left." Stacy shuddered and hugged herself tighter. "Blood all over the place."

"How were thy killed?"

"They were torn apart. I saw the bodies. One of the neighbors – Alan, the one who found the bodies when he went to let his dog loose in the woods – he wanted someone to go in and check on the baby. We could hear it crying. I was the lucky one they got to go. That was right before the police came."

"You went in? What if the killers were still inside!"

"Alan and some of the others had already been in. They just didn't know how to handle a crying baby. The bodies were really torn up. I was almost sick." Stacy looked at Paul, and there was a very sick look in her eyes. "Some kind of animal did this. It wasn't done by anything human, no matter what they find out."

Paul looked back at the house, taking on some of Stacy's fear and worry. She was obviously much shaken, but Paul could see trouble coming. He wanted to think of a way to hustle Stacy into the car, but nothing would come to mind that would not make him seem like some kind of nut case. So he just gave a weak smile as Samuels walked up with another man. There was no escape and, if Stacy had been inside, then there was a reason for Samuels to come over to them, though Paul would have preferred a quick getaway, graceful or not.

"Could it have been wild dogs?" Paul asked, mainly because that was coming out before he had noticed Samuels and couldn't shut it off without sounding like a fool. The cop took that for an invitation to step in and did so, walking right up to Paul and Stacy, answering Paul's question instead of the still-nervous girl.

"No way." Samuels' voice was flat and cold, hard as polished steel. "Ask the coroner. This is Doctor Rankin." Samuels turned to the man who had walked over with him and gave him a little nod.

Rankin was tall, over six four, thin as a rail, and he sported a handlebar mustache that had lost its popularity in the late eighteen-hundreds and only showed up as an anachronism since, if you discount some of the rock bands in the sixties. Even though he was still in his mid-fifties, Rankin's black hair was as well salted with white as his speech was saturated with a strong Western dialect. All in all, he looked and sounded more like a wrangler from a *City*

Slicker movie more than a doctor with enough degrees to land the job as city coroner or any one of a dozen other crime scene investigation specialties.

"It wasn't dogs," Rankin said absently, scratching a nose that, on a skinnier face, would have made W. C. Fields envious. "Ain't sure it was a mountain lion or a bear like some of your men have been sayin', either. Signs ain't right, wounds ain't right, time of the year ain't right."

"Maybe it was a dog that did it and ran off," Paul ventured, having only half listened to what Rankin had told Samuels just moments before. That earned him Rankin's full attention.

"Said it weren't no dog," he repeated forcefully and just a little louder, like someone speaking to a near deaf person or someone who couldn't understand English, as if volume could make a difference. "Nope, their dog was killed, too. Found pieces of it in the bushes. Whatever killed the people took most of the dog with it too. And that wasn't no poodle they had, either."

Rankin turned back and looked at the house. Two Air Force officers and a very pale female officer in what was obviously Army tan camo, along with several uniformed military police and a group of civilians – all with all the earmarks of government employees – had moved out from behind the house and were talking to the police forensic squad. The mystery of the blue cars was solved, but not why the Air Force – with an Army liaison – was poking around a Flagstaff crime scene. In the back of Paul's mind, a little voice began changing "Clay Springs, Toy Maker, Clay Springs, Toy Maker …" He couldn't help himself. As much as his mind said "flee the scene" his instincts said "dig, dig, dig."

"What do you think it was?" he asked, cursing his tongue, which was off on its own once again.

"Don't rightly know," Rankin mused, for the moment more interested in the conversation taking place just out of ear-shot between the military and forensics. "It wasn't anything that I've seen before and I've looked at a fair number of animal mutilations in the past thirty years." Rankin turned back to the group, pushing his worry about a military concern in this local killing aside for the moment.

"The claw marks aren't normal" he explained. "The spread's all wrong, too wide," he continued, spreading his fingers as an example. "It's more like a hand than a paw. Had to be strong and fast, too, since it took the dog without signs of a struggle. Don't think that dog ever set a fang on that creature, either."

"I know they used to say it was part wolf," Stacy added.

"Thought it was a big dog from the look of the droppings in the yard and the feed pan. Interesting about the couple, though," Rankin added, then let his voice trail off.

"What?" Paul prompted.

"Most of the body fluids are gone."

"Vampires?" Stacy asked.

"No, not in the Dracula vein," Rankin said, completely missing his own pun. "Something. Of course, they were left to bleed like stuck pigs."

"Bled to death?" Paul asked, fully aware that Samuels was not joining in and that his attention was focused almost entirely on Paul.

"No way. Death by, well, a lot of trauma. I'll know more after the autopsy."

Stacy looked over at the house and gave a shiver, hugging herself again, as if the temperature had dropped twenty degrees from one breath to the next.

"Do you think that's what might have been killing off the cats and dogs around here?" Stacy asked.

Samuels' attention was instantly riveted on Stacy.

"What do you mean," he demanded.

"There have been a lot of cats and dogs that have just vanished around here lately," she said and Paul nodded, remembering the large number of lost-pet posters tacked to telephone poles he had seen driving into the subdivision. He had thought that was whether odd when he had first noticed it, but had not thought much on it figuring that the people in Flagstaff were just lax about fences and leashes. Stacy had just made a whether chilling connection. "I think maybe they were killed by whatever did the killing here."

"They had the same problem up in Clay Springs, where those two girls and their dog were killed a few days ago," Paul said, suddenly connecting Stacy's thoughts with the odd sheriff and his son he had spoken with the day before.

Samuels turned back to Paul with one of the strangest looks Paul had ever seen on a human face. "What are *you* talking about now?"

"There's something that's killing off the livestock up in the hills," Paul said. "The sheriff mentioned it to me yesterday. Or the deputy did. One of them."

"What did he say it was?" Rankin wanted to know.

"Maybe a lion or a bear," Paul offered.

"No bear did this. Besides, bears don't drink blood," Rankin insisted.

"Drank blood?" Stacy asked, shivering despite the sun's warmth.

Samuels waved Stacy away, but Rankin answered anyway.

"The bodies are pretty well drained. There's not enough blood around her to account for all the fluid lost from the bodies."

"But there's blood all over the place," Stacy protested.

"Not enough," Rankin insisted. "Not near enough."

"The sheriff didn't say it, but the deputy did say something about drained bodies. And something about a couple of girls that were killed up there last week. He said that they'd lost a lot of blood, too."

"I heard about that," Rankin said. "But I didn't see the bodies. Anything else said?"

"No. The sheriff did grow a little upset when I started asking questions. Said it was a rogue bear.

Why don't you call up there and ask him yourself? He wouldn't tell me a thing."

"I'd do that, but we received word early this morning that the Sheriff and his Deputy were killed in a hunting accident last night."

"Sheriff Daniels, from the Kingman area?" Rankin asked in surprise.

"No, it was Rogers and his son from area around the Apache reservation. Clay Springs. Did you know them?" Samuels asked.

Rankin nodded, a bemused look crossing his face. "Several years. He and his son and I go elk hunting occasionally. What happened? Did he trip and blow his head off? He did have a bad habit of walking with his gun loaded."

"No. They were killed by wild animals," Samuels said flatly.

"I find that hard to believe!" Rankin said, truly startled. "Daniels might have been careless with a gun, but he was an excellent tracker. He had good wood's sense. He wouldn't've been killed by an animal."

Rankin shook his head. These figures just did not compute! "Do you think you can get his body down here for me to look at?"

"Yeah. I'll try, what's left of it anyway."

"And those girls that were killed… what, last week?"

"Yeah. Last week."

"And now this."

"Yeah."

"Any connection?" Paul asked.

"Maybe, at least on the surface. The report said that wild animals killed the girls. You said Rogers said it was a bear. These people were killed by a… a something."

"That sounds like an awful lot of work for mere animals," Paul ventured.

"What are you getting at?" Samuels demanded.

"I don't know. It's just that killings in two widely separated areas by what is supposed to be wild animals … It just feels … strange."

"Yeah," Samuels agreed. "Very strange. Clay Springs' a good way from here with some decent ridges in between and a lot of fences. If these are connected, it would be some very special animals. Know any animals that can travel fast enough to kill in Clay Springs and here in the same night?"

"Only the two legged kind."

"Are you saying this is murder?" Samuels asked, fishing for an official coroner's verdict.

"Not yet, but maybe. I ain't sayin' anything for sure. Not until I can see the bodies. All of them."

"But what do you think," Samuels pressed.

"Don't rightly know," Rankin answered, falling back on his down-home reluctance to commit to anything where there was still plenty of room for doubt. "It might be murder. Like those cult killings in California."

"What about the claw marks," Paul wanted to know.

"I saw an old Tarzan movie," Stacy ventured, "where the natives were killing people with gloves made of leopard paws. It's called *Tarzan and the Leopard Woman*. Is that what you're thinking of?"

The conversation came to an abrupt stop. The three men paused and just looked at Stacy: Rankin like she was some sort of specimen; Samuels like he was visiting the insane wards on the third floor of the County hospital, and Paul with wide-eyed wonder. He *loved* that movie!

"What?" she asked after a long moment.

"Well, I don't want to get too carried away," Rankin said at last. "But I guess it could be somethin' like that. I'd say somethin' would have had to have grabbed the woman's throat to have ripped it out like that. That means a hand. The rest could have been swipe wounds, but her throat looks like a grip. But I can't think of anyone with that kind of muscle outside the pro-wrestling circle. The grip required to do that kind of damage would be extraordinary. Weightlifting, a ballplayer... even a golfer would not develop a grip that tight. Maybe a sailor, a fisherman, someone who hauls in lines all day would fit the profile, but the nearest ocean is three hundred fifty miles west. A little far for a beached net-hauler."

Rankin's hand shot out with an accompanying growl, reaching for Stacy's throat. She jumped back with a startled squeal.

"Somethin' like that," Rankin finished.

"Well, damn it, should we be looking for an animal or a man?" Samuels said, his frustration creeping into his voice along with his irritation at Rankin's playfulness at a time when Samuels could see nothing playful at all.

"I wouldn't say that whoever did this was exactly *human*," Rankin retorted. "To rip out a throat like that would require the strength beyond that of even a super athlete. I wouldn't like to meet the killer without a .45 in my hand."

Samuels nodded. He knew exactly how Rankin felt. This was one crime scene that he would have gladly sat out. It all connected if the people were killed in a similar way and if there were diverse groups doing the killings – say a terrorist organization – or if a small group or person had good transportation. Like a car. Say, an '87 Cherokee.

"Not even a .45 would work, doc," Samuels said dryly.

"What's wrong with a .45?"

"Rogers had his .45 out and cocked when he lost his head," Samuels said.

"What does that mean?" Rankin asked.

"It means you'll get a body to examine in two parts."

The silence that followed the revelation stretched for what felt like an eternity.

"Where were you last week," Samuels suddenly asked Paul, very casually.

"In Phoenix, researching for my trip here. Why?"

"And what *are* you doing here? What kind of topic are you writing about?"

"Huh?"

"You seem to be popping up wherever there's a murder these days; first at Clay Springs and now here. What were you researching? What places you in the two places where people have died under strange circumstances when we don't even have a mysterious death in a decade around here?"

"Me?" Paul exclaimed, truly shocked. "I didn't know anything about this until I got here! I just came by today for a guided tour!"

"Nice to know I rate," Stacy said softly; but not softly enough that Paul could miss it.

"How's this connected with your story?" Samuels wanted to know.

Paul waited a few seconds before answering. One of the ambulances pulled out and hit the lights and siren right next to where the group was standing, making talking an impossibility.

"My date?" Paul countered, then waited for the second meat wagon to leave before finishing, "Like I said, that's just for sightseeing."

"Not your date," Samuels said, making it perfectly clear that this was not a good time for word games. "The murders. How do they fit in with what you are working on."

"As far as I know, they don't."

Samuels was not convinced. Here this big city fellow arrives and bodies start popping up everywhere. Counting the two from Red lake the week before – and Samuels had no way of confirming whether or not Johnson had been in that area before he walked into the police station two days ago – the body count must be six, at least. Maybe more if there were hikers or campers out in the woods somewhere just waiting to be stumbled over by some old fart out walking his cockapoo. Cats and dogs. Lions, and tigers, and bears, oh my. This was becoming too much like the South side of Chicago, a place he worked very hard to not remember.

Samuels let the silence drag on for several long moments. "Well, Flagstaff is a small town," he finally said. "Watch yourself."

"Yeah, sure," Paul answered, not entirely sure if that was a warning to be good, or a warning that there might be trouble waiting for him from one of the local red necks if he wasn't careful. "She'll be safe with me. It would be foolish to cause problems now," Paul said. He took Stacy's elbow and guided her over to the Cherokee and helped her in before moving over to the driver's side.

Paul had traveled a lot and knew that big cities did not exist. They were nothing but a large collection of small communities, each of which had its own personality, its own turf, and its own power pyramid. These invisible lines might not be recognizable even to the residents, but they were to the territorial dogs that roamed them. Any stranger was in danger in any town, small or large. Cross some invisible line and there was trouble. He didn't need that warning.

Samuels watched Paul help Stacy into Cherokee's the passenger side before moving back across the street, leaving Rankin still standing in the middle of the road. The tall doctor had a pensive look on his face, his well-disciplined doctor's mind was busy trying to sort out some very undisciplined facts and he was working on automatic at the moment. He watched as Samuels made right for Officer Fisher, and then moved over to the side of the car as Paul opened the door.

"Did you run that check I asked for?" Samuels asked without preamble.

"Yes, sir. It's on your desk. It came in first thing this morning. I dropped it there on my way here."

"I didn't ask for it on my desk," Samuels snapped, irrationally irritated. "I said give it to *me*. Well, what did it say?"

"Nothing," Fisher replied with a shrug. "Phoenix P.D. doesn't have anything on him. As far as they can see, he's clean."

Yeah. And Jack The Ripper went to the grave with a clean rap sheet, too, Samuels thought, noting that everyone was clean until they were caught.

"Stay with him," Samuels said, motioning with his head to Paul's Cherokee. "I want to know what he does and when he does it. Put in for overtime. I'll have someone relieve you as soon as the watch Sergeant can arrange it."

"I don't see why you …"

"You don't have to understand," Samuels barked, suddenly past his limit. "Something about all this bothers me more than just these murders. Something weird has been going on here for the last twenty-seven years and he thinks all this is connected. I want to know why. I want to know what he looks into. I'm not going to let go until I get to the bottom of this and I am not going to let any loose strings float around. Now move."

"Don't mind Samuels," Rankin said as Paul seated himself in the Cherokee and rolled down the driver's window when the lanky coroner walked over. "I've known him for a long time. He's a good cop and this mess will hound him until it's solved. And Samuels *will* solve it. He's very good. He says you're a writer?"

"Yeah," Paul answered, still distracted by Samuels' implied suspicion.

"What'd you write?"

"Now I'm just working on a factual article - something dealing with business and innovation," Paul said, turning his attention away from where Samuels was talking to a uniformed cop. "I was looking for the Caruthers place because I think the owner may be connected with some new technology and this young lady agreed to show me around."

"It's right over there," Rankin said, pointing across the Cherokee, toward the house where the activity was beginning to wind down. "The other side of the woods, a mile or so. The property borders this subdivision. Right behind the Biscotti place … The Biscotti's. Those are the people who were killed."

"Oh." Paul was silent for a minute, suddenly aware of another connection in a web that was increasingly putting him in its center. Or, whether, his research was pushing him into something bigger than he had anticipated. "Anyway, Stacy agreed to point the place out to me and show me some of the highlights of Flagstaff. We agreed to meet here. That's all."

"Ain't much to look at any more. Used to be a real nice house. But it was left to ruin and the new owner's not done much to improve it. Still a lot of weeds and it needs a good paint job. More's the pity, even if the new towers they added are interesting, they aren't exactly in the same style as the rest of the house and they don't look like they were added by any competent carpenter from hereabouts, either." Rankin looked around Paul to where Stacy had just fastened her seat belt. "You live around here?" he asked.

"Just down the block a little," Stacy answered, wondering why she felt suddenly cheap for agreeing to help out with a little sightseeing trip.

"Have you seen any animals or anything unusual around here lately?"

"No, I haven't. Just like I said. Over the past few weeks, there have been a lot of missing pets. That's all." Stacy bit her lip and gazed out the window past the Biscotti house, past the woods, and to the hills where the Caruthers House rested shrouded by trees. "You know, people say that Caruthers House is haunted."

"Well, this won't help the area's reputation any, I guess. I'll try to make a cast of the claw marks and see what I get. It was flesh and blood that visited here last night, not some ethereal spirit"

"You can do that? Make a cast from those bodies?" Paul asked.

"I can work something out. It won't be too hard. I'll get some of the University boys to help out, someone from the anthropology and the zoology departments. Off hand, though, I'd say nothing in the area here could rip out a throat like I saw. The only thing that could come close to making a swipe that would leave those kinds of marks would be a very, *very*, large Gila Monster."

"How large," Paul asked, not really wanting to know.

"Oh, six, eight hundred pounds."

"Do they really ..." Stacy asked, faltering over just the thought.

"Not since they quit making those B-rated sci-fi movies in the fifties." Rankin closed Paul's door with all the finality of a coffin lid slamming shut. "Well, be seein' ya."

Rankin crossed the street, walked past where Samuels was just finishing up talking to one of the uniformed police, and continued back behind the house, back to where the brush that separated the yard from the woods was crushed and beaten down. He automatically picked up a silent and armed escort as he entered and vanished in the woods. Stacy and Paul sat in the quiet, each lost in their own thought; her not a little uncomfortable with being in the Cherokee with a virtual stranger when stranger things were happening all around them than they could imagine. Paul was running around everything that had happened since he had unwrapped a toy fish. And who was this girl, anyway? The tension suddenly flew from the car as each realized that the other was just as nervous about the person next to them as they were themselves and that very nervousness was enough clear them of suspicion since, if they were the guilty party they would not be worried about the other.

Pretzel logic, Paul called it; thinking that twisted around on itself until it arrived back at its starting point without going anywhere; something you can chew on but it's better if you take it with a little salt.

Paul cranked the engine and began working the car around in the tight confines of the crowded street.

"Think he meant what he said?" Paul asked, motioning with his head to where Rankin had vanished into the woods.

"I hope not. That sounds like a dinosaur," Stacy answered.

"Yeah. *Jurassic Park* was set in the tropics. That was probably just his idea of a joke." Paul stuck his head out the window and looked up as a pair of OH-58 Kiowas thundered low overhead, Hellfire missiles and 50 caliber machine guns standing out in stark detail where they were attached to hard-points on the sides. Paul watched for a second until the pair Y'd off from each other, heading in different directions along the line of the forest.

As they banked, Paul had a good look at the mast on top of the rotors. It looked like a giant tootsie roll pop. But Paul had seen a Kiowa at an open house at Luke Air Force Base a few years before. He knew that the pod was an add-on unit that housed any combination of thermal imaging or television sensors, a laser range finder that could also be used as a target designator, or an optical bore sight system.

These were special helicopters; they did not have the same sex appeal as the Apache, and the resulting awareness in the public eye, but they were still powerful weapons, even if they looked like something no less dangerous than a news helicopter, if one ignored the modular weapons pods. The Army had pulled their first units from the Navy in 1991 to replace selected AH-1 Cobra's, those that acted as attack craft and scouts for air cavalry troops and light armored companies. Since then they had received major upgrades and were slated for major players in the Task Force XXI exercises scheduled for Fort Irwin, CA in March 1997. This was an exercise designed to demonstrate the Army's concept of the "digital battlefield" and the Army Warrant Officer with the Kiowa display at Luke had been very proud of the new Kiowa Warrior, pointing out an integrated cockpit control and display system, master control processor with digital map and video cross link, improved data modem, secure radio communications, and GPS embedded in the inertial navigation system. They had very advanced infrared jamming, infrared suppressor, radar warning receivers, and a laser warning detector, all of which would be very valuable in a high-tech arena. The wide range of sensor capabilities available to the Kiowa, when configured as an armed reconnaissance aircraft, was awesome. They could send a Video Image Cross link (VIXL) signal that gave the ship the capability to send and receive still-frame images over one of its FM radios.

There was something about the Improved Mast Mounted Sight System Processor (IMSP) mounted to the rotor, too. What was it? Right. It was a new high-speed digital signal processor that gave improved tracking capabilities by split-screen in both TV and Thermal Imaging Sight (TIS) modes, low contrast target tracking, simultaneous multi-target tracking of up to six targets, moving target indicator, aided target recognition, and automatic reacquiring of targets lost due to obstruction. Paul had learned that in an article he had written for *Government and Military Video Magazine* about new uses of video in tactical situations. The operator video display reflected real-time video zoom and still frame capabilities with an enhanced high-speed Gallium Arsenide-based digital signal processor that, with only software upgrades, allows for insertion of neural net automatic target recognition, identification of friend or foe (IFF), passive ranging, and real-time image enhancements.

More than that, the improved Allison 250-C30R/3 650shp engine had been equipped with an upgraded hot section to improve high-altitude/hot-day performance, perfect for summer operations in Northern Arizona. It was common, when a two hour ops plan – the Kiowa's normal operational limits – was in effect for the helicopter to go from the hundred-fifteen degree Phoenix daytime temperature to the fifty degrees Flagstaff could hit shortly after the sun dropped behind the mountains, a climb of over 6,000 feet. That was the main reason National Guard units in Arizona, Nevada, Utah, Texas, and New Mexico had tested the system that had started as a navy toy; it was why the Border Patrol had drooled over the units that politics had kept from their hands. Brad had written a piece for *Time* about that, how certain politicians did not want the borders protected so illegal aliens could cross easily and provide a cheap labor pool. They were less worried about the terrorist or drug runner or people smuggler who might also cross than in keeping campaign donations coming in. It seemed that the murders and rapes and robberies committed by habitual criminals were low on their priority list. *Time* had not published the three thousand-word article.

This Bell bird was as far removed from its cousin, the Bell Ranger, the stable of the media and entertainment and law enforcement helicopter industry. The Warrior carried air-cooled 50-cal Gatling guns that could rip a horse apart in less than twenty seconds. This was a bird designed to find, target, and destroy things that did not want to be found, were impossible to target, and even harder to destroy. It was a nasty character wrapped up in a package made more deadly by its similarity to the Ranger, a common sight in the skies over any American city. Deadly because it looked like its common cousin but carried a bite like a fer-de-lance viper.

But seeing these here, now, made Paul think that Rankin's six-hundred pound Gila Monster might not be far off the mark. The choppers were an unusual sight in public and Paul had seen them twice in two days. Military attack craft were seldom seen below 5,000 feet over civilian areas and these were at treetop level. Something was going on here that was more than a few murders or these deadly machines would not be so obvious and not be flying so low over populated areas.

As important as the military was to the U.S., people had a tendency to be hostile toward them when they disturbed the peace and heaven help and commander who allowed one of his prized possessions crash in a civilian population center. Everything about these past few days screamed at Paul's journalism senses.

"I don't guess we should be hanging around here today," Paul said as he pulled away from the crime scene. What a story! But right now there were some very nervous people around and Paul was not at all comfortable near an agitated cop and a few military types who had big enough toys to turn everything in the immediate neighborhood into instant confetti or, with the Hellfires, to turn them into crispy critters. Or pieces of crispy critters. Paul was not at all happy with the way his thoughts were going.

"I'm not sure I want to stay around here, either. What did you have in mind?"

Paul eased the Cherokee out of the side street and began working its way toward the main road back into Flagstaff proper. His mind was racing for something, a plan that would help lift the gloom that had settled in the car. Food. Women, who never admit that they are hungry, are still always ready to go out to eat.

"Tell you what. We're getting a late start, so I'll buy you an early lunch and you can show me Flagstaff. We can stop by the Caruthers place later this evening and see if anyone will talk to us."

Stacy suppressed a shiver.

"You want to go there after dark?" she asked, not a little incredulous and more than a little nervous.

"Why not? We are more likely to catch someone around dinner time."

"I just don't want to be on the menu."

"You don't believe in ghosts or six-hundred pound Gila Monsters, do you?"

"Not really, but I'm not sure that I want to be around that place after dark."

Paul had nothing to say to that, beyond pointing out that sunset was not expected until after seven-thirty that evening, so he kept still until they arrived at Granny's Attic, a restaurant with character near Northern Arizona University. He felt a little awkward taking a waitress out to dinner, but he figured waitresses needed to eat, too, and if the place was not worth its pricey menu, then she would be the one to know.

Paul was spooked before they ever made it to the house. He pulled off the main road and into the driveway, creeping down the dirt road just fast enough to say he was moving without lying. It was just a little after six - they had had a light dinner at the CoCo's since they were still a little full from the large lunch at Granny's - but the forest on either side of the road was already dark. The road was bordered by old growth pines, towering thirty feet or better. With the cut through the forest that was made for the road, enough light filtered through to permit the growth of bushes and vines and grass along the edges of the woods and the vegetation had taken the invitation with a vengeance. If Paul and Stacy met someone – or something – leaving the old house, there was no escape to the sides and backing up down the rutted and pothole-riddled driveway would be a nightmare all its own. A scattering of early rising fireflies, blinking like so many eyes in the trees and bushes, did not help any at all.

About halfway up the lane, Paul began fiddling with his mirror and watching his back trail. He didn't want to be caught unaware if something blocked his exit back there, if he could help it. He played with the angle a little, then grunted once and turned his attention back to the rough road to the house. It was almost a quarter mile drive before the woods ended and the yard, such as it was, began.

When they pulled out of the lane, the house itself was not much more encouraging. It was an old Victorian mansion, dating from the late eighteen-hundreds that had been added too and tacked on to, and then neglected. It boasted a large front porch that sagged its way across the entire front of the house. There was a balcony over the main entrance, set off-center to the left, and a third story dormer above that. The center portion of the house was two stories, with the second story being little more than a loft in front, but rising to a full height and attic toward the back of the house. Tacked onto the rear section was a three story hexagon tower, maybe forty feet across, with a peaked roof that rose at least another fifteen feet and that was capped with an odd array of antennas and dishes so that it looked more like something that surround the University television station or a large apartment complex without cable service than anything on a residence.

"Five thousand channels and still nothing to watch," Paul mumbled as he looked at all the receivers on the tower. That looked like a newer edition, but it was hard to be sure since it was already covered with vines. The whole yard was weed-covered and overgrown, especially close to the foundation where the bushes had run rampant and the weeds had invaded the flowerbeds with vigor. Whoever lived here now was no lover of yard work.

Off to the right was a separate two-car garage and an attached utility shed, but the grass growing in front of the garage suggested that it had been seldom used in the recent past, even though a pale light spilled out from a solar powered security light in front of the garage doors. Behind that, the backyard was relatively small compared to the half-acre front yard and it butted right against the forest where a thick growth of trees and brush seemed to create an impenetrable barrier more effective than a fence to anything larger than a rabbit.

Paul and Stacy took this in for a few minutes while Paul allowed the car to run. Finally, with a sigh, he switched off the car and stepped out, but remained in the doorway. Stacy, with more reluctance, did the same. For a minute they watched the main building from behind the psychological protection of the car doors. Nothing moved; nothing flickered; the house was totally dark and uninviting. The sun was still up but the trees effectively cast the house and yard in dark shadows.

"Well, it doesn't look *utterly* menacing," Paul ventured over the car's roof.

"It sure is dark," Stacy commented, never taking her eyes off the house.

"Maybe they have the blinds pulled," Paul offered in what was a poor attempt at bravado.

"Or maybe there's no one home," Stacy countered with false optimism. "Let's not disturb them if they are."

"Coward." Paul flashed Stacy a grin that was generally lost in the dark.

"Why not?" Stacy muttered back, looking around the house and yard that was beginning to appear more and more like a blind alley than a place where people lived. "Cowards live longer."

Paul closed the door and moved around to Stacy's side of the car. If anyone was watching them from the house, just standing around would not look too good.

"Come on," Paul said gently. "It'd be better not to stand here all night."

"You're right," Stacy said with a theatrical sigh. "I am a coward. You go, I'll watch. Just leave the keys."

"Silly, let's go," Paul replied, taking her hand and giving her a little encouraging tug. Stacy reluctantly let the car door close and went with Paul, following a slightly beaten down path through the overgrown lawn.

Neither of them noticed the car that followed them up the lane with its lights out. It pulled to a stop just shy of the yard and the driver, that intrepid Patrolman Fisher, switched off the engine once he had moved to the cover of a clump of Oleander.

"Central, this is Metro Four. Can you take a message for Detective Samuels?" Fisher asked quietly, as if speaking loudly in this darkened place might draw unwanted attention.

"Roger, Metro Four," the radio squeaked back. Fisher jumped at the loud volume and quickly turned down the speaker volume. "Go ahead."

"Tell him that this guy I'm following, he's at the Caruthers' place with the girl."

"Jesus, Fisher, you're out *there* after dark?"

"Yeah."

"Well, either you've got BBOs or you're just stupid."

"I don't have big brass balls and I am *not* stupid. How would you like to explain to Samuels that you'd lost a tail because you were afraid of the dark?"

"Yeah, copy that. Stand by."

Fisher sat in the car, studying the fireflies like they were some kind of weird mystical communications system. He was also scanning the trees for something more sinister. Like bears, he told himself; like bears that sometimes come in from the mountains, not like ghosts or goblins or nothing.

"You still there, Fisher," the radio asked.

"Yeah."

"Why are you whispering?"

Fisher cleared his throat and tried again. "I'm not whispering. I'm just in stealth mode."

"Right. Well, Samuels says he'll be there in fifteen and you are not, repeat, *not* to let them out of your sight or, if at all possible, let them know you are watching."

"That means I gotta get out of the car and go radio silent."

"Well, if you gotta go, you gotta go."

"Yeah, but I have to *get out of the car.*"

"There's no such thing as the boogieman, Fisher. What do you want me to tell Samuels?"

"This is the *Caruthers'* House. If there is a boogieman, he is *here.*"

"So what should I tell Samuels?"

Fisher sat a long moment thinking about his options. But in the end, he knew there really wasn't much choice. Samuels would never understand his reluctance to abandon the relative security of the car to follow the pair as they snooped around the Caruthers' place. Not Samuels; not in a million years. There was no other reply, besides "I quit," that he could give. So he confirmed, switched off the radio, stepped out of the car and into the cold black night of the Flagstaff woodland.

Paul stopped before he stepped up on the porch and looked around again. Something was bothering him, nibbling at the back of his neck like a persistent mosquito that had found a favorite spot and had the uncanny ability to miss the swatting hand. Besides that, the porch did not look particularly inviting. It had certainly seen better days and "rickety" would have been inferring sturdiness that Paul was sure was missing. It was in general disrepair and, where there was paint, it was peeling.

With a determined sigh, Paul set one foot on the first step and applied his weight. Much to his surprise, it held. So encouraged, Paul took the other two steps up to the porch proper. There was something weird about the porch. It *looked* like it was falling down, but it *felt* like he was standing on firm-set cement. And there had been a slight resistance when he had stepped fully onto the porch, like he had passed through a bubble wall or something.

Paul looked around again, then turned to look back toward the lane at the end of the yard. There was something out there, he was sure, but he couldn't see anything in the dark. He knew they were being watched, but by whom? Someone in the house or the person who had been following them? Or a third party, some nut case in the woods? The feeling persisted. "There's something out there. I can feel it," he said in a low voice that sent chills up Stacy's spine. And not good chills, like sex, but bad, very bad, chills.

"Stop it," she said in mock anger that was perilously close to the real thing. "You're just trying to scare me."

"No, really," Paul said, trying to stress his seriousness. He didn't want her to think he was being flippant. "I think that there's something out there."

Stacy was really nervous now. She didn't want to be where she was, but if there was something lurking in the woods? She sure as hell didn't want to make a run for the car. It was entirely too far away across the yard. Outrun something from the house? That she was prepared to do. But to try to reach the car if something was coming out of the woods... Well, that was another race entirely; one she did not believe she could win.

"Paul, don't play games with me." Stacy's nervousness was apparent, even to her, and she was a little ashamed at her own fear, but there have been just too many weird things happening lately and those girls had been killed … well, pretty close to here if one cut through the woods. This was no joking matter and if Paul was playing that kind of game, then maybe she had better call off this dating thing like, *right now*!

But Paul was still studying the yard. There was nothing about him that suggested he was playing a game and that was even worse, in Stacy's opinion than stupid pranks. "I'm not," Paul finally said. He made a small gesture with his head to the right. "Look, over there, in that patch of woods that sticks into the yard a ways. *Don't be so obvious*!"

Stacy leaned on Paul's shoulder and used that to cover her examination of the woods where Paul had suggested there might be a lurker. Sure enough, the bushes moved just a little. And there was not enough of a breeze to mention. And the bushes nearby and pointedly *not* moved. But she didn't really see anything and she said so.

"Well, I did," Paul said with determination. "Come on."

Paul stepped off the porch, passing back through the "bubble," dragging Stacy with him. He picked up a piece of a broken rake or shovel handle he had seen in the weeds.

"Come out right now," Paul shouted at the bushes near the opening to the driveway, "and I won't hurt you!"

"Paul," Stacy protested weakly as Paul took a couple of steps toward the bushes, still dragging Stacy with him.

"All right. Come on out of there. We're not alone. The police are right behind us!" Paul shouted to the bush again, though by now he was feeling whether foolish. If a poodle walked out of there, he didn't think he could ever look Stacy in the eye again. Of course, if it was something else walked out, he only hoped he would be around long enough to worry about that. His little stick probably would not stop a rogue four pound Gila Monster much less the six-hundred pounder Rankin hypothesized.

Paul brandished the weapon once more and shook it at the bushes. He hoped he looked strong and brave and not just foolish. "Come out now. If I have to come in after you or if the police show up, it'll be bad for you."

The bushes began to shake even more, then Fisher stepped out, gesturing for Paul to be calm.

"I guess you won't have to call the police," Fisher said. "We're right here. Lower your weapon."

"What are you doing here?" Paul demanded.

"I was told to follow you."

"No, no, no, I know that! You're supposed to be back there with the car. You're my back up. What are you doing in the bushes?" Paul demanded.

"How'd you know I was following you?"

"I've known ever since we went to Granny's Attic, I just didn't know who was in the bushes. You weren't that hard to spot."

"Oh. I was trying to be stealthy," Fisher said abashed at being so obvious.

"Yeah, but why weren't you back there in case I needed you? How could you help if you were stuck in the bushes?"

By now, Stacy had had enough. She slapped Paul hard on the shoulder. "Hey," she demanded. "Did you know that he was there all along?"

"Yeah, I suspected we were being followed a long time ago and I caught a glimpse of his car through the trees when he followed us up the lane."

"And you didn't tell me? You thought it was funny that I was scared out of my wits?"

"Well, no, that's not it… I wasn't *sure* it was the police back there, but …"

"Listen, you too, I am sure this is all very important to your future relations, but I want to know what you're… Holy Shit!"

Paul turned and looked in the direction that the patrolman's suddenly wide eyes were staring.

"What in the name…" Stacy started, then subsided into silence.

Just over the roof of the house, one of the alien ships was slowly sinking into the woods. It wasn't the sight that got to Paul so much as the sound: there wasn't any. If all three were not seeing it at the same time, Paul could have written it off as his imagination. But this wasn't a helicopter and it sure as anything wasn't swamp gas.

"That must be what they saw in Clay Springs," Paul said quietly.

"I'd better call this in," Fisher said, and started backing slowly toward his car.

"They won't believe you," Paul said.

"Yeah, but Samuels'll be here any minute. He can check it out."

"Oh, if Samuels is coming, we don't need to wait." Paul took a better grip on his club, then started toward the woods behind the Caruthers House. "Come on. Let's see what's out there."

The other two hesitated just a couple of seconds, but Fisher finally pulled out his service revolver and stepped out behind Paul. Stacy, determining it was better with two men, one with a gun and the other with a club, than being alone, scampered after them.

Paul made it to the back of the Caruthers House and stopped, waving the others to wait behind him. He cautiously squatted and looked around the edge of the house.

"What'd you see?" Fisher asked in a whisper.

"Nothing," Paul whispered back.

That was an irritant to Fisher. Here he was, skulking around someone's property in the middle of the night, acting like a scared rabbit, and there was nothing around to generate his fear except his own imagination. He boldly stepped around Paul and stood looking back at the forest.

Stacy made it to where Paul was still peering around the lower corner of the house and stopped where she would be hidden form the woods.

"Why are you down there," she asked in a stage whisper.

"If anyone was waiting to blow my head off, they would have been looking high. If I had stuck my head around the corner there, bam! I'm dead. But if I look low, they may not see me or I may have enough time to pull back."

"Oh. Where'd you learn that? In the military?"

"No. In a novel."

"Then why's he standing out there like that?" she asked, indicating Fisher.

"Maybe he doesn't read novels," Paul responded with a shrug. Satisfied that there were no waiting ambushers, Paul stood up and joined Fisher in his examination of the backyard. The backyard was as overgrown and neglected as the front. A few pines had sprouted as seedlings, testament that the forest was willing to spread up to the rear of the house if whoever owned the property allowed it that luxury. There were no lights visible in the house from the back, but there was a pulsating glow from the woods that was dimming even as the pair watched.

"I don't see anything, either," Fisher said, watching the woods in what amounted to an almost-trance.

"Well, there's a light back there in the trees, in case you dummies can't see what's right before your eyes," Stacy said as she came out from behind the house.

"Yeah. And it's getting dimmer," Fisher acknowledged reluctantly. "I was jis hopin' my eyes was playing tricks on me."

Paul grunted at that. Now he couldn't pretend he didn't see it, either, and not look like a fool in front of Stacy. He took a deep breath and put on a cloak of bravado. "Well, let's just go have a look," he said brightly.

"What are you so happy about suddenly," Fisher said, turning a baleful eye on Paul.

"Nothing," Paul replied more soberly. "I was just trying to boost my courage."

"Keep trying. It might help mine."

"Yeah, but you've got a gun and all I have is a stick."

"Right," Fisher responded unenthusiastically. He turned to Stacy and gave her a hard look. "You'd better stay here, miss."

"Are you crazy? You've got the gun," Stacy said with a little more fire than the occasion warranted. "I'm going with you."

Paul looked at Stacy, now, tearing his eyes from the woods. The light had faded to little more than an afterglow.

"Maybe you should go back. I only asked for a guide. I didn't figure glowing lights and strange aircraft into the bargain."

"So you can owe me another dinner," Stacy said, dismissing Paul's objection with a wave of the hand. "I just want to make sure I can collect… and this house gives me the creeps. And if you think I'm walking back to the car alone, in the dark, with nothing by my good looks to protect me, then you're crazier than I thought."

Paul didn't have a ready answer for that and, after thinking about the look in Stacy's eyes, figured arguing was not going to solve anything. Of course, he could walk her back to the car, but his desire to see exactly what was in the woods was a pull that was stronger than his will to fight with Stacy. He shrugged and gave her what she wanted which, in the long run, might be better if one considered his stick and Fisher's gun into the equation.

"Have it your way, but be quiet!"

"Probably just some kids smoking pot," Stacy ventured. "We'll probably scare the weejees out of them."

"Not with what happened this morning," Fisher said, shaking his head. "I doubt anyone is even *thinking* about being out in the woods around here tonight."

"Thanks." Stacy's sarcasm was thick enough even Fisher caught it. "I needed a little encouragement."

There was not much else to say and not much of a reason to stick around. About halfway across the yard, Fisher decided he was the military leader of the group and went into commando mode, just like he had seen in the movies. He dropped into a crouch and motioned the others to do the same, then finished running across the yard bent over like a Navy Seal with a bad back. Still in his persona as a trained special operations professional, Fisher made it across the yard and dodged behind a tree, using that for cover, and standing as straight as he could. He signaled the others to do the same, never mind that the eight inch tree did nothing to conceal his 40 inch paunch or even Stacy's thirty-five inch chest. But it made him feel like he was in control of the situation and false confidence can sometimes move things along where good sense would stall.

"What was that all about," Paul asked Fisher in a hushed voice. Paul had chosen a sapling whether than a full pine, and the small tree's outline completely hid Paul from the woods, unlike Fisher or Stacy who had chosen more mature trees where the branches began ten or twelve feet above the ground.

"I thought we should exercise a little caution," Fisher replied in the same hushed tone.

"Well, that was a fine time to decide to do that," Stacy said, her hushed tone not as quiet as she thought. "I thought you had seen something. I was so scared I almost wet my pants!"

Fisher rolled his eyes at Stacy. Women on a combat patrol! The world was becoming too Liberal.

He should have sent her back, was the message that he sent loudly with his body language. But she obviously wasn't buying the suggestion, and, with a shrug, Fisher started making his way into the woods, pushing through the undergrowth and dodging into cover whenever he could.

Once inside the woods, and away from the dubious illumination of the garage light, the forest quickly became very dark, the high tops of the trees cutting out even the weak moon and star light. In only a few steps, Stacy fell over an exposed root, toppling into Paul, who immediately fell flat on his face. The noise, combined with Stacy's suppressed nervous giggle, startled Fisher, who spun around with his gun ready. But then he froze.

Paul and Stacy had vanished! At least that's what he thought. A few seconds peering into the dark and he could see nothing until behind him, deeper in the woods, another light came on with the suddenness of an explosion. Fisher barely noticed their intermingled bodies on the ground as he spun toward the new light. This was not pulsing and it was *bright*. Behind him, Stacy and Paul untangled themselves and crept up next to the patrolman, quietly.

Stacy reached out and tapped Fisher on the shoulder. Fisher, who was trying to see through the trees to the light source, had all but forgotten the pair who had tripped up behind him. So Stacy's little tap just about scared him out of his skin. He managed to jump two feet straight up from a flat-foot start and he squeaked on the way.

"I thought you wanted quiet," Stacy whispered.

"Don't sneak up on me like that! I almost shot you!" Fisher's hot retort only elicited a snort from Stacy who knew that the only think Fisher almost shot was himself.

"I just wanted to ask how far you thought it would be. This army commando business is a little out of my league. You know that I'm normally a mild-mannered waitress, not Wonder Woman," Stacy chided.

"Just a little farther. The light's just ahead. Now be quiet!" Fisher said in a voice that was far from quiet itself.

"All right," Stacy pouted. "There's no need to be so pushy!"

Fisher just looked at her and shook his head. He was pretty jumpy and scared, but logically he knew there was nothing to be scared about; flying saucers and little green men were the stuff of novels and movies. There was something strange going on here, that was obvious, but it was something that would have a logical – and worldly – explanation.

The three pushed through the undergrowth until they were right outside a small clearing, hidden by some shrubs and tufts of Johnson grass. What they saw was strange indeed.

The clearing housed two of the strange craft, but there was no obvious landing field or other lasting structure. They knew the craft could hover, but they had been so silent that they made even the quietest Harrier or chopper sound like a brass band in warm-up. One of the ships, though, was popping, like cooling metal, and there was a little condensation on the stubby wings. That, Paul decided, must have been the ship they saw landing.

Set a dozen or so yards from the farthest ship was a geodesic dome made of some plastic-like material. It was about twenty feet in diameter. If the material was analogous to a tent, then the dome was dark, but from the shine, Paul suspected that the material was more solid than fabric and may not have permitted any light from the inside to leak through. If that was the case, there was no telling how many people were inside. Of course, having them inside was better than having them roaming the woods, Paul decided, since the clearing was otherwise empty. Except for the cages.

The cages were behind the hut and quickly drew Paul's attention. There were maybe two dozen of them, about half full. Each cage held a dog or a couple of cats. They looked domestic and several had collars.

The group worked their way into the clearing and nearer to the cages. The animals were lethargic and barely reacted to the trio's approach. Here or there, a head rose up to look. The eyes seemed interested, even pleading, Paul thought, but there was no energy to follow through. After a second or two, the head would drop, as if it was too heavy to hold up for long. A large golden retriever thumped its tail once, then laid still, the effort being all it seemed to muster.

"Now we know what's been happening to the animals," Stacy said. "They don't look so good, either."

"No," Paul corrected. "All we know is where they are. We don't know what's happened to them. And you're right. They look drugged or something."

"What are you two talking about?" Fisher asked, but he wasn't interested in the animals. There was something larger on his mind and he gestured toward the two craft across the clearing. "And what are those things, anyway? I haven't seen anything like them at the Guard site."

"Not surprising. They're spaceships and I doubt the Air National Guard has too many of them sitting around. I'd bet they weren't made locally, either."

"No?"

"No," Paul went on. "At least, not in this local solar system, anyway."

"You're crazy," Fisher retorted. "We've just stumbled on some kinda Guard exercise. They've been busy up here for a month."

"If you say so," Paul shrugged. He turned to Stacy as Fisher began walking toward the craft. "If this is our military, then there's no way we should have made it this far without being stopped by a patrol or guard or something. There's some surprises waiting and I think we should get while we can."

"I wanna look at those ships," Fisher said, already halfway across the clearing. Paul turned back toward the patrolman and looked on apprehensively. He didn't even notice when Stacy took his hand.

"Hold it!" Paul warned, stepping all over Stacy's "I think we should wait!"

Fisher turned and glared at the pair. "What's with you two?"

"Let's just wait a couple of minutes," Paul suggested.

"From the bushes," Stacy interjected. Paul nodded.

"Yeah. You said Samuels was on the way. If we don't see anyone in a few minutes, we can go back and get him. Something about all this… desertion just isn't right."

"Sounds good to me," Stacy said, backing up Paul. She just wanted away from the clearing, where they might have a few seconds head start when… "whatever" noticed that they were here.

"I think we should check this out *now*," Fisher said. "Something's gotta be wrong or they'd have somebody out here guarding the planes."

"Humor me," Paul asked. "If there's something going on, we can see it from the trees. Better than getting caught out there."

"Well, we should at least check out the hut."

"There could be a dozen people in there, smoking crack and armed. Want to face that alone? Let's watch and then go and see if we can find Samuels."

Fisher hesitated a moment then nodded. There was something very wrong here and crackheads could go off like berserkers. He didn't want to face that.

"Ten minutes," he said, not wanting to appear to have given up too much too quick. Pride was a pretty demanding master for Fisher.

"Ten minutes," Paul agreed. "Then we go back and get help."

"Ten minutes and then I go and check out that hut."

"I vote for ten minutes and help, not ten minutes and hut," Stacy added hopefully.

CHAPTER NINE

June 19, 2002
Flagstaff, Arizona

"China delicate; porcelain in purple
Hues touched with gold
Inlaid with amber and mist

Lingering memories
A touch, a whisper,
Nights are long without you."

"What's that?" Paul asked Stacy.

"Just a poem I wrote in Lit Class," she said.

"What made you think of that?" Paul asked, adding quickly, "At a time like this."

"The line 'nights are long without you.' I was thinking that this is going to be a long night and I sure wish my daddy was here."

"A love poem for your father? Isn't that a little... *too* Northern Arizona?"

"Don't be a jerk. The poem was for a guy I had a crush on years ago," Stacy said with more than a hint of disgust creeping into her voice. "No, my father's a big NRA guy. He always has *lots* of guns around and I wouldn't mind a few dozen of them now. Now *that's* Northern Arizona. You were thinking Georgia before," she added with a smile.

They lapsed into silence. The night was another typical Flagstaff summer evening: a little cool with a slight breeze, dark, and not a darn thing happening worth writing home about. The clearing, the woods, for all they could tell, were still, except for Fisher checking his watch every thirty seconds. Paul kept thinking that this had to be the most boring date he could have arranged when Stacy stiffened beside him and reached out grabbed his arms with both hands. She leaned forward and whispered to him: "Be quiet and look by the ships," she told him pointing, opposite from where their attention had been focused on the hut and cages.

There was some movement around one of the ships. Paul started to point that out to Fisher, but then something near the hut caught his attention. One section of the dome seemed to… shift and became translucent. There was light inside and at least four figures were moving around. A few seconds later, the translucent section appeared to melt into the sides and suddenly a door opened, spilling incredibly bright light into the forest.

What stepped out was straight from a fifties Hollywood horror movie.

At first, Paul thought it was the Creature from the Black Lagoon in spandex. But a closer look showed that it was more than Hollywood make-up. It stepped out in the light and scanned the clearing, but apparently didn't see Fisher, Stacy, and Paul in the shadows of the trees. The interior of the dome was much brighter than what one would expect, so it was probably that the creature came from a world with a brighter sun and could not see as well in the dark as humans or its eyes had yet to adjust to the dark night. Hotter or colder than Earth was anyone's guess. The scaled arms and head that were not covered by the uniform, for that was what the covering looked like, were greenish tinted in the light, but this was certainly not a little green man since it topped eight feet with an easy margin.

It carried a bucket. Why in the Hell did it have a bucket?

The uniform was a form-fitting affair that was tucked into sturdy boots. It was possibly one piece, though there were no seams or buttons or straps or anything else showing. The only decoration was a patch or embroidered design, similar to the hieroglyphics on the ships, on the upper left breast and a broad utility belt that held several unrecognizable tools and a holster that screamed "weapon," though that was not necessarily the case. Still, Paul would never have bet against the low-slung holstered object as being anything *but* a gun. The neck was protected by a metal band which might also serve as a locking ring for a helmet.

While the body itself was not much different than a human's, the face was like nothing that had ever walked the lands of Earth. It was larger than a human and there was no nose, just a set of large gill-like flaps that flared out from the creature's neck when it breathed. These were in front of two heavy ridges that anchored the muscles to the jaw. That face hosted a lip-less mouth full of large, wicked teeth. There appeared to be no scales on the face, though they could have been very fine. It was hard to tell in the light if the face was actually scaled or a smooth, rubbery skin.

The creature turned and said something to those still in the dome, revealing a short, stubby tail, also covered by the uniform. There was a general guttural sound that issued from those inside, which could have been the equivalent of laughter or something more profane. The "shit" that Fisher breathed when the creature came into view was certainly not profound in its own right.

"Be quiet!" Paul hissed at the fidgeting patrolman. "Let's see what it's going to do."

Stacy's grip grew much tighter on Paul's arm, but she remained quiet. Whether from fear or not, Paul didn't take time to analyze. He was fascinated by what he saw more than he was frightened, but he still had a feeling that things were about to fall from the pot into the fire quicker than later.

The creature walked over to a cage. The animals hunched back into the far corner of their cages and, even from across the clearing, Paul could hear a pitiful mewing from them. They were frightened, but their bodies did not appear to be under their control. They were either very weak or maybe they had been drugged. Paul believed from the reactions and the way the dog's teeth were showing that the dogs would have been at their cages, fangs barred and ready to fight, had then be able. The cats, well, the cats would have been looking for the nearest sandbox.

The alien selected a cage with a small dog, something that looked like a cockapoo from where Paul was standing. With a casual flip of the latch, the creature reached in and swatted the dog on the head. The hand, whose three webbed fingers and thumb were tipped with thick, wicked claws, all but ripped the dog's head from its shoulders, splattering the other cages with a spurt of warm blood that did nothing for the disposition of the animals still caged. The dog died with barely a yelp.

The creature pulled the dog from the cage and drained its blood into the bucket. Reason for bucket revealed, though Paul would have been happy to have remained ignorant. Before long, the dog had bled out and the creature casually tossed the carcass aside.

"*Now* we know what happened to the animals," Paul muttered as Stacy buried her head against Paul's shoulder, trying to suppress a sob.

Fisher, however, was less sanguine. He raised his gun and stepped into the clearing.

"I've seen enough," he announced. Though a portion of his brain was screaming run, his anger at the senseless killing of the dog had pushed him a little past good reasoning.

"No!" Paul tried to grab the patrolman's arm, but Fisher just shrugged him off.

"Hold it! This is the police! You're surrounded!" Fisher called, completely ignoring the fact that he was the only one doing the surrounding.

"Come on," Paul said, pulling Stacy slowly away from the clearing. "Let's get out of here."

"I thought you wanted to see this," she said, though not unwilling to begin a retreat.

"Maybe it wasn't such a good idea to not wait for reinforcements," Paul said. "This is going to get messy and when Fisher goes down, we've got nothing but a stick. We have to get help fast if Fisher's going to survive."

Paul really didn't believe Fisher was going to last three minutes, and he knew if they did not get out fast, they were going with him. The best they could do was to see if Samuels was poking around and have him call in the Marines.

"Now, drop that bucket and put your hands in the air, you alien freak!" Fisher was on a roll. He had the drop on them and they was all mother rapers. Father stabbers. Father
Rapers! Father rapers standing right there in the forest in front of him and this was not even an Arlo Gutherie song! So these dog-murdering-baby-raping--fathher-stabbing-motherless *things* were his. Not to mention the write up in the *Police Gazette*, Fisher was sure that capturing this group would lead to a promotion and he wouldn't have to share the credit with anyone!

"Damn! I wished he hadn't done that," Paul said softly. "We've got to get out of here. Now."

"We can't leave him," Stacy protested softly.

"We can't help him either and right now I don't think they know we are here," Paul replied. "And if they find out we are, there'll be no one to get help. Unless you want to try to get back to the road alone?"

"Oh, God, no."

"Thought so."

Paul grabbed Stacy's hand and began pulling her through the underbrush as quietly and as quickly as he could go. They had only taken a few steps when new voices rose from the clearing… voices like he had never heard before. They stopped and took a quick look back. They could barely see Fisher through the trees when a finger of light reached from near the ships and stabbed through Fisher's chest. Paul had seen something there after all. Where the light touched the uniform, both on Fisher's chest and his back, the fabric began to smolder, then burst into flame. Fisher, stunned and already dying, just stood still, even as the flames reached up for his face. Suddenly he let out a piercing scream and toppled slowly to the ground like a blazing torch.

"Son of a …" Paul breathed over Stacy's "Oh, my god!"

"This is no place to loiter," Paul said, shaking himself out of his shock. "Let's go!"

Paul took Stacy's hand and began an urgent flight through the woods.

Behind them, the alien who had shot Fisher joined the one by the cages. The other two from the hut emerged. A few moments of pointing and howling and looking at Fisher's smoldering body followed the shooting, and then three of spread out into the woods. Each alien carried one of the deadly pistols at ready. The original shooter returned to one of the ships, where he disappeared inside.

Paul gave over silence for speed. He figured – correctly – that stealth was no longer the main requirement. They reached the edge of the woods and began a flat-out run for the car when Stacy tripped over something hidden in the high grass. She went flying and bounced once when she hit, before sliding a foot on her stomach.

Paul stopped and raced back to her side. He grabbed an arm, heaving her to her feet.

"Are you alright?" he asked, anxiety plain in his voice. "You didn't hurt yourself?"

"Damn it!" Stacy's reply sounded shakier than she wanted. "Momma always said I didn't have enough grace to be a lady," she said, her hands flowing over her body while she searched for something broken or strained. "I'm OK. I just tripped over something back there. A root or wire or something."

"Let's see if we can get the car out of here. Then try to find Samuels. I don't think those… things back in the woods are the good guys."

Paul started off again, this time holding Stacy's arm for support. She was moving, but favoring her right leg. Exhaustion, fear, and the fall were taking a toll. They made it to the side of the house, when something made Paul look back to the woods. The three aliens were just emerging and there was no question that they saw Paul and Stacy. One of them snapped off a shot.

"Look out!" Paul yelled, dragging Stacy out of the line of fire.

Oh Lord, he was going to die and he'd never get to tell Jeremy good-bye. He'd just vanish and who knew what Janet would tell their son.

But the light never reached the pair.

The light streaked toward them… then hit something and dispersed across a wide area in dancing sparks and small lightning bolts. The other two aliens shot in turn, but both of those beams were also stopped.

Paul blinked a few times in the afterglow and took a step toward the point where the weapons had splashed against… well, nothing that Paul could see.

"Damn! Look at that!" Paul was drawn toward the spot where the beams had vanished, totally ignoring the danger surrounding them. "An energy screen!"

Stacy was not so impressed. "Let's look later. Come on, before they try a bounce shot or something!"

But the creatures that had chased Paul and Stacy through the woods were not advancing. In fact, they were backing cautiously into the woods. Whatever had stopped their shots had not been in the playbook. They were confused and maybe frightened. That the force screen had been as unexpected to them as it had been to the humans, was apparent and they were in a bit of a shock – like finding out that the boogieman you had been searching for in the attic is suddenly and solidly standing right in front of your way out from the dusty, forgotten refuge at the top of the house. Or maybe like a monster in a Steven King novel suddenly discovering that it is not the biggest monster on the block. Whatever they thought, the discovery of a force-field on a planet where force-fields did not exist certainly had the lizards excited.

And something, guided by monster or savior Paul had no clue, reached out from the house tower with a ball of orange fire that touched the nearest little monster, who promptly splattered its protoplasm all over the yard and near woods. The other little monsters did not wait for a second demonstration and vanished into the woods in a resolute retreat. Paul and Stacy did not wait for a second invitation, but took to their heels in the opposite direction, praying that the big monster was looking for something fishy and not chicken flavored.

Stacy ran to the car and jerked the door open, but Paul grabbed her arm and pulled her away before she could climb in. He was too winded to respond to her "Wha…?" but pushed her toward Fisher's car farther back down the lane. The night turned orange behind them and Paul pulled Stacy to the ground, but the ball was traveling in the other direction. Back in the woods, something exploded with a muffled *whoomph*. Not a ship, Paul decided which would have been a *ka-bam*!

"I don't think they like each other, back there," Paul observed, as several lasers flashed out of the woods from scattered points, probing the house's defenses. Paul looked Fisher's car. "No keys. Damn. I don't know if going back for my car is a good idea. Too close to the house."

"We… have… to… call… the… police," Stacy panted.

"And tell them… what? What can you think to tell them that they'll believe?" Paul demanded.

"We have to tell them… something!"

"But what? What'll they believe?"

"What would you expect them to believe?" Samuels asked, stepping from the woods and practically giving Paul a coronary. Stacy punctuated Paul's "Oh, shit!" with a gasp.

"Boy, am I glad to see you!" Paul exclaimed, standing up to dust off his ill-used pants.

"Are you?" Samuels asked, adding: "And don't call me 'boy'."

"I… uh…" Paul stammered.

But Stacy was far from wordless. "Well, *I'm* glad to see you. We were almost killed back there by those… those…" Stacy paused, suddenly at a loss for words, but not daunted. "Well, whatever they are, they killed… they killed… Well, I don't know his name, but they killed him and killed a defenseless dog and tried to kill us!"

"Yeah, but you won't believe how," Paul added.

"Let's start with what's important," Samuels said, scanning the woods while trying to keep an eye on the pair before him at the same time. "Who was killed."

"The policeman. The one you had tailing us," Paul said.

"Fisher?"

Paul nodded, adding a belated "I think."

"Oh? I was wondering where he was," Samuels said, not quite believing Paul. He let the silence drag a minute. "You were going to tell me why you killed him."

"Me? I didn't…" Paul sputtered a moment, suddenly feeling like the unintended hero in a Hitchcock thriller when he learns that the world mistakenly thinks he is a master criminal.

"It wasn't us!" Stacy shouted at Samuels, fear, anger, and ignition all wrapped in one heated burst. "It was the… the… those… those fish… them… the aliens!" Samuels' blank look did nothing to sooth her temper. "The *creatures*! Those *things* with the light guns and the super-planes and the cages and… stuff. Those… those *things* killed him!"

Samuels nodded once, then took a step back.

"OK," he said, then very calmly pulled his gun.

"Hey, what's with you? We need your help," Paul demanded.

"Why don't you two just turn around and spread your hands on the car." Samuels' voice was cold as ice, but it was like a warm summer breeze compared to the look in his eyes.

"Listen to me," Paul said urgently, waving his hand vaguely in the direction of the house. "They were right behind us. If you don't get out of here or call in reinforcements, they'll kill us, too."

"Damn it!" Stacy shouted. "Can't you see the lights? Their's an alien war going on back there!"

"Uh-huh. Now, just turn around and spread 'em. We'll worry about that later."

"Please," Stacy pleaded, "listen to us! It's true!"

"I said 'spread 'em' and I mean *now*!"

Paul looked at Stacy and shrugged. "I guess if they made it past the house they would be here by now."

Paul turned and spread his hands on the trunk of Fisher's car. Stacy, with much less grace, spread her hands over the roof. After a second, she shot Samuels a scathing glance and spread her legs, too. Samuels ignored her and began patting down Paul.

"You have the right to remain silent," Samuels said, jerking Paul's hands behind his back and fishing for his cuffs. "And from what I heard so far, that sounds like good advice."

Samuels finished with Paul and turned to Stacy. "You have the right to a lawyer. If you cannot..."

"If you plan to do to me what you did to him," Stacy interrupted, "then you'd better have someone watch. I don't want you running your hands over my body. Damn it, I'm not giving a free feel to anyone who calls me a liar and a killer without first checking the facts. You want to play with me you'd better be damned sure you got the right. Touch my booty now and you'll be working for the TSA tomorrow."

Paul looked over at Stacy. For an avowed coward, she was doing a good job standing up to the long arm of the law. Her vehemence struck Samuels as genuine. He still wasn't sure about this city boy, but the girl was pretty convincing. He considered his options for a moment, the spun Paul around and popped one half of a set of cuffs on Paul's wrist.

"OK. I'll check out your story. Let me indulge in a few idiosyncrasies..." Samuels quickly slapped the free cuff on Stacy's wrist.

"Ouch! That's tight," Stacy protested.

"... and take a few precautions. Just in case, you understand. Sorry it's tight." Samuels stopped and gave them both a long look. "Spunky girl you've got there," he told Paul. "She from Phoenix, too?"

"No. She's home grown."

"Home *fried* more like it if we don't get out of here," Stacy interjected.

"Restaurant humor. Look, if we run into those things again," Paul continued shortly, "I really, really, *really* don't want to be cuffed."

"If, and I really, really, *really* am not buying your story. We run into your walking fish friends, *then* I'll take the cuffs off. Right now, though, I'm not taking any chances."

"Fine. But we have a witness, you know," Stacy said smugly.

"Who?" Both Paul and Samuels asked at the same time.

"The house. Whoever it was in the house that turned on that whatever field or something, and blasted the alien. They have to know what's going on around here."

"Maybe," Paul admitted reluctantly. He could see a return trip to the house in his future and he was not excited about doing that without an army of more than one. "Of course, what you fell over back there could have been a tripwire and the rest could be automated."

"Oh. And we could get fried going back?"

Paul nodded thoughtfully.

"Oh." Stacy thought for a second, and then added "but can we take the chance that there's no one there? How're we gonna explain the dead cop if everything vanishes and the house is empty?"

"Good point. I guess we have no other choice."

"What are you two talking about?" Samuels demanded.

"We have to go to the house," Stacy insisted.

"OK, Stacy. I agree, but I think things are just going to grow more strange."

"How can they get more strange than this?"

"You haven't seen the toys this guy makes. If it *is* a guy. If it is *this* guy."

"Will you two tell me what in Hell you are talking about," Samuels demanded again.

"Look," Paul said, turning to Samuels. "Call for help and let's go talk to the people in the house."

"I think we have enough help."

"Aren't you even going to get help for the patrolman?"

"Fisher? You said he was dead. He doesn't need any help right at the moment."

"Well, maybe the house is full of crack heads. You'll need help then."

"OK. I'll call for a backup. We can talk to the people in the house," Samuels agreed. "Then you can take me to Fisher's body."

"No." Stacy's voice was firm. There was no wavering or doubt. *She* was not going back into the woods at night. Whatever fear Paul had of the house, Stacy's came with compound interest when she thought about what was in that clearing.

"What?" Paul was not expecting such a firm rejection from someone who had just suggested going back to the mysterious Caruthers House.

"I'll go to the house. Whoever is in there is friendly, I guess," Stacy said, waving away Paul's concern. "But I'm not going back into those woods without the National Guard."

"Yeah. I see what you mean," Paul agreed, looking back they way they had come with an almost vacant stare. Images of Fisher danced in his head just a little too brightly to make wandering in the woods appealing. Even standing in the lane was not something that seemed like a good idea. Who knew how many creatures were slinking through the forest right now, surrounding them and preparing the cooking pot? The house might not be much better, but recent experience suggested that it might be just the shelter they needed here and now.

"Well, I don't see anything. Let's go talk to the people in the house. Then I'll decide what to do from there," Samuels added, sourly. "Which may just be booking you two for mass murder and terminal lunacy."

"Whatever you say. Just do me a favor."

"What?" Samuels eyed Paul warily. Nut cases were supposed to be a cagey lot.

"You keep your gun ready and keep looking over your shoulder."

"Let's go," Samuels said. What a stupid suggestion. Any cop worth his salt would keep his gun ready when he had two suspected murderers in his sight and it was just common police policy to keep an eye out in any field situation. Of course, that excellent book-learning did nothing to explain the chilly feeling he had at the base of his neck. No, it did nothing at all to dispel the certain knowledge that there was someone may be watching his every move and that someone had ill intent written all over its psyche.

They made their way across the grass, passing through that slight resistance at the porch which made Paul's hackles hackle as far as they could. This night was turning into one of chills and thrills and not the circus type. Paul looked behind him at the cop and noticed that Samuels hunched his shoulders as he passed through the barrier. So, Paul wasn't alone in his apprehension, but, having witnessed the scene in the yard, the force bubble gave him a sense of security this time, not one of fear. If the house was going to eat them, it would have done it on their first visit, Paul figured. Or maybe the lizard men had whetted its appetite for warm-blooded victims. Well, there was only one way to find out. Paul raised his hand to knock, but Samuels pushed him aside. The cop banged on the door with the butt of his gun. Apparently, he wasn't going to take "I didn't hear you" as an excuse for not answering.

"Open up! It's the police!" Samuels yelled at the door, then thought that, if it was crack heads, they may just answer that with a shotgun. Well, nothing to do about it now. He banged the door a couple of times again. "Open up! I have some questions!"

A small Radio Shack intercom crackled into life near the door, causing both Paul and Stacy to jump. This whole place was just too creepy.

"Request denied. You may depart. You have a brief window of safety."

That brought all three to a full stop. The voice had a tinny, mechanical quality, strangely accented, and oddly phrased. But mostly it was the audacity to tell the police that they were not going to talk and to "depart" without a by-your-leave or kiss-my-ass. It wasn't natural.

Samuels took a deep breath and yelled at the innocent intercom. "I said 'open up!' Do it now. I want to talk to you. Face-to-face!"

"That is not possible," the box replied after a short delay. "You will please leave at once."

Samuels turned to Stacy. "Who lives here? Have you ever seen the owners?"

Stacy shrugged off the question. "No one has that I know of."

"That voice doesn't sound real. It sounds mechanical. Like the text-to-speech program I have on my home computer. Only odd."

Samuels turned back to the door and looked at it. Maybe he could kick it in and claim that he was in hot pursuit of a murderer. Well, he had Paul and Stacy and they weren't going anywhere. Besides, he only had their word that Fisher had been killed. Maybe he was being held prisoner inside. Samuels himself had not seen a body or blood or any physical evidence, beyond an abandoned car and there could be a dozen good reasons that it was sitting in the drive. Well, maybe not a dozen, but enough that a good lawyer would have his… shield… if he tried to use that as a case for entering without a warrant.

While Samuels examined the door and his thoughts, Stacy was watching the woods. Something was out there, of that she was sure, but she couldn't spot anything. She wasn't sure she *wanted* to spot anything, but she felt obliged to watch since the boys were busy playing with the… whatever inside. She was sure it was a "whatever" and not a "someone". There were too many "whatevers" running around and it wasn't even Halloween.

"Either we talk now or I come back with a warrant!" Samuels shouted at the door.

"I don't think that'll do you much good, somehow," Paul muttered and earned a glare from the frustrated cop. It had been a long day already and he had lost patience when he first found Fisher's car abandoned in the lane and the mosquitoes had gathered when he stepped back into the woods to see what the pair running down the lane had planned. Not like he had been hiding long, but he never claimed to have a strong stomach for stakeouts when the indigenous creatures considered *him* the steak.

"Your request cannot be authorized," the box squawked.

"Told you," Paul quipped, earning him another patented Samuels' glare.

"Analysis suggests that you leave immediately before you are harmed," the box continued.

"Oh, that's just peachy," Samuels said. "Threatened by a voice box on a haunted mansion." He turned back to the obstinate speaker and drew a deep breath. "This is the police you are speaking to! Are you threatening me?" Now, if the answer was "yes," a warrant would be superfluous.

"Negative. Our analysis indicates the probability of approaching danger from an outside agent. You should leave immediately."

"This thing is pretty stubborn," Paul said. "I don't think it's impressed with your shield and I don't think it's saying that it'll hurt us. I'll bet there are more things in the woods and it wants us out of here in case they show up. Look, this place is protected, somehow. I don't know *how* they are connected, but I'll bet the creatures in the woods were surprised to find the house armed and angry about it and I don't think they have the personality to be polite about it."

"You want to go back to the station and explain where Fisher is while I fill out a suspected murder charge?"

"Well," said Paul reasonably, "put that way, go ahead and get belligerent with a haunted call box."

"I will!" Samuels turned back to the door and rapped it again. "Open this door immediately!"

"I think we should leave and not come back without a full posse," Paul said slowly, the rush he felt earlier finally turning into a cold lump in his stomach.

"I think it's a little late to leave, anyway," Stacy said. "Hey, inside," she yelled. She threw that over her shoulder, never taking her eyes off a patch of dark that just didn't *feel* right. "I think our friends are back! Can you let us in? Please? I don't think we will make it back to the car."

There was a slight pause before the house answered, but when it did, it sent chills down the backs of everyone present.

"Your analysis is correct. You will remain outside, where you are, until told to do otherwise. So not attempt to leave the shelter of the EPT field unless told otherwise. Analysis suggests maximum levels. Sensors detect heavy weapons. To step outside the field may prove terminal."

"What's an EPT field?" Stacy asked.

"What's that light?" Samuels countered. The entire porch took on an eerie, blue glow, shimmering all along the border of the building.

"That's the light," Paul speculated. "But I want to know more about this 'heavy weapons' thing."

"Look!" Stacy pointed toward the woods, very near the spot she had been watching, but Samuels just shook his head. Paul strained to look, too, and he could see some movement, but Stacy obviously had better eyesight. Something was going on, but he couldn't tell what. He had the uneasy feeling that he had stepped into a bad science fiction movie only without the protection of a script. It was time to get the Hell out of Dodge.

Samuels couldn't see anything, so he stepped toward the edge of the porch for a better look, but Paul grabbed him with his free hand and pulled him back.

"I don't think you should do that. I don't think we know everything yet and the voice may be just a little slow on the details."

"What…" Samuels started, but the house – and by now, Paul was sure that it was a computer talking to them and not a living being – was not going to respond the way Samuels desired. No, this was from a program, perhaps something with a random search capacity based on input; he wasn't sure, just sure it was not a one-on-one with a living being. And it was not polite. It cut Samuels off in mid-sentence.

"Do not approach the Electronic Pulse Terminal Field," the house said. "You may be severally damaged at this level."

"Well, now we know what EPT is," Stacy volunteered helpfully.

"Yeah, but we still have no idea what it means."

"Look at the woods. I'll bet they're just about to demonstrate something interesting for us," she observed, pointing toward the aliens with her chin. "I sure wish we were inside now," she added with a sigh.

"I wish we were in Phoenix," Paul admitted.

"I don't see anything," Samuels admitted reluctantly.

"Look just a little left of the third dead rose bush from the front of the walk. See where the forest thins just a little?" Stacy asked. She had her difficult customer role running in high gear now, so patience thinly overlaid her earlier irritation. "OK. Now lift your eyes up. There are some silver things moving in the woods."

"Yeah, got it," Samuels said.

Paul had already tagged the group, but the confirmation was good to have. Or not, depending on one's perspective. He could see three of the aliens, just making out their silver suits. They were maneuvering something bulky through the woods. They were hard to distinguish through the trees, but even Samuels could see that there was something odd about the creatures, something not human, and he began muttering under his breath; something Paul couldn't understand, but it sure sounded like a sailor waking up after being rolled.

The group in the woods moved closer to the edge and it became easier to make out what they were doing… and to see that they were not human. Samuels gulped a couple of times, but Paul just watched, thinking about the great article he could write if only someone would buy it besides the pulp press. Two aliens set up something like a cradle with three-legged posts holding up each corner. The third alien laid a bar or tube of some sort in the sway-back center, then all three began fussing with the combined affair. They looked like they were connecting wires and tubes and setting dials, but the distance and the dark made it impossible to tell for sure. Whatever it was, Paul didn't like it a bit. He stepped back next to Stacy, who was pressed against the house like she was trying to merge with the walls.

"What are they doing," she whispered to Paul.

"I don't know, but I don't think it is going to be good for us." Paul reached out and pulled Samuels farther away from the porch edge. "See it now?"

"Yeah. I need to get back to the radio in my car."

"I have a feeling it isn't too healthy out there right now. Those suckers have some sort of laser gun and it does nasty things to people."

"That's what killed your cop," Stacy offered.

"Well, I don't imagine they are able to digest lead," Samuels retorted, lifting his pistol.

"I think those are flight suits," Paul said. "They have some kind of ship out in the woods and that silver isn't much of a camouflage pattern, especially for the nighttime woods. But it could be made from some sort of ballistic cloth and your gun would be next to worthless if it's true."

"What are you talking about?"

"Ballistic cloth would take the impact of the bullet and spread it across a wide area of the suit. That's the basic principal of interlaced force dispersion and conversion of kinetic energy into radiated energy. It might give them a kick, but it wouldn't penetrate. You'd have to make a head shot and I understand that's not so easy in the dark with a pistol… especially while you're running for your life." Paul made that last statement in a flat voice. He was making an observation, not a criticism, but Samuels was not in buying into any of that and just shook his head.

"OK. Think of it as advanced Kevlar."

"OK. I can buy that," Samuels said.

"Oh," Stacy exclaimed.

While Samuels and Paul had been talking, one of the aliens had stepped in front of the device they had set up and set out a framework about eight feet long by twelve high. It had just sprung into a brilliant shield that looked like mother of pearl made of light or the color of oil floating on a still pond. It was breathtaking and lovely and frightening, all in one. They could see the figures a little better in the light from the frame, but they were blurred, like being viewed through a frosted glass door. The group could still see enough to feel that something very wrong was going on behind the light curtain.

"Ahhhh!" Paul was not sure who cried out, maybe it was all of them. The light that struck out from behind the curtain was bright enough to cause real pain in Paul's eyes and the follow-up lightening as it dissipated across the energy field that protected the house was no less daunting. Heat radiated from the house's protective field and, had Samuels still been standing near the front of the porch, he might have been badly burned. As it was, his eye brows were singed and his suit jacket smoldered a little on the sleeve he had thrown up in front of his face.

But barely seconds after the aliens had fired on the house, the heat and light was gone. Then the house fired back.

Another of the bright orange balls that Stacy and Paul had seen earlier flashed out and struck the alien shield squarely in the center… and shattered across it like a paintball.

"Damn! Will you look at that?" Samuels asked. "Fireworks."

"I'd whether not look," Stacy offered, tears tracking through the dirt on her face. "That last one was quite enough. And those aren't fireworks."

"I guess we're vindicated. How about letting us go," Paul asked, holding his cuffed hand out to Samuels.

"Yeah. Sure." Samuels answer was slow and thoughtful. Right now, he just wanted out of here, but if they stepped off the porch, even assuming they could pass through the shield, the energy beam would toast them in a flash. Paul had the same thought.

"Damn," Samuels muttered.

"I don't like this at all," Paul said while Samuels was removing the cuffs, something he did without taking his eyes off the woods.

Stacy just muttered something about never dating a writer from Phoenix again, and that made Paul smile.

"You may never have another chance," he said, "if we don't get some cover. I don't think this is over yet."

As if on cue, the woods lit up again. This time, the shot hit considerably higher on the shield - as if testing out the strength at a different point - and the after effects were not as strong, but Paul knew it was just a matter of time before something gave and the three humans became collateral damage.

The house wasted no time in firing back, but this time the line of attack varied. Instead of aiming for the shield, the house threw several small balls of lightening in a scattered pattern around the shield. Immediately, the underbrush caught fire, setting up a fierce wall of flame in front of and around the sides of the shield. Paul could hear what must be the lizard equivalent of yelling and probably cursing. He could not see anything through the fire and smoke, but no more shots came from behind the screen, which was beginning to flicker. It was a good bet that the aliens had abandoned their position. Even if the immediate fire did not reach them, the increased temperature must have been less than pleasant.

Samuels turned to Paul with a slight smirk. "Well, that's a bonus. There'll be people from the fire department and forestry service here in no time. The woods have been dry for the last five years and there's no chance that they'll let this burn long enough to get out of control. Help is on the way," he concluded somewhat melodramatically.

But Paul had been watching the woods. He gestured with his chin. One of the aliens was spraying the area with foam. Where the fire had started to rage it was guttering out and the bright flames had turned into little more than embers. "If anyone even saw that, there's nothing now. I wouldn't expect any help from that. And if they sent anyone out to investigate, well, one or two people are just cannon fodder to these guys."

"We have to get to my radio."

"Where did you park your car," Stacy asked. "I didn't see it back in the woods."

"Near the road. I walked up the driveway."

"Brave guy."

Samuels just snorted. "If I'd known what was up here, I would've waited for a tank."

"Look, if it's near the road, someone will spot it soon enough. The department will have two of you guys missing and they'll put out some kind of an alert, won't they?" Paul asked.

"Yeah, but they won't notice anything is wrong until sometime around mid-morning and then who knows how long it will be before someone notices the car. Unless Fisher called in his location."

"How'd you find us?" Stacy wanted to know.

"Fisher called into dispatch. They tried to put me on a direct patch with his car but no one responded. Maybe someone will look at the message log; he told the dispatcher where to I should meet him. Or if the same dispatcher works tomorrow and if they find out that there is a search on, then we might expect help around sundown tomorrow, about shift change. I expect things will be much too interesting around here between now and then for that to be a comfortable wait."

"Well, I'll certainly have to pee before then," Stacy added. She turned back to the house. "Hey, inside, you got a restroom for humans in there?"

"I'm not sure if it would be better to go in there or in the woods," Paul commented.

"Woods are OK for you guys, but just any old tree doesn't work for me."

"Assessment indicates that there is a window of 10.1 time units before the next attack. You may enter quickly. Do not attempt to reach the street," the house said, making everyone jump, even Stacy who was expecting a response. "The door behind you will open. Do not leave the entryway. Quickly. I must reseal the building before the next attack or risk damage."

With that, the door swung open into a hallway made narrow by the racks of electronic and unidentifiable equipment humming and popping and glowing enough to give the space a dim light. Paul thought it looked like he was being invited into the guts of the Univac; the original Univac, the one personally constructed by the technicians with hand-blown vacuum tubes long before production models were available, and not something that was bought off the shelf of any worldly electronics boutique. But even with all the electronics, the breeze that flowed from the hall was dry and chill, almost crackling with static. If the rest of the house was packed with equipment as tightly as this hallway, then there was some mighty powerful something going on here. To Paul, it certainly did not look like an advanced stereo player for frat parties. It was daunting and, despite the known danger outside, they hesitated.

"Why this sudden change of heart?" Paul asked.

There was another slight pause before the house answered, as if the house was consulting another source. Or as if whoever was talking to them was distracted by something. Paul was not about to guess what was going on at this point. He remembered that old sci-fi movie where the robot went around saying "Johnny Five needs input." Paul Johnson desperately needed input, but he had a firm conviction that whatever input he received, he wasn't going to like it.

"You may become damaged by secondary radiation from the outer shields," the voice finally replied. "You must hurry. Seepage is dangerous. I cannot activate the inner shields until you are on the other side of the primaries or you will suffer terminal damage. And I cannot leave the door open if there is another attack since a static discharge could damage the equipment you around you. You must either come inside or I can briefly drop the primaries and you can attempt to reach your car before you are killed. I calculate you have a eighty-seven percent chance of failure if you run."

"Well, that doesn't sound very encouraging," Stacy said. "Stay here and get electrocuted, go out there and get zapped, or go inside and… or what? I vote on or what."

"Look, guys, we don't know who the good guys are in this. It's looking like this house is the target and they, those things in the woods, zeroed in on it when they tried to kill me and Stacy. But we don't know if they're the cops or the robbers."

"I'm betting the things in the woods are not on Marshall Dillion's team. You saw what they did in the dog and that cop. This guy at least saved us once and is showing some concern for us now. I vote for the 'what' again," Stacy said.

"Please decide now," the house insisted. "I must close up immediately. Sensors indicate activity with their ships and tight-beamed communication to their orbiting mother ship. The weapons they can bring to bear will be much greater than you have seen tonight. You must run or enter in two point six seconds or risk damage where you are."

"Well, that's good enough for me," Samuels said and stepped into the hall. Two point six seconds would not allow them much margin to clear the house and if they weren't a decent distance down the road when things began to heat up, then they were just as likely to become causalities as not.

Stacy was right on his heel. "And I don't need another invitation."

Paul took one last look around, then followed them inside. It wasn't that he was afraid, exactly. No, not really afraid of what was in the house, but afraid of what the existence of the house portended. He had spent a lot of time chasing down the toy maker, from badgering his Hollywood contacts about the *Star Wars* designs to hounding distributors and manufacturers into revealing the sources for their marvelous toys. Now that he was so close, he was not sure that he wanted to find the answer, not when it came cloaked in aliens, murder, and mayhem. As long as the toy maker had remained an object of his imagination, a wizened old man in spectacles working over a tiny basement workshop making toys much like Saint Nick and his elves, that was one thing. But to put a face on the creator that might be the face of a dog-eating monster was something else entirely.

This whole article idea had started with a toy for Jeremy. To have it finish like this was unbelievable for Paul. The fear, the violence, the panic that surrounded his search in Flagstaff and Northern Arizona just did not fit the feeling that Paul pulled from the finely crafted – if highly advanced – toys that he had identified and played with at that bar back in Phoenix so many years – no, it was only weeks! – ago.

Yes, Paul admitted to himself, he was afraid, but it was not fear of what might wait in the house. No, this was a fear that what waited was something that *should be feared* and not loved. Paul was afraid to see his dream shattered.

"Quickly," the house said. "They have called in their searchers. They are converging on this location. We must put our defenses in place or all is lost."

Samuels and Stacy had already made it inside the house, but Paul was still undecided, hesitant. But time waits for no man, and the door to the house began to swing ponderously shut. Faced between his own fear and the certain knowledge that remaining where he was would certainly produce one overcooked Paul Johnson was enough. With a leap and a skip, Paul made it through the door before it closed completely. The solid *thunk* the door made when it closed put "paid" on any idea that Paul and company may have had about breaking out easily. The door sounded as thick as eternity.

Paul and Samuels stepped in front of Stacy to provide what meager protection a club and a gun could against energy weapons and creatures that might be giant Gila Monsters. The house was a wonderland of consumer electronics, but Paul doubted that any geek Santa Claus sat as Lord and Master over the apparent clutter that marked that hallway. Whoever – or whatever – occupied the house was not what Paul had expected to find. Nor, he felt sure, were Samuels or Stacy any closer to guessing the nature of the occupant than he was. For Paul was very sure that whoever lived in this house, this ramshackle place with unkempt yard and consumer electronics transformed into force-field generators and military grade lasers, was not human.

The silence weighed heavily on them for several long seconds. It they were waiting for their host to present himself, the waited in vain. Once inside they were treated like they were not even there. It was eerie, but so was everything else that had happened since Paul had pulled into the driveway. Paul knew it was his insatiable curiosity that had brought him here, but he also knew the parable about the cat. Stay in the entryway? Not bloody likely.

"Well," Stacy said. "I guess we're all here. But where is the party?"

CHAPTER TEN
June 19 and 20, 1997
Flagstaff, Arizona

"I don't know if there's a party, but it does feel like we're going to rock and roll," Paul said as the house shuddered and groaned. Outside it sounded like a thunderstorm had rolled in and centered its attention on one square acre of Northern Arizona.

The humans stood together, huddling like sheep for the comfort of other bodies nearby. The hall was long, dim, and crowded. Where there should have been doors leading off from main hall into rooms on either side, there were only equipment racks or electronic gear uncaringly piled and wired into a semi-living mass, quietly humming. Any past elegance had been covered with wires and silicon components or was peeling from neglect. Whatever mad scientist lived in the house was not inclined to make minor repairs or worry about resale value. Cables ran everywhere and poked into walls and ceiling in odd places. There was only enough space to make a narrow path from the door. The smell of ozone was pervasive though not overpowering. There was a stiff, cool breeze blowing through the hall, pulling the heat away from the piles of equipment and replacing the air with something less stifling.

At the end of the hall, a broad stairway led to the upper floors. This too was covered with electronics from floor to ceiling with a curvaceous path winding up the stairs. The power and indicator lights cast a bizarre glow that was enough to provide a bare minimum of light for them to see; a good thing since the bare, dark incandescent that hung from a cord dangling from the ceiling looked blown out. Behind the stairs, in what was probably the kitchen, a stronger light crept out from around the electronics hugging the doorway. Something back there was using more light than just the glow from the equipment and that centered everyone's attention, though the speculation of what might emerge from there varied with the watcher.

Paul was giving the stacked equipment a close look, though he was careful not to touch anything. Accidentally hitting a power button could generate a response that Paul was not even interested in thinking about investigating. But he quickly tossed out the thought that this was some weird techno-geek junkyard. All the components seemed to be operating. There were no stacks of half-cannibalized, half-forgotten computers or stereos or receivers. Everything that he could see was powered and busy doing something, though at what he had no idea. The stereos were not making music and the computers had no screens, the receivers could be receiving, but receiving what? There were no speakers in the hall that Paul could see. Nor were the components stack as haphazardly as they appeared. The jumbled mass of stripped down computers and audio equipment had a strangely *complete* feel, like it was as well designed as a BMW.

When Paul looked closely in the poor lighting; he could see that many of the cases appeared to have been spot-welded or attached to its neighbors with small pieces of strapping similar to what construction workers used to secure two pieces of wood when framing a house. Those were easier to spot than the welds since no attempts to paint over the connections allowed their silver-gray color to stand out easily against the predominately black cases. It was also apparent that the owner did not have a brand preference. Sony was wired to Panasonic (deadly rivals in the corporate world), to Phillips to Casio to Gold Star; there was high-end wired to low-end wired to homemade Radio Shack component boards. And a few paces from the stairs, what must have been a hundred Ford car stereos with CD players were happily humming away, each with a CD spinning in its slot. Paul put his ear close to that stack, but he couldn't hear any music. He felt very confident that what the CDs were playing was not rap. Maybe heavy metal, he thought humorously, but nothing so reminiscent of the streets, or earthly streets, at least.

"When we get a forensic team in here, I'll bet we solve all the equipment thefts for the past twenty years in one fell swoop," Samuels commented dryly.

"Has there been a lot of that?" Stacy asked. She was not deeply interested but the quiet hall was nerve-wracking. She wanted to keep Paul or Samuels talking.

Paul already knew the statistics, but seeing this… well, no wonder the cases remained unsolved. Nothing ended up back on the market to give the investigators a trail back to Flagstaff. Who would ever believe that the hundreds of computers and thousands of audio power amps could all be *used* by the thief and not sold? He was interested in Samuels' take, since the news accounts were not well documented.

"My first unsolved case started with a shopping center robbery that wiped out every electronic component in a Radio Shack and the neighboring businesses in one night," Samuels said, looking around with a thoughtful expression on his face. "That was in the mid-eighties. Since then, there have been dozens of cases all over the Northern part of the state where electronics and other items have just vanished in large quantities. The FBI's been investigating since the early nineties, once the thefts began to spread into Nevada. Yeah, we found some of the missing equipment, but those all lead back to some clumsy armature and the ones we solved seemed to be isolated; there was never any connection to the major thefts, not a clue, nothing. Not in any of the major ones, anyway. Oh, they'd catch a few truck-jackers every now and then, shut down a few major crime rings, but none of them had the same feel as the one that started all this. Come to think of it, there was a truckload of dog food stolen at the same time. I never thought to see if there were any other thefts of pet food, though. Wish I would have thought of that. Not that I think it would have mattered."

"This place gives me the creeps," Stacy said, summing up the way Paul felt himself, but Samuels' comment about the dog food put a new light on what happened in the woods. Had they just stepped out of the skillet and into the fire? Were the dog eaters out *there* looking for a renegade dog eater in *here*? It was a chilling thought but it just did not jibe with the toy maker that Paul had been tracking down for a year. Of course, Paul reminded himself, he had yet to prove that this house's residents and the toy maker were one in the same. What if the actual toy maker lived on the moon or Saturn or somewhere and flew around in strange ships and ate dogs? That was not a pleasant thought at all and Paul rapidly put it aside.

"What's making the house shake?" Stacy asked.

"I think your friends from the woods have brought in the big brother of that cannon we saw earlier," Samuels said. "If the fire wasn't noticed, I'll bet the glow from those fireworks don't go ignored. Not with all the Guard troops running around these days."

"They aren't my friends," Stacy muttered, hugging herself. It was turning into a long night and the prospects of seeing the dawn were… questionable.

"It sure doesn't look like a millionaire toy maker lives here," Paul said. "I expected to see Nutcrackers and Trains and things. Not a house full of abused electronics."

"What do you mean, 'millionaire toy maker'?" Samuels asked as he began working his way toward the back of the hall.

"I've been tracking the designer of a series of toys and games. They all seemed to lead to a private post office box here in Flagstaff," Paul said. "I had a friend get the address of the box owner for me. It wasn't hard but it cost me five hundred bucks. The someone pays a courier to pick up the mail every day and deliver it here. I heard that the driver takes back any packages he finds on the doorstep and the mailbox company ships them out. This is the place. I think the toy inventor lives here."

"That's your proof?" Samuels demanded.

"Just guesswork," Paul admitted. "But it's based on some pretty good leg work. I've added a lot of loose ends together from old magazine articles and news clips, including the Flagstaff papers. They all seem to lead to Flagstaff and from what I could track, it ends here. I sent a letter to the inventor – I got the PO Box number from a store in Scottsdale, being such a good customer and all. It was returned refused, but the return postmark was from Flagstaff."

"So that's why you're here?"

"Yeah, I'm working on a story. It's just bigger than I thought."

"So that bit was true? You're here only to research a story?"

"Well, yeah. Partly. Partly I was just curious. If you saw one of this guy's toys, then you would be fascinated. But line a dozen of them up on a table and they'll blow your mind." Paul shrugged. He didn't want to admit, even to himself, that the research had almost become an obsession, something to distract him from Janet's obsession with punishing him for falling in love and marrying her. With the conversation they had when he had called earlier in the day, Paul almost regretted the loss of one of his most cherished distractions: the search for the illusive millionaire inventor.

"What about your friends outside," Samuels wanted to know. "Where do they fit in?"

"I don't know where they fit in," Paul admitted. "They're new to the equation. Nothing I have seen would suggest that they were part of this." Paul stopped himself in the middle of his own thought. "Except the video game. Damn! There is a tie-in! In the video game, the bad guys eat creatures and they look a lot like the lizard men!"

"What video game," Samuels demanded.

"It's a long story. I've got the video ball with my things at the 'Y'. I can show you later."

"If we live that long," Stacy interjected. "These things are murderers and monsters and I mean that last part literally."

"And the *Star Wars* thing. I'll bet that design from the death star was a message that someone had been there, seen that, done that."

"What the hell are you talking about?" Samuels was totally lost and it didn't make him happy at all.

"When I started this, I told a friend that I thought there were aliens living in Flagstaff. I don't think I really believed that until now. God. John will never believe this."

"No one else will, either," Stacy said.

"This time, there'll be enough evidence, I think," Samuels said dryly.

"And not just toys," Paul added. "I think we're in the heart of a computer that controls the force fields, the weapons, and who knows what else? I'll bet there's a power supply that the government would kill to get their hands on or this much drain on the electrical grid would have had investigators out here long before now. When we begin reverse engineering this, it will revolutionize the electronics industry and most of the stuff, from what I can see here, is just reworking what we already have. Forget the toys; this hallway is a gold mine. Add in the refined optics and voice controls that the toys represent, and this one house will change the world more than the invention of the internal combustion engine."

"These things are killers and monsters," Stacy repeated stubbornly.

"I find it hard to believe that the creatures outside are connected with the person who lives here. At least, not as an ally or even the same species," Paul said. He just couldn't reconcile what he had seen in the clearing with everything he had learned about the mysterious inventor in Flagstaff.

"What makes you think this is a *person*?" Stacy wanted to know, but she asked softly, almost afraid that she would get an answer. But she did not ask softly enough and Samuels picked up on the comment.

"What do you mean?"

"You didn't see what we saw in the clearing," Stacy said.

"That's my point," Paul said. "What first got me interested in this story was a toy I bought my kid." Paul turned to Stacy with a weak smile. "It's OK. I'm divorced. No horrible infidelity in taking you to dinner." He turned back to Samuels, frowning in concentration. "Then I found that there was a whole list of toys that had been filtering into the market over ten or fifteen years that were just fantastic. They're simple, but the designs are so comprehensive that they leave the entire toy market behind. For what they do, they're inexpensive, though that is relative."

"Toys? This entire thing is about *toys*?" Samuels asked incredulously.

"Hey, whoever it is really makes good toys. That's why I don't think… 'whoever' is connected with those things outside," Paul insisted. "But I don't think this is about toys, either. The toys are just a sideline. Maybe something the inventor uses for cash flow. Maybe a little more, if there really are messages interwoven in the things that we are just too dense to catch."

"'No one will know where to find you if you don't know where to hide.'" Tracy voice handled the quote with a slight lilt.

"What's that?"

"Just a line from an old song my father used to play on this old Motorola console a lot when I was a kid," Stacy said. "We can't find the messages because the sender didn't know enough about humans to know where to hide them. We just didn't pay enough attention to toys and movies. Is that what you mean?"

"Yeah. But more. If the inventor lives here, I'd trust him."

"You mean that any creature that could make those toys has to be all right?" Stacy asked, hoping desperately to be reassured.

"Something like that. He must like kids. Those lizard men don't seem to like anything."

"John Wayne Gacy liked kids," Samuels muttered, but the reference to the mass murder escaped Stacy and she made the mistake of asking Samuels just what he meant.

"Gacy was a homosexual that everyone thought loved children," Samuels said. "He had huge parties at his place near Chicago. He often dressed up as a clown to entertain kids at the local hospitals. Real kid lover. He committed his first murder in 1972. Over the next six years he murdered thirty-two boys by strangulation. Twenty-seven of the victims were found in shallow graves under his house. Yeah. He liked kids a lot. He had them for lunch sometimes."

"I would have placed this more in the annals of a Jeffery Dahmer," Paul said.

"Yeah. Maybe so. Now, that's a man that really *liked* people," Samuels agreed.

"I'm not sure I want to know, but who was this one?" Stacy asked.

"Dahmer lived in Milwaukee. Made the headlines in 92, I guess," Samuels explained. "He worked at a candy factory and rented a small apartment nearby. The neighbors complained of an overpowering bad smell and construction noise, but Dahmer explained all that away by saying that his refrigerator was broke and the meat spoiled and that he was building book-cases."

"And the police bought that," Stacy asked.

"Yeah. We're cops, not super humans. We make mistakes."

"So what made him so evil."

"You sure you want to know," Paul asked.

"No. But just waiting for something to happen is getting on my nerves." Stacy answered.

"Well, in 1991 police found a 14-year-old Asian boy bleeding and naked. He had escaped from Dahmer's apartment, but the police called it 'a homosexual lovers spat' and didn't do a thing. Forget that the kid was underage. Hell, he wasn't

American enough to count, I guess." Samuels shook his head. "Dahmer killed the boy later that night."

"That's awful! Didn't they even think about arresting this guy as a child molester?" Stacy asked, shocked out of her immediate fear and into outrage.

"Well, that's one of the reasons I live out here. People don't ignore things like that," Samuels said. "It wasn't until another one of Dahmer's victims escaped and flagged down a police car that things got interesting. The police used probable cause to check out Dahmer's apartment. They found photos of dismembered bodies, a head in the refrigerator, and a kettle on the stove full of hands and male genitalia."

"Oh, gross," Stacy looked a little green, but it could have been the light. The group had been moving slowly toward the back of the hall and the glow from the Ford CD power buttons cast a ghoulish pallor on them all.

"Yeah. Later, they noticed that there was no food in the apartment. Dahmer had been living off his victims. This guy Dahmer admitted to getting his victims drunk or drugged, photographing, strangling, and dismembering them. He also admitted to necrophilia and cannibalism."

"What a horrible person! But it sounds like a movie, not real life," Stacy insisted.

"Yeah. I read the book *Silence of the Lambs*. But Dahmer was no Hannibal Lector," Samuels went on. "Lector had class. Dahmer was an animal. Besides, we're all to think that Hannibal the Cannibal is still on the loose. Dahmer was murdered by another inmate while waiting on death row. He was found with a mop handle stuck in his eye."

"That sounds a lot like your lizard men," Paul noted.

"You know, if you throw in dogs, it sounds a lot like the deaths that have been happening around here for the past few weeks, too. Someone has been draining the blood from the victims."

"Well, that's a cheery thought!" Stacy said. "Are you suggesting that we were driven in here for some sort of dinner party?"

"I'd bet not," Paul said. "In fact, I'd bet we were just taken off the menu. And I think we're about to find out by whom."

Paul gestured toward the back of the hall. The light there began to grow brighter and a high whine could be heard from around the corner.

"That's the kitchen, isn't it?" Stacy asked.

"Yeah. I guess," Paul whispered.

"Are you sure we're not the main course?" Stacy wanted to know, taking Paul by the arm and gripping hard. Paul looked at her with as much confidence as he could.

"I'll protect you."

Stacy tried not to laugh at that, but she did feel strangely reassured, as if this mild-mannered reporter had a cape hidden under his shirt. When they looked back toward the kitchen, they could see shadows moving against the wall. Something was moving around in there, but the shadows made no sense at all.

"What's that?" Samuels asked, suddenly nervous at the prospect that there might be more here than he could handle with bluff and a gun.

"I think that must be our host," Stacy offered in a voice that sounded like her stomach had just dropped into one of the deepest canyons the world had to offer.

"Let's check it out," Samuels said, stepping forward and trying to replace stark terror with bravado.

"Nope, not me," Stacy said firmly. "The last policeman that said that – and, may add, in the same tone of voice – got fried. I don't intend to volunteer for a barbeque. Especially if I'm on the menu. We were told to stay in the hall and not following directions here might be very bad for one's health."

"Be reasonable," Paul said, patting her hand and trying to follow Samuels' lead, despite her resistance holding him back. "Whoever that's in there could have killed us outside. Instead we were saved. I think."

"So maybe they just want us to walk into the kitchen to make it easier to get us into the pots," Stacy said, not at all convinced that moving was a good idea.

"Well, I don't think it's a good idea just to stand around and wait for whatever happens to just happen," Samuels said. "I'm going to stir that pot and see what turns up."

Paul was not sure he agreed with Samuels metaphor, especially after discussing famous cannibals, but he did agree that just standing around was not a great idea.

"Come on, Stacy," Paul said gently, like urging a hesitant colt. "You don't want to be left out here alone."

Stacy hesitated just a second the relaxed her grip a little on Paul's arm. "You'd better tip big," she said. "This tour guide business is harder on the nerves than it looks."

Paul smiled at her and took her hand. That would give him a little more freedom of movement than her hold on his arm allowed. "I like your style," he said.

"I just hope we are around long enough for that to mean something," Stacy said softly, following along closely behind Paul, crowding him, even though intellectually she knew that his body would prove an inadequate shield if their host took a shot with one of those energy weapons the lizards used with such deadly effect.

Samuels edged himself into the lead, gun ready and finger just a little tighter on the trigger than needed. He paused by the entrance to the back room, which proved indeed to be the kitchen, though there were no boiling pots on the stove waiting for tidbits of humanity. Samuels waited for Stacy and Paul to join him, then motioned them to the left side of the jam, while he hugged the right side with his back to the wall. Paul thought that ideally the wall should be made of six inch steel plates. He didn't think anything less would stop one of those lasers. Certainly not the cheap cement board that made up the walls of this old house.

Samuels used the butt of his gun to bang on the doorjamb. The sound echoed slightly in the hall as the house shook once again.

"Come out of there with your hands up. This is the police!" Samuels didn't sound as confident as he should, but maybe it was still more confident than the situation warranted. His backup may or may not be on the way, since it all rested on the Dispatcher being curious when neither he nor Fisher responded. If, that is, they even tried to call. It all boiled down now on how much attention the racket outside was generating. The Caruthers House was set well back from the road and it was on the far west side of town on top of that. It was a lonely place at the best of times and these days most people were staying inside and away from the woods at night. There were too many strange things happening and the good citizens of Flagstaff were too spooked to be poking around a house with a haunting reputation. On the other side, it was the middle of summer and, even thought tourism was down, the sleepy college town normally swelled from its sixty thousand all-year residents to over a million people, many of them Phoenix residents trying to escape the sweltering Phoenix summers. *Someone* was surely out and about and *someone* would surely see what was going on and call in the Marines. Wouldn't they?

"You are instructed to remain where you are." It was the same tinny mechanical voice that they had heard outside the building. Paul briefly wondered if the voice was coming from another speaker or if the intercom had realistically reproduced a very tinny sounding voice.

"Still feel like playing super cop or do you want to wait this one out for the cavalry?" Paul asked.

"We are the cavalry," Samuels answered shortly. "Unless you haven't noticed."

Samuels wiggled his way around until he was almost facing the door, then took a two handed grip on his gun. "Come on out or we'll have to come in there and pull you out!" he yelled.

"There is no cause for violence," the voice responded. "There are no obstructions. Enter if you must but do not disturb us again. The situation is critical."

Paul and Samuels exchanged looks. Samuels looked a little deflated. He was not, after all, going to have to storm the bastions, guns blazing. It must have been a vaguely disappointing moment for him, though Paul was just as happy not to be around if there was going to be a fire fight. All he had was a stick.

Samuels wiggled his way around until he was almost facing the door, then took a two-handed grip on his gun. "Come on out or we'll have to come in there and pull you out," he yelled.

"There is no cause for violence," the Voice responded. "There are no obstructions. Enter if you must but do not disturb us again. The situation is critical." Samuels looked a little deflated. He was, after all, not going to have to storm the bastions, guns blazing. It must have been a vaguely disappointing moment for him, though Paul was just as happy not to be around if there was going to be a firefight. If you don't take a knife to a gunfight, you sure don't go in with just a stick.

"I don't trust them," Samuels whispered.

"Good," Stacy offered, and then scrunched closer to Paul.

"Look, just don't go in shooting," Paul said, more nervous than he wanted to admit.

Samuels took a deep breath and gripped his gun tighter. Plastering himself against the doorjamb, he gave Paul a short nod, then spun around and into the… kitchen. Gun ready and looking for trouble, all he found were pots and pans. Paul watched Samuels' back very carefully, expecting to see a ray of light stab through it like a finger from God. But nothing happened as Samuels swiveled from side to side looking – maybe hoping – for something to shoot. After a few seconds, his shoulders relaxed and Paul took that for a good sign, stepping into the kitchen with the improvised club at the ready.

It was, after all, just a kitchen. True, there were wires and pieces of equipment slapped around the room with mild abandon – or a plan that the humans could not recognize – but there were no man-sized pots bubbling on the stove or dog carcasses dangling from hooks over the island work station in the center of the large room. Just stacks of dog food in one corner and jars of some strange looking… goop filling a pantry. Nothing that Dr. Demento would use to dress up a ghoul's set for Halloween Eve or even a Ripper family picnic. Rather disappointing and drab after the hallway and the excitement outside.

Stacy crept in behind Paul and began opening cabinets and looking in the cupboards. "Well, we lived through that. Now what?" Stacy asked.

"What are you looking for?" Paul asked. "Body parts?"

Stacy shuddered. "I forgot all about that. I was looking for some Pringles or something. I'm hungry. But there's nothing here but pet food."

"Oh. I bought some Snickers this morning."

"OK. Give. I'm starving and it doesn't look like we'll make it to a drive-thru any time soon."

"Oh. Well, see, they're in the glove compartment in the car. But if you find a knife let me know." Paul winced at the look Stacy threw his direction.

"You two forget about food," Samuels snapped. He checked his gun and slammed the magazine back in place. "I think it's time we met our host. Or hosts."

"Look, just don't in go *there* shooting," Paul said, pointing to the other door leading out of the kitchen. He was more nervous than he wanted to admit. "Maybe these are the good buys."

"Right. No shooting until I see the whites of their eyes," Samuels snarled.

"If they have eyes," Stacy muttered, huddling closer to Paul. "They said they don't want to be bothered. Are you really going in there?"

She was answered by a high-pitched whine that came from a room off to the right of the kitchen, the one in the direction Samuels had chosen. It started slow and low, but grew rapidly and all three ducked down behind the dubious shelter of the kitchen island, expecting at any minute to be sliced and diced by light or engulfed in some strange alien conflagration. But nothing like that happened, either, and when the whine died, the three cautiously peeked over and around the work island to see… nothing. Just a swinging door innocently propped opened into another room.

"Now, that was exciting," Stacy ventured. "This place reminds me of that movie about the computer that wanted to make a baby."

"*Rosemary's Baby*? The novel?" Paul prompted.

"Yeah. That's it."

"I think this is getting a little carried away. We need to check out that room," Samuels said, motioning to the now-open door.

"What about this one," Stacy asked, pointing to a very solid looking door on the far side of the kitchen.

"Probably goes to a basement. These old houses usually had a root cellar or something. We need to go in this room because that's where the activity is," Samuels insisted.

"Yeah. Right," Paul sighed. "Let's get with it."

"Can I pee first?" Stacy asked, looking around for a powder room.

"No!" Paul and Samuels answered in unison.

They worked their way across the kitchen and into what was obviously a dining area and was probably still used as such. Except for the staggering amount of electronics, stacked around and over antique china cabinets, buffets, and sideboards, it was nothing more than a large, turn of the century dining room complete with a large dining table, completely devoid of anything sinister. In fact, it was the only flat surface in the house that they trio had seen that was not covered in some way with electronics or other gear. There was a large screen television in one corner of the room, but it was dark, and several smaller ones scattered around, but the only ones that were turned on showed scrolling lines of computer code and nothing else. Those were sitting next to computer keyboards or old typewriters that had been wired into the electronics around them and were obvious equipment monitors of some sort. The smaller dark ones could be anything from network fare to something more arcane.

"Do you think that's a sacrificial table?" Stacy asked, noting that there was nothing on it but space. That just earned her baleful glares from the two men. "Sorry. Too many viewings of *The Brotherhood of Satan*. I hope there are no evil spirits hanging around."

"You know that movie?" Paul asked incredulously.

"Uh-huh. I like off-the-wall films."

"Yeah. Me too," Paul admitted. "You're the only girl I've ever met with two brain cells to rub together that does."

"Hey, who said I had brains? I'm here with you, aren't I?"

"Point taken," Paul admitted, though her sarcasm was somewhat blunted when she stepped closer to him when the house shuddered again, grabbing on for comfort. The signs of an on-going battle had been apparent the whole time, so pervasive that they were easy to ignore, but the last couple had been more pronounced – almost like they had brought bigger guns to bear, Paul thought sourly – and that last one shook the entire house to its very foundations.

While the two had been talking, Samuels had been walking the around the room. He was stopped by a small door leading out the other side of the dining room.

"If you two PBS movie critics will knock it off, this looks like the only way out of here except back through the kitchen or through a set of double doors that probably go into the hall behind that china cabinet over there," Samuels said. "And there's something behind here."

"I wonder what's on," Stacy mused, walking over to the large screen television. She hunted for a second, then found the power switch and turned the set on.

"Do you really think we should go in there?" Paul asked. "We wouldn't want to surprise them and we were told to wait in the hall."

"Oh, I think they know we're here," Stacy said. The television set had warmed up and the three of them were clearly visible standing around the dining room. Somewhere there was a television camera aimed right on them but, though all three looked back at the place where the camera should be, they could see nothing that looked like a video camera, just another jumble of electronics with one piece that had a glass bead in it the size of the button. But that couldn't be a camera, could it? The case was too small and the color on the big screen was too vibrant and the details too precise to come from anything *that* small. Right? Everybody knew that the network cameras that produced similar quality were easily the size of a skinny footlocker.

"Then I guess they won't be surprised by the door bursting open," Paul said. "Maybe this time we can just knock."

"I guess," Samuels agreed reluctantly. "If they can see where we are with that much detail, they can just put a few bullets or lightning bolts through the wall and be done with it."

"OK. So, knock," Paul said again.

Samuels banged on the door with the heel of his hand. "Alright in there! We know you see us. We're coming in!" he yelled.

"Well, I was thinking of something more polite," Paul admitted, "but I guess that will have to do."

"You were instructed to wait in the hall." The voice came from behind them and Paul, at least, was so startled he almost wished he had a pair of Depends. They all spun to look at this new, unexpected threat, even Samuels momentarily forgetting that the real threat was just on the other side of the door.

But the room behind them was empty, making Stacy's comments about evil spirits ring ominously in everyone's mind. But Samuels immediately returned his attention to the door when Paul gestured toward some speakers partially hidden in the china cabinet.

"Intercom, again," Paul said.

"Yeah. Well, we're about to have a face-to-face."

"Whatever. I still think we should wait for the cavalry," Paul said.

"Look, I told you before, we *are* the cavalry," Samuels said, his impatience showing thorough his self-imposed calm. "I didn't call for a back-up. I don't think anyone else knows we're here. Whatever support we get from the National Guard that's been poking around here lately is likely to come in the form of bullets heading indiscriminately in our direction."

"Our own people wouldn't shoot us!" Stacy protested.

"Who knows what they'd do. How much training do you think those weekend warriors get in resisting alien invasions? They could just as well assume *we're* the bad guys and then sort it out later," Samuels said.

"Invasion of the Body Snatchers."

"Oh," Stacy said, catching Paul's reference to the classic film.

"This is up to us, here and now," Samuels said. "We either make common cause with whatever is on the other side of this door or common cause with whatever is outside."

"Or common cause with neither," Paul interjected into Samuels speech.

"Yeah. Maybe it's us humans against the Universe and there are no good guys, just bad and really bad. But any way you slice this pie, we're in a load of hurts and we don't know a damned thing about what's what and who's who. At least there are some answers in there and I'm tired of waiting for them to reveal what's behind door number three."

Samuels turned back to the door, determined that he was not going to stop this time, no matter what. Of course, Paul reflected, Samuels did not seem the type to have seen movies like *The Blob* or *Predator* or *Alien* or any other film that suggested that alien creatures that weren't bothering you were best to just leave alone and find the quickest way out of Dodge. *Not that the ways out of Dodge are free from rampaging lizards*, Paul reflected with a grimace, what he saw right then looked more like a free ride to those saucers in *Independence Day* than Oz's yellow brick road. So when Samuels started to beat on the door again, Paul stopped him.

"Let me try," he asked. After all, an avid science fiction fan would have a lot better chance in talking to an alien than someone whose library revolved around Mary Higgins Clark. When Samuels nodded, finally, Paul stepped to the door and gave a polite knock, though what an alien might think was polite would be anyone's guess. "Look. We are going to come in. We need to know what is going on and who you are. Maybe we can help and maybe not, but we'll just be a nuisance until we can see for ourselves what's happening."

"So maybe they should just kill us now and forget about calling the Truly Nolan guy with the funny VW outfitted like a mouse," Stacy muttered into the silence.

Suddenly, several of the televisions sprang into life. What they showed was not something that the humans cared to see.

"You can follow events from where you are."

For several minutes, they watched the televisions. What they saw was chilling. Ships, like the ones that they had seen in clearing, and other, larger craft, were swooping down on the house and pelting it with everything from beam weapons to explosives. The woods surrounding the house were ablaze and every time one of the menacing craft made a success pass at the house, they could feel the building shake. There was no question that the attacks and the impacts they felt were matched, no question that a deadly battle was raging just a few feet away and that any minute the world could come crashing in on them. Nor was there any doubt that it was sure death outside the protection they currently enjoyed from the occupants of the house.

But the battle was not one-sided. They could see light beams striking out from what must be the house's turret and an occasional ground-to-air-missile reach out to the invaders. Most of them were shrugged off by the craft's version of the house's force field or by anti-missile tactics, but while they were watching, one of the attacker's luck ran out and the diving ship vanished in a ball of flame.

"Mother f…"

"Yeah," Paul agreed with Samuels' choked off curse. "I think we're about to hit the evening news."

"How long before the military arrives?" Stacy asked.

Samuels looked at his watch. "You know, it feels like we have been here for hours, but it's only been a few minutes. I'd think help should be on the way, but I don't know how much time went by before they noticed something going on here and called it in. Then they'd have to scramble out of Vegas or Tucson and flying time would be just a few minutes, so not long."

"What about the Guard?" Stacy asked.

"There may be some ground troops rolling in trucks or coming in on Hueys, but I'd bet the choppers can't get too close," Samuels said.

"Yeah," Paul agreed. "The Army Guard has a few Apache's, but they wouldn't stand a chance against fixed wings and I'll bet there's no way that the military can get a radar lock on those suckers. They'd keep the Apaches out of this and wait for the real air force to show with their big guns."

"Think we'll last that long?" Stacy's question was punctuated by another shake that knocked dust from the ceiling and temporarily blanked out all the monitors.

"No," Samuels replied decisively. "There's too much going on out there and I'm not sure this home-made crap will hold up. We gotta get out of here and if those are the good guys in there," he said, nodding to the other room, "then they gotta come with us. Otherwise we're all toast."

"The Air Force..." Stacy started.

"The Air Force," Paul said, "is just as likely to lay a five kiloton bunker buster on us as not. Or a tactical nuke. No one knows who's here."

"Yeah. I wonder why those heavies haven't used something like that on us before now," Samuels said.

"Maybe they'll want whoever is in here alive," Paul ventured. "But I'll bet of the lizards don't crack the defenses before our guys arrive, they'll eliminate the evidence and boogie."

Samuels thought about that a second, then nodded. "Right. And the answers are still in there."

He turned back to the door and knocked – politely this time – again. "Listen up in there! We need to talk. We can either come in shooting and take our chances with the lizards or we work out an alliance so we can all get out of this mess alive. What's it gonna be? Guns or diplomacy?"

All three waited, not noticing that they were holding their breath, until the speakers came back to life.

"There is no cause for violence," the voice repeated itself once again, and all three eyes turned to the hellstorm that was raging outside and wondered exactly what these creatures considered violent. "The door is unlocked, but do not disturb us. The situation now is critical and all our lives hang in the balance."

"In the balance of *what*," Stacy wondered aloud.

Samuels thought that that might just be an understatement, but he didn't hesitate. With gun at the ready, he kicked in the door and stepped through, covering the room as his brain tried to take in what his eyes were seeing.

CHAPTER ELEVEN
June 20, 2002
Flagstaff, Arizona

The scene that greeted them was much like what they had found in the rest of the house. The room, lit only by the monitors and power lights, was obviously a library in a past life, complete with high ceiling and a rolling ladder. Like every other room in this crazy mansion, it was crammed with off-the-shelf computer and electronics equipment, many still with price tags on them, wired into each other and a series of computers in what looked like a haphazard manner. But some plan must have been at worked, since they all seemed to be on and doing something.

The major difference in this room was the large number of monitors. The ones in the dining room were just little brothers to these. There must have been fifty sets of phosphorus glowing away in the large room already made cramped by the electronics. Like the others, these showed scenes in and around the house in startling detail. There was no doubt in Paul's mind that they have been in the eye of one camera or another from the moment they entered the lane up to the house until right then with the possible exception of their side trip into the woods. There was not much showing into the depth of the forest, but every square inch of the wood's perimeter was covered and into the woods for a depth of a dozen feet or so and every room in the house was depicted on a monitor. From what Paul could see, ever room was packed with equipment. Some of the cameras were centered on banks of flashing lights, most blue but some yellow and flickering orange, but the rest just showed room after room of – presumably stolen – equipment.

One huge projector splashed a video-wall-like image on a screen that had been built across one end of the room, hiding the windows and the electronics stacked on the bookshelves that framed the windows along that wall. What they saw on the screen was not encouraging. The house was completely surrounded and not by the US Marines. The woods all around the property were crawling with lizard-creatures and each one was taking pot-shots at the structure that housed Paul and Stacy and Samuels. If one of the shields failed, there was no arguing the point that the entire building would be riddled like the nizzles in Swiss cheese.

What was worse werc thc spacccraft. Thc US had pioneered the concept of close combat support, but the way that these things were weaving in and out of fire patterns above the house would have made Top Gun pilots drool. Not a single shot failed to hit the shields. Everything from the ships hit the house. *Everything*. From the monitors, they could not see a single crater in the yard where something had missed its target. Talk about smart bombs… The creatures in the woods were not as accurate. Trees and bushes burned from missed laser fire, Paul's car and probably Fisher's car were in flames, though it was hard to see Fisher's car through the smoke. Still, Paul was pretty sure that both of those vehicles were worthless and he wouldn't have taken a bet that Samuels' car was in any better shape, wherever it was parked.

Any police or small military unit, especially a Guard contingent, in the area would think it was suicide to approach the house. They'd be right, too. Help from the outside was not happening unless the lizards went into hibernation or the our guys with the big guns showed up. Paul felt things would be over long before either of those options manifested themselves.

That this was the control room, the heart of the house's defense, was obvious. What was missing was a head. At first, it was impossible to discern whether there was a living being controlling the defenses or something mechanical, though the stacks of computer printouts and miscellaneous papers scattered around the room suggested that there was something more than artificial intelligences in the room.

But what really caught Paul's eye and held it like the hypnotic gaze of a snake was a little workshop at the opposite side of the room from the projection screen. Above the work bench was a shelf lined with toys. Paul recognized the voice controlled plane, the knight and dragon, the tub-toy fish, several miniature military vehicles on tiny pedestals, mostly tanks and armored personal carriers, that he had never seen before, and a dozen others that were almost-familiar, like the prototype of some of Jeremy's toys that Paul had bought in the past.

The workbench was as big a hodge-podge as the rest of the room, but Paul recognized some of the equipment from his short run in the Air Force. No question that the large box-like thing was a high precision soldering station, similar to the military version that Paul knew cost close to ten grand. There were various clamps and claws on stands and a huge magnifying glass, a microscope set to allow access to micro-miniaturized circuit boards (and who had hands steady enough to solder something *that* small?) and a rack of tools that had never been designed by men or for the hands of men was neatly mounted to the wall by the bench.

Paul had found his toy maker. Or at least his toy maker's workshop. Damned if he wouldn't have believed that elves were doing the work if someone had suggested it at that time. For all he knew, the lizards were just a bunch of poorly drawn Grinchs out to steal Christmas. That was a sobering thought. Paul was not entirely sure he would be around for Christmas to see if these lizards had found repentance and departed Whoville, formerly known as Flagstaff, without burning the entire mountain to the ground.

There was no furniture to speak of in the room, just a wide bank of monitors and consoles arched before the main screen like, well, remarkably like the control room in a *Star Wars* battle cruiser. From their vantage, these were largely hidden by a row of stacked computers. That was where Samuels, then finally Paul and Stacy centered their attention. That was where anything living would be hiding and Samuels held his gun ready to ventilate anyone or anything that tried to get nasty. Paul noted, however, that his gun was not exactly steady, even in Samuels' two-handed grip.

But what rose from behind the electronics wall was not a lizard. And it was not human, even though the shadow it cast vaguely resembled a man.

As the humanoid shape rose, the lights began to brighten just enough to allow the humans to take in the details. What initially faced them was a creature that had a torso like a human and a bump that served as a head. It had two arms that ended in… wiggly things. But it was only half there. It was similar to a mannequin riding a sewer cover floating in midair with nothing below the cover. It was cut off at the waist. Paul's first impression was of a gumdrop dressed up to look human. It did not look menacing. Just, well, the not-all-there look made Paul's stomach queasy. But those wiggly things. They could do precision soldering very deftly, Paul would bet. They didn't look like they had bones, so they could slip into spaces and around corners where human fingers could never reach. Some of the tools on the bench suddenly made more sense.

"Excuse me for a moment," it said, and the flying sled bobbed down and back out of sight. When the creature popped back up it had a complicated device over the top of its "head." A couple of "feelers" or sensory nodes extended above it, which he swiveled so they faced the large screen projection. Two more antenna -- antennii? -- popped up and centered back on the humans.

The Gumby creature sprouted two more tentacles that stretched down below the level where the humans could see. Samuels tensed and Stacy stepped back, pulling Paul with her. But when the creatures tentacles came back up, they were not pointed at the humans. Instead, they were covered with a sleeve that had wires running from the end, dropping out of sight below the hovering sewer lid, probably wired into something as crazy as the rest of the house.

The creature did nothing to show that's its attention had shifted from the humans to the large display, but Paul had the distinct impression that the sensors covering the group were no longer the center of the Gumby's attention. When the thing began waving its wired tentacles at the screen, Paul was even more certain that they were on ignore or somehow only passively in the creatures attention area. But the results from the creature's arm-waving were made dramatically obvious when the defenses from the house reached out and swatted one of the dodging ships from the sky. The creature's attention seemed spin back around and gave the humans a very disconcerting human-like shrug. It had plainly told them that it was intelligent and capable of defending its home.

"Holy shit," Samuels muttered, the gun now hanging limply, forgotten in his hand.

"My God," Paul breathed. "I knew, but… I still didn't believe."

"Well, this is no time for Halloween," Stacy said, trying to shake the two men out of their shock and awe. "There're lizards out there that're trying to kill us. We either need to help or get out of here."

Without warning, another being popped up from behind the electronics. This new arrival immediately began growling and hissing at its companion. This one had true hands, not wiggles. Unlike the gumdrop, it held a keyboard in its four hands and appeared to be conducting its own war with the keyboard and not with virtual reality gloves, as Paul labeled the gumdrop's decorations. And once it rose to its feet, it was nine feet of rippling muscle from the head to the haunches and probably stood a good four and a half feet to the top of its back, but with its torso extended, it was a good eight feet tall with a face full of teeth and commanded by steal eyes.

"Damn," Samuels muttered, taking in this new addition to the menagerie. What stood before them now was a cross between an escaped circus lion and one of Edgar Rice Burrows' green men from Mars. Four armed, four legged, a head covered with a course mane, and three-inch canine teeth that glistened in the light enough to testify that its ancestors were certainly not grass eaters. This new addition still did not push the fight or flight button in Samuels. His gun did not rise to cover the creature, nor did his feet seek the nearest exit. Despite its ferocious appearance, the new creature gave off an air of warmth and friendliness, something like the cartoon lion Mufasa from Disney's *The Lion King*: big, mean, ferocious, but kind and loving all at the same time.

"My friend says you are very astute," the gumdrop said. Or sounded. Paul wasn't sure since he could see nothing like a mouth and nothing moved, but the words were definitely coming from the gumdrop and Paul would have put down money that it was the same voice that had come from the speakers. Maybe it was a soft computer with manipulation appendages? No. Paul was certain it was living. Maybe a cyborg, he decided without conviction. "You are astute," it said again to Stacy directly. "You are vulgar," it amended to Samuels, just so there was no doubt about whose comment was astute and whose not. "It is unfortunate that you discovered us just when our enemies arrived. If we had not been forced to save you, we might have avoided detection long enough to complete our project or relocate to a new location. Now our lives and yours are at risk. You have endangered many thousands more with your snooping."

The gumdrop twisted back to the screen and directed more fire, this time at the gathering creatures in the woods.

"You forced me to reveal our true position when you foolishly invited attack," it continued. One could not say "over its shoulder" since the words now appeared to come from its back, but the effect was the same as being lectured by an irritated professor who was scribbling on a chalkboard. "The Aeolians suspected our presence, but had not yet located us. They were too uncertain to call overt attention to their presence, as surely your authorities will investigate this action tonight and perhaps learn much from the wreckage. You may have inadvertently destroyed many, many years of work and brought death upon us all."

The gumdrop let out a long sigh. Its tone was resigned, not accusing. It sounded like a far away freight whistle on a dark and lonely night. Perhaps it had expected this long before now and only wished for something better. Perhaps it saw the end of a long struggle coming out badly. Or perhaps it just had gas. Paul had no clue. It was, after all, alien.

"Are they the ones who have been killing people?" Stacy ventured.

"Regrettably, yes. They do not care much for the lives of others and I would think they believed their technology sufficiently advanced to allow them a free hand on your planet. They could have remained undetected for as long as they thought it would take to locate us or ascertain that we were not here. Then they would either leave or conquer you. Their thoughts are hard for others to judge."

"If you knew they were killing people, why didn't you contact the police," Samuels demanded, outraged that murder had gone unreported and unstopped when there was the chance that something could have prevented the deaths that had plagued Northern Arizona over the past few months.

"What could you have done?" the gumdrop asked. "Their ships are invisible to your detection devices, their weapons far superior, and their mind set much more steeped in blood. If they had not found us, they would have believed we died when they destroyed our vessel years ago and would have dismissed any of the signals they may have detected as an anomaly. In a few more days, they would probably have left."

"Or not," Stacy said. "They seem to like the local *Carte du jour*."

"Yes. They may have created an ongoing problem for your world. I do not think they came with enough force to take this planet. I do not think the politics in the Alliance would have allowed that, either," the gumdrop admitted. "But to raid for sport and food, that they can do. And you may have noticed that any warm-blooded creature is appealing to their tastes."

Paul had been watching the screens. The intensity was increasing, if that was possible, and the house shaking like a rock band was rehearsing in the basement.

"You say you've sent a signal?" Paul asked.

"We have been testing our sub-space transceiver. It has taken a long time to build and the process is clumsy with the primitive electronics your species produces, but I think we were having some success."

"Is that why the lizards are here, then?" Samuels demanded.

"Yes, probably.

"So it is your fault these creatures are here?" asked Samuels, his tone belligerent.

"Assessing blame for their presence is pointless. They may have left a few telltales in this system after they destroyed the Hiver craft, just in case there were survivors. Our first trial transmissions may have alerted them and drawn a scout team back to the area. They would not have left a full military mission here. I think that the Alliance would have detected. Your planet is interdicted, you know."

"Uh-huh. I just wanted our priorities straight," Samuels said, ignoring Paul's attempts to calm him down. "These things outside are in no way your responsibility, right?"

"It is possible we drew them, it is possible not."

"Yeah, well, these lizards may have killed one of my officers, I'm told."

"Regrettably, yes. They are also most likely the source of the other killings we have heard on your news broadcasts in recent days."

"Well, that could make you an accessory," Samuels said, satisfied that he had someone he could blame.

"I don't think that is important now," Paul interjected before Samuels could work himself up to giving the aliens their Miranda rights. "We need to worry about what's outside."

"Like to see you cuff the little guy, anyway," Stacy muttered. "Retractable hands."

"That looks more like a full attack than a scouting mission," Paul commented dryly, gesturing at the screens as the house defenses centered in on a group of aliens trying to rush the back porch. Their smoking remains littered the yard in the afterglow from the defense lasers.

"Yes. It does seem to be a recon in force," the alien admitted.

"Well, did your signal go through? Is there help from your people coming? And, hey! Hey! Why are we interdicted?" Stacy wanted to know.

The gumdrop let out a long sigh that sounded more like a steam engine venting than anything from a living creature. "We do not know if the signal was successful. We have sent trial transmissions over the past few of your months, but have not received a reply. It is difficult to tell if the signal failed to transmit or we are just not receiving. With this sub-standard equipment wired together without proper testing tools, it is more guess than science. We adjust a little and send again, but no one responds."

"Well, it looks like someone heard you," Paul said. He had been watching the screen. It was a fascinating display, like a video game on steroids, but Paul knew it was much more real than that. "And it looks like they will do whatever it takes to make sure you do not survive."

"Yes, they would not like us to contact our people. It would be most distressing for them. But they could have picked up our attempts with telltales and the signals still not gone through."

"You've been here for years," Samuels said, "things can change a lot in that amount of time. How can you be sure your 'people' are still out there."

"Oh, the Grand Alliance is still there. It has been for several centuries and even pressure from the Cescarian Theocracy could not have disrupted it over a few dozen years." Another aircraft mushroomed into a ball of flame over the front yard, scattering flaming parts through the woods, coincidentally disrupting what looked like an armored attack the lizards were trying to mount from the south. That cat let out a triumphant screech that sent chills down Paul's spine. "And even the Aeolians would not be so foolish to align with the Theocracy."

"So you've been stealing from our stores to set up your little radio all this time, huh?" Samuels wanted to know, the cop in him more interested in solving unsolved mysteries than in intergalactic politics.

"Well, that is only partially correct. It is difficult to purchase what we needed in the quantities we needed without calling attention to ourselves. Some we purchased by mail. But all the merchandise owners have been fully compensated or their insurance companies have. We are not thieves. Excuse me. It looks like they have decided to attack in force."

The gumdrop focused its full attention back to the screen, assisting the lion creature, who had been furiously banging away at a keyboard during the past few minutes.

The humans stood in silence, each watching the screens with their own thoughts churning over what the alien had said and what they saw before them. With the exception of the muffled explosions outside and the clicking of keyboards, there was no noise in the room louder than humans breathing and hearts pounding. Outside, the screen looked like the most exciting sequence Industrial Light and Magic could ever conceive of producing. The house was surrounded, but the shields seemed to be holding well. Most of the attempts at hitting the aircraft failed, either deflected by the craft's own shields or by superior flying. But not all.

The lizards on the ground, however, were taking a bit of a beating. The house's defense was chewing up little pockets of defenders and, now that everything looked like it was on line, the lizards' portable shields were only partially effective against the larger weapons the house was able to throw at them. The woods were burning in several places and nothing was helping the creatures where the forest had caught on fire.

Certainly, Paul thought, the skies above this part of Flagstaff must look like the Fourth of July over the Statue of Liberty. God help the Guardsmen that stumbled into this fight.

"I feel like we are in the Alamo," Stacy whispered after a particularly intense exchange.

"I don't like just standing around," Samuels responded, hefting his gun nervously. "If this is the Alamo, I want to do something before we're overrun."

"Remember the Alamo," Paul said.

"Cute," Stacy muttered back.

"No, I mean *do* you remember the Alamo?"

"Yeah. The good guys got slaughtered."

"Yeah. That's what I was thinking, too. We need to get word out to the Marines or somebody. The Texans could have won that battle if the reinforcements had arrived just a little earlier," Paul said.

"What reinforcements? I don't remember anything about them getting help." Stacy twisted around, looking for a phone, damning the cell companies that had created an industry that everybody needed but priced themselves to a point where the people who *really* needed the phones couldn't afford the charges for extra minutes. Like her. Like *now*. Someday, the cell companies were going to pay for that.

"They didn't. That's the point. Of, a few trickled in before the Mexicans launched their final attack, but not enough to make a difference. But Sam Houston and a bunch of Texas Army folks took on the Mexicans and later wiped out General Antonio López de Santa Anna's army at the Battle of San Jacinto."

"They really kicked some butt," Samuels added. "Best numbers had the Texas out gunned two to one, the Mexicans had cannon, and they were an experienced Army while the Texans had not had much training as a group. I guess you could say that the Texas forces were militiamen and volunteers governed mostly by whim. Mostly just Indian fighters, barely aware there was supposed to be a chain of command. But they really stopped old Santa Anna."

"But that didn't do William B. Travis, Davie Crockett, or Jim Bowie and the Blue Ridge Boys any good 'cause they was 'already deed,' as they would say in Texas," Paul said.

"Oh, you're just such a comfort." Stacy lapsed into silence and Paul and Samuels joined her. Samuels played with his gun, passing it from one had to another, but Paul was lost in his thoughts. From what Gumby had said, there was a lot at stake here. Perhaps more at stake than the Battle of the Alamo had been for Texas. And the Alamo had made America. Paul remembered *that* lesson well from when he was a kid Biggs Air Force Base in El Paso. It was almost a litany: Without the Alamo there could have been no Battle of San Jacinto. Without the Battle of San Jacinto, Texas could not have existed. Without Texas, the westward expansion of the U.S. would have been thwarted. Without the West, the U.S. would have remained an Atlantic power, and not risen to become a world power. Without the U.S. as a world power, the world as we see it today would not exist. A logic chain.

One could argue that, if the US was meant to be a major power, then it would have made it another way. But one could not argue with history. It was the Alamo that set the stage for the expansion of the United States from sea to shining sea and any other "what if's" were just intellectual exercises. Or, at least, that's what the Texans would say.

"You know, the Texans took a full day of cannon bombardment and didn't lose a man," Paul muttered. "They held out for thirteen or fourteen days. Maybe 187 or as many as 250, no one's sure, but 250 max against about 2500 regular Mexican Army members is pretty heavy odds. History says only 1500 or so made the attack, but six-to-one or ten-to-one, doesn't seem to make much difference to me."

"In the end, it didn't," Samuels reminded him.

"Yeah, well we probably won't have two weeks to worry about it. Even the Georgia Guard could get here in that time. But this'll be over pretty quick," Paul said. He had been watching the screens. The lizards had finally mounted something like a coordinated offensive. A group of ground pounders had been hammering away at a corner of the house nearest to the woods. From what Paul could see, the air cover was also pouring a lot of their fire into the same area and, if Paul could judge by the monitors, it looked like the defensive screen was weakening.

"What do you mean," Samuels demanded.

"Don't look at the main screen," Paul directed. "Look at the pile there to the right. Third row down, second in. That's the back of the house near the woods. See how the image is flickering?"

"Yeah. Looks like a bad set."

"It's not. I've been watching it," Paul said. "The set isn't flickering, it's the images we're seeing through the shield. The shield isn't holding well there and the lizards have been working on it."

"Oh!" Stacy gasped, pointing to the main screen.

One of the attacking ships had not managed to dodge the house entirely. Paul had not seen what made the hit, maybe it was even one of its own side's weapons that had sliced through one of the wings, but the ship was falling right toward the house, growing in the camera as they watched. Paul glanced over at the secondary monitor and held his breath. The weak spot was right where the craft was headed. If it fell into the house and the shield failed …

"Get down!"

Paul grabbed Stacy and Samuels and pulled them to the floor right as a tremendous explosion shook the house. Dust and plaster rained down on them, stacks of equipment toppled in several places, sparking and smoking and dying.

"What happened!" Stacy demanded, as she stood up, dusting herself off.

"One of the attaching ships crashed into the house. It overloaded the shields."

Paul looked at the monitor, but several screens were black, that one in particular. The cat-thing was pounding away on two keyboards at once, hissing and growling as it tried to bring the screens back on line, but Paul didn't think it was having any luck.

"We are breached. I can cover that approach from other directions for a few minutes, but I do not think the screens will come back up with the wreckage in the way," the gumdrop said.

"How can we help," Paul asked.

"Do you have weapons?"

"I've got a gun," Samuels said, though he was pretty sure that they already figured that out from the way he had been threatening them earlier.

"I've got a stick," Paul said, knowing that that was one of the lamest things he had ever said.

"I gotta pee," Stacy said, which at the moment was the most important thing in her life. The screens might have held enough for them to be protected from the full impact of the spaceship hitting the house, but it had sure not been enough to protect her bladder from the sudden impact of fear-driven adrenalin.

Paul pointed back the way they had come. There was a small bathroom off the kitchen. The door had been open and Paul had noticed that, while it had its compliment of electronic equipment, it otherwise looked functional.

"Be careful."

"Watch the door," Stacy demanded, but Paul just smiled. Whatever was going to happen, watching the door was about the best he could do.

The cat thing let out a howl and a series of hisses that raised the hackles on Paul's neck.

"They are preparing to rush the house. We can stop most of them before they get inside, but we are likely to be invaded. The monitors are not giving up a clear view. You must stop the Aeolians before they reach here."

"Look, you got a plan B?" Samuels demanded.

"We have an escape route, but it will take a few moments to activate. They must not reach this room before we finish preparations."

"OK. I'll go." Samuels turned to Paul. "You wait here."

"Sure. Not like I can do much with a stick."

"You could poke 'em in the eye," Samuels offered.

"I could. Oh, hey, you'd better be good with that thing."

"Why?"

"Those things are wearing some kind of armor or ballistic cloth suits or something. It'll take a head shot to take one down."

"You must hurry. They are crossing the lawn now. Systel will go with you," the gumdrop said. "She will guide you."

With a few hisses and growls, the cat unlimbered itself and stalked around the electronics wall to lead the way past Samuels into a far part of the house. She was a massive creature, rippling muscles and fiery-eyed. As she moved past, Paul could feel her body heat, something well over that of a human's. Whatever fires she had inside burned hot.

"Good luck," Paul called.

"Don't worry about me. I'll be right back," Samuels said, popping a full cartridge in the automatic's firing chamber as he ducked out of the room.

"Well, good luck, anyway."

"You must hurry! This is difficult for me without Systel's assistance and sensors indicate that there is movement in the back of the house!"

"On it," Samuels said, and ran out of the room behind the giant cat.

Paul stood in the middle of the room, just him and the gumdrop, and felt a moment of panic. If the aliens had been trying to split them up, then they had just succeeded. Paul had never felt so alone or helpless in his life.

"I must concentrate on the main defenses," the gumdrop said as a row of monitors flickered into life. "You must monitor their progress. Inform me at once if an Aeolian manages to get past the kitchen."

Paul grunted and turned his attention to the row of nineteen inch monitors. At least it was something to do and it might even be productive. He absently noted that even the bathroom was monitored and he was glad to see Stacy was alright as she washed her hands at the sink. Paul was not sure he would have bothered washing up at a time like this. He wasn't even sure that he might not have opted for a corner, then shrugged that off. Going in any corner in this place would likely electrocute him. He wondered briefly what the aliens used for a toilet but shrugged that off, too. At the time, it wasn't important. He could just pretend this was a sci-fi movie where no one ever worried about the facilities.

Paul watched Samuels and the cat creature – what was its name? Systel? It sounded like an Internet or wireless company, Paul thought – make their way through the house. The Caruthers House must have been elegant once, but it was hard to tell now in the dim light and under the mounds of equipment. It must have taken a lot of Sony Walkman's to generate the parts that *keeps* this place running, Paul thought. Force fields, lasers, some kind of projectile weapon that could toss deadly fireballs, monitors everywhere. And speaking of everywhere, where did the power come from? The lizards would surely have destroyed any power lines running to the house. There was probably some sort of nuclear reactor lying around somewhere made out of old televisions and laser printers. Maybe the alien just kept a few things running off the grid so the power company wouldn't wonder where the house was pulling its juice and send someone out to investigate. Paul was willing to bet that the pair he had seen thought about and covered all the bases miles ahead of anything he could think of in a decade.

Samuels and Systel were slowly making their way to the back, moving in closer to the area that had been blacked out when the ship hit the house. They stop by a closed door. Paul watched as Samuels started to open it, but the cat stopped him. The monitors in the room behind the door are either out or the cameras were no longer pointing in a useful direction. Paul thought he could see some shadows moving on the one camera that was tilted directly down toward the floor, but he wasn't sure.

"They will have help soon from the mother ship and the shields are weakening," the gumdrop said, pulling Paul's attention back to the main screen for a moment. "I had to use regrettably poor quality electronics and the break in the parameter shields weakens the entire system."

"This is the stuff that was stolen in that famous shopping center heist years ago. The dog food – what, for the cat?

"Systel. Yes. Her metabolism is closer to your dog than your cat. Though it has been hard on her since there are certain elements she cannot manufacturer from the proteins on your planet. We have been luck with some vitamins, but her time here grows short regardless of the outcome of the fight."

"Right. I hadn't thought of that."

"We were able to make the emergency rations stretch, but we have been out of those for some time. Perhaps this is more fortuitous than it appears. If we escape, the Aeolians have already broken the interdiction, so we might call for help openly without violating Alliance protocols."

"The rest of this? Was it stolen, too?"

"We regretted the initial theft, but we needed to establish ourselves. The rest was bought with proceeds from the toys and designs we sold or, if we took something in bulk, we made arrangements to pay. I told that to your dark friend."

"Yeah. I guess your royalties have been pretty high."

"One might say so, yes." If the alien had been human, Paul thought, that would have come out very smug.

Stacy walked back into the room and stopped next to Paul. She handed him a large kitchen knife and showed him that she had one of her own. She had evidently made a side trip on her way back from the bathroom.

"Everything OK," Paul asked her.

"Fine. I don't think these will do much good, but if there are lizards in the house, I want something more than my good looks and charm," she said, making it plain that the knives were not for carving up gumdrops.

"I think things are going to get interesting pretty quick," Paul said, motioning to the monitor. Samuels and the cat were backing up, away from the door. They crossed the room and took up positions outside the room they had just entered, using the doorjamb as cover. That was fine with Paul. The monitors gave him a good view of the room and he had no desire to be in a guessing game when it came to the state of the invasion.

"What'd I miss?"

"We have company. Samuels and the cat are acting as greeters." Paul motioned to the monitors. "I think there's something behind that wall there. When it comes through the door, Samuels should have a clear shot. He'd better make it good, too. I don't know if he'll have a chance for a second one."

"That's comforting."

Paul was silent for a few seconds, then his eyes lit up. He hated to bother the gumdrop, who was directing fire at the aliens outside, but this might save their lives. "Uh, excuse me, sire. Or madam. Or whatever. I hope you don't mind if I ask a question."

"Ah, yes. That might work. You may call me Ingram. Here," Ingram said, not waiting for a reply. He wiggled his virtual reality glove and a monitor close to Paul came to life with an outline of the house. Shortly, red dots popped up around the schematic and began flashing. "The flashing lights indicate the location of the intercom boxes we installed. That is a touch screen monitor. Touch the one you want. I have turned on a directional audio pick up and it will activate when you speak. Please do not speak until you are ready."

"How…" Stacy began, but Paul quickly covered her mouth.

"Shish!" he whispered in her ear. "He said that was a voice activated, directional microphone. We don't want to give anything away."

"But you haven't touched the screen yet," Stacy whispered back, reasonably. Men could be so dense sometimes. "And how did he know what you were going to ask?"

"Question for another time," Paul said, still whispering, eyes on the monitor. Sure enough, he could just make out the door opening slowly. He touched the monitor near where he thought Samuels was standing. The light turned a steady read. "Samuels," Paul said, still whispering. He was rewarded by seeing Samuels jump. He had been standing right next to the intercom. "Good. I see you. Don't say anything," Paul continued. "When the bad guys move into the room, I'm going to yell at you from an intercom behind them. That should distract them and let you get off at least one good shot before they react. Nod if you can hear me."

Samuels nodded and stuck his thumb up in the air. Paul touched the screen again, guessing correctly that the intercom he had selected would turn off. He smiled without humor when the light started flashing again. He glanced back at the monitor. The door was fully opened now but there was nothing to be seen. Then, in the dim light behind the door, Paul caught a flash of silver. He held his finger to his lips and reminded Stacy to be quiet, then pushed a flashing light in the room behind the door. He hoped the gumdrop had the volume up loud. The louder the better.

Slowly, three alien lizards made their way into the room. These three were dressed similar to the ones he had seen before, but their uniforms were more serviceable, crisscrossed with weapons belts and studded with utility pouches. Paul guessed that this was the alien version of the Marines while the ones he had seen in the clearing were probably Air Force types. Those aliens had cleaner uniforms and they had not carried anything near the weapons load that these three had. The bad news was the helmet. Perhaps they wouldn't hold up to a police special, but Paul thought these soldiers would be much better equipped than any army he knew about. The silver uniforms threw him for a second, but he figured that they were designed to deflect laser blasts more than for camouflage. If they were made out of some sort of ballistic cloth, and surely they were, then Samuels was going to have a problem doing anything more than pissing them off with his .38.

Well, they could only try and hope for the best. Maybe the cat had something in mind that would save them all. A super rail gun or something, but her hands were empty.

The lizards were moving slowly, checking out the shadows and looking in corners and searching behind any furniture or equipment that might hide a gumdrop. The cat was too big to hide behind anything in the room and Paul figured that these guys were hunting specific targets, that they knew what they were looking for, and not just looking for the random pussycat snack.

Paul waited until they were about a third of the way across, and then started yelling. "OK Samuels! They're into the room! Three of them! Go for it!"

The noise had the desired effect. Thinking they were flanked, the three spun around and covered their backside. But these were professionals and one of them quickly turned back to the front while the third scanned the room. Still, there had been a second when all three were looking the wrong way and Samuels had taken his cue well. He dove into the room, rolled just like they had taught him in the Academy obstacle course, and tapped off two shots in quick succession. Bang-bang! Precise and measured, more like an Israeli Mossad agent than a small-town cop. Two quick taps on the trigger, then go to the next target. The theory was that at least one of the two shots would hit – if you were well trained – and that both should. The first one to the torso to stop the target, the second to put "paid" on the job. Of course, he might be trained in the Mozambique Drill, commonly referred to as the "two in the body, one in the head strike-out". However, if Samuels had been military trained all shots would be body shots. The Geneva convention forbid head shots, Besides, Paul's Air Force small arms instructor had said that making a headshot in combat situations was like trying to hit the bouncing head of a bobble head doll head in a dust storm. But close range... where would Samuels choose to strike?

Samuels had spent a lot of time practicing that on the firing range. He had never pulled his gun before in anger – but boy was he pissed now! – and he had never expected to draw down in a firefight; it was a sense of personal pride that kept him on the range practicing. That and the fact that there were very few blacks in Flagstaff, which had curtailed his social life significantly. The Flagstaff folks were pretty nice, but it was still a small country town and people talked. There were a lot of liberal girls at the college – mostly white – but they were all too young for Samuels and, boy howdy, would the town talk if Samuels had taken up with a white girl a decade or more younger! Except for his weekends off, which he often took in Las Vegas, there wasn't much else to do but pop a few caps at targets that he often called "Bubba."

Samuels preferred an Olympic Arms 1911 pistol. Forget the cute scorpion blazed into the handle, this was one tough pistol. His .38 mm version of the standard .45 mm gun had the speed, reliability, and accuracy he felt he needed, should he ever needed to use a gun in the field. It also had decent stopping power, the number one criteria. The weapon is manufactured with a true case-color hardening, a process that makes metals sturdier, enhancing performance and giving a longer life to the material. The normal Rockwell hardness for a standard carbon or stainless steel slide is about 38c. Good, but under stress, maybe not good enough. Once case hardened, the same piece of metal will Rockwell in the high fifties to low sixties, depending on how the process in controlled and the type of metal being treated.

The ability to control hardness is in fact critical with most firearms. A manufacturer cannot heat-treat a slide stop to the same depth of a slide or frame or the slide stop becomes brittle and can easily break. Besides, the process makes the gun metal mottled and, Samuels thought, if you're going to shell out almost nine hundred dollars for a pistol, it should be functional *and* pretty.

Now, there was plenty of pressure to perform and Samuels' careful choice in weapons and his practice paid off - so did his choice of ammunition. What's the point of shooting someone if the bullet doesn't stop them? And Northern Arizona has more than its fair share of cowboys built like bulls... and just as hard to kill. So Samuels used the .38 S&W Super Police bullet to British specifications: 200 grain, lead bullet propelled by 2.8 grains of "Neonite" nitrocellulose powder. The lubricated shell hit 630 ft/s when it left the 4-inch barrel. The aliens were not far enough away for any noticeable drop-off.

The first shot hit the center alien in the shoulder, spinning him around so that the second took him square in the chest. That threw him back, knocking him into the second lizard that had just begun to cover the interior of the room. But Samuels' luck wasn't as good as his aim. The third lizard, the one that was turning to cover the main part of the house, was completely out of that little mix up and his aim was dead on.

Except that Samuels was already moving again and the laser that shot through the space where Samuels' torso had been was just a little too high and a fraction too late. The heat scorched Samuels' jacket, but did no other damage to him. However, it took out a chunk of wall behind him and a fair amount of electronics with it. Samuels only hoped that those components controlled the house electric can opener or something, and not the defense network.

Systel was not idle, either. She sprang into the room a fraction of a second behind Samuels and made for the two lizards that were tangled together. Ignoring the one Samuels had shot, she pounced on the other one and knocks its gun hand so hard that the weapon flew across the room, smashing against the wall and falling behind an equipment rack. She grabbed the creature by the throat and twisted, snapping its neck just as Samuels let off another pair of shots, this time at the alien who had shot at him.

The first shot went low, square into the chest, but the second shot was higher, raised up buy the gun's recoil, which Samuels was trying to control with one hand from his position on the floor. That shot made a cracking impact on the alien's helmet's faceplate and staggered the creature back. Samuels saw a satisfying spider web of cracks form across the creature's faceplate, but he also saw the bullet wedged in the thick material that covered the creature's face. Moving quickly to his knees, he braced the gun with two hands and popped off another pair of shots, this time aimed directly at the faceplate.

The first bullet completed shattered the screen and before the lizard could jerk away, the second smashed into its head, splattering the inside of the helmet with a grisly combination of gore, bone fragments, and electronics. The bullet, slowed by the skull, hit the helmet's super-hardened backside and deflected back into the creature's brain. Before the bullet came to a stop, after bouncing around the helmet three or four times, there was nothing inside the helmet resembling a living organism, just a stew in a fountain of blood.

Samuels turned toward the other fight, but Systel had completely dismembered the alien she had grabbed and was turning on the one Samuels had shot initially. Samuels took aim but he was not fast enough this time. The alien, protected by fabric of its uniform that had gone rigid when the bullets hit, was back on its feet again. It was moving a little slow and stiff, but it was moving. It took a wild shot at

Samuels, which missed, but managed to set a buffet along the wall on fire, sending flames into the electronics that it held and a cloud of acrid smoke into the room. Samuels ducked away, rolled and popped back up to take another shot at the creature, but Systel was already bearing down on it like a locomotive with a mission.

It took a shot at Systel, aiming low, and sent a bolt through the cat's foreleg. The scream that Systel let out was enough to raise the dead, and enough to stop the alien from reaching the lizard as she crashed to her side in a pile of televisions and fur. With the immediate problem solved, the lizard turned back to Samuels, but the cop had dodged back into a corner where the shadows gave him good cover in the low light. The lizard looked around and slapped its helmet a couple of times, like it was trying to bring some bit of arrant equipment back on line. Failing to achieve its goal, it flipped open the visor.

Samuels had one shot in the chamber and one left in the magazine. Two shots then reload the spare magazine on his belt. If these two did not count, he might not have time to reload before he became a crispy critter.

The creature crouched and scanned the room, looking for Samuels, its yellow eyes glowing in the low light from the fire. If the cop did not act quickly … but behind the alien, Systel was struggling back to her feet, something easier to do with a shot out leg when there are three left on which to stand. But she was not steady and she knocked against an equipment rack. The lizard spun on her and took one expert shot, right through the center of her torso.

This time when she went down, she went down permanently.

But like Paul's yelling before, the distraction was just enough to allow Samuels to move into a firing position and take aim. As the alien turned its attention back to the room, Samuels tapped out his last two shots, slow this time, but lethal. The two bullets entered into the helmet and the explosion from the creature's head tore it right off the body.

"Never did like snakes," Samuels said, starting to stand up.

But like a snake, the lizard's nervous system was not ready to die just because the head was gone. As the body staggered backward, the muscles in its hands twitched, trying to bring the weapon in line where the pesky human had taken its stand. The gun jerked once and fired, hitting a row of shelves above and behind Samuels, bringing the ubiquitous equipment crashing down on top of the hapless cop. As the light from the fire began to die out, so did the energy in the alien body, but there was enough left for a final trigger pull as the gun slumped to the floor. The laser slashed through the foot of a cabinet next to Samuels and that, too, toppled over on the cop who already had been knocked down by the falling shelves.

"Damn," Samuels managed to mutter right before he passed into darkness, never seeing the weapon drop from the alien's lifeless fingers.

CHAPTER TWELVE
June 20, 2002
Flagstaff, Arizona

"We have to help them!" Stacy said, tugging on Paul's arm, pulling him toward the door.

"Just a second!" Paul replied, digging in to keep from being pulled off his feet. "Is it safe out there?" Paul asked the gumdrop. "We need to help them, but are there any more lizards in the house?"

"No," was the alien's curt reply, as it concentrated on the screens and the firefight outside. "Your friend is injured, but not badly. Bring him back here."

"What about your friend?" Paul asked. "I'm not sure we could handle the weight without causing more damage. "

"Do not worry about her," came the cold, emotionless reply. "She is beyond our help."

To Paul's eyes, it was totally unaffected by what had just happened. But when Paul was a kid, his Scout troop had gone camping near Cottonwood. A group of younger Scouts had taken off and gone down to the creek where there was a colony of frogs and spent a couple of hours pelting them with rocks. Paul tossed a few rocks himself, but quickly backed away from the slaughter. The frogs had shown no emotions, no awareness, nothing, as their friends died around them, but Paul was still impacted by the cold eyes that watched every companion as it was splattered or crippled. Animal rights was his one

Liberal cause. Well, that and conservation. This was no time for either.

Paul had never told on his fellow Scouts, but he had also separated himself from the group and shortly after that he quit Scouting, right after receiving his Life ranking. The bright red heart on the badge always reminded him of Cottonwood and Cottonwood to him was a subject of guilt. It was more, too. Over the days after the Massacre at Bumble Bee Creek, as Paul came to think of the camping trip, Paul came to believe that the eyes were not necessarily the windows to the inner being. He learned to accept whatever went on around him, like those stoic frogs, and tried not to think about what it did to the soul. The cold, unforgiving eyes of the frogs, Paul believed, held more than he could read. So he learned to take life a little more as it came, taking people a little more at face value.

In the world of workplace politics, that proved to be a strong disadvantage. But in just living, it gave Paul a chance to learn more about people before he made a critical judgment. He never assumed he knew what someone was thinking or feeling just by the look in their eyes. Because he, at least, could not read minds. Well, the gumdrop, he guessed, had eyes in the stalks he shot up, but damned if he could read anything in that even if he had been a gypsy boy. So, for his own peace of mind, he assumed the gumdrop was in deep grief and would reserve judgment for later.

Stacy, however, did not care one way or the other. Someone needed help and they were just standing there. She started tugging again on Paul, but stopped when a flashing blue light appeared right in front of her nose.

"Follow the light," Ingram said. "There was damage to the house. This will take you through safely. But be quick. Time is running out for us."

The pair raced out of the control center, following the light back into the kitchen, then out a door on the other side. But behind them, haunting Paul's every step, were the alien's last words. "Time is running out for us." What in the name of all the Gods of Babylon did that mean? And how fast was it running? And when it ran away, what would happen then? The shaking of the house by enemy weapons did nothing to settle his thoughts as the pair worked their way through dust-filled narrow passages lined with electronics. Here, the house's air conditioning suffered an airflow problem and the close confines of the passages were hot and uncomfortably close. These back rooms had been filled with so much equipment that their passage was a zigzag around stacks and columns, over bundled wires and fiber runs that sparkled with light flashes.

Paul rubbed his nose a couple of times, trying to prevent a sneeze. He was sensitive to house dust, and he expected that he would have a sneezing fit sooner or later, but he was relieved that nothing had happened yet. He did note that the equipment was fairly dust free. Maybe the little gumdrop spent its spare time dusting and vacuuming.

The rows were set so close together that Paul was positive that the cat could never have negotiated these aisles. All of the wiring and stacking and welding and, well, everything, must have been done by the gumdrop – by Ingram, Paul corrected himself, trying to humanized the creature a little – and Paul couldn't even begin to consider what effort that might have taken.

The light ended at a closed door. Paul and Stacy pulled to a stop and Paul tried the handle. It turned, but he couldn't open the door that would normally have swung into the room behind it.

"There is a rolling rack against the door. It looks like it shifted when the plane hit the house. You must try to open it," Ingram said through the intercom near where the pair stood. At least Paul knew where they were, but it didn't make him very comfortable knowing that there was a vulnerable entrance just on the other side of the wall. But Samuels needed help…

"Here, help me with this," he said, putting his shoulder against the door. He started a slow, steady push and moved the door enough that he could let the door handle go when Stacy slammed her weight into his efforts. The rack shifted and the door sprang open, dumping the pair in a heap on the floor. Fortunately, Paul had enough presence to twist himself so he landed on the bottom. Stacy, while not exactly heavy, came down hard on Paul, knocking his wind out.

"You OK?" Stacy asked, raising herself up with one hand, observing Paul's heavy breathing with some concern.

"Yeah," Paul panted, "just trying to catch my breath."

"Well," Stacy said, standing up and offering Paul a hand. "Save the heavy breathing for later, when we have time to enjoy it."

Paul's look, as Stacy hauled him to his feet, was a mixture of surprise and reevaluation. Perhaps it was true that danger drew people closer together. Then again, he didn't know Stacy well enough yet to judge whether or not that what she said meant what he thought (hoped) she said. She was certainly more animated than a frog, but right now she was looking at the light as it floated in the doorway of another room.

"I think this is the way the alien's got in," Paul said, surveying the area near where the ambush had taken place. He moved stiffly toward the door. When he approached, the light sped across the room and bounced above a pile of rubble right where Paul expected to find Samuels.

The room was a mess. The wall where Samuels was buried was blasted and crumbling. More equipment clogged the doorway and there were sparking and smoking CD players and video units everywhere. Paul was trying to see a safe route through the tumbled and shattered electronics, but Stacy was already working her way over to the light. Well, that was fine, but they would still have to get him out. It looked to Paul that the only reasonable way was back through the equipment maze. The wall behind Samuels was smoking and cracked and the ceiling was sagging. No telling how much weight it was holding in equipment from the second floor. If it was even half what was in this room, Paul was sure it exceeded the architect's anticipated load capacity. Paul seemed to remember stories from the sixties, when waterbeds were first introduced, about second floor apartment bedrooms suddenly ending up as first floor units. He couldn't recall if that was *after* a bed leaked out or not, but the ceiling above Samuels looked none too promising for long term survival.

"You must hurry," the intercom beside Paul blasted, proving that the gumdrop – no, Ingram – was watching the monitors in addition to fighting. "My outer shields will not hold much longer. There has been too much damage to the equipment inside the house."

Paul worked his way over to Stacy, who was trying to shift shelving and units away from Samuels. Paul looked over the situation and directed Stacy to a pile of Hitachi VCRs that had toppled over when the shelves fell.

"Work on those," he told her, motioning to the units that were pinning Samuels' legs. "I'll move these."

Paul worked gingerly on the Sun amplifier heads that were sitting on a shelf above Samuels' head. The shelf was precariously held up on the topside by a stack of what looked like IBM 486 mixed in with Commodore 128 computers but Paul doubted the cases contained anything that slow, not at least if they were connected to what looked like newer gigabyte hard drives. They were tilting a little outward and if they toppled, they would add their weight to the Hitachi's on Samuels' legs and, worse, let the very heavy Sun Spectrum II amps crash down over the cop's head. The end nearest Samuels' head was sitting on a little side table that held an old rotary phone that was wired back into the series of amplifiers. Whatever in the world that dial-up controlled was beyond Paul, but he did know that the spindly legs of the table would not take much more before they gave way and turned Samuels' head into so much mush.

Paul worked slowly and carefully, trying not to disturb the delicate balance. He turned off each Sun amp and unplugged the power cord from the rear input and then set the electronic unit aside. They were heavy, old tube-style units made to take the rugged life of a road trip, but they were some of the most reliable and powerful guitar amplifiers ever made. They could easily crush a head with a three foot fall.

Stacy, however, was not so constrained. The Hitachi's were unceremoniously jerked off the stack and tossed as far as the power cord and video leads would allow, often ripping the video leads from the unit. Once, Paul had owned a computer program for his Amiga computer that stored data on video, creating a massive memory system for only the cost of a high quality video tape. In fact, he could store a hundred thousand gigabytes on video for far less than he could on a one-gig Jaz drive. Paul looked as Stacy indiscriminately, unknowingly, tossing trillions of bits of information into a smoking pile and wondered, around an odd bit of nostalgia for his Amiga, just how the loss of that data was going to impact the alien's ability to maintain its computer controls – and with that, their screens which were the cornerstone of their survival.

Well, no time to worry about that. Paul emptied the shelf of its three Suns in about the time it took Stacy to move the dozen or so Hitachis. Paul tossed the shelf aside and bent down to check Samuels' head, ignoring the ominous creak from the shelf unit that still remained attached along the very top of the wall.

"He's breathing OK," Paul said. "Looks like a bump on the head is all. Or maybe the excitement was too much," he added, trying for a little levity.

Stacy was not in the mood right then for jokes. She was busy ripping off the bottom of her blouse to staunch a freely bleeding wound on Samuels' leg caused by one of the falling Hitachis gouging out a chunk of flesh. She worked quickly and precisely and Paul kept one eye on her and one on the door that lead to the breach in the shields. She moved efficiently and soon had a workable bandage wrapped around the leg. It looked like it was working, too.

Finishing that, she stood up and quickly tied the remnants of her blouse off just below her breasts. Paul supposed that this was not precisely the proper time to notice just how good she looked like that, but he noticed anyway. She was a pretty girl and Paul was sure that it wasn't just the situation that made her look more attractive. On the contrary, the dirt and grime and tousled hair were enough to make most girls just look a mess. To Paul, Stacy looked more like one of those tough girls that helped win the west without benefit of Maybelline or Max Factor or The Gap. If they lived through this, he was going to make one serious attempt at talking her out on a real date without cops or lizards or intergalactic wars.

"How did you learn to do that?" Paul asked, still admiring Stacy but pointing to her work on Samuels' leg. "Were you a nurse?"

"No," Stacy said, brushing the hair out of her face, then settling into her new outfit with purely feminine gestures. "I just watch a lot of old war and cowboy movies." She bent down and casually tucked the gun into the waist of her pants.

Well, how could one argue with that? Movies were where Paul had picked most of his survival techniques, too. That and old television shows like *Combat* and *Desert Fox* that were his favorites before the Liberals began taking body counts and forced those shows off the air for the pabulum that dominated the airwaves from the seventies on. If not for that new show, *Space: Above & Beyond*, that had just premiered last fall, there wouldn't be anything decent on television at all. But Paul didn't expect that program to last any longer than *Tales of the Gold Monkey*, another show that was geared for production quality and an audience with more than a sixth grade education. It had only lasted for the '82 and '83 seasons.

Yeah, *Space: Above & Beyond* pretty much hit the nail on the head, from what Paul could see. Combat with aliens was dirty, gritty, and deadly. Not at all like the antiseptic stories from *Star Trek* or its spin-offs. Paul had seen ample proof that people hit with beam weapons leave very messy remains behind and don't just vanish in a sparkle of little lights. And speaking of deadly…

"We'd better get back to the main control area," Paul told Stacy as he lifted Samuels to his feet. The cop was coming around a little, just enough to be more difficult to handle than dead weight, and Stacy stepped in to take Samuels' other arm. "I don't think this place is going to be safe much longer. I think the alien has a back door out. At least I hope he does, because we'll never make it out the front."

They started across the room, back the way they had come, dragging Samuels over the debris where the path wasn't clear. About half way, Paul came to a sudden stop.

"You got him?" he asked.

"Yeah, I guess," Stacy answered, resetting Samuels' weight and taking a firmer grip on his arm that she had draped over her shoulder. "Where're you going?"

Paul nodded to the downed form of the large cat creature and slipped out from under Samuels arm. He worked his way through the mess to the body and stood a few feet off. He wasn't sure if he should get any closer, but he knew he still had to check. But Paul had raised Irish Setters when he was still married to Jane and he knew a little about first aid. Not that this creature was an animal, but Paul figured the same things applied. When he worked on his dogs, and one, a cagey old male, was always hurting himself on barbed wire or something, he tied off the muzzle with a scarf. Even though he knew the dogs would not hurt him, he also knew that poking around on a wound was a sure way for the dog to forget just who was a friend and who was causing it pain.

But Systel had a very large head and Paul was not at all sure he had anything he could use to tie off her mouth in case she decided to snap at him. Besides, her face was closer to that of a human: flat, with only a very short muzzle, but wide to compensate. Well, he had to risk it, he told himself. If there was any chance that the creature was alive, they had to try and do something for her, even though he could not imagine how they could move her back to the main room.

"Is she alive?" Stacy asked, from where she was struggling to hold Samuels up all on her own.

"I don't think so," Paul said, examining the body for a few more seconds before moving closer. If she bit him, he thought she could take an arm off and not even choke. Systel resembled a mythical Centaur with the way the torso and body connected. She was crumpled in a lifeless heap, nothing like that statuesque being that he had seen earlier. No, that one had all the power and presence of the Centaurs from that artless television series *Hercules: The Legendary Journeys* that Fox was running late at night. The animation was pretty good, but the dialogue… Well, Paul was sure that this was flesh and blood and not a computer generated image. The cooked-meat odor in the room us unmistakable.

There was a quarter-sized hole though her chest that had oozed a little blood from around its charred edges. The laser had probably cauterized most of the blood vessels, preventing more bleeding. Paul had no idea what was behind the wound in the creature's chest. For all he knew, the vital organs were all in the body with nothing but muscles and sinew in the torso. She sure showed enough muscle there and what looked like the rudiments of mammalian glands under a soft fur covering. But she was alien and Paul shrugged off guessing.

She did have what looked like a nose. He couldn't see anything else where she could breathe, except through her mouth. That made him nervous, but he bent down anyway and put his arm on the front of the nose and then the mouth. He watched the fine hair on his arms to see if they moved and tried to feel if there was any wind blowing across his arm.

Nothing. He felt around the neck under the theory that any creature with a head would need to get oxygen and nourishment there, but he was less hopeful of finding a pulse; the main blood vessels could be deep inside and protected by bone or cartilage, so not finding a pulse did nothing to challenge his belief that she was indeed dead.

"Anything," Stacy asked, growing increasingly nervous and burdened by Samuels weight.

"No, nothing yet," Paul answered. He rolled back the lids on her eyes and all he saw was a glassy milk-white orb, not the fierce blaze he had seen earlier. If eyes could in fact reveal the soul, then this soul had undeniably fled. He felt around her body and even his inexperienced hand could tell that the heat he had felt from her as she moved past him earlier was ebbing away. He stood up with a sigh.

"Let's get out of here," he directed Stacy as he took his place beside Samuels.

The trip back through the electronic maze was torturous and tedious. They often had to move sideways to pull the unconscious copy along, ever vigilant least they trip over a wire run or bump into a precariously balanced stack of components or have an elbow hit a power switch which could have dire consequences. And Samuels grew heavier with every step, making both Stacy and Paul break out in a heavy sweat in the close confines of the equipment room. For Paul, that meant constantly wiping the stinging sweat out of his eyes and wiping his hands on his pants so the moisture wouldn't permit Samuels from slipping from his grip.

His clothes were sticking to his body and he could feel the sweat running down his sides by the time they emerged into the relatively cooler kitchen and the air conditioning had a chance to catch up. Paul glanced once at Stacy as she moved up next to him, then he concentrated on maneuvering Samuels into the control area, where they propped him up against the side of an equipment rack that looked like it wasn't going anywhere.

For Stacy, the tormenting trek following the little blue light though the jumbled equipment room had generated much the same results for her as it had for Paul; but Paul decided, in just a quick glance at her when they entered the kitchen, that he had better concentrate on what he was doing and not the way her sweat had plastered her blouse to her body or the way the material became slightly transparent when wet or the way her nipples were poking through the fabric, or… no, Paul realistically decided that the situation called for his entire concentration on other matters than those generated by biology and body chemistry. Why were women so much of a distraction, anyway? And why were they distracting when things were most likely to fall out of the pot and into the fire?

Paul shrugged off those questions and compartmentalized them with things like: why do babies cry? And why do kids scream when they are playing? These were all questions that made one wonder how humanity ever made it out of the Ice Age, a time when noise and distractions were a sure invitation to lunch for Mr. Saber-tooth and Mrs. Cave Bear. If people bred like elephants, then humanity would have gone the way of the Wooly Mammoth, a two year gestation being entirely too long to repopulate a species that insisted on having young that advertised the availability to the first hungry belly to pass along. Human babies were like a barker in a carnival screaming "come and get it! Dinner is served!"

Things did not look too promising back in the control room. Many of the indicators had changed colors and, while Paul did not know what color scheme meant to aliens, a change in these circumstances could not be good. A couple of monitors now had alien hieroglyphic symbols scrolling down the sides and a few had large, bold symbols flashing on them.

"What's happening?" Paul asked, even though he was not sure he really wanted to know.

"Sensors show that there is a fire in the area near where the Aeolian craft crashed through the shields. That is not good, since additional damage will only degrade my defenses there. Some of my power amplifiers for that end of the house went off line."

Ooops. The Sun amps, Paul thought.

"We must depart as soon as I finish programming the automated defenses."

"Why not just turn them loose and let them kill whatever they can," Stacy asked.

"I must randomize the sequences so it will look like I am still in control and not the computer."

Paul was less interested in Ingram's reasoning than he was in getting out. Dodge City was rapidly becoming an unhealthy environment. In fact, it was more like Hadleyville, New Mexico Territory, in *High Noon*. But before he could speak, another large monitor flashed on with a graphic overlay of what Paul recognized as Flagstaff from the time he had spent studying his map earlier that week. The map had seven triangles on it, all aimed at Flagstaff, or, more precisely, the site just off the city limits where the Caruthers House was located. Each symbol had a series of letters beneath it and one was about twice the size of the other six.

"What's that," Stacy asked before Paul could query the alien.

Ingram shifted its attention to the monitor, pausing in his work as he studied the screen a few seconds.

"Those are preliminary projections from my long range sensors," he said, turning back to programming the defenses.

"And…" Paul prompted.

"Preliminary readings indicate additional forces from the attackers should arrive shortly. They have been in transit, from the vectors, from the other side of your moon," Ingram said, absently swinging a tentacle that resulted in a ball flashing among a group of icons on a screen far to Paul's right. From the master screen, Paul saw a fireball flash out and land back in the woods, perhaps near the clearing, where he assumed Ingram had just made hash of a rally point.

"Wonderful. More lizards," Stacy breathed softly and it was not a breath of relief.

"You mean these guys come from the moon? We've been there and didn't see anything," Paul protested.

"You have not been there enough and you have not been there recently. Your space program is pathetically under-funded and under-supported.

There are a lot of bad people out there and the Alliance cannot always protect you, as you are seeing now."

"Yeah, but they came from the *moon*?"

"No. They probably have a small observation post set up now, trying to locate the source of my transmissions, but these would have come from the far side of the moon where the mother ship is probably hiding in its shadow."

"Just one?"

"One should be enough. I doubt they would risk an armada, which even your primitive technology should detect and certainly the Alliance observation buoys would see. They cannot disable the buoys, either, since that would also attract an Alliance investigation. But even a single mother ship has enough striking power to equal that of your nation's entire Navy."

"Damn…" Paul muttered. The US still had the most powerful navy in the world, despite the Democrats systematic attempts to rape the military. One *ship* with that much firepower was an awesome thought. An *armada* of such ships could that the world easily. He looked again at Stacy, drinking in as much of her as he could. He figured there probably wouldn't be much of a chance later.

Stacy didn't notice. She had been watching the screen with the Flagstaff map and she was the first to notice two other groups of much smaller icons spring up on the display. "Are those more bad guys?" she asked, pointing to the bottom most grouping.

Ingram spared a glance at the screen, but only a moment. "No. Those are your military air forces.

They are coming from two of the installations we have identified in this area."

Paul's look, as Stacy hauled him to his feet, was a mixture of surprise and revelation. Perhaps it was true that people in danger were drawn closer together. Then again, he didn't know Stacy well enough yet to judge whether or not she had meant what she said about breathing heavy later. Paul looked at the screen and considered their orientation to Flagstaff. "Davis Monthan out of Tucson and probably a unit out of Las Vegas," he guessed. "Will they be here in time?"

Ingram took another look at the monitor and made a little fluttering motion with one of this tentacles. "Maybe shortly after the others arrive. Not in time to help us, but it may keep some of their ships occupied for a few minutes while we try to find a place to hide. Maybe enough time to survive. They will not last long though."

Even as it was talking, Paul saw a pair of icons angle toward each of the oncoming human formations. A pair against, how many? Two? Four? Six? The monitor only showed one round icon without designating individual planes. Paul wondered if the humans would stand a chance even with ten-to-one odds. If the aircraft on-board radars were not up to seeing the enemy, he didn't think the pilots were trained well enough in fighting without instruments to do much good, especially at night. Maybe with heat seekers, they could make the odd lucky shot but the alien seemed to think even the powerful ground based radar scattered the around southwest could not lock on to these lizard planes and if that were true, it *would* only be the odd lucky shot that hit.

Even with the advantage of height, he did not think the AWACS, those highly advanced radar planes that the military used for vectoring in its fighters during battle, would paint the craft attacking the house. If any of the incoming military planes made it to Flagstaff, they might, just might, get a few cannon rounds off or a heat seeker or two (which Paul was fairly comfortable in believing would zero in on the house itself) before they became so much flaming scrap metal. Those ground crews back at the Air Force bases could just as well stand down and go home to watch the action on CNN or Fox.

Paul was pretty sure that by now the local stations were set-up around the area and his friend at Northern Arizona University sent tape occasionally by satellite link to the cable news networks, so he'd bet that one of the local stations would make arrangements for a feed pretty quick. Forget the Phoenix stations, which Flagstaff fed as a regular course; this was national, no, worldwide news. He knew sci-fi fans, much more so the UFO crowd, would be burning up the lines to the local authorities and heading out with camcorders and cell phones and welcome signs or shotguns and "alien go home" posters.

Paul wondered if a news helicopter would survive for long in the air around the house, but he doubted that any of the Flagstaff stations had choppers, other than something private and on-call. He hoped someone would have the brains not to call. It was going to be bad enough if help arrived who could shoot back, but an unarmed helicopter would be a sitting duck. Maybe the Governor would call Maricopa County Sheriff Joe Arpiao. Paul had read somewhere that he had purchased a military armored troop transport, complete with a .50 mm machine gun. Maybe he had a few portable rocket launchers around, too. It was only a three hour drive from Phoenix. How long before Sheriff Joe brought his Maricopa County illegal alien crime sweep posse north to Coconino County? These lizards were sure illegal as hell and they were about as alien as one could imagine. Whatever that answer, Paul was convinced the good Sheriff would not be here soon enough.

That would be interesting, though: Sheriff Joe busting a bunch of lizards, sticking them in pink underwear, and dropping them in a tent city. The Phoenix Zoo would probably have a fit with all the concessions they would lose to people driving by the jail. He could imagine the run on *America's Most Wanted* followed by a special on *COPS*. Bad boys indeed.

Paul turned away from the screens. He smelled something burning. He walked back into the kitchen and risked a look out the window through the slats of the shutters that covered them. What he saw made him blanch and rush back into the control room.

"We're going to have to do something fast or risk being toasted," he told Stacy.

"What's new? I thought that was the plan all along."

"Not really. But right now, the back of the house is burning pretty good. It won't be long before the insides are on fire and then we'll have major problems."

"Like we don't now?" Stacy looked over to the monitors that showed the back of the house but that row had gone blank while her attention was elsewhere. But she did notice that there was a haze in the room where they had gone to retrieve Samuels. Smoke was already filling up the back part of the house and, one thing she did know about medicine, carbon monoxide intoxication killed people well before the flames reached them.

"Point taken, but let's not invite more problems."

"Well, at least Samuels got the ones in the house and if the backside is going up as good as you say, then there won't be any more coming in that way. So look on the bright side for a change," Stacy said, though there was no bright lilt in her voice like there had been before they started this whole crazy adventure. It would have been a good day to start at the beginning and take Stacy to the rock slide in Sedona, where she could show off in a cute little two piece, not bothering with mysteries and millionaires, Paul reflected. But it was too late for that. Somehow he would have to find a way to survive and then get Stacy to someplace quiet, and to that end he began examining all the existing monitors, looking for an opening where they could, maybe, bolt for freedom. It was not promising.

Behind him, Samuels groaned softly, pulling his attention away from the screens. Paul could see that Samuels was coming around and he joined Stacy, who had moved to his side with the first whimper.

"Good. At least you're alive," Paul said to the blurry-eyed cop. "We need to figure a way out of this place and do it now. I don't think we're going to like what's cookin'."

"I smell wood smoke," Samuels moaned.

"Alright, your nose is working. That's a start. Come on and see if you can stand on that leg," Paul said, reaching down and helping Samuels to his feet.

Paul turned back to the screens. Something was bothering him, but he couldn't put his finger on… No, there it was. There was nothing going on. Paul looked from one screen to the next and there was no sign of the alien ground force, no beams reaching out to the woods, no scaly things huddled around strange implements of destruction. Except for a single enemy aircraft dodging in and out for quick potshots at the house, there was nothing. Even the return fire from the house seemed weak and ineffectual. It was like the calm before the storm or the eye of a hurricane, and Paul had lived through a few of those when he was younger and lived in Baton Rouge and Biloxi. This did not look good from any angle, and anyone who lived along the Gulf of Mexico knew that the back side of a storm could make the front side look like a cakewalk.

The yard certainly looked like a battle zone. Paul could see his car and part of Fisher's in one monitor off to the side. Neither one would ever take to the road again; even if the fires were put out quickly. The yard nearest the house was pot-marked with small burning craters where fire from the woods or aircraft had missed or splashed off the screens. Anything standing out there beyond the screens had been razed to the ground, including the weeds and the runaway bushes. The yard looked like a manicured version of the Devil's Paint Pots in

Yellowstone Park: grass leveled in neat lines where the lasers had slashed in low around bubbling cauldrons spitting out smoke and an occasional flame. No, this did not look promising at all and Paul was sure the backyard was worse.

He could hear sirens in the distance. On the main screen, he watched the remaining fighter make a last pass at the house, then stand on its tail and accelerate straight up. That must have put some g-force on the crew, Paul thought. In a couple of seconds, even the glow from the engines was invisible.

"Well, it looks like a reprieve," Stacy said.

"Yeah, I guess," Paul replied, but he had a nagging suspicion that the storm-front was just about to break over the house, the yard, and everything.

"Well, let's get Samuels and get out of here," she said.

"That is not advised," Ingram said, cutting off Paul's cautionary reply.

"Is that a threat?" Samuels mumbled, trying out his injured leg. He could put weight on it, but not much. He would need help getting out of the house.

"Watch a minute. Now, I must work extra hard. The reinforcements will soon arrive and the defenses will not hold even for a few minutes," Ingram said, centering his concentration on the controls he had been fussing with a few minutes before.

"It looks like the Calvary is here, kid," Samuels said, centering Paul's attention back on the screen.

Three police cars and a matching number of fire trucks were pulling into the yard. Two of the trucks pulled around to the back and began setting up to put out the fire. Paul could just catch their activity from one of the side cameras. A police car went with them, but he could not see where it finally stopped. Probably near the wrecked fighter, Paul surmised. The other two cars pulled up out front and the officers got out, using the doors as shields to cover the house. A Park Ranger's dull green pickup arrived as well and about half dozen men jumped out and began attacking some of the smaller blazes by shoveling dirt on them. Paul could see some civilians milling around in the background.

"Come on. Let's go," Stacy said. She was growing antsy and fairly prancing in her eagerness to leave.

"I think we should wait a minute. I don't think it's safe out there yet."

That stopped her cold. The last half-hour had been chilling for her to say the least and she shuddered to think what would happen if those people outside were caught without protection. "Can we warn them? Bring them in here," she asked.

"I don't think they'll be very safe in here for long," Paul said. "Maybe we can warn them away. I don't think there's much…"

Suddenly hell seemed to erupt outside. The fighter made a dive bombing pass on the house, stitching the front yard with short bursts of laser fire much like a machine gun laying down parallel path's of death in the movies. But this was no movie, the people out there were not paid stuntmen, and the laser bolts were nowhere near as gentle as a 50 caliber machine gun.

As the ship's fire raked though the yard, more weapons opened up from the trees. Whoever had sent these people had no idea what was going on behind the trees that screened the house from the road. The book that said "do this" if "that" happens had not been written for alien invaders attacking a semi-sentient house. The explosions from the house and the fire in the woods were the "this" and the Forest Rangers and police cars were the "that," no matter how inappropriate the action to the reality of the situation. People were reacting "by the book" and people were dying because the book was wrong.

"…time," Paul finished lamely, watching helplessly as the ship continued its run centered on the approach lane, sending bolt after bolt into the milling crowds that were scattering into the woods. Where, Paul knew, they would be met with a more personal kind of death.

In the first strafing pass, the ship hit both police cars, sending one skyrocketing into the air on a geyser of flame. The second was hit immediately after, completely shattering the engine compartment. All the cops were down and only one was moving, but that was only feebly. Samuels clutched Stacy's arm in a death grip. Those were people he knew.

Behind the house, some small arms fire answered the lasers from the woods, but that was rapidly silenced. Paul could see the firemen trying to take cover behind the trucks, but one exploded into flame and he could see the other shattering from the force of the hits, scattering bodies like, well, like frogs pounded with rocks.

The men from the forestry department were quickly cut down and their truck rendered useless by the smaller laser bolts fired from the woods. Within seconds, there was nothing moving at all out front. Even the cop that had survived the initial attack was not moving, his uniform smoldering in several places. Maybe some of the people in the lane had survived. Paul hoped so. He would lay a solid bet that no one who ventured into the woods lived through the night, though.

He thought he saw flashing lights from near the road, but they came no closer. Apparently the lizards were content with clearing the area of potentially bothersome locals. They wanted to destroy the house, kill everything in it, and then perhaps they would take out all of Flagstaff or maybe just go on their way. But now they were concentrating on the house again with renewed fury.

"I think we're in trouble," Stacy said.

"What makes now any different from two minutes ago," Paul wanted to know.

She pointed back to the main screen. There were no longer friendly circles approaching, just unfriendly triangles.

"More of the lizards are coming and there's no sign of the Mounties," she said.

"I hear more sirens," Paul offered without much hope. He figured there should be more police on the way. *Someone* must have survived; someone a little farther away from the house would have called for more help, wouldn't they? But Paul had seen the pieces fly when the bad guys had let loose with their lightning guns. If they had coordinated with the ground forces a little, then it was a good bet no one close enough to have seen anything would have made it back to the main road alive. Still, anyone on the main road should have seen the aircraft, the fire and smoke from the explosions. Too many would-a, could-a, should-a's. Paul was beginning to think that it was time to be a little more proactive.

"Look, I've been shot at, dumped on, and slow smoked," Samuels said from his position on the floor. "But I'm still not convinced these are the good guys." He eyed Ingram cautiously for a reaction.

"I think they are," Paul said, with Stacy's nod of approval. "If you had seen what we say in the woods, you would know that, too. OK. Maybe not they are not the 'good guys' but they're certainly better than the alternative."

"Yeah, but they admitted they are thieves. There ain't no honor among thieves, and that's a fact," Samuels insisted. "What do you people say about that?"

They all looked over at Ingram.

"It is true we stole when we first arrived. But we have repaid those we took from with, as you say, a sizable interest."

"I still don't know why you're here and I don't know why you're in *my* town."

"I have been working on an interface with our memory systems and your tele-production facilities. I have completed the story of our arrival, but that is all so far. I will give that to you and the device we made to display it. But we have no time now for discussions. I must finish my preparations."

"Look, he says they paid for the stuff they stole. Reimbursed the companies somehow," Paul whispered. "Cut him some slack. Right now we are all in the same pot."

At Paul's and Stacy's urging, Samuels reluctantly agreed to put aside his doubts. The gumdrop scooted his sled back into the other room, then returned with a small cube with coils and knobs seemingly haphazardly attached. He made some connections with a fiber optic cable to an old Amiga and the little device began to hum and various lights concealed beneath the transparent shell began to flicker and glow. In a few seconds, it went dark and quiet.

"This is from Systel's report in her own words. It is designated for the Alliance Security Council. We have been transmitting the entire report since the attack began, but this is all that is in a form humans can read." Ingram snaked out a tentacle and snagged the device, offering it to Samuels.

Samuels began playing with the projection device, absorbed with figuring out which protrusion was the ON button. He wanted to know the answers *now*.

"Leave it alone," Stacy said. "I want see if we can get out of here. Come on, I'll help you up."

"I guess surviving today is more important that what happened over twenty years ago," Samuels said, reluctantly, tucking the cube into his shirt. He held out his hands. Stacy grabbed him and pulled him to his feet. He wobbled a little, then leaned heavily onto her.

"Where are you thinking of going?" Paul asked. They were in the middle of the house and one option seemed as good as the next.

"Maybe we could sneak out through the woods," Stacy offered. Samuels was not up to thinking yet; his head was still spinning and his thoughts a little fuzzy. He was unsteady and forced to use both Stacy and an equipment rack for support. Paul had grown quiet, thinking. His eyes had taken on a faraway look. She wasn't sure if he was just thinking hard or had locked himself in a little room and didn't want to come out. Besides, she couldn't see that all that finger… hand… ah, tentacle… uh, whatever waving that the little alien was doing in the other room was doing *them* any good. So between her and the men and the aliens, who pretty much came down to the same thing, she figured she was the only one functional. Typical of men to become useless right when they were needed the most.

"We can *try* to make it out through the woods. I'm sure our little ET here has something that we could use as weapons and there are the weapons from the dead lizards, if we can get to them before the fire does." She was trying. Someone had to start thinking.

"There is an Aeolian camp in the woods," Ingram reminded them, scooting back into the room. "My defenses did not have the range to destroy it, only to cause a little havoc at the near edge. There are still significant forces in the woods, as you can tell from the weapons fire on the house."

"But it's a lot less now," she protested.

"When their attack ships come, there will be enough massed-fire to destroy the building. The larger icon is a close support attack craft. It carries about the same weaponry as ten of the fighters. It is slower than the fighters, though. Of course, the house is not going anywhere, so speed is not a factor. The fire from the woods now is just to keep us inside."

"Oh." Stacy didn't have any real desire to go stumbling around in the woods, anyway, but it felt like everyone was just going to roll over and give up. She pointed to the screen, were there were flashing emergency vehicle lights could be seen reflecting off of the trees and the clouds that were beginning to build up over Flagstaff Peak. "There are cars out there and probably people with guns to go with them," she said reasonably. "If you turn on your automated defenses full blast, we could probably make a run for it and get to the streets."

"Perhaps you are right," Ingram replied after a second of thought. "My automatic defenses should cover your movement. Perhaps you could escape. I estimate the odds that one of you will reach the road alive as one in seven hundred eighty-four thousand nine hundred thirty-two and point fourteen."

"That good, huh?" Stacy asked dryly.

"Maybe a little better if the wounded one stands and dies in a holding action," came the prompt reply.

Stacy turned to Paul and grabbed his arms and gave him a quick shake. "Hey, you in there? Think we can make it?"

"Why not? We only have to dodge laser bolts and walking snakes," Paul said, proving that he had been listening to the exchange all along. "You're a fast runner. Samuels can hold them off for awhile and when they take me, it'll slow them down a little. You should get out."

"You make it sound so simple," Stacy said with more than a hint of bitterness in her voice. "And you make me sound like a real ass."

"Not really, but I've been thinking."

"Oh, is that where you were doing?"

"Yeah. This little guy has been tinkering with the programming for a while and insisting that we all get back to this room for some reason. I don't think we're bait for the bad guys and I don't think we can make a run for the street and have a snowball's chance of getting ten feet if the gumdrop's with us and that little fellow is what this is all about. If we don't get him – it – out of here safely, then we might as well just turn him over to the lizards for lunch."

Paul looked at Samuels and took a long look at Stacy. Yeah, they both understood. But neither of them had a clue how to go about saving Ingram. Paul, at least, had a clue.

"I think the little guy needs us for something. But I don't think he'll force us to help. I think we either go along with whatever he has planned or run on our own. He'll… it'll… hell, it's a *he* for now because I'm tired of getting confused. *He* – will help us escape. And he'll either die doing that or die trying to escape on his own, but I'm pretty sure the choice is entirely up to us." Paul turned back to Ingram. "Am I right on that?"

"Yes. You must help me on your own choice. I cannot ask it at this point."

"Right," Paul said, turning back to the others. "I'll bet there's some religious or ethical or maybe even legal reason for that; after all, we are savages by their standards I'm sure."

"Not savages," Ingram corrected, "just not advanced enough for Alliance membership. There are restrictions on our level of contact, which I may have violated several times with the toy designs. Talking with you now is regrettably forbidden. Asking your assistance is prohibited."

"OK. There you go. We help or we run alone. Either way, it looks like a death sentence to me, but I'm thinking that dying helping to save the galaxy from lizard cannibals is a little better than just dying while running away."

Paul looked long and hard into Stacy's eyes. This was a moment for soul-searching and he had already come to his conclusions. Death had never bothered him or been something he feared. Not that he relished dying; no, there were too many things he wanted to do in life, places to see, stories to write, things to create. He would not welcome death because there was so much unfinished work here, but he was not afraid of death, either. He was, in fact, curious about what was on the other side. His view of God was largely tempered by the philosophies and beliefs from the Orient, where he had spent time as a teenager, with a good healthy dash of Missouri "show-me" State "I won't believe it until I see it myself" thrown in.

But he was afraid of pain. Pain bothered him. Pain was to be avoided. And death, so often as he had seen it in his life as a writer and in military service in the Middle East, too often came with a whole lot of pain. Right now, he wanted to avoid both. Something told him that dying now would be like starting a book and leaving the last chapter – or two or three – unread. There was a lot more to this story to unfold and, though the night was no longer young, the day had yet to begin.

"Well, when you put it that way," Stacy said after a moment, "you really don't give a girl much choice. If the gumdrop has a plan, and it doesn't involve anything slimy, then I'm in, I guess."

"Samuels, what about you?"

"I don't guess I'm gonna walk out of here alone anyway you cut it. What's the alien thing have in mind?"

Ingram produced two small items from somewhere on its body. Maybe it had a pouch like a kangaroo or some kind of body cavity where it could store things, because these just popped out of nowhere, it seemed. One was obviously a weapon, designed something like the laser pistols that the lizards were using. The grip and trigger guard were larger, probably designed for Systel's hands. The other was just a box shaped device with two small antennas on the top, something like a *Star Trek* tricorder with Mickey Mouse ears.

"What's that," Paul asked, pointing to the tricorder or whatever.

"This is an emergency signaling device. I salvaged it from the escape pod that brought us here before it dissolved," Ingram said. He hefted the other object. "This is a fairly powerful weapon, as you deduced. It is designed for long range use and would have not helped us with the Aeolians who made it inside the house. However, it will help us with their ships. The Aeolian prefer to fly without shields when they are in the atmosphere. Once we are out of the house, they will think we have no weapons powerful enough to damage a ship. There are four shots in this at full power, each can take out a fighter and maybe their close support craft if it is hit in the right place. At a lesser setting it can terminate ground personnel."

"Let's hope we don't need it," Paul said dryly, taking the gun. After a second, he handed it to Samuels. No question who the better shot would be and Paul was more interested in maximizing survival potential than in becoming a hero.

"How is your friend?" Ingram asked.

"I'm better," Samuels said, answering for himself. "It was just a bump on the head and it is clearing up pretty good. Just a headache. The leg is a problem. I can hobble along with help, but I'll not be doing any running."

"That shouldn't be necessary," Ingram replied, "but it is better that you are mobile. We must leave quickly. My sensors indicate that the reinforcements are almost here and the defenses are prone to collapse. I have set the weapons to full automatic with one of my Artificial Intelligence programs. When the shields collapse, I have set the house to self-destruct. If all goes as planned, it will look like the shields failed and the house was destroyed by their fire. They will believe me dead. But we must get to the transportation we have secured in the out building."

"Go outside?" Stacy protested. "That's suicide!"

"There is no other way to reach the building," Ingram said reasonably. "But the way is short. There is a passage through the sub-structure."

"There's a basement here?" Paul asked. Basements in Arizona were very unusual. Soil conditions in the sandy Phoenix Valley area were not conducive for sound construction. Likewise, blasting basements out of the rocky mountains in Northern Arizona was cost-prohibitive. But the Caruthers House had been there a long time and the original owner was known to be a Yankee with a lot of money. A basement seemed reasonable, and Paul had already postulated that one of the exits from the kitchen would lead to a root or wine cellar.

"Yes. It is not large, but it houses the power supply and some storage areas that I deduced were for food and bottled beverages. There is a short tunnel and a ramp to the surface that leads toward the garage. Originally, the house was fueled with coal, and I have deduced that the ramp was a delivery area for the fuel and bulk food stuffs. It has served us for much the same, though the reason they put such a small elevator in the kitchen is beyond me. I fit fine, but Systel could hardly manage just her head. This is a strange thing and it even goes to the second floor. Some day you will have to explain that. But it was useful in moving components from the basement to the levels where they were needed."

"But there are lizards with guns out there!" Stacy insisted.

"Yes, it will be most unpleasant for a few moments, but the house will provide a distraction. Those who stay here will surely be destroyed."

"Well, I guess outside isn't so bad an idea after all."

"The way is short and their sensors will be blinded by the house weapons. We only need to escape and then to stay out of their claws for a few of your hours."

"Does that mean that there is help on the way?" Paul asked.

"Yes. I just received a response from a Vegan patrol that was sent to investigate the signals I had sent earlier. They could not read them clearly, but subspace transmissions from this planet were enough to have them dispatch out a survey team. They are not heavily armed, but if I can get to them or they can get a shuttle to me, then we should manage Alliance space without a problem. They are calling in full Patrol support, so the Aeolians will not be eager to stay in-system for long."

"How long?" Samuels was concerned with practicality. "Not long" could just as well be "too long" for this motley group to survive, and that included his hide, which he was sure the lizards would want for the stew pot. Damned Arnold Schwarzenegger and his stupid film *Predator*. You couldn't meet an alien these days without wondering if they were going to pull out the trophy case or chopsticks.

"The Aeolians have probably intercepted my communications with the Vegan survey ship. They will know that the Alliance has been warned. They will want to destroy me and what evidence I hold before they leave, but they will leave before the Patrol arrives and sooner if they think I am dead. Failing that, they will need to report back to their leaders on their failure since the consequences to their worlds will be severe. It is possible that they will leave their fighters and assault craft behind and depart with just the mother ship, but I think not.

Those elements will not all chose suicide to prevent interrogation and they cannot assure that their equipment will be destroyed completely. To leave you large amounts of personnel and equipment to examine would be… counterproductive.”

“This is all insane,” Paul said.

“War, no matter where or how fought, always is,” Ingram replied. “Sometimes it is necessary, but it is never sane or desirable. There will likely be a large conflict when what I have reaches the Alliance Ruling Counsel. There will be much debate and delay, but eventually the Aeolian leadership will have to be removed. It is unlikely that they will leave willingly.” Ingram adjusted the height of his sled to about eye level with the humans and floated back toward the kitchen. “Everything is in motion. We must go.”

Ingram spun around and scooted over to the master control. There he very carefully removed a briefcase-sized object from the master array. It was obviously too heavy for him and the sled had trouble with the added weight, bobbing a good two feet. Stacy scooted over and took the case from the alien and looked at it closely.

“Wow, this is heavier than it looks,” she said.

“Yes,” Ingram acknowledged. “It is quite full after all these years and the power for the environmental controls is an older style, therefore heavier. I did not wish to risk the contents by building a newer container from your questionable electronic products here, though I had always expected Systel to be around to assist in carrying the case in needed.”

"What's this?" Stacy asked,

There was a small window on it and her curiosity overpowered her common sense. She looked.

Inside was what looked like a pool of bacteria swimming around happily in some sort or liquid. It looked like the biology slides from swamp water that Stacy had studied back in high school.

"Oooo. Bugs," she reported. "Biological warfare?"

"No. That is a microbe memory case. The viewer lets me assess the condition and activity level of the memory microbes," Ingram explained. "Such things are impervious to tampering. It contains all the evidence that Systel and I were trying to get to the Alliance. You must guard that with your life. Without out it, the Aeolians can argue that this was just a minor infraction of Alliance regulations. They might call it a hunting expedition by nobles for exotic wildlife."

"Dogs?" Stacy asked.

"Yes. They would be exotic to Aeolians."

"And cats?"

"Certainly. They would like very much to feast on Systel's race or your felines."

"And people?"

"Yes, but you taste like chicken," Ingram said through the flat, metallic translation device. Paul groaned. An alien with a redneck sense of humor.

"Yeah, but people are not that hard to hunt. Not very sporting," Samuels groused.

"The Aeolians are not here for sport. They will do whatever they can to muddy the waters. Even if I live, they could conceivably convince enough on the Council that there was nothing to what I say but lies. This they cannot argue against; only destroy." Ingram put the sled in motion and shot past the humans. "We have no more time to delay," it said, swiveling an antenna to see if they were following promptly.

The three did not have much choice but to follow. Samuels pocketed the alien weapon and, after a brief hesitation, handed his pistol to Paul. "There's a full clip in there," he said. "I'd save the last four. You know what I mean."

Paul just nodded. He did not have a clue how many bullets were in a full clip, but he did know that he was not going to put one in Stacy or himself. He still had the knife and he would go down swinging if it came to that. However, he was pretty sure that "captive" was not on the collective alien mind. It would be dead, alone or with company. He figured he'd take a few lizards into the afterlife with him. At least, that's what Paul thought. But, he reminded himself, he wouldn't know until the chips actually hit the table whether he had enough grit to play the hand or fold with a whimper. He was, after all, a writer, not a warrior and, even when he had served in the military, it had been as an information specialists, not as a shooter.

They entered the kitchen but Paul could not see a door that would lead into the basement until Ingram swung out a shelving unit that had been built over a very stout wood-plank door. As Ingram passed the door, the basement lit up automatically.

The hover sled the alien road took the stairs without problem, gliding down at a constant height, like it rode on a rail.

Paul followed, gun ready, just in case the lizards had made it into this part of the house unknown to Ingram. Paul doubted it. The little creature almost seemed psychic, but Paul was taking no chances. Behind him, Stacy and Samuels started down the stairs, but stopped while Stacy closed the door at Samuels' direction. There was no need in giving away more than they had if the aliens managed to slip a few commandos thru the hole in the house. They were probably pretty good at dodging lasers and Paul had the impression that the house's automated defenses were more predictable, and therefore less deadly, than those that were directed or augmented by living controls. From what Paul had seen, a kid that was good with one of those joystick controlled game systems would be a whiz at defense.

Paul noticed that the stairs had been reinforced in the not too distant past. When he reached the bottom, he saw that the pillars supporting the house had also been beefed up. The basement itself was spotless, like no other basement Paul had ever seen. Everything was clean and there was not a speck of dust in the air. Moreover, the space was virtually empty. Near what was once the main heating unit for the house was a contraption not much larger than a footlocker made from one-gallon glass jugs, and what Paul recognized as plastic fish tank tubing, and, of course, a stack of electronic components. From the base there snaked off several very large power cables that connected to several equally large circuit panels that had been added to the wall next to the furnace. There were also three separate sets of duct-work, but they all lead to the old furnace system. Paul guessed that one was heating, one cooling, and one the return air, but in this crazy house they could have been a new plumbing arrangement.

The only other items in the basement were two large floor-to-ceiling things that looked something like giant evaporative coolers, but there was no water, and what must have been a filtration device for the return air ducts. There was a small conveyer belt at the bottom of each wall-thingie moving very slowly. Occasionally some caked dirt would fall off one of the units and the conveyer hauled it over to a lift arrangement that crossed the ceiling. There was a similar lift near the return duct and Paul assumed that it was also collecting and depositing dirt, except this one scrubbed the air in the rest of the house. It was pretty full right now, but it would be with the mess created by the crash, the fire, and the blasted plaster from the firefight upstairs. There was another track there, made out of G-gage model train tracks. These are the large ones that Paul recognized as running around inside some restaurants like Judge Beans or Ruby's, not the HO-gage that he had played with as a child. The tracks ran from each side of the room and over the top of the gizmo where there was a kind of miniature train yard.

It was hard for Paul to see because it was near the ceiling and the tracks ran largely between the rafters, which provided the supports. But the trains on the tracks, Paul spotted four, though there could have been more in the "train yard," each had a single locomotive and three replicas of the 65 foot mill gondolas. The train would pull up to a loading platform near the wall. A series of shoots and hoppers would gather the dirt from the wall-thingies and load the cars. Then they would chug off to the yard while a second train pulled up and began loading.

At the yard, they gondolas dumped their load then were sucked clean by some very tiny vacuum hoses that could have been made from plastic straws. The larger pieces were ground up and mixed with the dust from the vacuum in a large clear work area. From there, the dirt was fed into a funnel and down another tube into the top of the contraption near the furnace.

Paul could not take his eyes off the system as he crossed the basement and into a tunnel that was about six by nine and maybe twenty feet long. He wasn't sure, but he would almost have sworn that the contraption was fueled by the dust from the room, collected by the wall-thingies and delivered by the trains, and *that* is what powered most of the house, provided the air conditioning and heating, and juiced up the energy weapons. General Electric would drool over that device for hours, but any housewife in the world would love it: no dusting or vacuuming.

Other than scuff marks on the floor around the dumbwaiter, there was little evidence that the room had any function other than to act as a collection chamber for dust and dirt used to fuel the house. That explained why there was very little dust in that maze of equipment upstairs, something Paul's nose was very happy to report as a verifiable fact. All the power one could ever want, from household dust. Idly he wondered if using up dust for energy would eventually make the world grow smaller. But since he wasn't much for his physics, and the conservation of matter theory made no sense to him since once matter was turned to energy it dissipated and once the Ever Active battery ran out, then the energy was gone. *Nothing* seemed like it was conserved. Stupid physicists. Maybe the cosmic dust falling on the planet would balance out the matter converted to energy.

The tunnel ended in a gentle ramp that was covered by a flat roof. Ingram and Paul waited for Stacy and Samuels there. They were making slow progress; Samuels on his bad leg and Stacy hobbled with Samuels and hampered by the weight of the memory case. Paul had tried to take Samuels from her but she waved him away. He had the gun and shouldn't be impaired if he needed to use it she said. Martyr, he returned, and earned himself a fierce scowl.

"This opens into a small shed," Ingram explained once everyone was there. "The entrance is screened and I do not believe it has been detected. Opening the passage door will trigger the program I wrote before we left. The house will go into full offensive mode and a hole in the shield will open to allow us to safely exit to the large structure facing the door to the shed. That is outside the shield. We must get there quickly as the shield will only be open for a short period."

"Is the garage locked?" Paul wanted to know.

"Yes, but the program will command the small door on the side to unlock and disable the passive defenses in the building. The Aeolians have not bothered with it since the defenses there have not been active. Had they drawn near, I would know."

"Then what?" Samuels, having just caught his breath, wanted to know.

"There is one of your conveyances in the building. I have repaired it and modified the engine somewhat, but it has been more of a hobby. The piloting controls have not been modified. One of you will have to pilot it."

"Anyone here knows how to fly, now's the time to speak up," Samuels stated flatly, making it plain that he was not the pilot they were seeking.

But Ingram forestalled their responses. "No," he said, waving a tentacle at Samuels. "I may have used the wrong term. The vehicle should not leave the pavement."

"Well, I guess I'm it, then," Paul said, looking at Samuels' injured leg. "Unless you want to drive, Stacy."

"No. Racing around in the night with aliens and wounded cops seems more like a guy thing. I'll sit in the back with Samuels and play nurse."

"Well, that's settled. When do we go?"

"Now," Ingram said, snaking out a tentacle and hitting a switch near the bottom of the ramp. Instantly, a large section of the roof tilted quietly up, revealing the interior of a small shed, complete with gardening equipment on the walls and cobwebs in the rafters. It looked like an abandoned or forgotten utility room.

The group worked their way up the ramp quickly and stood aside as Ingram played with a flowerpot holding a dead something. The floor quietly replaced itself, revealing an old, rusted wheelbarrow partially filled with rotting potato sacks. Just like something from Disney World's Haunted House, once the floor was back in place, you could not even see the cracks. Paul looked down and noticed that a breeze was blowing gently across the floor from hidden fans in the walls, stirring the dust, erasing their footprints, and making the humans stifle sneezes.

During the time Systel and Ingram were unloading their supplies and purloined equipment into the basement for distribution into the house, the used the shed to avoid activity around the house. They also had the dog food and other items from town delivered and stored in the shed. When the delivery people had left, the trap in the floor would open and the items shifted to the house. After the shed was emptied, the floor would close and within seconds there would be no evidence that anyone or anything had passed through. Creepy, Paul thought, but he was still very impressed with the details. Still, they had spent almost twenty-two years perfecting their system. But the details... no wonder they had succeeded in staying undetected all this time.

"Now, quickly to the vehicle enclosure. The House will create a distraction, there will be an abundance of fire and smoke to hide us, but we dare not risk being seen by the Aeolians or all will be lost."

The humans did not need to be warned twice. They had already seen the damage the aliens could do and they wanted no part of a closer examination. Ingram was quiet for a few seconds, as if using some sense they could not see to assess just how ready they were, then the door flew open and his sled darted across the yard to the garage. Paul was second out, but stopped by the door, holding Samuels' gun in two hands to provide what cover he could. If he couldn't hit anything, maybe he could keep them ducking and not shooting.

But his worry was not necessary. The house had set up a wild barrage, blasting into the trees and sending multiple shots after the ship, which pulled out of the area, rockets glowing brightly as it zigzagged away from the house's deadly beams. Paul forgot covering the fleeing group and ran off after them. There was enough fire and smoke to blind anything living and probably any sensors in the woods. Maybe the aliens would know something was up or maybe they would think that Ingram and company were just putting up an offensive to drive them farther back into the woods. Paul didn't care. He just ran like a bat out of Hell.

He didn't go far, though. Before he caught up with Stacy and Samuels, he slowed to a stop. The back of the house was something from a Hollywood horror flick. Where the alien craft had slammed into the back wall, there was a blazing fire raging. It looked like the house had some firefighting capability, which had obviously retarded the flames' spread, but the craft's fuel and exploding weapons were more than enough to overcome what Ingram must have installed in case of a forest fire. One whole corner was blazing away, sending flames hundreds of feet into the air and blasting out heat waves like a pizza oven on overload. That should block any infrared surveillance, anyway.

The fire only held his attention for a second. What caught him up was the destruction that littered the backyard. One fire truck was nothing more than a burned out hulk, resting on pools of melted rubber. Its companion was shattered, blown to pieces by enemy fire. It looked like someone had cut it in two with pinking shears. The police car strangely looked fine. The lights on the top were still rotating, but when Paul looked close, trying to understand what his eyes were seeing, he could tell that the car had been neatly sliced in half and the two pieces were offset by a few inches. If the two halves had not have been holding each other up, the car would have slumped like a tent with a broken center pole.

Bad as the scene was, however, it was nothing when compared to the toll in life that testified to a violent fight at the back of the house. The ground was littered with the firemen's lifeless hulks whose slickers, reflecting the flames from the house, looked like the caprices of so many dancing bugs. Paul could see a dozen or so lying on the ground, unarmed firemen cut down by the lizards. For a second his blood raced hotter than the house fire. He almost wished he had something to shoot at and not just a wall of fire and smoke between him and the forest.

He couldn't see the bodies of the people from the Forestry Department. But then there were the two cops from the patrol car. From the way their bodies looked, the Aeolians had continued to shoot them even after they were down. They bodies were riddled by quarter-sized holes, as if the frustrated lizards had decided to punish the two with the guns for the failure of the house defenses to just roll over and die. Paul was a gentle person at heart. He didn't hate easy or hate long, even when he had seen how some humans treated others in the hell that could be the

Middle East. He had shot enough photos and reported on enough cases of torture and rape that he had no illusions about man's inhumanity at times.

But this, this was worse than anything he had seen before. Or maybe it was worse because it was not humans doing humans, but aliens treating humans like so much meat. Paul didn't know. He didn't care. He just wanted a chance to do something to even the score. He knew he wasn't a soldier. Oh, he was pretty good at tactics and strategy, at least in simulations. But he knew he did not have the conditioning or training to go in head-to-head with professional soldiers. Or professional killers. There was a difference and he would swear that the Aeolians were the latter.

So maybe laying down his life to protect the gumdrop would help a little. But if he could do more, if he could find a way to carry the battle to those that would create the psychological atmosphere where the common soldier felt that mutilation was acceptable and would go unpunished... He had learned one thing in his checkered working career: a company takes its personality from the top down. If the owner was honest and trust worthy, caring about his employees, his managers would be the same, right down to the bottom. Oh, sure, there might be one or two lower level employees here or there that were jerks by nature, but they would either change or be weeded out.

On the other hand, if the owner was two-faced, cheated his employees and took advantage of them that is how his staff would treat others around them. Slow pay on reimbursements, lies, misdirection, office politics, all of that could be traced to the top.

If the owner only paid lip service to his philosophy of fair and equal treatment, then the few who were honorably in the company would be left time and again out on a limb, holding a bag of empty promises. Eventually, the good and talented people would go or be replaced and the company would suffer. It all started at the top and worked its way down. But, as John Stewart once said, "I never had a job where the boss wouldn't steal the drum from his own brass band." That, largely, was why Paul was a freelance journalist. He had a sense of honor and fair play that wouldn't allow him to fit in with the corporate crowd.

And his sense of honor was up in full arms. If he lived through the night, there were going to be some lizards that learned that the power of the pen was a mighty thing. There would be enough evidence left scattered around Flagstaff to put proof to his words and put the story on the front page of the *Post* or *The Times* and not lost in the back pages of *Fantasy and Science Fiction*. Or some other magazine. *F&SF* never bought anything Paul wrote, no matter how good it was, so this wouldn't even see their automated rejection system.

"Paul, are you coming or are you trying to get a sun tan?" Stacy called from the garage. That shook Paul out of his meditation and sent him on a fast trot toward the open door. Both Samuels and Stacy were waiting inside and both gave him a very strange look. But it was Ingram that surprised him.

"You must speak loudly about this, though many will not believe. It is, as you know, all you can do." Now what the *hell* did that mean and why the *hell* did the gumdrop say it when he did? Paul was already suspected the little fellow was a mind reader, but he kept proving it at the oddest times.

The volume of noise from outside suddenly increased. Ingram looked at his hand-held communication device for a second, then turned to the others.

"We were just in time. Their other ships have arrived and are attacking the house. When the main door to this building opens, the house will begin another barrage, but we must hurry. There is little time left before the house is destroyed."

Ingram moved out of the way and the humans got a good look at the car he had been modified.

"Will you look at that," Paul said. "A 1965 Ford Mustang. The first car I ever owned. Yeah, I can drive one of these," he added, a slow smile coming to his face. "But you know it doesn't have a lot of power, especially with all of us in the car."

"The engine was missing when we found the car, so I put in one of my own. I believe it has more than enough power for our needs. The speed will be considerably greater than that to which you are accustomed."

"Well, if it steers the same, and you haven't messed with the controls too much, I should do fine."

"If it gets us out of the free-fire zone I'll be satisfied," Samuels said.

"Then you must enter it and go quickly."

No one needed a second invitation. Stacy helped Samuels into the back seat. It was easier than it might have been, since the passenger side seat had been removed, obviously to make room for Systel's larger frame. Ingram, however, did not follow them. He hovered right outside the door, watching as Stacy stored the vital memory on the floor behind the driver's seat. Paul stopped on the other side of the car after he opened the door and saw that Ingram was not moving.

"Go on. Get in," he said, leaning over the roof of the Mustang, yelling across the car.

"You have the memory. I am not sure I should continue to endanger your lives," Ingram replied, piping the words in tones that sounded like a wind singing through a lonely canyon.

"Well, hell, if he isn't going I'm not going!" Samuels exclaimed from the back. "For all we know, we're a diversion and he's got a better hidey-hole around here. Damned if I'm going out to be target practice."

"No, no, please, your best hope for survival is in fleeing," Ingram said. "Besides, you don't believe there is a safe place here or that I have another means of escape."

"Then get in," Paul said again, softer and without the urgency that he felt. "We're in this too deep to worry about that now."

The little alien dropped his sled low to the ground, where he could easily sense each of humans in turn. Then, without further comment, he slid into the car and settled the sled on the floorboard.

"Yes. I see you will risk yourselves to help me. This is a good planet to save."

"Well, I guess that means it's time to go," Stacy said.

Paul climbed in and looked to start the car, but there was no key. Ingram grew a tentacle and sent it to a small pad mounted next to Paul's door on the dashboard. Something happened; it was not like a normal car starting up, but they could feel the power in the little 'Stang even though it did not rumble like the little six cylinder engine that Paul knew so well.

"Anything else I need to know about this?" Paul asked.

"The engine is different, as I said. There are some stealth units built in to help us avoid detection, but the control and guidance should be normal."

"Gas?"

"No, but acceleration is controlled by the same mechanical foot device."

"Let's do it, then."

As soon as the garage door began to open, the outside exploded in a violence that made the earlier distraction look like a lame warm-up session. Bolt after bolt shot out and into the woods and there were enough shots into the dark sky to keep a dozen enemy ships at bay.

"Damn," Samuels breathed from the back. "I hope we don't get toasted by friendly fire."

"Everything is programmed to prevent that," Ingram responded to the rhetorical question. But as the garage door rolled up, none of the humans were *that* confident in running the laser gauntlet unscathed.

When the door barely reached four and half feet, Paul stomped on the accelerator and the Mustang shot out of the garage like a Minnie ball from a musket. His old Mustang could move, but he thought this one just might fly. He had a moment's problem handling the car as it fishtailed around the remains of one of the fire trucks and he let off on the gas. Or the whatever. Paul was sure there was certainly no Ford V-6 under the hood. He would bet that whatever Ingram had replaced the engine with would rival the horsepower on the most powerful Mercedes 12-cylinder ever built. Or a fighter plane.

Paul swung the car wide around the still burning hulk of his old '87 Cherokee and dodged Fisher's car heading into the lane. He tried to ignore the bodies scattered alongside the road and tried his best to avoid hitting them with the car, with pretty good success. Whatever suspension was holding the car to the road was also not standard Ford issue. It flew over the potholes as if this rutted, country driveway were a newly opened Autobahn.

"Damn," Stacy said as they passed the Cherokee.

"It's insured," Paul said over his shoulder.

"I was thinking about the Snickers," Stacy replied sardonically.

"Where do we go?" Paul yelled, though there was no need for that. The inside was quiet enough that a whispered conversation would work. He decided to ignore Stacy.

"I think we should head for the police station," Samuels opted.

"Well, I think we should get out if town," Paul said. "If those ships try to find us, I don't think we should be around people. Help's on the way. If we can stay out of sight until then, we'll save lives."

"No, we need to…

"Avoid the city," Ingram said, cutting off Samuels and putting an immediate end to the argument. "If they do find us, we want to avoid additional causalities. The other attack craft, the ones that dispatched by your military, should arrive in the area momentary. They'll join in the confusion around the house, distracting the airborne Aeolians. But if the ground forces saw us – and they probably did – those four other ships might be sent out hunting. They will not take chances that we have escaped with the data microbes."

That made sense to Paul, but he still didn't have any idea where to go or what road to take, but Stacy came to his rescue. "Take a right," she directed from the backseat, just as they came up on the road.

Paul slammed on the brakes, spun the wheel, and fishtailed off the dirt and gravel and onto the pavement. There were a couple of police cars – these looked like the highway patrol and not the local Flagstaff variety – parked across the street. Someone shouted something, but Paul was out of the lane and gone before anyone could react.

"That was easy," Susan said.

"But this won't be," Paul returned, looking down the road. The light from the fire had been so bright that Paul had not thought to turn on the car's headlights. He held off now. The road ahead was barricaded by the National Guard or Army or somebody with big trucks. They were quite close before anyone noticed them and Paul was around the roadblock and shooting down the road at well over 90 before anyone could take aim. Paul caught a quick glimpse of a trooper trying to shoot an M-16 from the hip, but that just didn't work with those highly accurate weapons. Spray and Pray was a tactic untrained terrorists used with an AK-47. Weekend warriors! The 16's had sights and were meant to be used *with* the sights, unlike an Uzi or an AK. All the soldier managed to do was expend a full clip shooting up some pine trees. Those units that had fought in the Gulf knew better. Aim-shoot, aim-shoot. It was one of the reasons the US military had a much higher kill ratio than the terrorists despite using a fraction of the bullets. Maybe it didn't look as cool as standing in the middle of the street spraying bullets but it was deadlier.

"If they start following us with flashing lights, then I'll bet the lizards will get curious. They'll see that from the air pretty easily," Paul said over his shoulder.

"Slow down a little. You're going to turn pretty soon," Stacy said. She turned in the seat and looked out the window. "I see some lights back there, but we;re going to make some quick turns to get on another road. I don't think they'll be able to follow us."

"All we need is a chopper in the air with look down radar and they'll pick us out with no problem," Samuels said.

"They will not see this car on your radar," Ingram told them. "And you can leave the lights off."

The alien dropped open the glove compartment and fiddled with some controls that had been mounted inside. A heads-up view of the road before them painted itself across the windshield. Paul could see and drive as well as if it was daylight. It was almost like driving one of those racing games at the mall, except he didn't think he would just bounce off if he ran into a wall.

"How accurate is this?" he wanted to know.

"Details are down to less than an eighth of one of your inches. It is created by a highly efficient laser."

"Can the lizards detect it?" Stacy asked, peering out the back window and into the night sky. "I don't see anything there."

"And you won't, either, unless it's sitting on the roof," Paul responded.

"No, the laser is not something the Aeolians can easily detect and the car is radar and scanner proof, both to them and to your local police."

"What were you building this for?" Samuels asked. "More robberies?"

"No. There was a good chance that a rescue team could not land close to the house without detection. We needed a quick way to reach the coordinates of a good landing spot. This was my planned means of transportation."

"Left here and a right at the next major street," Stacy directed.

"Do we need to head to that landing site now?" Paul asked as he followed Stacy's directions at a sedate 60 miles an hour.

"No. It will be morning, three or four of your hours before the Patrol can insert forces into the system close enough to send a shuttle. They will not risk a rescue in daylight because they will not want Humans to spot the craft. And they do not have the coordinates. We will need to contact them when they arrive and make arrangements for a pick up later.”

“In the meantime, we need a place to hide,” Paul said.

“Not in the city. We don’t want to endanger innocent lives,” Ingram said.

“Well, I sure don’t know any place this side of New River,” Paul said, referring to a small down about thirty miles north of Phoenix.

“The Indian Reservation’s rodeo wrapped up last month. The Fair Grounds will be deserted,” Stacy offered, somewhat hesitatingly. “We can probably hide in the horse barn.”

“How far is that?” Paul wanted to know. He was swerving through traffic aiming for I-40.

“Oh, about a hundred seventy-five miles…”

“I don’t know that we can last over three hours before we're spotted,” Samuels said in a voice so dry that it would make the Gobi feel humid.

“This place is remote from inhabitants?” Ingram asked.

“Yeah, the houses aren’t real close to the Grounds. Only place I can think of that’s remote and a shelter,” Stacy said.

“Do we have any other options?” Paul asked.

Samuels sighed. “I guess one place to become a human torch is as good as another. Go for it. Stacy, can you give him directions? I’ve never been there.”

“Turn right here,” Stacy said. “This will take us to Historic Route 66. It’ll take us out of town in a couple of minutes, and then there’s nothing for a long way.”

Paul made the turn onto North Switzer Canyon Road, a beautiful tree-lined drive that eventually turned north into the Historic US 66 and then on to I-40, where Stacy sent him east.

"Go ahead and open it up," Samuels said. "If we get stopped I'll flash a badge and see if I can't get word back to headquarters. We should probably go there now…"

"It is too dangerous. We need to move away from our base as quickly as we can."

Ingram reached into the glove compartment again and made some other adjustments. "You may relax your pressure on the accelerator," he told Paul. "You must still guide the vehicle, but I have initiated a program that will allow the maximum speed for the road conditions. It will adjust to keep the vehicle on the road. Do not worry about turns. It is scanning the road far enough ahead to allow for safe maneuvers."

Paul took his foot off the "gas" and sat back. He kept an eye on the digital speedometer displayed in the heads-up. As the numbers began to climb, his eyebrows went up. The speed increased past sixty, moved steadily past eighty. At one-twenty, the scenery was beginning to blur and, though the traffic was very light that time of the morning, Paul became nervous about his reaction times. But Ingram assured him the computer looked for obstacles as well as turns. The numbers kept climbing until they hovered around two-forty. In less than five minutes, they had made the forty-minute trip and were whipping around the curve I-40 took as it passed the city. But even at two hundred and forty miles an hour, it would be another five or ten minutes before they reached the turnoff for US-180.

"If one of those truckers we pass calls in a report the State will be on our ass pretty quick," Samuels said.

"Well, then you can see about contacting your headquarters, right?" Paul said. What the hell, not much they could do about avoiding eyeballs. "Does the radio work?" he asked Ingram.

"No, it only picks up your local stations."

"That's what I wanted. Stacy, what's the local news channel?"

"I listen to The Mountain. Classic rock," she said, impressing Paul who thought the best rock ever recorded still came from '65-'75, with a few exceptions in the early 'ninties when Pearl Jam and Nirvana first came out. Beyond that, not much impressed him, except when people like Santana released a new single. "I'm not much on news, but I think 600 AM is an all news station. KVNA."

"I know that one," Ingram said and turned on the radio.

"…to be one of the worst wildfires in the city's history and reports of fatalities from both the fire department and local police keep trickling in," a reporter was saying.

"Why is that, Jack? And what about rumors that the military is involved?" the station anchor asked.

"That's just what we're hearing on the scene. But look at what's happened already tonight. We have a blaze that started shortly after dusk and already it has engulfed almost six acres on the edge of town, including the old Caruthers' House. Something is flying over that area and there are explosions reported and sightings of fireballs in the sky. I have seen the fireworks myself. It is like an illegal bottle rocket factory caught fire, but worse, much worse. Everything off the road is gone, is what I am hearing from the firemen who are rotating off the line. But right now, no one is willing to go into the woods. They are holding the line at the road."

"Any idea what started the fire yet?"

"No, nothing has been said about that yet. There have been some National Guard activities and what may be Air Force or Marine fighters up here over the past couple of weeks, and they seem to be back as well as National Guard helicopters. Right now, there are a lot of Guardsmen helping fight the fire and there are Guard helicopters circling the area, but these are military helicopters, not search and rescue or choppers equipped with water buckets. This story is a lot bigger than the fire, but nobody is talking. No one knows what set off the explosions. It's another mystery to add to the many things that have been going on around here for the past few weeks."

"OK, Jack. We'll check back with you after eight. Call in if you know more."

"You got it!"

"And speaking of mysteries, there is more going on right here in Flagstaff, where the National Guard are blocking roads near the Route 89-66 merge..."

And that was about all they could hear as the vehicle rapidly passed beyond the station's signal.

Ingram turned down the radio and braced himself as Paul swerved between two semi's that looked like they were standing still but were probably rolling at over a hundred. The car held well, not skidding an inch as it flew through the curves.

"Why were those things after you? What's so important in there," Stacy asked, tapping the case with her foot, "that they would risk attacking us to destroy it."

"Systel was an Ambassador on one of the Aeolian fringe worlds. I was her aid. She gathered information for her home government and came across some Aeolian practices that would not be approved in the Alliance. She and I were on our way to carry that evidence to the Alliance in the hopes that the Council would prove an ally in stopping Aeolian aggression. Our diplomatic mission was attacked and our Hiver ship destroyed in a space battle. Systel and I escaped in a life pod, which crashed in the mountains near Clay Springs. Our colleague was killed in the crash, though the Hiver would not have survived alone here in any case."

"Clay Springs? Where the UFOs have been seen? And the murders?"

"Yes. The life pod melted near there and we made our way to the city. We originally moved toward Clay Springs but the town was too small so we moved west. We established ourselves in an empty house and have been working to build a communications system to call for help. That is a difficult task, so we also built defenses should we be located before the radio – you would call it a radio, but it is much more than that – before the radio was completed."

"But Clay Springs. There's UFOs there again, isn't there?"

"Yes. I fear the Aeolians may have detected our test signals. I am sure they found the residue of the pod and searched for us first there before moving on to Flagstaff. They could not be sure where we were hiding in relation to the signal we sent."

"So how did they find you?"

"They would have traced the messages we sent and found a general location of the transmitter. Since the house was defended, we had the transmitter located there. It seemed a better idea at the time. They knew the general area within several hundred square miles. I know they have been trying to pin down the exact location for some weeks. They would have detected some strange readings at the house, though our cloaking processes would have left them uncertain until our next distress call. Unfortunately, the shield that I used to protect you earlier is not a product of your species. That confirmed that a non-human controlled the location, if not our exact presence. Yes, they would have razed the house and every dwelling near there for insurance, then kept searching after us should the house have been only the transmission site. That is logical and fits the facts we have."

"You just let them…" Stacy began.

"No, no, you don't understand. We thought the Aeolian forces had abandoned this system after they gave up their search when we originally landed. It has been many years since we crashed. Had we known that we would draw their attention to you, we would have found another way to make contact or moved the translator to a remote location," Ingram protested. "Understanding the logic and action after the fact is not the same as understanding it before it happens. They must have detected the distress call," he said after a short pause. "We couched it as a general call from an unaligned species, to simulate a new crash here, but the Aeolians must have decided to investigate anyway. It was a gamble that needed to be taken."

"Yeah. Nice of you to invite us to your party," Samuels grumbled, rubbing his leg.

But what difference would it have made? Paul wondered. Would the government have helped or thrown the aliens in a dark hole someplace for study? That's what a lot of people believed happened at Roswell. And if they did that, wouldn't we have pissed off both the good guys and the bad guys? Well, probably only the good guys; the bad guys would be happy that we had locked up the information that condemned them. Yeah, the saying was pretty true: he who condones evil, supports evil. Had we not helped Ingram, we would have helped the Aeolians. Hindsight was truly a wonderful thing. Unfortunately, most governments didn't even have now-sight, much less hindsight or foresight. Just power-and-greed-sight.

The highway had wound though the foothills and Flagstaff was almost sixty miles behind the car. Paul kept glancing at the mirrors. The fire in Flagstaff was still visible against the clouds over San Francisco Peaks like someone had dropped in landscaping lights. Paul snuck a quick look again in the rear view mirror. What he saw made him slam on the brakes and swerve to a stop on the side of the road.

"What…"

"Look back at Flagstaff. See them?"

"Wow, look at that," Stacy said, seeing what had grabbed Paul's attention. Clearly etched in the light cast by fire was a large aircraft, plainly larger than anything every produced on earth and certainly not manufactured by Boeing or Lockheed or Northrop Grumman or Mitsubishi or Mikoyan-Gurevich. No, this could easily have been the *Millennium Falcon's* big brother and Paul once again saw what he had thought only his imagination proven something in reality. But where the *Falcon* had been a ship used by the good guys, this was not. Or had the *Falcon* started out as a good-guy ship? Didn't Solo get his hands on it from the criminal element? Maybe there was a train of alien logic in there somewhere, but Paul could not follow it.

Whatever the intention Ingram had in sending off the designs, that was the *Falcon* hovering over the house, blasting away as its shields easily deflected the house's defenses, while the little fighters wove their way in, adding their own weapons to the hell storm surrounding the house. And where was the US Air Force? Probably in smoking ruin in the deserts of Nevada and Arizona. This was not something that a B-52 could handle and the interceptors they had spotted at the house were long overdue. But Paul believed that the military – the human type – would make their appearance sooner whether than later. If the first interceptors had been trashed, then better believe that there were more on the way.

These aliens moved fast, but they were stopped now, sitting over the house. Drop a few hundred Rafael Python-4 air-to-air missiles and watch them try to scramble, then come back and talk about Earth

Military. Or at least the US military. Right now, the bad guys were only fending off energy weapons from the house. Paul didn't believe that the same shields that worked with energy would have the much effect against a swarm of seeker missiles and he doubted the point defenses on those smaller birds would hold up to a mammoth assault from long range followed by a short range barrage of AGM-65 Maverick or AIM-9 Sidewinder heat seeking missiles. There was no way Paul believed that those ships ran *cold*.

Suddenly, the close support attack craft, *Millennium Falcon* to Paul, was engulfed by a huge ball of flame mushrooming up from the ground. For a few seconds, all that they could see was a massive ball of flame. Out of that, one of the fighters that had been attacking the house staggered, faltered, and fell. A second, streaming flame, shot straight up, probably seeking to return to the mother ship, but it became a rapidly expanding ball of flame of its own before it could vanish into the clouds.

Slowly, the fireball dissipated and there, in the center, was the *Falcon*. It looked untouched as it continued to hover for a few seconds. Then it slowly began to settle from the stern, until it was at about a forty-five degree angle. Then it slid rapidly out of sight and a second later, another fireball rose toward the clouds.

"The people…"

"They are dead."

"I meant in the houses near there. That explosion…" Stacy choked on her words, thinking that the blast that had taken the alien ship was surly large enough to have laid waste to a large area around the house.

"They are fine. The blast was designed to go up, not out. The house and everything in about 100 feet around it are gone, but the road is three times that far or more and the nearest houses farther still, so there should have been no human causalities from the house. Only the Aeolian ground forces in the area. Of course, where the Aeolian ships fell may be another matter. But your rescue forces should have little trouble entering the area now. The bulk of the attackers are gone."

They stayed parked for a few more minutes, looking at the firelight reflected from the mountains and clouds. It was over, Paul thought. They were free and could wait out the arrival of Ingram's rescue team with a little peace.

"We should continue now," Ingram finally said. "There may still be scouts searching the area."

"Why? Wouldn't the destruction of the house be enough? Won't the other ships leave now?" Stacy demanded, feeling like someone had dumped a bucket of ice water over her right out of a hot shower. "Aren't we safe now?"

"The disturbance from the blast should have distorted the Aeolian sensors for now. We should have time to escape." Ingram did not sound encouraging.

"I thought you said this car was undetectable," Paul said.

"Normally, yes, and to their atmosphere craft, most certainly. But if I was in command of the Aeolians, I would have a spotter ship in orbit above this area. They will be using optics, scanners, radar, and other sensors tied to a computer system. Our departure from the house would have been noted by the ground forces and probably recorded by their computers. The orbiting craft will see that it cannot read us with its other sensors and, now that the house is gone, they will investigate anomalies. The sensors will see the heat from the tires on the road but not see the vehicle. They will vector a craft this way I am sure. But if we can find a place to hide where the optics cannot see us, we should be safe. They will be splitting their attention across a large area. We have a chance."

"I hope the lizards agree with that," Stacy quipped, leaning back into the seat, total exhaustion washing over her like a wave cresting in Fuerteventura.

Paul reluctantly got back in the car and pulled away at a more sedate pace. If they were being tracked by optics, then a radar-proof car going 120 or better would be a dead give away with emphasis on the dead.

"We should go back now," Samuels said. "There will be police about. They might be of some help."

"If we approach them, they will be killed." Ingram's simple, unemotional statement sent chills down Paul's spine. There was no equivocation, no doubt at all. The humans would not stand a chance if the Aeolians came at them with their fighters and almost no chance if they attacked with ground forces. Maybe the Rangers or one of the special ops groups could hold their own, but Paul was sure that even the US military's elite, unquestionably the best in the world, could not even hold their own if they were not given time to prepare and work through new techniques, new weapons. To come at the aliens now, unprepared for the battlefield conditions that they had never dreamed about, for which they had never seen a second of training, well, that would be worse than a massacre.

No, Paul agreed with the little gumdrop; if they were going to survive, it would be through stealth and invisibility until help arrived that understood this type of warfare, who could stand in combat against the aliens on their own terms. From what Paul had seen so far, the human military could probably whip the aliens any day on equal footing, or even a little less than equal. But the disparity in weaponry made any likely encounter in the near future a foregone conclusion and one that was not promising for human survival.

"Those aliens blasted everything that came in their way," Paul told Samuels. "I don't think a tank could even stand up against their lasers. The closer we are to the city the better chance they have of nailing us."

"A tank could not stand and fight," Ingram said with certainty. "The Aeolian weapons are concentrated energy weapons. When they hit the armor of one of your tanks, the outer surface would vaporize, but the inner surface would only turn to liquid. The temperature differential would blow the liquid metal into the enclosed area at high speed. Any living tissue would be incinerated. Certainly covering any moving parts with liquid metal would either destroy them outright or clog them when the liquid hardened. The liquid 'bullets' would eat right through any soft or thin metal, like the coverings on most of your electronics, and destroy the circuitry inside."

"Well, don't we have weapons that could hit back?" Stacy remembered the Gulf War, where American tanks had made mincemeat of the best the Iraqi's had to offer. And she had read a *Time* or *Popular Mechanics* piece in a doctor's office about little rockets that floated around on parachutes and then shot off when they spotted a target. "I mean, if we can hit them, are they armored that well?"

"Not the fighters," Ingram admitted, "and maybe not the close support ships. Their defenses are designed for more modern weapons, energy weapons. There are few projectile weapons used any longer in the Alliance or our traditional adversaries and the ships have thinner armor to reduce weight and increase mobility."

"Yeah, but our guys wouldn't stand a chance with shoulder-fired missiles," Samuels said, flatly.

"Why not?" Stacy was interested. They were cruising along at two hundred miles an hour or more and there were no problems that she could see. At least for the moment, she could relax and, in an odd sort of Tomboy way, this was interesting. Maybe because her life might depend on whether or not the military could mount a defense against these lizards if they ran for help or maybe just because she needed a distraction, so not to think about what might be zeroing in behind them.

"They'd be instant targets. If these lizards know where our guys are, their dead meat," Samuels explained. "Take the Army's Dragon missile. That's a shoulder-fired anti-tank weapon that the Army uses a lot," he explained, thinking back on the work he had done with the Guard a few years back. "The soldier's gotta keep the weapon's sights on the target and direct the missile's flight if he wants to hit anything. But those puppies often make a lot of noise and 'back-blast' – that's smoke and debris that shoots out the rear of the missile's launch tube. Don't bet your life that these lizards don't have the technology to spot where the missile came from and fire back, and if that happens our guys are gone. They've either gotta destroy the ship or ground vehicle the enemy sends before the hostile fire reaches them or break away from the attack. If they break, they'll miss the target."

"Don't miss the turn," Stacy said as they flew past Joseph City. "It should be soon."

"Wait a minute," Paul said, looking at Samuels in the rear view mirror and acknowledging Stacy's comment with a nod. "I did an article a few months back about Lockheed Martin's new Javelin. That's a true 'fire-and-forget' missile; once it's launched, it guides itself to the target. I saw the video. It took an M1A2 and turned it into scrap metal that had to be dug out of a six-food deep hole."

"Yeah, but you can't get a radar lock on these things. Something like that would never work," Samuels objected. "You still need a driver and that driver can be spotted and knocked out before his missile hits."

"No, no, not these things," Paul said. "I work with video. The Javelin has an internal TV camera to find the target."

"That can be jammed," Samuels said, not giving an inch.

"No, it's totally internal," Paul explained. "First you have to prep the Javelin for launch. If you are not detected there, once the missile is locked, it's on its own. It uses a set of digital imaging microchips that detect infrared light bounced off the target. There's a separate optical or infrared viewer attached to the launch tube for spotting. Once the target's locked, you push the fire button and the missile's imaging chip grabs an electronic picture of the target before it leaves the firing tube. In flight, it has a camera that takes new images of the target every second or so and compares it to what's stored in its memory. The internal computer keeps the missile locked on until the very end, even if it's moving."

"I don't know. These ships can move pretty far in a second," Samuels said, carrying the argument further.

"OK. You got that point," Paul admitted. "The Javelin's designed to attack a ground target, like the old Greek Javelins. Once it's launched, there's a secondary rocket that kicks in to take it into a high arc so it can slam into the target from above. That's harder to defend against, I guess, and the tank's armor is thinner and more vulnerable up there. It also makes it more difficult to follow the trajectory back to the launch point. It's got good range, about 7,500 or 8,000 yards, or with a minimum of about 80 yards, so it's pretty good for close-in fighting, too. And there's no back-blast because it uses a small explosive charge with just enough force to push the missile out the launch tube a few feet. Once it's about twenty feet away from the launch tube, the motor kicks in to send it to the target."

"Sounds like a neat thing," Samuels agreed, "but I don't think these guys have a lot of assets on the ground."

"No, but it might have taken out that ship that was just hovering and it sure would have taken out the fighters on the ground back in that clearing," Paul insisted. "I think ground fire is our best bet. I don't think our aircraft have much of a chance against those things we saw back there. But the British have a system that might work pretty well."

"But that's in Britain," Stacy protested. "The lizards are over here."

"I know that the US has plans to test them on the Apache, a modified version of the two-man portable system," Paul said. "They're pretty good against fast moving targets. Called a 'Starstreak' I think."

Paul would certainly like a Starstreak about now. He had been writing quite a bit for a military magazine last year and the Starstreak, the UK's new close range anti-air guided weapon system that they had developed as a defense against helicopters and high-speed ground attack aircraft, had been pretty big news. The system was produced by Thales Air Defense Ltd., formerly Shorts Missile Systems, of Belfast, Northern Ireland. The self-propelled, high-velocity missile system had made quite a ripple when the Brits announced that they planned to place an Irish weapon service with the British Army in 1997. Paul knew that a shoulder-launched version was in the works, but he didn't know how far along it was, but he had read that the British government was in the process of negotiating a five-year production contract with Shorts early this year for three batteries of thirty-six systems. That had prompted the takeover by Thales, a French company, which could ultimately degrade the product, Paul thought, especially since Thales had bought, or was in the process of buying, out every other manufacturer who made components for the system. Yeah, a big problem. You just couldn't trust the French not to sell you cheap junk or sell it to your worst enemy, especially if they controlled the entire production process.

The Starstreak relied on a two-stage, solid propellant rocket motor, a separation system and three high density darts. A power pulse from the missile firing unit ignited the first-stage motor, giving the missile a pretty hefty initial acceleration before it is jettisoned. Canted nozzles put the missile into a roll, using centrifugal force to unfold the fins for aerodynamic stability in flight. When the second-stage motor ignites, it kicks the missile to a velocity greater than Mach 4, which should be enough to hit one of those alien ships as it was coming in for an attack run.

The three darts automatically separate when the second stage motor burns out. They keep a high kinetic energy and, with all three guided by a double laser beam riding system to the same target by independent guidance and control circuitry, the fused high-density warhead, designed to penetrate the target before detonation, can wreak havoc on the aerodynamics of any atmosphere craft it not destroying it outright. And with three darts launched at the same target from close in, the final sprint almost guarantees a hit by one or more dart.

Typically, the Starstreak was mounted on a tracked Alvis Stormer vehicle with eight rounds of

Starstreak missiles primed and ready to fire and with a backup of another twelve missiles. It reportedly relies on a Pilkington infrared scanner and processor that automatically slews the weapon sight onto the target from a stationary vehicle. But the launch vehicle only need to be stopped for a few seconds, then the driver can get the hell out of the firing range before retaliation can strike. Mobility was the key to survival and with the lizards.

Up to this point, Samuels was fully intrigued. There might be some of these things as near as El Paso or maybe even the Yuma Proving Grounds in Southwest Arizona, he suggested. And, yes, Paul acknowledged, he knew from a source in the Pentagon, that ATASK, an airborne variant of Starstreak, was scheduled for tests by the United States Army on the Apache attack helicopter sometime in October or November of 1998 in Yuma. But that was more than four years and Paul had not read anything about the outcome or deployment. And they needed help *today*. Now. Pronto. Of which Samuels reminded Paul, without much humor and with absolutely no soft words, when Paul mused that he had no idea what had happened with the weapons.

"Yeah. OK. Just thinking," Paul said.

"Well, think about this," Samuels reminded him. "The National Guard is playing around these parts and they're likely going to get here way before the Army or the Marines or the Coast Guard or even the Boy Scouts, right?"

"Yeah. Probably. If they're here already."

"They are. They've been all over the area recently, playing real army," Samuels said, suddenly wondering if the war games the Guard was playing was something more and if the observers from the regular army weren't here looking to observe little green men. Or big lizards. "Yeah," Samuels continued after a second. "The Guard. Now tell me, how many Guard units have *today's* equipment, much less *tomorrow's*? In fact, most Guard units are using equipment from the day *before* yesterday. Now, how much chance do you think they'll have against the lizards?"

"Not much," Paul admitted.

"Right. Our SWAT team is better equipped than the Guard, even the ones who were sent to Iraq," Samuels stated flatly. "And when we need help, how soon do you expect them to get to our aide?"

"Probably after everything is over," Stacy offered.

"Right. We can have Flagstaff SWAT, as small as it is, ready on 20 minutes, if they aren't already mobilized. I'll kick some ass if they aren't. So we have police help *now*. Why not use it?"

"Because they will all die and you with them," Ingram stated flatly, in a tone that left no room for challenge.

"There is that," Stacy agreed.

"Well, we still need to get some fire power," Samuels insisted. "I've got my gun…"

"Against energy weapons and force fields? That's like tacking on a tank with a rubber band gun!" Paul interrupted with a shocked protest.

"What I was saying is that, if those guys start tracking us and find us, my peashooter isn't going to do much good. Hell, it only knocked that one lizard over and it takes two to the head to do any real damage. I'm pretty good, but I don't know anybody that's *that* good with a pistol, especially if they're shooting from more than ten yards away and I sure don't want to get even that close again if I can manage it," Samuels concluded, leaving absolutely no doubt in anybody's mind just how much he had enjoyed his last meeting with the lizards.

"And rubber band guns or not," he added, "we should be doing something besides running!"

"We are," Stacy said quietly.

"Yeah, and what is that?

"We're staying alive."

"And our turn is coming," Stacy added. "That's Holbrook. The turn's near the far edge of town."

Paul tapped the brakes and watched the numbers begin a rapid decent. He would go through the little town at a sedate speed, knowing that it was a prime location for radar traps. He had to smile at that. Radar? Not with this baby! He was tempted to blow on through but getting to shelter was not something he could risk with teenaged nose-thumbing at the Highway Patrol.

He made the right turn onto SR-180, doglegged around Navajo Boulevard onto SR-77 and began to take the speed up again. Half-way there. But he had no sooner left the city and entered the barren desert south of Holbrook when he saw a streak of silver light crossing the night sky behind him. It wasn't a bird or a plane and it sure as Hell wasn't Superman. No, it was trouble and it was looking for him.

CHAPTER THIRTEEN
June 20, 2002
Near dawn, in the country,
Outside Flagstaff, Arizona

The road outside the Caruthers House was growing crowded. There were half-a-dozen police cars, the SWAT van, three fire trucks, and maybe a hundred heavily armed National Guard members wandering around looking serious. They were serious. The officers had just been given the real bullets for their M16s. This was no drill, soldier boy; playtime's over, shoot to kill, don't bother waiting for the whites of the eyes, and all that jive. But no one was exactly eager to join the dance.

Four strange ships hovered over the area, blasting away at anything that moved near the house. They had made one recon patrol National Guard *flambé.* Just a few minutes ago, and a mother of an explosion had ripped the clouds apart. There were murmurs of atomic weapons. Guys were wandering around in radiation suits, bio-hazard suits, and FBI men in black suits. There was a party at the Caruthers House and humans were not inviting guests. Something the size of a small aircraft carrier had flattened about eight acres of forest just north of the Caruthers property. There were strange things going on this night and for the typical weekend warrior, well, home sounded pretty good. This was not like it said it would be in the book. Not like Iraq. Good God! They were the 158th Combat *Sustainment Support* Battalion, not the 158th *Combat* Battalion! No, not front line fighters at all, and not interested as an 11x secondary MOS. And now four new ships, the little ones, were flying over the area, and blasting away.

Lieutenant Samantha Jamison was talking to Police Sergeant Mark Untermeyer, trying to get a better handle on what was going on and what the brass might expect her platoon to jump into. Captain Blankenship had been on the radio to someone for twenty minutes, but she had no idea what was being discussed. Whatever it was, she had a sneaking feeling that her ROTC days were about to come back and haunt her. So far, nobody knew nothin' except that three police cars with six policemen, a half-dozen forest rangers, a team of Rural Metro firefighters, and a heavily armed recon team had gone in before the explosion and not been heard from since. That they had not been heard from for a long time *before* the explosion did not go unnoticeable, either.

When the black sedan and three additional police cars pulled up next to their observation post, she expected trouble and that's just what she got, in the form of one newly appointed Chief of Police, Mathew Ragsdale, a New Yorker and Yankee to the bone.

"What's the hold up, Sergeant," he demanded of Sergeant Untermeyer, not wasting a second for politeness as he emerged from the high-powered sedan.

"Guard won't let us in," Untermeyer said, gesturing to Jamison. "Says it's a matter of national security." Not that Ragsdale was in any great rush to investigate. The ships hovering in the air and the silence when they flew were not something to encourage curiosity. And there were still fires burning in there. He wanted the fire department as a back up and those boys weren't even lifting an eyebrow to the Guard's prohibition.

"What the hell's going on," he demanded, turning to Jamison, gesturing at the hovering spacecraft. "And what the hell have your helicopters been doing in my town."

"Those aren't helicopters, sir, you'll notice if you look close. They aren't US military, either," she responded politely. She had dealt with assholes for a long time. A woman in ROTC had to get used to it.

Ragsdale snorted and turned back to Untermeyer. "OK. The Guard doesn't know anything. Nothing new there. What do you have and what are you doing?"

"I don't know, sir, but it looks like we've got some kind of private war here," Untermeyer replied, a little cautiously. Ragsdale was not known for his patience with poor quality information.

"Yeah? Well, I hear we got officers down," Ragsdale said, leaning into Untermeyer's face. "That makes it no longer private! We're going in."

"Sorry, sir," Jamison said, again quietly and politely, "but my men have orders to shoot if anyone tries to cross the line. The Captain, sir, he made them understand that they he would shot *them* if they allowed anyone to pass. He's quite serious and quite capable of carrying out his promise. No one will go up that lane until Washington authorizes it."

"Just what the hell is going on here!" Ragsdale demanded.

"I think we just got in the way, sir. No one's bothered us since we've been staying back. It's those crazy ships," Untermeyer said, letting his control slip just a little. "They're fighting the house! Or what's left. It went up pretty good a couple of minutes ago. It seemed to blow out most of the forest fire, too, sir."

Ragsdale looked back at the aircraft that just sat above the smoldering forest like balloons tied above a used car lot. They were raking the grounds behind the trees with some sort of blue light, but nothing seemed to be exploding or catching fire. The lights looked like the search lights on police helicopters, stabbing through the smoke and dust rising from behind the trees.

"Who are the good guys?" Ragsdale muttered more to himself, but Untermeyer was ready with an answer to this question, anyway. "Our people I know, but who are the other players here?"

"I think the people in the house are… were, the good guys. I guess there's not much left of the house now."

"And you think that, why?"

"Well, a little while ago, there was a lot of activity."

"Yeah, I was that on the news while we were organizing this relief team."

"OK," Untermeyer continued. "Right in the middle of that, when we were all watching the fireworks in the sky there, this old Mustang comes ripping out of the house and tears off down the road."

"Why didn't you stop it?" Ragsdale demanded.

"Uh, it caught us by surprise and it was moving pretty fast."

"OK, you screwed up. Why do you think they were the good guys?"

"Because I saw Lieutenant Samuels in the back with a chick. He flashed a thumbs-up when they spun out of here. I don't think he was a hostage or anything."

"Samuels? How the hell do you know it was Samuels?"

"Well, that's his car over there," Untermeyer said, pointing at a gray Chevy smoldering on the side of the road, "or what's left of it, and he had radioed in that he was going in on foot to look for Fisher and some suspects. Besides, how many Blacks are there in Flagstaff? He's not that hard to pick out."

Ragsdale just grunted. Samuels. What kind of mess had he managed to rake up this time? Ragsdale had read his folder and it was not a pretty sight. That boy got into more unusual cases than Clinton got into interns. "The others in the car… do you think they were Arabs?" Ragsdale asked, 9-11 still very fresh in his mind.

"No, Sir," Jamison replied. "The guy driving was a white guy. There was something else in the front, but I couldn't tell for sure what. Anyway, no A-rab's got planes like those," he finished, pointing at the alien craft still zipping over the woods.

"Why didn't *you* stop the car?" Ragsdale demanded of Jamison.

"Like he said, sir, it was pretty fast and we had just established our periphery positions," Jamison answered reasonably. "Besides, we were told to shoot people trying to get in, sir, not *humans* trying to get out."

Ragsdale snorted again. What was this Guard weenie trying to say, anyway. That there was something *nonhuman* back there? These Arizona people were a little farther off the track than he was used to, even coming from New York City. "OK.," he said, then turned back to Untermeyer, where he hoped to get some sane answers. "Go with that and assume that Samuels left with someone from the house. Where is he now? What's your evaluation of the situation?"

"I don't know where Samuels is, sir. All air traffic is grounded, so we couldn't use the chopper to put a tail on the car. In fact, word is that every airport in the Southwest has been told to divert flights north and east for an unspecified time, so we couldn't even call in help from outside the area. But whoever was driving sure boogied out in a hurry, like he had someplace real important to go," Untermeyer said, thinking that the "someplace real important" was anyplace but here. "I think we ought to hang tight until the Guard says otherwise. This seems just about over and the guys aren't too eager to go in there while they're throwing around fireballs and explosives." Untermeyer looked at Jamison. The skies had been pretty quiet, from the local standpoint, he thought. "Has anybody called the Air Force?"

"They scrambled a long time ago. The first flight didn't make it. They're putting together a squadron of twelve now to send in. It'll take awhile to arm and prep more than just the standby birds," Jamison reported, figuring these cops were front line troops now, too, and had a right – a need – to know what was going on. "They are sending in more ready birds now, but they're from much farther away and will need to refuel in flight. Don't expect them soon. Washington was not willing to strip the ready birds off too many border bases," she added, letting them know that Washington was also worried about the coast and Mexico's border, not just a mountain in Arizona." *Do you get the drift, guys*, she was trying to say with her eyes and body language. *This isn't a local peyote smuggling ring.*

Untermeyer and Ragsdale let that sink in. If the Air Force had sent their ready planes in and they had not even made it as far as Flagstaff…

"I called the Governor. She was busy and her aide told me to call back in the morning. I told him to dig her out of whatever hole she had crawled in and to get on this. Damned if she doesn't know. There's footage of this fire and those… those… those planes all over CNN," Ragsdale muttered, cursing Democrats as a whole and this one in particular. "I've got my aids trying to reach the Senator. Now there's one *man* who'll know what to do."

"Which Senator, sir?" Untermeyer asked.

"There's more than one in Arizona?" Ragsdale asked. So much for public education, Jamison concluded, herself a product of a good private school. She knew there were two Senators for Arizona, she just didn't know who they were.

"Well…" Untermeyer began.

"Wait until this hits talk radio," Ragsdale smirked. "That'll shake the Governor up."

"We've lost some civilians, sir," Untermeyer said, steering the Captain back toward the issue at hand. "There's some on the road, but the ships won't let us near enough to recover the bodies. Also, the house blasted a couple of those ships. One crashed in some houses near here and those bastards went over and fired on that ship until it was confetti. We've got civilians down there. A news chopper from Phoenix that was covering the forest fire flew over, and it was dusted. So were three or four Army helicopters. Apaches. And our first units on the scene are still in there, but I don't think they're alive."

"How long before the Guard's going to let anybody in," Ragsdale demanded again, turning on Jamison like a sidewinder striking at a rabbit.

"About now, I'd say," Captain Gearson, Arizona National Guards said as he walked up to the group. He nodded to the house. The four lizard planes had stopped hovering peacefully and had rotated to face outwards, like spokes on a wheel. Even as they looked at the alien craft, the four took off in different directions. "I guess they didn't find what they were looking for, so we can go poke around."

"That's a crime scene, Captain. My men go in to protect the forensic evidence."

"No, Captain," Gearson replied. "That's a battle zone and *my* men go in with weapons hot. They are also going in with radiation detectors, biological detectors, chemical detectors, and a couple of cages of canaries. *Your* people will wait until the area is cleared from contaminant risks and after we have secured any national security interests."

"But…"

"You want to argue jurisdiction?" Gearson asked. "This is a live, direct-link field radio," he said, handing over a handset receiver attached to a phone the size of a large textbook. "There's a Navy yeoman on the other end. Just say hello and he will connect you directly to the Secretary of Defense who *can* connect you to the President, if your career means so little that you would disturb *him* at 4:48 am, Washington time."

Clinton was known for his temper with people who disturbed is routine and he certainly did not like the military. But Bush was another matter. He was a military man and had already started working to fix the damage that Clinton's meddling had done to the CIA, FBI, and Military Intelligence services. Bush respected the men in uniform who upheld the law and protected the public while Clinton only respected the men in suits who played with the law. But Ragsdale had no desire to see President Bush pissed off at a Chief of Police from Flagstaff, Arizona, by way of Queens, who was not yet ready to retire. Better not bother anyone in Washington quite yet until he knew more. Of course, he should have realized that by the time the first military jet lifted off the runway on full emergency power in response to a terrorist warning, President Bush was already awake and headed for the situation room.

"Why do these damned… things always pick the middle of the night to mess with innocent people?" Ragsdale asked rhetorically.

"Yeah," Untermeyer agreed, noting that his shift had ended almost two hours ago.

"Damned inconsiderate bastards."

Paul was thinking just about the same thing that Ragsdale was saying. They were nearing the halfway mark to the 180/64 juncture. The trees were thinning, which was their cover from an air search, and one of the alien craft had just swooped over the car. Paul could see it stopping ahead and spinning for a return pass. An earth craft would have required a fair amount of time to climb and pull around. But this thing just slammed to a stop, spun on its axis, and headed back without ever clearing the treetops.

Paul punched the accelerator, and boy, howdy, did that little Mustang take off. If the gumdrop had added wings, it would have flown, but as it is, the little 'Stang jumped from 65 to 280 – then more, the speedometer was pegged, the digital indication whirling in a blur – in the blink of an eye. Paul almost lost control, so unexpected was the charge, but he gripped the wheel and aimed the car down the center of the road.

The sudden acceleration must have been as big a surprise for the pilot of the air ship as it was for Paul and his passengers, since the two blasts that ripped through the night were a good hundred yards behind the car. Maybe he was shooting anything that moved, or maybe it was shooting cars with no headlights and no radar signature, but he must have known that he had a hot one when the car acted like it could teleport.

Stacy was watching out the back window, caught between the greatest thrill she had ever had and a fear so strong it made her forget to breathe. But when the enemy craft stood on its tail and did a flip, completing the maneuver with a roll, she squeaked once before she could get the warning out.

SR-77 was about as straight as a mountain road could hope to be. There was no traffic and the car worked its way up to nearly three hundred miles an hour, the desert flashing by like the landscape of a blasted moon. The miles ticked off but the car was no match for the alien spacecraft. It had some kind of lock on them, but had only fired once. Why was it waiting?

"The small craft does not have a full sensor suite," Ingram stated flatly. "They need to fire with manual aiming devices until the sensor craft in orbit has us identified. Then it can fire piggybacked on its readings."

"So what is stopping it now?" Paul asked.

The answer came quickly. SR-77 passed out of the high desert into a sparsely wooded area. The road began to take on the hills, and the rolling terrain forced the vehicle to slow, backing off to about two fifty-five. It was still flying over the low hills, but the lower speed brought the wheels down faster to grab the highway again. Why the wait? Why was Paul not trying to dodge laser blasts on the narrow road, where a wrong move could send the car crashing into an embankment?

Then he saw the sign: ten miles to Snowflake. If they stopped in the town they would be an easy target. And it would alert local authorities to the presence of the alien, perhaps something it did not want. Well stopping was not an option.

Paul flew threw Snowflake and the neighboring town of Taylor in under two minutes, the alien not backing off. Past Taylor, the road curved and took on some mountains, slowing Paul even more than the towns. But in just a few minutes, Paul blasted into the town of Show Low, forced to slam on the brakes as the Mustang skidded through a ninety degree turn onto AZ-260. Seconds later, Paul was on White Mountain Boulevard, screaming into Lakeside, his speed drastically reduced on the twisting, narrow mountain road that was now winding through thick forest as Paul raced from Lakeside and through Pinetop. Now on SR-73, coming out of Pinetop, the road began a series of twists and turns… and the alien moved in closer. Thank God it was in the middle of the night and there was no traffic! Paul had a little room to dodge and the laser bolts began to churn up the pavement around him. The car was automatically slowing and surging forward as the road turned into straight sections altering with winding mountain stretches. A couple of shots were close enough to peel paint, but the combination of stealth technology and the slight maneuvers Paul could make were enough so far to keep them safe.

In no time they blew through Whiteriver, but apparently the alien thought the sleepy little mining town was not worth worrying about; its attempts to blast Paul's car set businesses and automobiles along the main street on fire. Paul saw the road straighten out and applied speed, but Stacy warned Paul that they were close to their final turn.

Paul was splitting his attention between the road ahead and the side mirrors. They were dead meat if they stayed on the road. He was not going to bet that the fighter did not carry some sort of missile to augment its lasers. If it did, and the missiles were heat seekers, then surely they would be able to lock on the car and follow it wherever it went. They needed an escape route and they needed one fast. It would be a matter of timing and luck…

"There's the road!" Stacy yelled, pointing to a small side road off to their left. Paul skidded the car onto Fatco Road, a two-lane stretch of tarmac that jumped across the White River and quickly moved out of town.

The alien, taken by surprise with the turn and anticipating that its prey would accelerate on the straightaway that began just out of town, overshot the fleeing vehicle. The sharp turn was enough to shake the visual lock the lizard had on the car and the fugitives were momentarily free.

Paul curved onto Route 44, going much slower now than before, and Stacy said they were almost to the Fairgrounds. Could they get into hiding before the fighter returned? Paul prayed so as he saw the sign for the Fairgrounds parking lot. His blood racing almost as fast as the car, Paul made the left-hand turn into the desert rodeo grounds, moving quickly toward the shelter of one of the horse barns. Stacy hopped out of the car trough the rear window while the Mustang was still moving. Landing fast from her gymnastic feat, she slid open the door. Paul pulled in and stopped the car. He hesitated to turn it off, but finally did just to help reduce any emissions and to let the engine begin to cool.

"That was some fancy driving," Samuels said.

"Fear is a powerful motivator," Paul replied.

Stacy approached the car after closing the door and stuck her head in. "Do you think we lost it?" She asked no one in particular.

"We may have," Paul answered. "It went right over us when I turned."

"It knows your direction. Do not relax," Ingram warned. "They have very sophisticated sensors, even on their attack craft."

"It's a tin roof," Stacy pointed out. "That should help hide us."

"Do not be overconfident," Ingram stated. "If we are still…"

He never finished his sentence. The back end of the barn exploded as two laser bolts ripped the doors off and blasted away the wall.

"Oh, shit," Paul said, starting the car.

Stacy struggled to get into the backseat again as a series of blasts walked up the barn, systematically leveling the building. Paul slammed on the accelerator and, not bothering with the closed door, blew out the far side. He hit a left on Fort Apache Road, but by the time he was a hundred yards from the barn the alien was peppering his tail again, leveling the Theodore Roosevelt Indian School as it took wild shots while trying to line up on the once-more fleeing car. Behind him the Rodeo Fairgrounds was a roiling mass of flames. The fire rapidly spread from the demolished stable to the other buildings, moving outward from there and into the forest. In seconds, the area around the Rodeo Fairgrounds was a blazing infernal.

Paul flew back over the White River and onto Chief Highway (SR-73) while picking up speed. In seconds, the town of Canyon Day was a memory, hardly noticed. For the next three miles, covered in less than a minute, the road was relative straight though irrigated farm land before it hit the mountains again and began a steep climb into the pass that lead to Silver Butte, a dormant volcano.

The road wiggled like a sidewinder, making it difficult for the alien to lock onto his target. But the narrow mountain road was treacherous in and of itself and when the alien's blasts went into the mountain sides in front of the car, Paul found himself dodging boulders and rock slides as well as laser beams.

Paul was not sure how he made the thirty miles from the first inclines of the pass to State Route 77, but he did and he made it in less than ten minutes. He made a hard left onto SR-77, not at all sure now where he was going or where the road lead. Just a few feet behind him, once he was on SR-77, the alien had blasted the bridge over the Salt River. It wasn't much of a bridge, just a span over a culvert, but had the blast been in front, there was no way Paul could have avoided going into the gulley.

Just yards before SR-77 became SR-60 in a hairpin turn, Paul slammed on the brakes and cut the wheel hard to the right. He had seen a sign flash by that looked like a road juncture and here it was, almost quicker than he could consciously register the importance of the sign. The Mustang fishtailed and threatened to roll, but the suspension upgrades held it to the road and the tires quickly caught, shooting them down a side road at ninety miles an hour. Once again, the lizard pilot misjudged his target and the lasers stitched large holes in parallel lines down the highway, just about where Paul would have been if he hadn't made the turn.

"Where are you going?" Stacey demanded.

"Hell if I know," Paul replied, his voice cracking with stress. "That sign said Cibecue and Chediski Peak. Maybe we can get help there!"

"Don't count on it," Samuels said. "Cibecue only has about 1200 residents, including dogs. It's on the Fort Apache Reservation, and I'm, not even sure they have telephones. It's nothing but scrub brush and tumbleweeds. If we're going to find a place to hide, it'd better be soon while we still in the forest!"

Fortunately, the lizard was a little slow in catching Paul's sudden change of direction. Maybe the trees that lined the side road helped hide the car from him momentarily, or maybe he was just playing it a little more cautions. Paul figured the alien was probably totally pissed right about then, having missed two easy shots. He wondered if there were gun cameras and if he would be the butt of peer jokes for missing an unarmed automobile with his super-charged fighter. Well, Paul intended to make sure that he was the butt for a long time, but he wasn't sure if his luck would hold or not. This road was much narrower than SR-77 and it twisted like a snake. It quickly crossed a rickety plank bridge then dissolved into unimproved gravel. The Mustang barely slowed.

Almost immediately, they were back into trees and winding mountain roads. Paul could see the fighter pull down into the lane created by the trees behind him, following as the road dipped and twisted through the Reservation's mountains beauty. They were in the foothills, surrounded by taller peaks. A few more minutes and Paul thought the road would straighten out and the trees vanish as the hills turned into the plateau. The trees would return, but not for another mile or so on the other side of Cibecue. By then, they'd all be cinders if they could not shake their tormentor.

The lizard pilot must have felt he had the rhythm of the chase now. He started popping short bursts at the car, tearing up the road behind and to the side of the speeding Mustang. A hundred miles an hour would have been harrowing on this back road at any time, where anything could pop up in front of you with only scant notice. Paul thought he saw a speed limit sign go up in a ball of flame telling him that thirty-five was about all that was safe. He was easily tripling that, but the hairpin curves forced him to slam on the brakes just to rocket around the corners at sixty. How the pilot was able to stay between the trees and still take shots and negotiate the curves and maybe eat a bologna sandwich, for all Paul knew, without pulling above the tree line was beyond Paul's imagination. But that he had a deadly foe slowly creeping into tailgate range was an undeniable fact. And he didn't need Stacy and Samuels yelling at him to "go, go, go" for him to go, go, go as fast as he could.

The lasers bracketed the car, sending geysers of dirt and rock into the windshield, lighting up the night as trees, dried from the long dry spell that normally precedes the late-Summer monsoons, went up in flames like the Olympic torch. Without thinking, Paul hit the wipers, but the view was the same computer generated heads-up display that he had been relying on before. A little rock and mud didn't make much difference. What he really worried about was a laser hitting a tree a little ways in front of the speeding car. That would just about settle things then and there without the pilot needing his Marksmanship Merit Badge.

Either the pilot was getting luckier or he was getting better or he was getting tired of the chase. The shots were growing closer. One near miss blasted the road near the passenger side front tire. The car took a quick dip and then a bounce, jerking the wheel out of Paul's hands. Paul scrambled frantically for the wheel, ignoring the calls from the back, telling him to do just exactly what he was trying to do.

The tire didn't blow, but it did catch the edge of the grated part of the road right as Paul caught the wheel. Instead of slamming head-on into the pine – spruce, aspen, pinon, oak, whatever; it happened too fast for Paul to make a formal introduction with the foliage – Paul managed to jerk the car to the left just enough to wipe out the side mirror and decorate the powder blue finish with long, squiggly scratches.

Screams from the back. He was glad Stacy had hit the bathroom before they left. He wished he had, but he had been too busy being scared as to wet his pants. He wondered how Samuels was doing. He could see Ingram from the corner of his eye and whenever he glanced to his right. That little guy had not budged an inch. From somewhere, he had produced six tentacles and was anchored so solidly to the car that he could have been part of the frame. Paul wondered if its silence was courage or if its ridged hold was a sign of *rigor mortise*, as in, "death by fright."

The brush with the tree had slowed the car to about seventy-five or eighty, and the alien ship slipped right over the top of the trees, not more than a few feet behind them. Paul slowed and the ship flashed over the top of the car. If the Mustang had had a sunroof, they could have reached out and touched the spaceships underbelly. The lizard tried to slow down, to get back into firing position, but Paul slowed with him, staying right under his fuselage. This was a game of highway asshole; speedup, slow down, but don't let the other guy pass. Paul had never played that game, but he had been the victim of many jerks who did, so he could do a passable imitation. From the way the pilot reacted, he had never played that game before either; at least, never speeding down a dark highway between two rows of very close trees, on a road that might dip or suddenly rise up or swerve around a hill without warning.

It didn't take long, but the lizard decided to start this one from go. He hit his afterburners – or whatever served as afterburners – and went into a steep climb. Paul figured this was it. Had he been the pilot, he would have stood off and plastered the road until something hit. Of course, had Paul been the pilot, he would have started with standing off and saturation firing and never played shoot-the-canyon with obstinate humans who refused to die.

Stacy flung her arm across Paul's shoulder, almost scaring him to death.

"There! There! A side road! Try that!"

Paul almost missed the turn, but he sweet-talked the Mustang into a wild slide and down the lane to his right before the lizard had brought the fighter around and reacquired its target, but it sure did a good job of destroying the cattle guard that marked the entrance to Bureau of Indian Affairs Road 12.

Paul had all but flown over the grating after completing the turn. It would be on them again as soon as the pilot could break and lay his eyes on the target again. That target, Paul reminded himself, was them. And this time it look like his luck had failed him. This was not a side road maintained by any division of the State Highway Department, charged with keeping up the highways and byways in the Nation's second largest, though one of the most scarcely populated, counties. No, this was a dirt road to some rancher or farmer's house or nowhere and they were about to bring death and destruction to visit. What followed was a wild and crazy run north, toward the isolated Chediski Peak, leaving a trail of burning trees behind them.

This could easily have been the road to the Caruthers House, rutted and pitted, but it was longer and the tree cover was much thinner. Paul had to slow down dramatically to keep control and he knew he just made them a better target. But there was no help for it. There were too many trees to make a run across the countryside and too many rocks and boulder to make that a sane option in any case. No, they would have to find a place where Paul could spin the car and make a try for the road again. Or not. He was pretty sure that cattle guard was just now a smoking pit. He'd never get out that way and trying to run a barbed wire fence was sure to set them up for a clean kill.

"We got trouble people!" he yelled. "I need ideas!"

About then, the car flew out of the woods and into a drive past a small horse pasture fronting a typical Northern Arizona ranch. There was a small, white, two-story house with a porch and a swing and decent landscaping. A real Andy Griffith scene. There was a small silo and a water tower to the left. There were a few horses in the front pasture they were passing and a small herd of cows out back. The heads-up display painted it all quite pristine. To the right was a barn with the door open and a tractor sitting…

"There! There! Go right! The barn! Park in the barn!" Samuels was yelling. "They're not back behind us yet. They may not see us!"

"Their sensors will spot us. Remember, they can track the heat of the tires on the road right to the barn."

"Damn their sensors!" Samuels yelled. "It's the only chance we have!"

Paul wasn't sure what the chance was, but he knew that going back was not an option. Maybe there would be a root cellar and they could hide in that while the lizard destroyed the barn and everything else for miles. Their only real hope was that the fellow wasn't sure Ingram was with them and that he wouldn't call his buddies in from their search to help him with the pesky group in the car.

The Mustang flew into the barn and Paul got a good demonstration on how Ingram had improved the brakes. But before the car had stopped rolling, Paul was out and racing toward the barn doors. Stacy clambered over the slow moving Samuels and reach Paul just in time to help him slam shut the second door. But Paul put the brakes on when the door was still about a foot open.

"Don't close it all the way," he told her, trying to catch his breath.

"Why not?" She was still trying to tug the door closed, but Paul's foot was in the way.

"It may think we have left the barn. There're a lot of animals around here, that'll clutter its infrared detectors. I think it's going slow to check out all the life forms. It may give us a little more time if the lizards aren't sure if we are still here or gone."

"Or maybe they'll just kill everything. They're running out of time before someone reacts to all the explosions and fires and I'll bet they know it."

"Yeah. So they have to be sure they've got us. They could blast the car and that'd be that. But they don't know who or what is here and just blasting away won't guarantee that we haven't escaped. I don't think they will want to take that chance if given an option," Paul said, finally catching his breath. "They may land and poke around. If they do, we've got better options."

"I sure hope those lizards reason like you do," Stacy answered.

Samuels had made it out of the car's door on his own and hobbled over to the door. "What's wrong with the door. Why didn't you close it," he demanded.

"I wanted to see what happens," Paul replied.

"Good idea," Samuels said, and backed away to where he could watch while still remaining in the shadows.

"You guys are nuts," Stacy said, throwing her hands up in disgust and moving off into the bar to look for something she could use to stick lizards.

"It's your life," she muttered. Then it dawned on her: it was her life, too.

Paul could see the blue search lights before he saw the ship. Ingram had explained that those were scanners that could detect bio forms or some of the more esoteric emissions used in advanced electronics. He suspected they could distinguish easily between equipment designed and in use by humans from that designed by extraterrestrials even if it was built largely with earth technology, but that the lizards would have more difficulty separating the earth bio forms. In other words, they couldn't tell a cow from a pig from a dog from a human, but they could quickly spot the zapper Ingram had given Paul if it was left unshielded. Ingram had taken that back from Samuels and was scooting around the barn looking for a metal container that would hide the weapon and his communicator.

The theory was that the lizards would pass over the barn, scan it, and miss the Mustang because of the stealth technology that Ingram left running when they bailed out. But it had to be someplace that still allowed them to get to it if the lizards were not fooled or if the scanners did not miss the zapper even if it was shielded. Ingram wanted to have the communicator close at hand in case the lizards decided not to cooperate.

Paul had asked Samuels why he had not shot the plane earlier and Samuels replied, simply, that he had forgotten he had the weapon during the chase. Paul couldn't argue with that; he had forgotten about it, too. Stacy, however, was not so forgiving until Ingram commented that destroying the fighter would be a sure indication that alien technology was riding in the target vehicle and that the pilot would surely have reported chasing a potential high value target. The other ships would flock to the area and, if the scanner ship had not already been tasked to search their area, it would undoubtedly do so if the fighter fell off the grid.

Stacy shut up, but not with good grace. She figured that vaporizing the fighter was a good thing and that in the time it took the others to zero in on that location, they could be gone. Except, Ingram pointed out, that they would know that an alien not associated with them was running around on the planet, something he hoped to avoid. Right now, all they knew is that a very fast ground vehicle with a peculiar lack of sensor readings was in the area. Maybe that was an Earthling military vehicle as yet unseen or something else, they didn't know and the other fighters would continue their search patterns. Ingram felt there was a greater level of safety in their ignorance than in destruction of the fighter.

Not that it mattered. Samuels had not shot the fighter and now it was making its way toward the isolated ranch. Ingram speculated that its slow approach would allow the heat for the car tires to dissipate enough to fool the sensors, since the night itself was warm and the path was dirt and gravel, which would not hold the heat signature long. Perhaps the Aeolians would not be able to follow it directly to the barn. It sounded like wishful thinking. But then, Paul reflected, Ingram's thinking had been pretty good so far. Maybe they would have a little luck.

And maybe not. The two-story house was no longer quiet. Paul could just make out the patio from his vantage point and the front light had come on. Now a rancher was standing on the porch stairs, looking toward the barn. He had a dog with him and what looked like a shotgun or rifle. This could be trouble. But before the rancher could move further into the yard, though, the slow moving fighter glided silently into view. The lights from its scanners flickered over the rancher, the ranch house, and the barn briefly, but there was no other reaction from the lizards.

Like a slowly drifting balloon losing its helium, the fighter quietly settled on the ground, scattering the horses like leaves in a monsoon. It was not until after it had landed that the dog began to bark furiously, while pressing itself tight against the rancher's legs. The frightened horses, lead by a barrel-chested mare, crashed into the gate, snapping the main support post, leaving the fence a cantered nuisance as the equines bolted off into the night. A woman and a young girl appeared in the doorway behind the man, a frozen tabloid of amazement and disbelief.

This is not the same style fighter that Paul knew from the assault on the house. He had not noticed it before, but this was a larger adaptation, more like a beefed up version of the Sweden's Saab JAS 39 Gripen, with a delta-winged, canard configuration, with the small stabilizer wings jutting out right behind the cockpit, well forward and above the sweeping lift wings, which helped explain the ship's amazing agility. Paul could spot two barrels under the wings, figuring those to be the laser units and not machine guns. He didn't see any missile pods, which had probably saved their lives back on the road. The ship looked fatter than Paul would have thought - certainly fatter than the T-38 look-alikes he had seen in the clearing - but he initially tossed that off as something to do with the requirements pressed on the plane for fighting both in and out of the atmosphere. He was quickly proved mistaken, however, when a ladder folded out from the body on the far side of the craft and four lizards - the heavily armed Marine variety, not decked out in the fighter pilot garb - stepped into the rancher's yard.

Trouble for sure, Paul thought. This was Northern Arizona, a place where people were fiercely independent. He had even heard news stories – not urban legends – about farmers blasting away at Forest Department helicopters dipping into their ponds for water to wild fight fires. He wondered how this one would take to lizards scattering his horses. Not too kindly, Paul noticed, as the rancher brought his gun to his shoulder.

"Hell and damnation," Samuels exclaimed. One of the aliens, shooting from the hip, drilled a hole through the rancher before the human could squeeze the trigger. The man collapsed in a heap. The girl slammed open the door screaming "Papa! Papa!" and tried to reach the downed man. But the woman, perhaps showing a little more sense, grabbed her, lunged back inside the house, and slammed the door. Paul could not imagine the terror going on behind that closed door right then. He had a hard enough time dealing with the terror going on inside himself. But his terror was encased in a cold shell of fury.

"We have to do something," Paul said, looking desperately at Samuels. "The lizards probably think we're in the house!"

"Yeah, but do what? Don't think crazy, man," Samuels retorted, holding Paul back but at the same time keeping a close eye on the lizards, which had split up and were surrounding the house as a pair of them cautiously approached the front door. "We can't do anything to help them. It's ourselves we gotta think about now!"

"He is correct," Ingram said, gliding up to them. "There are more in the ship."

"We have that alien ship killer," Stacy said, looking pointedly at Ingram.

"Yes, but that is a matter of desperation. Use of it will be detected. Then all of the Aeolians will converge on this location before we can travel far enough to avoid destruction. And the Aeolians will surely kill any living creature in a large radius around this location as insurance."

"We can't just do nothing," Stacy protested.

"We'll have a better chance if we can catch them when they check out the barn," Samuels said. "If they don't know we're here now, then we can surprise them."

Samuels' words hung in the silence of the barn like closing time at a slaughter house. That just wasn't good enough for Paul, and Stacy's confused and concerned look didn't add to his belief that Samuels was right.

In a sudden burst of what Paul would later call stupidity, he grabbed Samuels' gun from the other's lax grip and darted out of the back of the barn before Ingram could sense his intention and voice a warning.

"Cover me!" he shouted over his shoulder.

Pandemonium erupted in the barn.

"Hey, you can't do that!" Samuels yelled, ignoring the obvious fact that he *had* done exactly that.

"Paul!" Stacy yelled at his back.

"If they are not distracted, your friend will surely die," Ingram stated flatly. He extended a tentacle toward the ship, which had lowered something from the nose on a swivel mount that appeared to be tracking toward the barn. Their voices had been heard. "He is too close for the sensors to lock in, but the pilot can direct the antipersonnel defenses itself. When the switch is moved to manual, it will be too late."

"Damn!" Samuels. Stacy started to bolt after Paul, but Samuels grabbed her. "No way, lady. You're staying out of the way," he said, pushing her back into a stack of baled hay. "You know how to use that thing?" he asked Ingram, pointing at the weapon the other held.

"In theory, yes, but I have never partaken in personal violence," the alien replied.

"Then give it here," Samuels said, taking the weapon from the alien. "How does it work?"

Ingram pointed to a stud on the side and told Samuels to aim and press there and whatever was in the way would no longer be of concern. "However," the small alien warned, "try not to destroy the ship. Its destruction will alert the others. Using this weapon will probably be enough to give us away, but that will eliminate all doubt."

Samuels was watching Paul as the writer took refuge behind a tractor. Surely the lizards must know he was there if their ship was tracking him. Maybe if he ran the other direction, he could circle the ship and in their confusion get inside the gun range and…

"Wait," Ingram instructed, warping a tentacle around Samuels' arm before the cop could make his dash. "I sense that the others are leaving the ship. Yes, even the pilot. There is a chance now," he said. "They may not have their sensors on repeater to the mother ship. Stop them from recovering the ship without damaging it. Their arrogance has led them to a dangerous mistake."

Samuels nodded. He understood that. These lizards were the big kid on the block, like a lot of gang members he had known when he was younger. They ruled the turf, but they were not very smart and that made them even more prone to mistakes than the average dumb criminal. As a rookie, he had busted two gang bangers by tracking their footsteps in the snow from where they had heisted a television set right from a neighbor's house to their pad. He found them drinking beer and watching the NBA on the heisted set. They had thought they were too clever to get caught, ever, but they were especially surprised at being nabbed just a few minutes after they had dropped out a back window form the other house. Yeah, if these guys were bullies, then there was some hope they were as stupid as any criminal.

He watched for a second to see what their game plan was. The two that had made the porch had stopped and were looking in the direction of the tractor where Paul was hiding. The other two were out of sight in the back. The ones from the ship, however, were walking toward the barn. They were obviously planning on getting around behind Paul and just as obviously, not worried about weapons. Well, that made a little sense. If Paul had anything that could punch through their armor, then he would have used it already. But Samuels had the big guns. Give those scaly things a few more feet and he'd see what this little toy Ingram had made could do.

Samuels took a long aim and slowly pushed the button. He expected recoil, but there was nothing. Nothing at all. No light, no sound, no smoke. Nothing. But the closest lizard seemed to… blossom… as everything from the waste up vanished in a rapidly expanding cloud of blood, bone, and flesh.

"Damn," Samuels said, looking at the gun in his hand. This little thing had a *punch*.

"You got the bastard," Stacy said, moving away from the stacks of hay to get a better look.

"Nice language," he replied.

"Well, you won't hear it again if you don't shoot the another one!" Stacy exclaimed, pointing out to the yard where the lizards were just coming out of their shock over discovering that there was a new kid in town with a bigger stick.

The Marine from the ship had spotted the opening in the barn door and was taking exception to having his partner vaporized next to him.

"Look out," Samuels yelled, pushing Stacy back into the hay and throwing himself into a roll in the other direction. Ingram had long since glided to the back of the barn where it was observing from behind old tack and hand tools. So when the front doors to the barn exploded, his soft body was not riddled with flying splinters. Samuels and Stacy managed to escape with just a few cuts, but the barn was in sorry shape. The doors were gone and the front had caught fire.

Through the flames and smoke, Samuels could make out the surviving alien walking toward the door. He had no clue where the others were or what was happening to Paul, but he had a bad feeling that things were going from worse to impossible rapidly.

Paul had the same feeling outside. From his vantage point, he could see that the two lizards from the porch were splitting and coming at him from opposite directions. The flyboy was headed for the barn with the remaining Marine. Okay. Maybe he could empty the clip into one and hope that enough hit the helmet to make a difference, but no way would he have a chance at the other if they were spread apart. What to do, what to do. Paul suddenly remembered that he was an out of shape writer with no – none, zip, zero, nada – training in small arms combat. He had two days on the firing range with an M-16 in the Air Force, but they hadn't even shown him a pistol. So it would have to be brains over firepower, but right now, Paul felt like it would be more like mush over lizard spit.

He could barely make out the two coming from the ship if he watched the feet under the tractor. Left was not good, then, since that way had three sets of feet, so that meant that his best chance was right. Or would surprising the ones on the left work better, since the three might not have any worries about shooting at the one?

Paul was just about to make his break to the right when he saw the body of one of the aliens topple over and into his line of sight below the tractor. Well, half a body. That cinched right. Whatever was shooting at the aliens with something that could take out half a body through that armored cloth was probably not safe to be around.

Paul crouched low and made a dash for the alien. He surprised it and the lizard's shot went high, hitting the side of the barn and starting a fire there as the beam passed through the wood and into the stored hay. Paul didn't have much time to notice that the front half of the barn was a solid sheet of flame, but he knew there was a pretty good fire nearby because he had plenty of light. What he didn't have was enough strength to knock the alien over like he had planned. His shoulders slammed into the lizard's legs like he was slamming into a fence post and pain shot from his right shoulder all the way to his fingertips. His arm and hand went numb for a second and then the gun slipped from his nerveless fingers.

But his early days on his junior high wrestling team came back and may well have saved his life. Before the alien could recover and cook Paul on the ground, the human's left arm flew out and wrapped around the alien's legs. With a twist of his body, using the momentum of his rush to add additional force, Paul rolled behind the alien and staggered him enough that the shot he had tried to send into Paul's prone body only cooked whatever insects were blasted out of the ground three feet from Paul's chest. Then the alien toppled, crashing over Paul as he continued his turn and twist.

Life came back to Paul's right arm and he scrambled for the gun while the lizard was trying to untangle itself from the rose bushes by the side of the porch. Paul grabbed the gun and threw a glance toward the other two aliens. One had started to trot his way, but someone was shooting from the burning barn and streamers of earth were silently cascading up across the yard. Instead of making for Paul, the second one from the porch was making for the other side of Paul's former shelter. He probably figured his partner could handle one little human alone. And he was right. One swipe from those clawed hands driven by other-worldly muscles and Paul was through.

Paul found the gun and brought it up just in time to catch the lizard rolling over in the bush, swinging his gun around for a finishing shot. Paul pulled the trigger three times, the gun only a couple feet from his target. At least two hit the alien's faceplate. It shattered and gushed blood and gore. But the lizard still had a little life, or at least momentum. The gun hand continued around and the finger continued to squeeze and a final shot lanced out toward Paul before the human could do more than jerk a few inches to his right.

But luck was still riding with Paul and the shot missed him. Instead, the laser stabbed through the motor housing of the tractor. The engine exploded with a muffled *whoomph*! It was not a grand and glorious Hollywood explosion, but it did mark an unlucky turn for Paul. The other alien was now aware that he had a problem at his back. Instead of sending more bolts of artificial lighting into the burning barn, he turned and turned his attention to Paul and his downed companion. Maybe the two who had circled the house could take out the puny human and maybe not. The silly creature was trying to pull the laser from the dead lizard's grip and it sure was not the time to take chances with some soft, weak creatures that had proven unacceptably hard to kill.

The lizard aimed at on Paul and squeezed off a shot, but Paul was already rolling away, still trying to free the dead alien's grip on the laser. It was frozen tight and Paul had no illusions about hitting the helmet of the shooter with the pistol from the greater distance. Behind him, he could hear glass breaking and screaming from inside the house. Things must be getting hot in there. They were outside, at least.

Paul swung the alien's arm around and began pressing the dead alien's trigger finger. He sent bolt after bolt toward the other alien, but only managed to hit the broad side of the barn, the tractor, and the ground around the lizard. But that was enough to keep the creature off balance and its return fire was not much better, peppering the porch and bushes enough to set the front of the house ablaze. Paul suddenly felt very warm. If the alien didn't fry him, the fire would unless he could get away pretty soon.

But the cavalry arrived from around the corner of the barn. In one silent second, the tractor and alien vanished in a ball of debris. The flyboy alien was nowhere to be seen. For a few seconds, silence rained down on the ranch, broken only by the crackle of the fires, now fully engulfing the barn and doing a good job of eating away at the house.

The house. There were still two aliens and at least two humans in the house. Maybe more. Maybe a dog. Paul pointed that out as Stacy, still lugging that case Ingram had given her for safe keeping, and Samuels rushed over to help him to his feet. He figured Ingram already knew something was still messing about, since the gumdrop had not moved its sled from the dubious cover of the barn. That side was not burning fully yet, but the fire would be there in seconds rather than minutes. Part of the roof on the near side had already given way and sparks were rising hundreds of feet into the air. Someone would be here soon to investigate, Paul knew, since they were far enough away from Flagstaff that the police and fire departments would not be tied up there. And they would be looking for something. The fire that was destroying the Rodeo grounds, the string of burning trees along their former escape route, and the one that must be burning around the Caruthers House in Flagstaff would have every police and fire official on pins and needles this night. But there was no way help would arrive now before the other aliens had either killed everyone or escaped. They had to move while they still had the initiative.

Before they could more than think about moving into the house, then entire back side blew out in an explosion that nearly shook them from their feet.

CHAPTER FOURTEEN
June 21, 2002
In the country, outside Flagstaff, Arizona

"Damn. The fire must have hit a gas line or something," Samuels said, watching in awe as the windows blew out of the front of the house in front of a sheet of flame.

"More like a propane tank," Paul responded absently. His mind was on the people in the house. If they were still in there, they would need help.

"Paul… the people…" Stacy said in a small voice. "We brought those aliens here."

"Yeah. I was thinking that too. We need to see if they're trapped inside."

"Getting in and getting out isn't gonna be easy, especially if there are any more aliens inside," Samuels said.

"There are no more alive here. The two inside perished with the explosion," Ingram said with a certainty that no one thought to argue. "But there are still some people inside. On the second floor."

"Is there a ladder around here," Paul asked, casting his eyes about for one near the house. They could get to the porch roof and from there get inside the house with no trouble if they could do it before the fire spread too much farther. Maybe they could reach the people inside.

"There was one by the side of the barn," Stacy offered.

"Right, I saw it," Samuels confirmed. He turned back toward the barn to get the ladder, but that fire had spread across the entire structure. There was no way that he could possibly retrieve the ladder from where it lay next to the fiercely burning wall.

"How about I boost you up,' he suggested to Paul. "Or how about that sled of yours," he turned to Ingram. "Can it get that high?"

"Yes, but it could not take the weight to assist anyone," the alien said. "Be patient."

"Patient! Hell, the whole house will be gone…"

Samuels was cut off by a chair flying out of a second floor window. The chair was followed a second latter by the top portion of the body of the woman who had stood in the doorway. She was helping the little girl out over the glass.

"¡Ayuda! ¡Necesitamos ayuda! ¡Por favor! ¡Ayuda aquí!" she called out in Spanish, pleading for help.

"Anybody speak Spanish?" Paul asked. Stacy nodded.

"Just a little. Kitchen Spanish from the restaurant. She wants help. What can we do?"

"*¡Ayuda! ¿Puede usted ayudarnos?*" she called down, relieved that she could see humans and not creatures dressed in silver with big heads, but not understanding why no one was answering.

"Tell her to get out on the roof. We can help them down from there," Samuels said.

"*Tengo español muy pequeño. Necesario para moverse a la mesa. Ayúdele de la mesa. ¡Haga aprisa!*" Stacy called out, waving the little girl over toward the edge of the porch roof, but the little girl just shook her head and stood by the window.

"*Sí! Sí!* Yes, yes, hus' a second!" the woman yelled back in heavily accented English, then vanished back into the burning building.

"*Venido aquí. ¡Mucho rápido!*" Stacy tried again, waving at the hesitant child, but without luck. She backed up so she could see better, while Paul and Samuels moved to the edge of the porch, ready to help them off the edge when it dipped over the porch when, if, they made the move.

It soon became apparent while the girl waited. A minute later, the mother was back, holding a young boy out the window to the girl, who helped him onto the roof, then gave her mother a hand out as well. Smoke was billowing out the broken window now and Stacy could see light from the flames behind them. The fire must have chased the woman down the hallway from wherever she had left the boy. There wasn't much time left, but the woman was bending back inside the house. This was no time for retrieving lost possessions!

"*¡Mucho rápido! ¡Mucho rápido!*" Stacy called, encouraging the woman to move quickly, the fire was eating away at their time as well as the house. "*El fuego está viniendo. ¡No hay hora!*"

"*¡Sí! ¡Sí! Comprenda. Momento. Momento. Mi perro,*" she called back, waving one hand at Stacy. The other was inside, fishing for something. A moment later, she had both hands inside, even though she was beginning to cough in racking hacks. But a second later she straightened up, pulling the front end of the dog with her as she came. "*Mi perro,*" she said again, helping the large dog out the window. It was evidently not very excited about being on the roof, but Stacy would bet it would be less excited to have its tail singed. But then, it would probably die of carbon monoxide poisoning long before it burned. At least, Stacy did not think dogs were as dumb as horses who often ran back into a burning barn if frightened.

"Okay! She's out and she has a dog," Stacy called over to Paul and Samuels. This should prove interesting. Maybe even comic.

The woman moved to the edge of the roof in the direction Stacy was waving, and looked over cautiously. When she saw Paul and Samuels, she said something in rapid fire Spanish and the young girl brought her brother over. She continued talking to Samuels and Paul. It apparently didn't matter that they did not understand. She just needed to hear her voice, reaffirm that she was still alive and, maybe judging from the men's reactions, believing that they were real and human.

She handed the little boy over the edge of the roof. He was easy to take. The girl was a little heavier, but again the men had no trouble. The dog, however, had absolutely no desire to get down off a perfectly good roof into the arms of some stupid *gringos*, no matter that they did not smell like the lizards. But the woman was determined and, accompanied by a great deal of cursing and struggling, she finally managed to wrap her hands around the dog's chest and walk it over on its hind legs to the edge of the roof. Once there, she straighten up a little, just enough to get the kicking hind legs off the shingles, then bent over and dangled the wiggling canine over the roof.

This was not a good thing in the dog's mind. It started whining and twisting. The ranch wife dropped to one knee, almost tumbling off the roof, and lowered the dog until Samuels could grasp its hind legs. That's when she lost her grip and the front end plummeted into Paul, knocking him over and onto his back.

Fortunately, that was enough of a cushion that the dog was not hurt, but it wanted no part of its benefactor. Wiggling out of Paul's arms, which he had automatically tossed around the dog when it fell into him, it ran off a dozen yard and then sat, watching what was going on with soulful eyes and wounded pride.

The woman was the easiest to help. She sat on the roof and then pushed off, only needing Paul and Samuels to steady her as she dropped the seven feet to the ground.

"Gracias, gracias mucho. Usted ha ahorrado mis niños y mi perro. El dios le bendice. Gracias. Usted nos ha ahorrado todos," she kept repeating, hugging everyone in turn and then in turn again.

"Ask her if there are any more inside," Samuels told Stacy between hugs.

"*¿Quién está adentro? ¿Cualquier persona adentro?*" Stacy said, complying with some hesitation over the wording.

"Solamente las serpientes en la cocina. El diablo los ha tomado de nuevo a infierno," the woman answered, then went back to her litany of "gracias" and "mucho gracias."

"What did she say?" Samuels demanded.

"I don't know," Stacy answered somewhat petulantly. "Something about snakes in the kitchen and the devil wanting a 'to go' order. Or something like that. I mean, *para ir* is 'to go' and *no aquí* is 'not here' but that's not quite what she said. I think the lizards were in the kitchen when the house exploded. I think that's what she means."

"*Sí! Sí!* Dee-vil snakes locked in *la cocina*," the woman confirmed.

"Well, so there you have it," Stacy confirmed, crossing her arms, not even noticing that neither Paul nor Samuels had a clue what was just said, but they could tell from Stacy's body language that she was no longer worried about lizards coming out of the house.

Samuels, however, was more cautious and moved around the house, now collapsing into itself much as the barn had done while they were rescuing the woman and her children. Ingram glided over to the alien craft, cautiously studying it for signs of damage to its airframe. And dog. Mustn't forget the dog, who had moved over to be with the children and woman as they stood a little apart, watching the home burn, taking everything they had with it, including the body of their husband and father.

Stacy moved over to stand next to Paul and watch the house burn. He absently put his arm around her and she moved in closer to the comfort of his embrace. She shivered a little, not from cold since the house and barn heated up the chill Northern Arizona night quite nicely, but from delayed reaction.

"Are you all right," she asked.

"Yes and no," Paul answered quietly. "I'm just singed a little and a little bruised. I guess they barricaded the hall from inside the kitchen. That blast probably took the lizards by surprise. They must have had a strong motivation to track down the gumdrop there," he said, gesturing with his head to where Ingram was floating up into the alien craft. "Maybe he can find a radio he can use in the ship. I'm not real comfortable staying here. Sooner or later, they'll come looking for their friends and I'll bet they know exactly where that craft is sitting and I wouldn't be surprised if they knew their people were out of commission. Or maybe not. Our people are pretty tight on human life, but I guess I shouldn't count on the lizards being the same. Yeah, I'll bet on the plane, but not on telemetry for their pilots or marines or whatever."

Paul looks over at the three people standing off to the side. Their life wasn't going to get any easier anytime soon. The girl was sobbing into her mother's dress and the boy was in a state of shock. Paul didn't think they had seen Ingram yet. He wondered what that would do to their already-frayed grasp on reality. "The kids look in bad shape," he said. "I don't guess there are any blankets or anything left."

"How about the mother?" Stacy asked, shaking her head "no" after a baleful look at the barn. No horse blankets either.

"Probably not letting it hit her now. She's pretty happy the kids made it out. The rest will get her later."

"And you know this, how?" Stacy asked.

"Hey, I'm a writer, remember? I know a little about everything," he answered airily and received only a sock to the arm for his effort.

"So, has this been an exciting date," he asked after a moment's silence.

"I'm not home yet. Ask me then," was her answer, but she snuggled just a little closer and did not object at all when Paul gave her a squeeze while she was wrapping her arm around his waist. She still held onto Ingram's box with the other hand.

After a while, Paul grew tired of watching the house burn. Samuels was still out back, looking for living lizards or doing a body count. Or maybe taking a leak, something Paul was thinking sounded pretty good right about then. But he couldn't see Ingram. He gestured to the ship with his free hand. "I think the gumdrop is inside. What do you think he's doing in there?" he asked.

"I don't know. ET calling home, I hope," Stacy answered.

Samuels was just walking back to them and suggested that they go see what the "damned little gumdrop" was up to while it was out of sight.

They had just made it to the craft when there was another explosion from the house, followed shortly by one from the barn.

"Damn!" Samuels said, brushing himself off from where he had thrown himself to the ground. He gave the house an accusing glare. "Must have been a second propane."

"And I guess that was the Mustang," Paul said sadly. They were going to need wheels, but there was probably going to be some help arriving fairly soon and he could arrange a lift back to Flagstaff for him and Stacy he was sure. He didn't know how he was going to explain all this to the insurance company and he wasn't sure if they covered vehicle loss from alien invasion. Well, USAA had treated him well, *most* of the time.

Back at the Caruthers House, things had also been getting a little exciting. After the remaining ships had sped off to the four corners, there had been a period of silence, but not for long. Three of the ships had returned and it looked to the human observers that they had landed. Members of the National Guard 2220th Transportation Company, headquartered in Flagstaff, had arrived to help out. They weren't sure why. There was nothing to move and their trucks were parked mostly as roadblocks and not deploed for hauling water or troops. Then some bright boy had begun passing out night vision equipment, video gear, and special monitoring devices and told the soldiers to go play Special Ops. Yeah, okay, they were in uniform and on government time, but, hey, this wasn't what they had trained for, was it? Well, soldiers were soldiers and they are all supposed to be trained in everything, unless they were Air Force, and everyone knew that every Army job description included the term "rifleman". The Captain, hearing exactly those words from the Governor, shut up and handed out the gear.

Now, drivers and shotgun riders were out in the wood, working their way slowly and cautiously through the underbrush, using night vision gear they had never worked with before, trying to play stealth like real Marines or something. Damn! Didn't anyone know that's not how you run a war?

The fires were dying down, but they had no idea where the enemy was or what it was, or exactly what they were supposed to do when they found it. But that there was an enemy around somewhere, oh, yes, of that they were sure. There were enough civilian bodies scattered through the woods on either side of the lane all the way to the house to make that abundantly clear to the soldiers. What was not clear was why they were moving ahead instead of waiting for *real* Special Ops guys from the regular Army and *where in hell* were those weenies from the Air Force, anyway, who should be providing air cover?

So it was that the Guardsmen, tasked with setting up observation posts to detect and report "enemy" activity, were under the cover of the thick growth of pine and spruce that silently surrounded the remains of the Caruthers House when their objective returned. If you could call a smoking thirty-foot deep, two-hundred foot wide crater "remains."

"Something's happening!" one of the police officers assigned to crowd control shouted, pointing to the pre-dawn sky over the old Caruthers House. He had been scanning the heavens since there was no crowd to control; anyone with any sense was secured in their house with whatever weapons were at hand and, this being Northern Arizona, that was a lot of fire power waiting behind locked doors.

The patrolman's call was picked up and other eyes locked on the strange craft that converged on the Caruthers House. More of the smaller ones and one or two of the larger units, a sizable chunk of firepower in and of itself.

The word went out and Guardsmen found cover in the undergrowth and tried their hardest to be invisible. Some of these men had gone to the Gulf when Iraq decided that it wanted Kuwait and Kuwait's access to the Persian Gulf. Oh, and oil, of course. The war was about oil Iraq wanting it, Kuwait having it. That conflict had been a cakewalk but even the US military had not had a get-out-of-jail-free card and they remembered the wounded and dead, twenty-eight of them the Guardsmen had hauled from a Scud-hit barracks to a make-shift Morgue and they helped move most of the ninety wounded to a field hospital. Others they had seen coming back from the front. Four hundred and twenty-four dead Americans, about four times that seriously wounded.

From what they had seen so far this evening, the Arizona Guards looked to be in the position of the Iraqi troops facing the 101st Airborne (Air Assault) Division out of Fort Campbell, Kentucky. Better known as the Screaming Eagles, those troops took to the air in January, 1991, in a flight of Black Hawks and support ships. The air cavalry's mobility allowed the 101st to conduct the deepest ever combat air assault into enemy territory. The 101st sustained no causalities in action during the hundred-hour Gulf War and captured thousands of enemy prisoners. Yeah, the Guardsmen felt like they were up against a superior force like that.

These troops had not seen a lot of combat. Of the hundreds of Arizona Regular Army and Guardsmen sent to the Gulf in 1990 and '91, only four were killed and three out of those were killed by friendly fire. About 170 guardsmen and women from the Arizona Army National Guard's 2220th Transportation Company, headquartered in Flagstaff, were sent to the Gulf and tasked with transporting both dry and refrigerated containerized cargo, general non-containerized cargo, and bulk water by truck in support of the 3rd Infantry Division out of Fort Stewart, Georgia. Along the way, several of them got to know Private Dorothy Fails of Taylor, Arizona, in Navajo County's White Mountain area, best known for the Painted Desert and Petrified Forest and the only paper mill in Arizona. But with only 2,700 residents, those who did manage to get out of town tend to be whether gregarious.

Dorothy was a little different from most teenagers from rural Arizona. Her outlook was broadened by her Army experience, her mind sharp, manner friendly. She was more than happy to spend time talking to the Guard unit from her home state while most of the other regular Army treated them like second class citizens. Most of the Guardsmen had wrangled trucks, some had rode shotgun, but few had even fired their weapons in practice, much less in battle. For the Guard, it was a support position and the One Hundred Hour War had not given them much time to worry about combat or snipers or getting lost in the desert. So when word came back down the line that Private Dorothy Fails was a causality, it had hit hard. It had made them angry, and it had reminded them about their own mortality.

Now, here they were, on the front line with loaded weapons on the outskirts of Flagstaff acting like real soldiers against what some were calling an Alien Invasion. Every single one of them had seen the movie *Independence Day* and this was just a little too scary for guys who were accountants and clerks and fry cooks stock boys. Maybe this was a Hollywood movie and they were unknowing extras to make it more real? Not with real bullets. Not Hollywood, not with Hollywood still talking about the *Twilight Zone: The Movie* accident that had taken out Vic Morrow, every soldier's image of a real combat warrior, Hollywood hype or no.

So they froze and waited for word, sweat trickling down their faces in a cool August dawn.

Behind them, reinforcements were gearing up. The cops and SWAT team members had seen *Independence Day* too and they remembered that it wasn't just the hot-shot military that had taken out the bad guys, but every day common Joes like themselves. They adjusted the scopes on the rifles, passed a shotgun or ammunition to a buddy, or stood talking in quiet whispers, wondering whether or not they should charge in. These were not combat soldiers, nor were they big city police where crime was a matter of course. These were Flagstaff cops, tasked mainly with bringing down the unruly drunk college student; Reservation cops, tasked mainly with bringing down the unruly drunk tourists or locals on the reservations; Forest Rangers, who were tasked mainly with making sure the drunk campers didn't get the bears drunk and unruly; and Flagstaff's eighteen member Special Weapons Assault Team members, who were mainly unruly cops who had gotten drunk one night and drafted a report to the Flagstaff City Council outlining all the reasons the small college town needed a SWAT team (except for the main reason: they wanted to play with bigger guns). And now they were all here, about to take on aliens who could, for all they knew, be the forerunners of a *real Independence Day*. Of course, had that actually *seen* an alien, they would have been thinking *V*.

Slowly they began to work their way up the lane. They knew the soldiers were in the woods and they had no desire to be shot by accident. They would stick to the road.

Ragsdale had had enough with waiting and this was getting out-of-hand. Or out of *his* hand, at least.

"Gimme that," he snarled, grabbing a megaphone from a nearby officer. "This is the police," his voice boomed into the night, scaring the Guardsmen and everyone else half out of their minds. "You back there in the trees! We have you surrounded!"

Ragsdale ignored the chuckle he heard from behind him. He would find out who that was later and deal with the (soon to be former) patrolman at his leisure. "The Army is here and prepared to eliminate you if you resist," he continued, completely ignoring reality and surprising the Guardsmen who were prepared, really, for nothing, but willing to do what they had to do if they had to do it at all, though preferring, of course, to leave the eliminating to the professional, full-time Army when they finally drug their slow asses up here. "Lay down your weapons and come out with your hands up!" Ragsdale commanded, then, as an afterthought, added "And land those damned ships, too!"

There was a pause for a few seconds, then one ship shot into the air. A second, then third followed, and in under a minute, all the ships had lifted off and vanished into the night sky.

"Damn. How am I going to explain that they got away to the mayor?" he asked no one in particular.

"Damned if I'm going to," an officer muttered, taking back the megaphone before Ragsdale did something stupid, like issue a challenge.

"I saw Samuels' car. Where is he?" Ragsdale suddenly demanded.

"I heard that he got out in a Mustang. But someone else said he was inside the house," the Patrolman answered whether reluctantly. The house was gone. There had been a massacre in the woods. And he had liked Samuels.

"Great. Just when I can use him, he goes and pulls a bonehead maneuver like this," Ragsdale said, with no more concern for Samuels' life than he would have had for the dog he hit in the road the week before. "Well, if he's there, then this is his mess and I can tell the mayor to talk to his ass about it."

Ragsdale nodded, satisfied that he had solved the immediate problem: where to lay the blame. "Well, let's call it a night," he continued. "Secure the area and get forensics to work. You can have the Guard haul out the bodies. We can sort all this out when I get back to the office around noon," he concluded, turning back to his car and waving his driver over. Fortunately, the lizards were not returning to Flagstaff.

The dawn was coming and night had been their friend so far. Would the daylight help or hinder them? Not that it mattered. The family car had been destroyed during the fighting. They were pretty much stuck here or they could try to catch some of the frightened horses. They would have to make a break bareback; the tack had gone up with the barn.

"With some difficulty, yes, but I can fly this ship," Ingram was insisting again, forming a pretty solid defense against Paul's verbal onslaught for a little guy that looked like he was made mostly of jell-o.

"Now that you've won, why not stick around and wait for help," Samuels offered, a voice of calm reason against Paul's more emotional storm.

"That is not possible. We have won the battle, but not the war. If the ship does not lift from here soon, it will draw the others to investigate and another battle will rage. One we cannot win, I fear. And there are still Aeolian ships out there. We do not know how long before someone swings by to assist here."

"And go where?" Paul demanded.

"I listened in on their communications while I was inside. The Vegans have entered the system. They are engaging the Aeolians outside your moon's orbit. That has pulled away most of the fighters but there may still be Aeolian ships searching for us or on the way to see why this one has not moved. Time is still against us."

"Look, what is all this fighting about, anyway? What's so important about that box?" he asked, pointing to the case Stacy had finally set down by her feet.

"The Aeolians are a war-like race. They are particularly repugnant to my race. And even more so to that of Systel's."

"That sounds like a rotten reason to start a war," Stacy observed. "I mean, these guys are creepy and disgusting, but you can't go off and fight just because you don't like someone's table manners."

"It is their table manners that are the problem," Ingram insisted. "You have noticed that they have a strong taste for your domesticated pets. Systel's race is related to your cats and dogs, in flavor if not evolutionary history."

"Oh," Stacy gasped, catching on to Ingram's drift.

"Yes. The Aeolians use them as food whenever they can. We have reason to believe that they prefer the flesh of several other sentient beings as well," Ingram continued. "And you may have noticed that they prefer to kill their own meals and to eat them fresh. There is no quick death for their victims."

"Disgusting," Stacy said with no equivocation.

"We feel the same," Ingram stated. "My mission, while attached to Systel's staff at the Embassy, was to determine the extent of the problem, gather evidence, and prepare a report that would unite the intelligent races against the Aeolians. The goal was to cut them off and confine them in their own systems. Permanently," Ingram said. "We do not want beings that live on the blood of others given free rein to roam the galaxy at will."

"Maybe a little holy water and a good stout wooden stake…" Stacy said, trailing off with a shiver. Vampires, cannibals, things that go bump in the night; these Aeolians were creatures for nightmares.

"I must go. I must try to reach the Vegans. I dare not use the Aeolian radio now for fear they would intercept my transmission, but I can contact the Vegans once I am in space. They will send an escort. Please, just set the case inside the airlock. I will secure it there," Ingram asked. "And thank you my friends. I believe now that the Aeolians would have found us this day no matter what happened and your help has surely saved the information we have struggled to protect and so many have died trying to conceal from our enemies."

Paul hesitated just a bare second, then took the case from Stacy and held it like a shield across his chest. "Take me with you," he said in a rush.

"Are you crazy?" Samuels exploded. How did they know that these aliens were not the bad guys? Paul was virtually putting his head in the lion's mouth!

"What's wrong with staying here," Stacy demanded. "Someone got bad breath or something?"

Paul's first rush was on impulse, but he was beginning to understand what it was that had prompted him to blurt out his offer. He had been lost for a long time. And though the events of the last few hours had pushed the pain aside, he knew he had pretty much lost Jeremy, too. At least for a few years and who knew how long after that? He had a chance to do something now, a chance to do something that might make a major difference in his son's life, whether Jeremy ever knew about it or not. Here was an opportunity to achieve something significant, something world-changing that most men only dream accomplished. And what a story!

It was not that what had happened since he first set foot on the Caruthers' porch had been insignificant. Just getting Ingram this far had been a major accomplishment, perhaps something world-changing in and of itself. But here he had taken whatever actions he had not because he had decided to take them, but because circumstances had forced them on him. Now was a chance to move forward under his own will, his own determination, to take a step and go "boldly where no man has gone before."

This was, ultimately, not a choice. It was an imperative. So maybe Paul was still being pushed. Maybe he liked the direction, though, and was not going to resist the flow.

Paul turned to Stacy, looking deep in her eyes. Yes, there might be a reason to stay. In time, he could fight his way back into Jeremy's life, be a part time father, and do what he could. But that fight could go on without him for a few months, while he pleaded with this Alliance to open itself to Earth. He could go and be back, with a little luck, before the courts could even schedule a hearing on Janet's move. In that time, he could make a major difference in the world, maybe even saving the lives of thousands if the Aeolians decided Earth needed their personal attention.

"There's nothing wrong with staying here," he told her. "It's just that this is the chance of a life time. I came here to write a story about a toy maker. I don't have the ending yet. And waiting to find out whether we win or lose in a court somewhere out there in space is more than I can handle. Think of the story this'll make! Think of how much it can change everything, how far we can go if we can finally reach the stars!"

"If you live to tell it," was her somber reply.

"I'll live," Paul said, suddenly sure that this was the truth.

"Man, this is crazy!" Samuels insisted, himself fully believing that Flagstaff's six thousand foot elevation was about as high above sea level as man was meant to go.

"Maybe," Paul agreed, then turned back to Ingram. "Take me with you. You said handling the ship will be difficult. Maybe I can help."

"I cannot," Ingram protested, though not strongly. "I must wait until your race has been formally contacted."

"Why stand on formality," Stacy wanted to know. "Just kill a few people, eat a few dogs, and go about your business is alright just because it's *informal*?"

"Look," Paul said, picking up her thread. "You said you were an ambassador or at least on the ambassador's staff, right? You said that you were charged with gathering evidence, so that makes you a spook – an intelligence officer to be politically correct. Isn't that true, too? The Alliance has got to start making contact somewhere and you've already contacted us and, by implication in using us to save your life, made us agents *pro tem* of the Alliance," Paul said. It was a weak argument and he knew it, but so what? It was still an argument and he was looking more to giving Ingram excuses than to convince him. It. "You brought your war to us. What if these… vampires decide to eat humans as a steady diet? When you leave, we'll be defenseless. It seems that the Alliance at least owes us a hearing. If it were not for you and the Ambassador, these lizard things would not be bothering us now."

"It is not my place to decide," Ingram said, but still considering Paul's argument. "However, you have helped me." He paused again. "And you are correct. Members of the Alliance are responsible for the death and destruction visited on your planet." Ingram paused and thought some more. He seemed to focus on Paul at some length before he spoke again. "Yes. I will leave this to the council. And I shall present your case myself."

Paul was not sure whether he should cheer or regret his rash remarks, so he just nodded and started for the ship, not noticing Stacy standing off to the side, looking somberly at Paul and Ingram. "Good," he said before he could change his mind. "Let's get going."

"Hey, you can't go!" Samuels protested. "Who's going to explain this to the chief?"

"You know as much about this as I do," Paul pointed our reasonably. "You know I'm staying at the 'Y'. My notes and laptop are there. All the background you need is in a file called 'ToyMaker.' But you have a lot more information now than you did before. At least you can explain that shopping center heist and all that missing equipment. You couldn't do that before."

"No one will believe it, no one at all," Samuels insisted.

"And who took all the cat and dog food," Paul finished.

"You did that," Samuels demanded of the gumdrop. "You and that crazy cat?"

Ingram fluttered his tentacles, but Paul nodded an affirmative. "And you have some bodies and some technology to back up your story," Paul added, pointing at the lizard zapper Samuels had tucked into the top of his pants.

"Look, man, this is pure crazy," Samuels continued his protest while Stacy stood quietly, measuring Paul by some personal yardstick. "You could be killed! You might never come back!"

"I could slip in the shower and die tonight," Paul said. "Hell, I could have died anytime in the last twelve hours and done it pretty easily. Just because there is risk doesn't mean that the job shouldn't be done. Would that stop you from being a policeman or a soldier for protecting the country?"

"There's no need to go out and borrow trouble," Samuels insisted, falling back on the philosophy his grandmother would spout when we talked about joining a gang way back when.

"I think I'll be back," Paul said, and the conviction in his voice was real. "Maybe six months, maybe six years, but I will be back. Besides, there's nothing to keep me here anymore and if I go I stand a chance of making this planet a little safer for my son. This is probably saner than trying to fight with my ex over custody."

"You gotta be crazy," Samuels said, not letting go.

"Staying and fighting with my ex would be crazy," Paul said. "This gives me something to do that can help everyone and, ultimately, that could be the best thing I could do for my son."

"I still say you're nuts."

"Maybe, but look what is at stake here: There's a chance to protect the Earth, to keep it from becoming the lizard's private game preserve., maybe to enter the intergalactic community! Think about it! Who is better to pitch for help for mankind: a man or a gumdrop?"

"A gumdrop, man, that's easy. Who's gonna listen to you out there?" Samuels said, waving his arms at the universe.

"Maybe no one, but I still need to try. What chance did Columbus have of convincing anyone the world was round? It was hopeless; but somebody listened."

"Man, all I can think about are those lizards," Samuels admitted.

"OK. That's enough reason in itself. What if they decide they want as a private convenience store? Do you think we could stop a hundred of those ships? A thousand? How about one really big mother? Think we stand a chance without outside help?"

"Well, maybe we can't take them today, but..." Samuels said, wavering a little.

"So someone's got to go for help. This is a government we're talking about, an alliance, not a dictatorship. If someone doesn't go and push, they could take so long deciding that help wouldn't matter much. Look at Bosnia. Look how long it took the US to go after Hitler and how many died while we debated. Look how hard it was for Bush to pull together an alliance to toss Saddam out of Kuwait! Do you really think that aliens are going to move that much faster without someone pleading our case? And it doesn't matter! We have to start the ball rolling sometime. The gumdrop has other obligations."

"Maybe we could hold the lizards off, if we pulled together…"

"You know the world governments will be too busy scoring political points to do much good. Damn! I bet they have liberals out there too. I bet there are those who think they can talk to these things. And while they talk, how many die?

"I think a human has to be the one to ask for someone to take us seriously. And someone's got to stay behind and try to convince people that what happened here is real. There are real Aliens and real Predators and real ETs that have been trying to phone home. They're out there and, in case you didn't notice, they're down here too. We need the ET's help if we are going to keep the Queen Alien from having us for lunch," Paul argued emphatically. And in the back of his mind there was the hope that if he were successful, the publicity would help him win Jeremy back. Just going might be enough. He was sincere in his motivation, but few people do things for one reason only.

Paul wanted to save mankind; he also wanted to see his son, to write this story, to see the stars…

"Man, nobody's gonna believe this," Samuels protested lamely.

"Right. People aren't going to believe until the proof is shoved down their throats," Paul said. "That's your job."

"I'm a cop, not a messiah with a message?"

"And that means bringing in help and making the aliens visible to everyone. I don't think this 'Alliance' will do anything for Earth on their own, except maybe set up a blockade or something. They may not have the political will – or the courage – to try and stop this lizard land grab. Someone has to ring the bell and there is only one person here who is willing to try."

"And you think *you* can do it?" Samuels' sarcasm was thick.

"Who else can go? The farmer's wife? *You?*"

"No way, man. I like having my feet on the ground."

"There's no time to find a real diplomat. Sometimes the average person just needs to stand up and do what is right. Isn't that what started the American Revolution? Just average people standing up for their rights?"

"Yeah, yeah, I guess," Samuels said, relenting after a moment's reflection. "Yeah, I guess someone does need to go. I'll be more believable here, being a cop, than you would be as a writer. I guess you'll do. You've got the fire and conviction that just might be enough to pull this off."

"Right. And who better than you and Stacy to stay behind and bring the light of truth to the people of the world?" Paul asked, clapping Samuels on the shoulder. Then Paul turned to Stacy with a mixture of sadness and longing that he didn't fully understand. But she did.

"I'm going to miss you," he said.

"No you're not," she responded with a little shake of her head.

"What do you mean," Paul asked, perplexed, but expecting some stupid reply about being a hero or too busy to worry about a one-night stand or something.

When she said "I'm going with you," it took him a second for it to click into place. But Samuels' "Another Looney Toon" comment, delivered offhanded and too the sky, locked her meaning into place. He agreed with Samuels on that one.

"That's crazy!" Paul protested, echoing Samuels' thoughts. "I may never come back!"

"I'm still coming. Hey, I don't want to be the one left here to explain all this, either, and if you think I've found you just to wait patiently for your return, then you're crazier than I am!"

"But you don't know what you're getting yourself into," Paul continued, completely forgetting that he, too, had no idea what the future held.

"And neither do you," she promptly pointed out. Paul looked at Samuels for support, but the cop just shook his head and moved off a few feet. "Besides, this is your toy maker, isn't it? The one you've told me about, right?"

"Yeah," Paul admitted reluctantly. He had the strong feeling that his big mouth was about to turn around and bite him on the ass. Never say anything to a woman. They never forget and they'll use every word you ever utter to their ultimate advantage and your ultimate disaster.

"Any creature that makes those toys and kills snakes, must be all right," she said with the firm conviction of the dedicated believer.

"Not snakes, Lizards."

"Snakes. Lizards. Snarks. Whatever difference does it make?"

"Really, Stacy, this is crazy," Paul said, unable to fend her argument so falling back on is first protest. "Why would you want to go, anyway."

"We're going to go out and make a difference for everyone, you said that yourself," she pointed out and Paul was forced to nod his agreement, suddenly not sure if she was arguing for going or his staying. "Well, I want to be a part of that too. It has to beat being a waitress."

They looked at each other for a long time, then Paul held out his hand, which Stacy took, a little shyer than her words suggested.

"We must go. Now," Ingram interjected into the silence. "I sense it is right for you both to come. But it must be now."

Paul turned to Samuels. "Thanks," he said simply.

"Good luck, man," the cop said with a mixture or respect and amazement. "I really should arrest you, you know."

"For what?" Paul asked in amazement.

"Hell, man, I don't know! For being an escapee from the Basket Weavers Guild. Something. Anything to keep you here!"

"Well, thanks again. There's another file on my computer called 'Buddy.' It has notes and contact information for a friend in Phoenix. Talk to him and he'll take care of my apartment and bills and things. I've known him a long time. There is a power of attorney on file in his office. He works in my agent's office. Just make sure you get the story right: off on an extended business trip, not dead."

Samuels nodded and looked at Stacy.

"I moved back in with my folks a year ago. You know: It's the economy, stupid. Just stop by and tell them something. They sure won't believe what really happened. But don't let them toss anything. Tell them I eloped. Tell them I'll be back."

"What, do I look like Arnold Schwarzenegger?"

"Maybe if he got a tan," Stacy quipped back.

Samuels smiled and watched them walk up the ramp to the ship.

"Oh, man! Hey! How am I gonna explain all this," he yelled again. It was really beginning to dawn on him that the Feds were going to want to have a long, private talk with him. "Ain't nobody gonna believe me!"

"Have them ask the girl," Stacy suggested.

"What makes you think they'll believe *her*? She doesn't even speak English!" Samuels protested. "They're gonna haul my ass back to Area 51 and nobody's gonna see me again."

"If they don't want to cooperate, shoot them with that fancy gun you have," Paul said, sticking his head back out the door. "Then sell the patient to Smith and Wesson and retire!"

Samuels pulled Ingram's ship blaster out of his pants. That was the second time he forgot about that thing.

"Yeah, the gun," he said, then looked back at the ship. "Say, thanks…"

But they had already vanished inside and the port was closing. Paul and Stacy and that little gumdrop were gone.

The alien craft rose slowly into the dawn, the first rays of the morning sun striking the silver finish and making the craft look like it was made of gold. And for humanity, Samuels thought, maybe it was, maybe it was a golden chariot that would herald a golden age. Then the ship tilted almost straight up and aimed for the dark skies where a few stars still showed overhead. Just before it vanished from sight, three more craft streaked after it and Samuels could see the craft with the hopes of humanity begin to weave and dodge the enemy fire. It would be close, but the escape vehicle had a good head start and Ingram had said help was waiting.

"I sure hope they make it," Samuels said to the empty heavens.

"They will, mister," the little girl said, taking his hand and surprising him with her English. "*Ellos vuelan con los ángulos*"

"Huh?"

"I said they are safe. I said 'They are flying with the angles.'"

CHAPTER FIFTEEN

June 21, 2002
Flagstaff, Arizona

Samuels leaned back in his chair, toying with the strange device the gumdrop had given him before it left with Paul and Stacy. It was, the gumdrop said, his story written for his home world and roughly translated into English. It would explain how the aliens had arrived on Earth and perhaps answer some lingering mysteries. There was also information on the alien's bank accounts.

Apparently, all parties had been compensated for the stolen equipment. There was some money left over. Well, quite a lot left over. The gumdrop - Ingrid - had wanted it divided and put in trust for Paul and Stacy, the family at the ranch, and of course Samuels. After donating a chunk to help the families of those killed at the house, that left a few million each for the rest. Samuels could retire. He could retire anywhere in the world. And maybe still have enough left to hire a good lawyer to keep his ass away from the Men in Black.

Of course he had to be careful. Sure as shit the government would grab it all if they found out about it. Maybe it was time for a vacation in the Cayman Islands. He could afford that from his personal savings. Set everything up in numbered accounts. Yeah, put some of the knowledge gained in fighting the drug smugglers to use for a positive cause.

Samuels keyed the *on* switch and jumped slightly in his chair. The gumdrop had said it was like a movie, but what popped up in the center of the room was much more than that. It was a holographic image appeared. It was hard to believe that this was animated and not filmed live. Pixar would be amazed.

*　　*　　*

Ingram's Story
March 2-26, 1975
A short distance from Saturn,
on Luna,
and near Clay Springs, Arizona

"One comes."

Systel stirred from reviewing her report and looked over at Ingram Three. It was pulling its body, which had flattened to a lumpy blob while it rested, into its normal gumdrop shape. It extended an antenna and assumed the Position of Careful Listening.

Systel waited patiently for it to speak. Ingram Three would not have stirred from its post-jump depression for a minor disturbance. Systel consciously willed herself calm. It never did any good to hurry Ingram.

"A messenger," it said after a pause that Systel counted in multiple heartbeats. Systel looked directly at the eye that Ingram extruded on a slender stock to watch the Ambassador's reaction. Her species was one of the few with minds closed to its *psi* receptors. Her skin crawled, which was her normal reaction whenever Ingram studied her body language closely, trying to gauge visually what its other senses normally conveyed. It was an uncomfortable experience for her, this scrutiny by a telepath. But, except for twitching her nose – a habit she had whenever she was disturbed – she showed no outward sign of her thoughts.

The image of the report Systel had been reading shimmered in the air then blinked out as the reader detected the loss of eye contact and disengaged the holographic projection and audio system. Systel glanced at the chronometer and squinted to make out the notation; the cabin's walls, painted amber, hurt her eyes, making it hard for her to see the numbers projected on the plastic surface, and she scrunched up her nose in concentration. *Let it try to sort* that *expression out!* she thought. She did a quick calculation, translating ship's time into Standard. It was too soon for break-out from non-space but, conversely, break-out was too near to expect a summons by the Captain. The approach of a Hiver now could only herald trouble. Her tail twitched with her disquiet, but she stilled it, fully aware of Ingram's interest in her species involuntary muscular movements.

"Ingram, please give me a reading," she asked her assistant, a little more curtly than she intended. "I need details."

"Yes, Ambassador."

It extended an antenna almost to the cabin's roof, withdrawing its eye stalk into its boneless body. It transferred the mass from the eye stalk to the antenna, providing a thicker receptor base, and expanded the top of the antenna into a spoon-like disk. It slowly rotated the disk until it locked in and tracked the Hiver moving through the ship.

Quuoral hated the alien section of the ship more than any other and she hated the stark metal ship very much. She was part of the Quartermaster Section and, due to her low rank, had carried messages before to non-receivers, despising every step she took outside the dirt-covered floors of the Hive ship's main living section. She was agitated, angered, bored.

She was also distracted and did not notice the gentle mental nudge when Ingram, its antenna twitching, sent soft triggers along the fragile bridge it built between itself and the Hiver. Subtly, it tried to coax her message to the fore-front of her thoughts. But Quuoral's agitation was too much and her own inner turmoil overrode Ingram's attempts at delicate penetration.

Try to keep tight control over your errant cogitations, she berated herself in what amounted to a mental shout, effectively overriding Ingram's attempts to sort through her individual shots. *Your feelings leak into the communal thought pool! Hive Captain Yanni orders me below because of my lack of discipline. But it's not fair! I hate this part of the ship!*

"She does have a leaky mind, Ambassador," Ingram told Systel several corridors and two flights away. "She is easy to read and does not detect me at all. She is worried about her crew rating and this overshadows all else… Now she wonders how Hive Captain can equate the hard ship's corridors with the soft earth tunnels of home-world hives… This is dangerous for her, Ambassador. It is unthinkable to question Hive Captain, but Quuoral's thoughts run wild. Yes, she has a leaky mind -shield, even for a Hiver... She believes Hive Captain gives her an endless list of make-work chores. This does nothing to improve her disposition."

Ingram chuckled, a sound that originated deep in the air cavity that nestled in the inner core of its form. Air eventually passed from the cavity through one of several diaphragms originally designed to maintain inner pressure in equilibrium with an outside atmosphere that fluctuated greatly on its home planet, which was riddled with volcanic action. As a side effect, its system also produced sound in wondrous variants. While Diaddians had some form – organs with prescribed duties and such – their boneless bodies were flexible and their strong minds could form various appendages when needed from the plasma that comprised most of Ingram's body mass.

If only the aliens had communal minds, then this trip to their quarters would not be necessary, Quuoral thought, completely ignorant of Ingram's presence inside her mind.

"She doesn't suspect that I can eavesdrop on her. This is humorous." Ingram chuckled again, then hurried on when it detected Systel's growing impatience, which she demonstrated by twitching just the bare tip of her tail, a movement Ingram knew was allowed and not involuntary. "She thinks we are handicapped by our inability to speak mind-to-mind like Hive Sisters; that we are as brain dead as Hive Brothers, and so courtesy is necessary. – Watch this one, Ambassador. She borders on xenophobia. She does not understand why Hive Captain Yanni expects her to *like* carrying messages to you and why the Captain expects her to take it as a privilege."

"The purpose of her visit? Do you have that yet?" Systel felt impatience grow. Ingram often sprinkled its reports with too much personal commentary. For the hundredth time she cursed the Hiver's espier power, a power that made ship intercoms unnecessary on their ships. Convenient for the Hivers, but a nuisance for any other species.

"I will search deeper. She comes quickly and is much agitated. Is this important? We will have the message soon and I do not detect hostility toward you. Just a general dislike of species without *psi*."

"Ingram, I know how you prefer not to read other's thoughts without permission, but we are in a desperate place here. The messages we carry are important. I need to understand the Hivers to properly evaluate the situation and I would like forewarning of any problems. That last raider attack nearly sent us to our ancestors."

"Yes, Ambassador." Ingram sent a stronger nudge to the approaching Hiver and was immediately assaulted by a new wave of self-pity and anger.

Quuoral's claws rattled off the metal deck and this annoyed her. She passed through the air lock and into the Ambassador's Corridor, feeling the sudden drop of air pressure; and this also annoyed her. She did not like it here at all. Not liking annoyed her.

Even the air smells of aliens on this side of the lock, she thought. Not bad, just... odd. No smell of cool earth, no acidic tinge from the larval beds. Barren. Boring. Alien.

Quuoral quickened her pace. While she did not detect Ingram, except, perhaps, as nothing more than a light buzzing in her receptors, she was still an upset Hiver. More, she could pick up tension from the communal mind, probably, she thought, originating with Yanni, the strongest mind on the ship. In her anxiety, she thought the disquiet was aimed directly at her.

"You will need to ease her tension some for me to obtain a true reading," Ingram reported to Systel.

Systel rose and walked to one of the cabinets built into the cabin wall. She pulled a small vial from a carton on the floor and opened the bottle. The fragrance of a field covered with fresh flowers on a soft summer day slowly filled the small cabin. Systel motioned Ingram to continue. It had stopped talking as Systel rose.

"She arrives, Ambassador."

"Her message?"

"She does not have it yet. I can follow the communal mind to the Hive Captain, if you wish..."

"No. Her mind's too complex, her senses too strong. I don't want to risk detection."

"The Hivers are allies, aren't they?"

"Yes, of course, but these are dangerous times. Few outside the Council knows of your species psi ability. For now, it is better if it stays that way."

Systel sighed and splashed more of the scent around. Better to be over liberal that to risk and agitated Hiver. "We'll know soon enough, I suppose. I think I have enough with which to work. Thank you."

Ingram brought the antenna down close to the top of his body until the spoon was only a knob resting on its 'head.' With Quuoral so close it could 'listen' more discretely with the antenna withdrawn.

In the corridor, Quuoral shivered and her wings rattled dryly beneath their cases. *Funny smells, too humid, too cold, just plain unpleasant.* She twitched her left feeler in disgust before stepping to the ambassador's door. Reluctantly she extended a hand, extruded a claw, and tapped on the portal.

Immediately, the door dilated and she was face-to-face with the Ambassador, trying hard to hide her disgust over the soft-shelled creature's appearance and odor.

"Noble Ambassador," she said in the Brother Tongue, her voice scratching against her feelers like sandpaper. She hated using the Brother Tongue. It hurt the throat and it hurt the feelers. Spaceships were a female's world despite the cold metal walls. Metal walls were male things and male creatures were like dead metal walls with metal dead minds. Their harsh spoken languages were unsettling, and should not penetrate female domains. It was a blasphemy to twist tradition, this use of male things on ship, this building a section of the ship that would comfort a male. Of course, this was an emergency. The ambassador was an important creature, carrying an important message to the Galactic Council and the Hive was part of the Alliance, so the unpleasantness must be endured. At least the ambassador was a female, even if she was a mammal.

Quuoral took a deep breath, calmed herself a little – the scent of fresh flowers inside the cabin was pleasantly unexpected and masked the alien odor somewhat – and opened herself to Yanni. She took another deep breath, her nostrils filling with the sweet perfume of flowering plants, not the mustiness of the alien and the male creature that accompanied her. She relaxed some and Ingram slipped a little deeper into her thoughts.

"This is Hive Captain Yanni speaking through my Mouth," Quuoral began, relaying the message as Yanni sent it to her. "Be informed that we will drop out of non-space shortly. I am putting the crew on battle alert. Please prepare yourself for action."

Systel motioned her aide to her side. The small Diaddian extended one thin pseudopodia. It slipped into a tiny hole in the base of the gravpad on which it rested, branching into several "fingers" which wrapped around a series of micro-switches. It pulled on the power and the thin pad glided forward. Its fingers delicately adjusted the gravity repulsion forces, weakening the side of the pad in the direction it chose to go, strengthening the field in the direction opposite from its desired destination. Pad and Diaddian moved silently across the cabin's floor on a thin layer of pulsating gravity waves.

It stopped by Systel's larger form and increased the repulsion equally around the pad's circumference, rising to just below Systel's shoulder. It extended two eye stalks, being careful not to raise them above the level of Systel's mouth, so she was not forced to look up to look it in the eye. It focused one eye on the ambassador; the other on the Hiver, and with one, it quickly examined the gauges on the gravpad's data pod.

"Ask her where are we," Systel said in Galactic Basic. Her vocal cords could not work around the clicks and pops that composed the Brother Tongue but her aide could imitate almost any form of audio communication in the known Galaxy. Its species' versatile agility with languages and excellent memories for dialects made them unquestionably the best translators for the Galactic Council and they served as such galaxy-wide. Their psi characteristics, however, were a closely guarded secret, revealed only to the highest level ambassador in Council service.

Ingram Three dipped an eye toward the waiting sailor, while still keeping both parties in focus. This seemed to disconcert Quuoral immensely and add to her discomfort at being the ambassador to the Ambassador, so Ingram politely kept its other three eyes nestled under their protective lids, fully hooded.

Ingram clicked and popped the question in passable Brother, then waited for a reply. Hivers were always difficult to deal with since the underlings often delayed answering a question until they received their superior's mental directions. When questions or problems became complex, the pause grew longer as more voices joined the communal mind with opinions and comments until the top Hiver in easy receptive range responded back down the line with a definitive answer. Fortunately, this was a small ship and not a small planet. The question would not go to a Hive Queen; the nearest Queen was too many light years away to receive the mind-thoughts. This Hiver only responded to the Hive Captain piloting the ship. But it still took a few seconds and Systel fidgeted impatiently.

"I am to inform you the Captain Yanni is no longer available for direct communication. I have been directed to answer from the communal knowledge pool. We are entering the field of a small, unimportant star on the fringes of Council space. There is one habitable planet harboring a primitive, warm-blooded, oxygen breathing, sapient species. The Hive Captain has blocked further details from the common knowledge pool, since we are in proscribed space."

"If this is a proscribed system, why are we here?" Systel asked through Ingram. She sighed when the Hiver's eyes vacillated as they always did when Hivers used the communal mind. Though she herself had a good grasp of the Brother Tongue in its spoken and written forms, she usually permitted Ingram to translate and then compared its answers to her own.

Again, the delay before the Hiver's eyes focused.

"Hive Sub-Captain Salzie reports that we are here because here we are."

Unprompted, Ingram asked for a clarification.

Hivers could be obtuse sometimes, Systel thought, then corrected herself. No, most of the time.

"Hive Sub-Captain informs you that we took a random jump while avoiding the last encounter with the Aeolian pirates. This is where we are. We shall leave when she is sure it is safe and Hive Navigator has plotted a course to the nearest Alliance system or outpost sufficiently large enough to thwart the pirates."

Exasperated, Systel was about to demand more information when the corridor light turned a pale blue and a low hum vibrated through the ship, the Hive equivalent of a danger klaxon.

"Hive Dub-Captain informs you that it may be some time before it is safe to jump out of this system," Quuoral spouted in a rush. "Hive Sub-Captain informs you that violent evasive maneuvers will commence in seven clicks and that you should seek shelter in an egg. Hive Crewwoman Quuoral bids you peace."

Abruptly, the Hiver turned and raced down the corridor to the air lock, leaving Systel and Ingram standing in the open door.

Systel growled softly. "What was that all about?"

"The Hive mind was informed by their surveillance units that a mother ship and a squadron of raiders materialized along our spore. I do not think the Hive Captain expected the raiders to follow so closely through the jump. I sense they did not expect the raiders to have the technical ability to track through non-space. They expect a fight soon. Hive Sub-Captain suggests you shelter in an escape pod."

"You can be sure that these are not Aeolian pirates, Ingram," Systel stated flatly. "A mother ship with tracking capabilities is military. The Aeolian government wants us stopped, not a ragged band of pirates."

Systel growled again, this time louder. Her race evolved from predators and the urge for action when danger arrived still flowed through her blood. Here was action and she, thirty-three seasons out of the nest, was relegated to hiding in an egg! Slowly she forced the tension from her body, calling on ancient mind games to cool her heated blood and racing hearts. Deliberately, placing her rear feet directly where her forefeet had stepped, a habit learned eons ago when her feline race hunted with spear and sling and were, in turn, hunted by the vicious fliers of her home world, Systel stepped to the side-board and picked up her reader with her right hand.

"Gather whatever you think we will need, Ingram, including all the data and images on this system that you can download from the Hive computer. Use the microbe memory unit. It has the most capacity. I'll take the dispatches and we will go to the egg like good little cubs. If Hive Captain flies like she did the last time, the inertia suppressors in the cabin won't be enough to keep our fur unruffled."

Ingram nodded and glided to a cabinet. It felt some sense of urgency even though the fine filigree covering its body were technically taste buds and not fur. However, high-g maneuvers were still whether uncomfortable. It found a small duffel, threw it open and tossed in items of its special interest: a small tool kit, an emergency medical computer and supply pouch, a few personal items for itself and the ambassador, a text reader and cache of classical literature memory microbes in their climate controlled cubes. It also selected microbe cubes on arms and armor, cooking, and electronics, slipping them into the mounts inside the case. It added a few final tools to the duffel, then slumped looking at the heavy bag, unsure how it would lift it. Though its pseudopodia were capable of delicate work, Ingram's appendage strength was negligible and the duffel was too heavy for its personal gravpad to manage. It could probably drag the satchel along the floor if it could safely remove it from the small table. The same with the duffel. But Systel stepped over and took the bag and case from Ingram, easily lifting the weight the Diaddian's small frame could not handle, and, incidentally, solving Ingram's dilemma. She carried a large brief in her other hand, crammed with photo memory microbes in their cubes, blank data microbe memory cubes, and hard-copy reports covering Aeolian activities in Hive occupied space and incursions into adjacent territories.

Watching carefully with the pair of eyes at the rear of her skull, she settled the small microbe environments in the cases with strap across her back, secured between her shoulders. Systel's arms rose from joints just behind her forelegs. Their double elbows permitted her to work on projects either in front of her, where the sharper pair of eyes were located, on her back, if absolutely necessary. She was far-sighted in the rear eyes, which had evolved as an early warning system against the flying predators of Systel's home world and were not well suited for delicate work.

She braced herself as the ship lurched suddenly, slapping a hand over the open lid of the black-box. The microbe cubes were sturdy enough, but the memory beasts inside were fragile. If they were banged around too much or if their environment was changed drastically from the norm, they would die before budding, losing their memory.

"The Hive Captain launched a salvo of long range seeker missiles," Ingram said, unconcerned over the violent shift.

"Are you sure?"

"Yes." Ingram raised an eye-stalk to look at Systel. "If that lurch had been evasive, well, this Hive Captain is much harsher than that little shock. Long range missile attack is action consistent with Hiver battle tactics. Besides, the gunner's joy over firing first was impossible not to read."

It blinked once, slowly, automatically, its mind racing along the ship's corridors.

"We have little time, however, to reach the egg before evasive maneuvers begin in earnest," it added.

"Fine. I have everything I need. Let's go."

Ingram dipped the eye stalk and extended an appendage to dilate the door again. It floated through with Systel right behind. They turned down a side passage leading toward the ship's escape pods. Behind them, from the direction of their cabin, came the sharp echoing klack-klack of Hive claws on metal.

"Quuoral returns," Ingram announced absently.

"You go on ahead and prepare the egg. Remember, the one supplied for us is the forth down the port side. I'll see what the Hiver wants."

"You do not delay much with that Hiver, Systel. Hive Captain will not wait for you when the raiders get close."

"I understand. Just power up the egg and prepare the systems. I'll be along directly."

As Ingram sailed off in one direction, Quuoral came scurrying around the bend in the corridor, in such a hurry that she ran both on her hind legs and her middle set of appendages which, while suitable for locomotion, were generally reserved for gesturing and light utility work. When she saw Systel, she skidded to a stop, her claws screeching most unpleasantly against the corridor floor, sending shivers all the way to the tip of Systel's tail. Systel stood patiently waiting for the Hiver to realize that Systel did not speak the Brother Tongue and that Ingram was not present. After a brief interlude, which undoubtedly meant messages and instructions were flashing back and forth, the Hiver spoke again, slowly.

"Noble Visitor-With-Honor," the Hiver clicked in simple, Maggot Brother Form, having heard from the Communal Mind that the Ambassador was thought to understand elementary Brother. "Hive Captain has assigned this unit to your service. Please hasten to your egg."

When Systel did not move, the Hiver continued, guessing at the question Systel was unable to voice.

"Hive Captain worries over your inability to communicate if a problem should arise." Quuoral paused. Systel noticed her antenna vibrating in urgency and mild anger at being, once again, the Ambassador's ambassador. "Hive Captain says most assuredly this vessel is out-gunned and outnumbered but it is not out-thought. Hive Captain says she is a careful pilot. But she wants me with you to relay messages if needed."

Fine, Systel thought, understanding double talk in any language. She turned and headed toward the egg, the Hiver falling in obediently behind.

The first evasive maneuver shook the ship just as Systel and Quuoral reached the egg. Systel braced against the lurch, but it was still just a mild jolt. The suppressor fields held the inertia displacement to a minimum, but Systel knew worse was coming. Quickly she threw her bundles in a storage locker that Ingram had left open and settled into the chair custom-designed to cradle her against violent accelerations and high-g stresses. Quuoral pulled herself into one of the pilot's chairs, Ingram watching every move from one eye or another without turning its head. It was already strapped into its own custom couch in the egg which also could fly the egg.

Quuoral looked over the board, then settled herself into the chair's padding as it wrapped around her, adjusting to the form of a wide variety of species. Everything was set as it should be. The little one did a good job of readying the egg for emergency evacuation, if required. Quuoral closed both sets of eye lids and tried to get a feel for what was happening from the ship's movements. Ingram listened in on the communal mind, but it wouldn't report to her with at present. At least, not without orders. There was much going on with this new attack and Ingram was more interested in what Hive Captain was doing than in what was transpiring in the egg. Everything Ingram caught it remembered, since it knew Systel would want a full report later.

Hive Captain Yanni did not have time to worry about the safety of the unit sent to shepherd the cargo. There were more important matters to claw now... like survival. To a species tied by communal thoughts, individual survival was not important to the race as a whole, but Yanni cared about her pod, nonetheless. They were too far from the nearest Hive Queen or Hiver outpost to commune with the Hive mind. If she failed in defeating the Aeolian raiders, or, if the Hive ship was damaged too much to permit escape, her pod would die without sharing its data with the Hive mind. All that knowledge would die forever. That was an unthinkable thing and her pride pushed her forward with all the skill and craft she could muster.

She knew little about the third inner planet, except that it sheltered a life form taking its first steps into space. In a few hundred revolves these savages might meet Galactic standards and a delegation would approach them with offers of membership in the Galactic Council and the gift of faster-than-light travel.

But contact was strictly forbidden before then. She took a big chance in running for the planet's single satellite, hoping the Aeolian would back off for fear of triggering the planet's detection devices.

Her plan was working, a... little. The mother ship settled into orbit around the larger ringed planet, but the raiders kept coming and sensors showed the mother was disgorging flight after flight of the small attack craft. Yanni must immediately dispatch the raiders harassing her now and find shelter on the blue planet's moon before the next flight of Stingers arrived.

She launched a series of distress beacons through non-space toward Galactic Central with little hope that Aeolian hunter-seekers would not destroy them before their messages arrived. She also commanded the Communications Officer to set up a repeating beam on the Galactic non-space emergency channel, but she knew the jamming from the Aeolian mother ship was strong. Much stronger than a Raider should have been able to field. There was some unease in the Communal Mind. Units in the Analysis Section were pondering if the Aeolian Raiders were not, in fact, Aeolian Military.

The easy work done, Yanni turned her mind to the guidance of her gunners, leaving the ship's dodging race for the moon's shelter to the Steering Officer.

There were only five raiders in the advanced flight: lightly armored Stingers, but they were fast and their aim deadly. Yanni kept a close watch on the shields but they were holding well.

The Steering Officer functioned admirably at her station. She threw the ship into tight turns and jumps at precisely the last second, disturbing the enemies' aim enough so that they only scored glancing blows on the shields, while all the time keeping the ship moving as rapidly and as directly toward their hiding place as possible. The raiders could not cut them off or make enough direct hits to overload the energy shields at this rate. The tactical computers on Stingers were not up to the complexity of the Hive ship's navigational and avoidance computers and Aeolian biological reflexes were no match for the Hive programmers, but if enough ordinance was thrown their way, enough would connect to make continued existence problematical.

The Hive ship was small, much smaller than a mother ship or a cruiser. Its shield generators would not stand much abuse. While armed, the Hive ship was primarily a diplomatic transport and not designed for extensive combat roles. The ship's firepower had been upgraded for the mission but the Hiver's had counted more on stealth than arms and shields to move the Ambassador though Aeolian lines.

It was a ploy that failed early in the game and the desperate Hivers had fought the doggedly trailing raiders through several systems and a series of random jumps, valiantly trying to break free or find a safe hiding hole. Ammunition was running low, the laser cannons were in need of overhaul, and the jump engines were under strain.

Good! Number Three gun, well done, Yanni thought, as a careless raider moved in too close and a short burst from the aft rapid-fire pellet gun shredded the enemy craft.

Four and two, watch for a raider coming under the belly!

The ship jerked violently to port but the two gun crews locked on and their combined laser fire vaporized the Stinger. Seconds later a third was knocked out by a seeker missile, thought-guided from the mind-linked fire control center deep inside the ship.

A sharp bounce up deflected a missile but a thought later the ship rattled as the blast's concussion wave passed through the shields. Ugly blue lights sprung up on the boards as some systems shut down and minor fires ignited. Worse, the marauder escaped the Hive ship's answering fire.

Quickly, quickly, reset the power! Another attack approaches! Yanni's mind screamed at the technical units who were scurrying to secure the damage.

But the expected attack did not come. Rather, the other raider peeled off and joined with its more successful brethren.

They do not see the damage, Yanni thought. We have some reprieve! Quickly, they form to attack again!

The raiders moved in, this time close together with their shields overlapping, providing a strong frontal guard. But their maneuver was too late, the Hiver ship was back in battle trim.

Steering Officer punched in a set of pre-determined; computer controlled evasive stratagems and fed the data to the gunners. At the last second, just as the raiders entered range, the Hiver ship slammed into a series of twists and turns that the raiders could not match or anticipate. But the ship's guns knew what was coming and, with the accuracy of a battery launching from a rock steady platform, lasers, missiles, and pellets struck the shields in precisely the same place, overwhelming the protection, shattering the shields, and vaporizing the pair of ships. Then, at full military thrust, the ship dove for the little moon, aiming for shelter on the dark side before reinforcement Stingers arrived. Once sheltered, the Hiver ship should be undetectable without an exhaustive infra-red and visible light search and Yanni doubted the little raider's equipment would handle that detailed an examination of a large area and they would be undetectable by the time the mother ship could arrive to add their massive scanner arrays to the hunt.

But the action must be fast and decisive. First, the Hiver had to detect a crater with a deep dust bottom. Then the craft had to settle in with a long enough lead time for the heat from the ship's gravity boosters to dissipate into the cold of space. The moon would shield the Hiver craft from the long-range scanners now plying over the transport from the mother ship and from curious lookers on the planet. Yanni hoped the beings in the system did not yet have bases on the moon or satellites that would detect her approach. But for the safety of the Ambassador – or at least the Ambassador's material – Yanni would risk censorship by the Council.

Yanni was confident that the dodge would work. Their lead time over the chasing raiders was enough for hiding if not enough for escape. Since the mother had sent out some raiders in a boxing pattern, the Hiver ship could never move far enough from the gravity well to return to non-space before more raiders were on them. The moon was their only hope.

Yes, hide, Yanni thought. Hide and repair our wounds. The raiders will grow impatient. We can run for home soon enough.

The situation lasted for several days. The problems facing the Ambassador needed to be out into the open.

"Quuoral," Systel asked through Ingram, "I tire of living in this egg. When will Hive Captain Yanni take us out of hiding?"

"It is soon, honored Ambassador. Even now, the Hive Captain's preparations draw close to completion."

"You said that two revolutions ago."

"This shall be the last. Patience, please, honored one."

And it was, truly, a short time later that the ship moved again.

The crater lit up with the intensity and suddenness of a high-powered searchlight, sending a beacon of graviton energy into the darkness of space for any waiting sensor to note. Slowly the beam widened as the Hiver ship struggled to rise from its hiding place under tons of dust. Finally, telescoping sensors rose above the crater's rim to see if danger lurked in the vast emptiness that surrounds the dark side of Luna.

Heartened by the readings, Hive Captain Yanni applied more anti-gravitational pressure, preparing to flee the moon's desolate, airless surface. But the attempt was in vain. When the lightly-armed transport cleared the crater walls, a flight of four Stinger attack ships swept over the horizon, just meters above the terrain, locking in and firing on the ship struggling to rise far enough from the moon's surface to dump the dust covering its upper hull and atmosphere flight planes; what had been their earlier salvation was now a chain holding them to the moon.

The Hiver ship still floundered on lifting gravatonics, now kicking in thrusters, making little forward progress. Yanni could run or fall back into the crater. Running would drain shield power but the ship would be easy prey in the crater, trapped and ripe for boarding. Yanni ordered full power to the lifters and full thrust to the in-system engines.

Shields flaring under the raider's salvo, the transport struggled to gain enough height to maneuver, its crew valiantly returning fire. The accuracy of the mind-linked Hive gunners took its toll and two of the attackers flared into brilliant balls of rapidly dispersing energy.

Hive Captain's excitement rose. They may yet escape, she thought, and her excitement spread to the crew. Then two more Stingers streaked onto the transport's sensor screens from starboard and another one just port of forward. A sixth Stinger blipped on the screen and streaked for a high cover position. The raiders boxed in the ship, efficiently trapping the Hivers. The mother ship had waited, probably sending flights of raiders over the moon's surface in a pattern guaranteed to spot the Hiver craft when it lifted, not even searching diligently. The Aeolian knew – or guessed – that the Hive Captain would not hide too long or stay on station for more than a few days. The mother ship's captain had quelled his impatience and waited abnormally long for an Aeolian… and an unbelievably long period for a simple Raider. His patience paid well.

Angrily, Yanni thrust thoughts of logistics and tactics aside. When they escaped the Aeolian raiders, she could worry about battle plans and deviations from racial stereotypes. Now, she just needed to survive. Or at least insure the survival of a single egg...

In a desperate move, Hive Captain stood the little ship on its tail and applied full rocket thrust. But that took power from the shields, power from the lasers, power from the fire control pods, and the pursuers were too many, too hungry for the kill.

With a blinding flash of light, the Hive ship blew apart, taking three of the raiders with it, their combined debris flying off in all directions. Hidden by the blast – a blast, incidentally, precisely timed to take as many enemy craft into oblivion with it as possible and a blast not caused by enemy fire – a powered-down egg was launched into escape orbit. Shielded by the Hiver ship's debris, it fell toward the distant, cloud-speckled blue planet that held the moon in its grip. It plummeted unnoticed by the raiders with a thousand other pieces of junk captured by the cloud flecked planet. They fell into the atmosphere, lighting the night skies in streaks and flashes of falling stars.

Triumphantly, the three remaining Stingers took the short jump back to the mother ship then fled the scene of their crime. The escape pod fell undetected toward the planet, just a large chunk of space debris falling, falling, flaring into a ball of fire, not starting its anti-gravity pulses until hull temperatures reached critical levels...

* * * *

Systel awoke slowly, forcing herself to take an inventory of all the aches that played her body like an army of mites on maneuver. Alive, apparently. No sharp pains, nothing plainly broken. She sniffed cautiously. No smell of fire, but that might change with any heartbeat. She pushed aside the cocoon formed by her crash chair when the egg struck the ground and squinted at the bright light entering through a large rent in the egg's side.

Immediately, she looked over at Ingram. Its couch appeared fine, a dull gold glow along the seams, a positive sign that it was alive and well in its cocoon. As soon as it awoke the cocoon's fabric seam would dissolve and it could emerge or Systel could claw it out. She decided to let it rest.

The force of the landing was still with Systel. The pilot Hiver must have waited a little too late to apply the counter thrust, or the egg would still be in one piece and she and Ingram would not have blacked out from the excessive gravitational forces caused by the reverse thrust.

She turned to the Hiver and had taken only a couple of steps when suddenly the Hiver sat up and screeched a series of loud wails mixed with rapid clicks and pops, waving her hands in the air, kicking with her legs. Then, as abruptly as it began, the Hiver slumped in her seat, antenna drooping, limbs frozen in a parody of a Racine Holy Dancer.

Ingram's voice stopped her as she started once more toward the immobile crewwoman.

"She is dead," Ingram said impassively.

"What was that noise about?"

"Something about all the other Hivers being gone. She died of horror at being cut off from the communal mind, I think," Ingram said as it finished pulling itself out of its couch. "I have read where Hivers die if isolated. None of the other pods launched, I guess. Just ours. She was alone. Their Communal Mind is different from my race's *psi* ability. We tend to go mad with too much noise; they go mad with too much silence."

"Alone. Like the rest of us and it killed her."

"Yes, Ambassador. But I do not think now is the time to ponder Hiver psychology. We crashed on a proscribed planet so there is no help from the locals. And the Aeolians may still be out there looking for us. We must remove our grip and find shelter before discovery."

"And then what, my little friend?"

"We must raise capital and purchase or build a null-space radio to call for help."

"You make it sound simple."

"It is not simple; it is what we must do if we expect help, if we hope to survive, if we dare dream to end the Aeolian curse. Come, Ambassador, we may not have much time."

"Yes, of course." Systel turned to the locker and pulled out her brief and Ingram's kit. "Take from the pod anything you need that I can carry."

"Nothing is retrievable, Ambassador. Just our kits. Shortly the material of the pod will begin to break down. By night fall, if this sun is almost at midday, as I suspect, there will be nothing left of the egg but a puddle of slag. This will keep the aliens from learning of Council technology. The countdown began when I emerged from the cocoon. We must hurry. The breakdown elements are corrosive once they combine and leak from the shell."

"What about the emergency radio?"

"This is a forbidden planet, Ambassador. The ship's computer surely told the egg that before launch. Everything will melt now that we are safely out of the shells. We must be away from here soon or the chemical reaction will damage us."

Systel and Ingram grabbed the brief and duffel from the locker and all the packets of emergency rations they could carry. They picked their way out of the craft through the large rent. Already the sides felt soft and pliable. Systel tried to remember her studies at the diplomatic school about survival techniques on potentially hostile planets, but her mind refused to work. She would rely on Ingram for the time being since the little blob never forgot anything. And it was right. They must move away from the egg before the raiders or the local fauna discovered them. Systel mentally listed her new set of priorities: find shelter, discover what she could about the local social structure, raise capital, if that was possible, purchase what Ingram needed to build a null-space transmitter, and survive until help arrived. But foremost she must remain undetected by the locals until rescued. She could not risk exposing herself to Council censorship for violation of non-interference regulations. That would over-shadow the news she carried about Aeolian activities, which must not happen.

The egg had landed well up the southern slope of a serpentine series of ridges. By the time they had gathered their supplies and moved away from the crash site it was about midway through the local dark cycle. The terrain was rugged, rolling, and dry. Scattered trees and succulents with spiked leaves struggled to survive on the barren slopes. There was almost no ground vegetation, but what there was also had thorns, though not like the trees. It was hot, dusty, and isolated; uninviting.

They would need water and shelter, though that was just the beginning of their needs. Somehow, they must find a civilized place to hide and begin trying to find a way to contact the Council without attracting too much attention from the locals. They could not be seen because, surely, the interest from the native media would bring disaster.

The little Diaddian quickly established that it could "read" the local intelligent species and many of the lower forms that inhabited the woods. Ingram detected a cluster of intelligent minds some distance to the south from where the pod was slowly dissolving. They could see the lights from Aeolian ships playing over the area where the egg had crashed. So far, they had moved fast enough to avoid detection and the Aeolians. Since the egg would dissolve everything, there would be no physical evidence that the pair had escaped.

With resolve, though not with eager anticipation, the pair started their journey. The lower life forms avoided them and it was not until near dawn when they neared the thought cluster, a town Ingram had determined was named Clay Springs. They rested on the outskirts while Ingram sorted through the thought impressions from the locals. He did not understand the language, so the work was slow, but he was able to determine that the nearest city of any size was be near the base of the peak on a tall mountain some distance to the west. While the residents were still struggling to awaken, they began the journey west, toward a town that Ingram thought was called Flag on a Stick. Later, they would learn that the thought images Ingram had captured referred to the town of Flagstaff: somewhat isolated, but large enough to provide a base for their needs.

They found an isolated cave, not much more than were water had undercut some harder rocks along a dried river bed, and decided to stop. The sun had been up for only a couple of hours and already the heat was taking its toll. That day and the next they rested in the relative coolness of the shadows and watched for reactions from the Aeolians.

The second night, noting that the Aeolian over flights had grown sporadic and scattered, they set off through the high desert, working their way carefully through the thin forests, toward the promise of shelter and a civilization that, though primitive, may have the technology to allow them to build a sub-space transmitter and call for help. In time, they would reach that goal if the technology available was anything beyond the Iron Age. Systel knew it would not be easy, but she also knew that every hour lost the Aeolians were killing more innocents.

Several days later, Systel worked her way through the tall evergreens and sparse underbrush. She was tired and irritable. They had subsided on small mammals that Ingram had lulled with his mind long enough for Systel to make a kill. That was a very dissatisfying experience, for an Ambassador who only sought peace. But they needed the nourishment; though Ingram could metabolize just about any organic matter, Systel was beginning to feel the effects of a diet out of balance.

They worked their way up the mountain, using Ingram's ability to detect the intelligent beings as the area began to become more densely populated. The desert scrub had given way to thicker woods, though the way was no less rough. Sometimes Systel was forced into letting Ingram ride on her back when the trail grew too rugged for the gravpad. That further wore her down, though Ingram was, after all, not much more than a bag of wind. She had no set plan or final destination in mind, but when the sun set behind the towering mountains ten days later and she could detect the glow of a large town's light against the night clouds, she knew that this Flag on a Stick would have to be their resting place for awhile. She was, after all, civilized now and not used to wilderness treks.

It looked only a few hours walk away; it took two more nights of hard hiking to reach the outlying residences.

She would need a city's resources and food supplies to survive and to begin the work of rescue. So she moved steadily through the forest. Before long, she reached the outskirts of a fair sized city, nestled at the foot of a tall, snow-covered peak.

That night and the next day they rested and watched for reactions from the Aeolians and tried to make sense of the civilization they had encountered. They skirted the city, looking for shelter, until they found, sitting forlorn and isolated in a stand of overgrown trees and bushes at the edge of town, an old, abandoned house. The roof look sound, but the paint was peeling and the porch sagged and the shutters hung loose and the turret room had a broken window. A weather-beaten sign rusted in the front yard, partly obscured by weeds and rubbish, its chain squeaking softly as it swayed in the light breeze.

"This looks like a good place to start, Ingram."

"It looks abandoned. I detect no higher life thoughts. Do you think we can occupy it without complaint?"

"I suspect we need to learn a little about the inhabitants of this planet first, but we should be safe here for a while. If they are in space, then they probably have radiated communications, most likely in wide disbursement. We can tap into that for information. You should be able to absorb the language quickly."

"Yes, if they transmit visuals and audio to the populace, I can learn quickly."

"Good. We must research, see how their economy works. Perhaps this shelter is available for purchase. Let us settle here for the night and rest. Tomorrow night we shall enter the town and see what we can find."

"I need electronic parts, Ambassador."

"Yes, and we both need protein. Tomorrow we go shopping."

Someday, and someday soon, Samuels decided, he would have to find Paul's kid. There was a lot he needed to know about his father. He would turn over the writer's notes and this disk and have a long talk so the kid would know his father did not abandon him. But give it a year or so. Give Paul a chance to succeed and return. Who knows, maybe the kid would have a half-brother or -sister by the time two healthy humans returned from the fringes of space.

Meanwhile, he put them away in his office safe. He turned on the television in his office and caught the report on the Rodeo-Chediski fire. It was now one of Arizona's most notorious wild fires. Blame was being placed on a stranded motorist for the Chediski fire and an arsonist for the Rodeo blaze that had quickly burned far enough east to merge with the Chediski. But Samuels knew better. He knew the Rodeo fire was caused by lasers blasting into the Fairgrounds as they tried to fry a fleeing gumdrop and the Chediski fire was caused by a barn going up in flames for the same cause.

But who would ever believe the truth?

The End

About the Author

 James B Brandt is a writer and film/video producer living in Phoenix, Arizona. While he prefers science fiction, his work covers everything from documentaries to romantic comedies to action adventures.

Mr. Brandt has worked on a number of major motion pictures and numerous local productions in addition to writing scores of television and radio commercials. He is currently represented by the Canton Literary Agency.

Other Publications by Brandt Media

Join the discussion on Facebook!

Print: 978-0-9862815-0-1
Extended eBook: 978-1-312-54906-7

A SENSE OF DUTY

A hard hitting story of one man's determination to fulfill his duty... even if it kills him.

Suggested for mature audiences.

Print:
978-0-9862815-2-5
eBook:
978-1-312-55271-5